TALES FROM THE TOWER

Fairytale Anthology 2

Ye Olde Dragon Books

www.YeOldeDragonBooks.com

Ye Olde Dragon Books
P.O. Box 30802
Middleburg Hts., OH 44130

www.YeOldeDragonBooks.com

2OldeDragons@gmail.com

Copyright © 2022 by the participating authors

ISBN 13: 978-1-952345-67-8

Published in the United States of America
Publication Date: May 1, 2022

Cover Art Copyright Kaitlyn Emery 2022

All rights reserved. No portion of this book may be reproduced or transmitted in any form or by any electronic or mechanical means, including photocopying, recording or by any information retrieval and storage system without permission of the publisher.

Ebooks, audiobooks, and print books are *not* transferrable, either in whole or in part. As the purchaser or otherwise *lawful* recipient of this book, you have the right to enjoy the novel on your own computer or other device. Further distribution, copying, sharing, gifting or uploading is illegal and violates United States Copyright laws.
Pirating of books is illegal. Criminal Copyright Infringement, *including* infringement without monetary gain, may be investigated by the Federal Bureau of Investigation and is punishable by up to five years in federal prison and a fine of up to $250,000.

Names, characters and incidents depicted in this book are products of the author's imagination, or are used in a fictitious situation. Any resemblances to actual events, locations, organizations, incidents or persons – living or dead – are coincidental and beyond the intent of the author.

TABLE OF CONTENTS

Foreword

The Royal Treatment
    Pam Halter   1

A Baker's Guide to Fortune and Folly
    Rachel Dib   11

Rapun Zel
    Michelle Houston   29

The Lost Princess
    Kaitlyn Emery   39

Operation Breakout
    Stoney M. Setzer   59

Blood Gold
    Etta-Tamara Wilson   73

Down the Fire Escape
    Kathleen Bird   87

Tower to Tower
    Michelle Levigne   99

The Safe Tower
    Beka Gremikova   119

Starchild
    Abigail Falanga   **143**

Deserted
    Cortney Manning   **161**

Fairy Cursed
    Lindsi McIntyre   **179**

The Princess of Callanway Broch
    Meaghan Elizabeth Ward   **185**

The Dragon Keep's Servant
    Michaela Bush   **203**

Ocean Shackles
    Cassandra Hamm   **215**

The Tower
    Deborah Cullins Smith   **227**

Meet the Authors   **251**

Foreword

Before you begin...

Last year, Ye Olde Dragon Books premiered two new series of anthologies. Very ambitious for "two old dragons." But we bit off that chunk and savored every bite.

Readers enjoyed our unique take on the Beauty and the Beast tale, and later the Wolfman legend. So this year, we tackled Rapunzel and waited for the stories to roll in.

They were slower to arrive this time. After a year of lockdowns, everyone reveled in the chance to spend the holidays with family and friends, and storytelling was placed on the backburner until after the New Year festivities had died down.

Then the floodgates opened. What an incredible multiverse we have to share with you!

We have zombies and werewolves; we have an orphan in space, and orphans in the woods; we have the emotionally battered and abused, and we have those shackled by the expectations of others. Some of the towers are physical, and some are emotional, while some are complex combinations of the two, and a couple of stories don't have an actual tower at all! We leave it to you to sort out which stories are which, and enjoy the journeys along the way.

We have many returning authors this year, so you may recognize some names, but we also have a lot of newcomers to the Ye Olde Dragon Books family, and they are wonderful additions to our roster of writers. Our family is growing, and we are looking forward to many more editions of fabulous, far-out fairy tales.

Now pull up a chair and a nice cup of tea. It's time to dive into the deep end of the pool!

Deborah Cullins Smith

Before you dive in ...

Keep in mind that we do fairytale ... ahem ... "adaptations" in the spring, and we do classic monster movie rewrites and twists and turns in the fall, just in time for Halloween.

This fall, 2022, our theme for you to twist and warp and turn on its ear is .... (drum roll, please) .... Frankenstein!

If you're daring, you can play with Dr. Frankenstein, and you can play with the monster. Your choice in the story you want to write and submit for consideration.

Or you can just sit back and wait in eager anticipation for our authors to amaze and delight you again.

Either way, it's gonna be fun!

Thanks for stopping by and visiting our many and varied playgrounds of the imagination. We couldn't do it without you, our readers!

Michelle Levigne

The Royal Treatment
Pam Halter

Rapunzel gazed out the bedroom window that overlooked the flower gardens. One year. One entire year had passed since Prince Armel had rescued her from the tower and brought her to his castle, where they were married. Rapunzel had felt she couldn't be happier. Until she learned Armel had wanderlust. After their first week together, he rode off with his knights on some quest. She couldn't remember the purpose.

Rapunzel longed for more of her husband's company. When he returned from the first quest, Armel spent one night in her bed. In the morning at breakfast, he announced he was leaving that afternoon for the next one.

"My love," Armel said as he set down his goblet of pomegranate juice. "I'll be leaving this afternoon to search for the perfect sapphire earrings to enhance your lovely eyes."

"But, my lord," she stammered. "You have only been home one night."

He gave her a loving smile. "I want you to have the best of everything."

And off he went that afternoon, leaving her with no husband, and as she learned not too soon after, no baby.

Rapunzel paced the castle. She looked in every room. She visited the kitchen, where she was banished because her long hair kept getting into the food. She was also banished from the weaving room (her hair ended up in a royal rug), the arts room (her hair got into the paint), the pottery room (same reason as the arts room), and even the koi pond in the rock garden.

Her long hair.
Her long hair!

The more she paced the castle, the more her hair got into things. She tried keeping it braided. It dragged behind her like a drawbridge rope. She put it up into a spiraling bun. It hit the top of every single doorway. Every night, she went to bed with a headache because of her hair. Who knew that would happen? In the tower, there was only one room and very little furniture to catch it on.

After the next quest, for the perfect flowering Delphinium (the tall bloom reminded him of her tower and how he rescued her), and still no baby, Rapunzel braided her hair into six strands, grabbed a pair of scissors and cut them off. She gazed in amazement at her now shoulder-length tresses, which waved and curled on the ends. Not only was her head lighter, she loved her new look. Perhaps Armel would also love it and stay home.

But being a man, he barely noticed, so after his post-quest husbandly duty, and a "Lovely, lovely" comment when she asked him about it, he left once again.

"My lord," she said before he left on his fourth quest, a stunning jeweled hair comb (to enhance her natural loveliness), "I miss you so. Might you stay home a bit longer?"

Prince Armel drew her into his arms and kissed the top of her head. "I miss you, too, my love. But I must accomplish these quests. It's my princely duty!"

And off he rode.

Rapunzel went to her room and wept. Even with a castle full of people, she felt almost as lonely as when she was locked in the tower. If only Armel would give her a baby!

Some days, Rapunzel would distract herself by brushing and braiding the long locks of hair she had cut off and put in a trunk. She loved the feel of it, and how she could braid it into intricate designs. The more she played with the hair, the more intrigued she became with what she could do with it.

During a royal pedicure, Rapunzel mentioned this to Cara, one of her ladies-in-waiting. Cara looked up from Rapunzel's feet. "Why, Your Highness, you could make a wig."

"What would I do with a wig?" Rapunzel asked. "My hair has no problem growing, and it's quite healthy."

"No, no. For women who may have problems with sickness or age," Lady Cara said. "I know of many noble women who stay inside because they're embarrassed about their hair."

Rapunzel frowned. "How do you know about these women?"

Cara began to rub violet oil into Rapunzel's foot. "Why, we ladies talk to each other, Your Highness."

Rapunzel thought and thought about it as Cara finished up her pedicure. "Thank you, Cara," she said.

Cara curtsied. "You're welcome."

~~~~~

Rapunzel lost no time. She summoned the wig maker, Mergig, from a neighboring kingdom and pleaded with him to teach her. At first, he balked at the idea. But she won him over by showing him the beautiful tresses of her own hair she kept in her trunk. Mergig taught her the basics and left, a bit miffed at her refusal to give him some of her hair.

Rapunzel wasn't thrilled with so little instruction, but she practiced. And she came up with ideas of her own. The hardest part was sewing the leather band inside the wig that would hold it on someone's head, but she got it done.

After Prince Armel left on his latest quest, Rapunzel invited Lady Cara and the other ladies-in-waiting, Abbi, Rhonda, and Jess, for tea. After the tea was served and they were left alone, Rapunzel spoke.

"Girls, Cara has given me an idea of something I can do while Prince Armel is on his quests."

They all looked at her with rapt attention.

"We are going to open a hair salon."

The girls gasped. "Your Highness, what a wonderful idea," Cara exclaimed. "I knew you'd come up with something."

Rapunzel set down her teacup. "Thank you. Now, you all take expert care of me, my hair, nails, and skin. I believe there's a place for all of us."

"Your Highness," Abbi said. "Pardon my question, but what would you be doing?"

"How about this?" Rapunzel got up and opened her trunk. She lifted out an intricately braided wig and held it up.

"Oh, Your Highness!" Jess exclaimed.

"It's fabulous!" Rhonda cried.

Abbi just squealed while Cara smiled.

They spent the afternoon designing the salon on parchment.

"I think we can use the room to the right of the front entrance," Rapunzel said. "All the hours I spent walking the castle, I've been in every room. That room is mostly empty, but it has a small side alcove containing a cloak and cape rack and a couple of armor stands."

Abbi nodded. "And the windows capture the morning sun. It's so bright!"

"We'll have to talk to the royal gardener about another well for water, close to the salon," Cara added. "And enlist the kitchen maids to bank the fire and fill the cauldrons."

"And the royal seamstress," Rhonda said. "For towels."

"I'll speak to the royal laundress about shampoo, soaps, and lotions!" Jess exclaimed.

Rapunzel clapped her hands. "Girls, we can make this work!"

~~~~~

Three months later, after practicing on all the servants in the castle, Rapunzel opened up *The Royal Treatment Salon*. Prince Armel had given his approval on his last visit home. Rapunzel didn't even mind that he rode off on yet another quest.

The royal heralds had traveled to all the neighboring lands to leave parchment flyers in all the castles and surrounding hamlets. It soon became known that Princess Rapunzel welcomed anyone who wanted the royal treatment for their hair. And they didn't have to be royal. She even gave discounts for the elderly and children.

While Prince Armel quested, Rapunzel and her ladies snipped, set, and styled. She was especially delighted when the Twelve Dancing Princesses came in. Each one showed her a different trick of the trade.

"We princesses stick together," Princess Number Six told her.

After that, Rapunzel was able to offer coloring and other hair enhancements. Her ladies-in-waiting were quick studies, each one specializing in something. Lady Abbi was a whiz with color, helping Snow White keep her ebony black hair. And Princess Sondra from the kingdom to the south loved her purple tresses. Abbi spent many hours experimenting with spices and flower petals to create new colors.

Lady Cara excelled in manicures and pedicures, becoming extremely popular with her creation of fingernail guards. These were especially in demand with all the royals, as they deemed them a sign of status and power. As queens, princesses, and other royalty did no real work, they loved having nail guards on the ring finger and little finger (only the showoffs wore them on all fingers). The guards were usually made from silver and/or gold and inlaid with jewels or had carved designs. Only queens were allowed to have rubies or garnets in their nail guards, as red showed their top status. The orders for fingernail guards were so numerous that Cara needed two assistants of her own to fill them.

Lady Rhonda created intricate, extraordinary styles using ribbons braided in with hair. She became an expert with *braids and beads* after Princess Senate Mary Seeiso from Africa visited the salon while traveling. This style spread like dragon fire, and braided hair competitions sprang up all over the kingdom. Princess Marvel Violet was a fierce competitor, winning many competitions. After she won her twentieth competition, Princess Senate Mary decided to sponsor her, and they spent many hours creating better and more unique styles and, of course, winning many more awards.

Lady Jess curled and teased such elaborate and high styles, she was always in demand. Besides red jewels in fingernail guards, top status was also determined by the height of a queen's hair. No princess, or any other lady, was allowed to have hair higher than a queen's hair.

Princess Rapunzel's talent making wigs kept her busy night and day. After she came up with a way to keep the wearer's scalp cooler, she could barely keep up with orders, even with extra help. But she did hit a snag when the Snow Queen requested a way to keep the tips of the icicles on her crown from chipping.

"Rapunzel, dah-ling," the Snow Queen said as she handed Rapunzel her crown. "I simply *must* find a way to keep my crown straight and my icicles intact. Can you help me?"

"I'm not sure," Rapunzel said. "This is a hair salon. Your problem needs a jeweler."

The Snow Queen crossed her arms. "But crowns sit on *hair*."

She laughed. "That's a good point. Let me think." She turned the frozen crown around in her hands. The icy cold felt hot, as if it might burn her fingers, so she grabbed a towel to hold it. A couple of drips of water fell to the floor. She handed it back. "Well, you're going to need to put it back on so it doesn't melt entirely. Then we can talk."

They sat in Rapunzel's tearoom. After the footman left the tray, she poured them each a cup. "If you don't have to have *real* icicles, maybe I can work with the royal jeweler to incorporate crystals into a crown that I can attach to a wig."

The Snow Queen took a sip. "*Fake* icicles. I'm just not sure, dah-ling. What would my subjects *say* if they found out?"

Rapunzel smiled. "Snowy, you need a little faith in me. I promise, if the wig and crown do not meet your standards, we'll think of something else."

Three months later, the Snow Queen left the salon happy.

Her subjects never found out the icicles were fake.

~~~~~

As the months progressed, so did the clientele for *The Royal Treatment Salon*. And when Princess Rapunzel celebrated her one-year anniversary, she unveiled her *Wall of Hair Fame* with great fanfare and lots of cake and tea.

Guests *oohed* and *aahed* over the before-and-after portraits of Snow White, the Twelve Dancing Princesses, Princess Sondra, Princess Senate Mary Seeiso, Princess Marvel Violet, and of course, the Snow Queen. And many, many more.

Rapunzel had to clear out the two rooms next to the salon: one for waiting and the other for changing clothes. Because the *big* announcement during the party was that she was branching out into gowns. As she was not an avid seamstress, she employed village maidens to do that work. She, however, discovered a knack for design after Princess Angela of Liechtenstein (who was already famous for *her* dress designs) gave her some pointers.

The newly engaged Princess Winnifred (of *The Princess and the Pea* fame) was Rapunzel's first wedding gown.

Prince Armel put his arm around his wife when everyone had gone after the party. "My love, I am so proud and delighted. You are an amazingly talented woman!" He gave her a sound kiss. "In fact, this calls for something special. I shall go directly tomorrow to look for an appropriate gift."

Rapunzel smiled all the way to their bed chamber. Still, with all her success, she had an empty space in her heart. A baby-shaped space.

The week after Prince Armel left, Rapunzel was sitting at her desk, doodling on parchment, trying to capture in ink the design she had in her head for a Summer Tea Dress. Laughter and conversation drifted into her study from the salon. It was a happy and comforting sound.

Suddenly it went quiet. Before Rapunzel could get up to investigate, Lady Cara came bustling into the room. She gave a half curtsey. "Your Highness!" she exclaimed. "Your Highness, come quickly!"

Rapunzel rose. "What is it?"

Cara, still a bit out of breath, was rushing back out the door and didn't answer.

Rapunzel followed. "What—?"

She gasped. There, standing at the sign-in table, was Medusa.

Rapunzel avoided looking Medusa in the eyes, even though Medusa was wearing a shield over them. And while no one had been turned to stone, no one moved. Fear felt as thick as frozen fudge.

"So," Rapunzel said, "how—how can I help you?"

Medusa sighed. "I'm so tired of everyone fearing me. I literally have no friends. I think it's the snakes."

She blinked. "The—snakes?"

"Of course! I mean, I have the eye shield. As long as I wear it, I can't turn anyone to stone. It has to be the snakes, right? I need something to make my snakes more—well, attractive."

"Let me think," Rapunzel said. She tried not to panic. It would not do to have Medusa as an enemy. She rubbed her forehead. How did one make snakes attractive?

"I also have a large number of snakeskins," Medusa went on. "If you can use them."

She smiled and gave a little nod. "I'm going to have to think. Can you give me a week?"

Medusa stood. "Of course, of course." She moved toward the door and turned back. "Thank you for not running, shrieking, from the castle. Most do, you know."

Rapunzel smiled again. After Medusa left, she put her head on her arms for a moment, feeling overwhelmed. Then she sat up. "This will not defeat me," she said. "I *will* figure this out."

~~~~~

When the day was done, Rapunzel called her ladies-in-waiting together. She explained her dilemma and asked them all to come up with ideas. Then she asked Lady Cara to draw her a hot bath and dismissed the others. As she soaked in the warm scented water, she couldn't stop thinking about how in the kingdom she could help Medusa. There must be something she could do.

The next day, Rapunzel went to the royal library after breakfast to read up on snakes. It was a fascinating study. *Snakeskin is made from the same thing as fingernails*, she read. That gave her an idea.

A week later, when Medusa came back to the salon, Rapunzel had a full color drawing to show her.

"Do you think it will work?" Medusa asked.

Rapunzel winked. "I'm positive."

~~~~~

Five hours later, Medusa looked at her reflection in the mirror. "I don't know what to say. It's incredible! I don't know what to say!"

Rapunzel and her ladies admired their work. Each snake was dyed a different jewel-like color using manicure products. Rapunzel created thin braids from the snakeskin and attached them to the base of each snake. She didn't want to cover up the colors, so she wound the braids around just the base of each snake. As the snakeskin was shimmery, the effect was mesmerizing.

The royal jeweler crafted gold hoop earrings for Medusa, which also reflected the colors of the snakes. And Rapunzel had commissioned Princess Angela for a sleek gown for Medusa's long serpent-like body.

The transformation was complete. After sobbing into a towel, Medusa thanked everyone and left. She promised to let Rapunzel know how her new look worked. A year later, Medusa came back to the salon for a wedding makeover. Yes. She was going to take the blind minstrel, Bartholomew, for her second husband. Poseidon had been her first husband, but the two were forced apart by the goddess, Athena, many years ago.

Rapunzel felt pleased and proud of this success, but there was still that empty place in her heart. How she longed for a baby of her own. But she was not one to brood, so she continued to make those who came to her salon feel beautiful. Prince Armel, when he was home, was loving and attentive. Rapunzel, even though she had an empty womb, chose to be thankful for all she had.

Still, there were times when she gave into her sorrow. One evening, as she wept in the small garden outside the library, she felt a hand on her shoulder.

"Oh!" she cried, surprised. She had thought she was alone.

An old peasant woman smiled kindly down at her. "I'm sorry, Your Highness. I did not mean to startle you, but I heard you weeping. What's wrong?"

Rapunzel was too filled with despair to wonder how the woman got there. Something about her eyes invoked trust. "I—I want a baby!" she burst out. "It's been over two years and I still have an empty womb."

"Oh, my dear," the woman said. "My dear. I understand. If it please Your Highness, I can bring an herbal tea blend that may help."

Rapunzel grasped the wrinkled hand. "Would you? I would be so thankful."

"Aye, I'll bring it tomorrow morn." The woman stroked Rapunzel's hair. "Have no more worry, my lady. All will be well."

"Who are you?" Rapunzel asked.

The woman stared at the night sky for a moment. "Why, I'm your fairy godmother, my dear."

Rapunzel blinked. "Whaaa—" she started to say, but the old woman had vanished.

~~~~~

The next morning, Rapunzel paced the small garden. She had left the gate open, but so far, the woman had not shown herself. Of course, it was barely past sunrise, she chided herself. Still, she paced and wished and dreamed. After a while, just as she sat to rest on a bench, she caught the aroma of cinnamon and something else she couldn't place. The garden gate creaked.

Rapunzel jumped up. "Godmother? Is that you?"

"I am here, my dear."

The old woman from yesterday stood in the gateway, holding a steaming mug. "I made the first cup for you," she said. "And I have more herbs so you can drink a cup every morning before breakfast and every evening before bed."

Rapunzel took the warm mug. The scent, while unfamiliar, was pleasing. "What's in it?"

Her godmother's eyes sparkled. "Oh, just a mix of herbs that are known for preparing the womb for life."

That didn't answer her question, but Rapunzel didn't mind. She took a sip. Not bad. It wasn't sweet. It wasn't bitter. Earthy, grassy, and a little spicy. She drank the whole thing.

Her godmother pulled a cloth bag from her cloak. "Put two good pinches of these herbs in hot water. Let it steep for five minutes. Then strain out the herbs and put them out here on the ground for the birds to enjoy."

Rapunzel followed her godmother's directions faithfully. She didn't really believe it would help, but she did enjoy the tea.

Two months later, Prince Armel returned from his quest to bring home a rare night blooming orchid. Rapunzel knew exactly where she wanted to plant it -- in what she now called her "Tea Garden." She and Armel, who did not leave immediately for a new quest this time, enjoyed many pleasant and loving nights. Their intimate times seemed different than before. In a good way.

One month later, Rapunzel was pregnant. She and Prince Armel were delighted, and Armel, of course, vowed to find something special for the baby's room. So, off he rode, and this time, Rapunzel was content to let him go.

The news spread rapidly throughout the kingdom and beyond. Rapunzel was such a beloved princess for her kindness and generosity, many gifts were sent to the castle as the months progressed. As her time grew near, she retired to her chamber while her ladies ran the salon.

She didn't have long to wait. Just one week after she confined herself, Rapunzel gave birth to twins, a boy and a girl! That evening, as she held her babies close, she wasn't surprised when her fairy godmother appeared in her bed chamber.

"Godmother!" she exclaimed. "Thank you! Thank you so much!"

"Oh, my dear, I am so happy for you," said her godmother, taking the baby girl in her arms. "What shall you name them?"

"The boy will be christened Orlando, which is Prince Armel's middle name," Rapunzel answered. "I have not decided about the girl. If I knew my real mother's name, I would choose that."

Her godmother blinked back tears. It took her a moment to speak. "Why, I can tell you your mother's name," she said. "It was Deborah Michelle."

Rapunzel was astounded. "You knew my mother?"

Her godmother handed the newborn princess back to Rapunzel. "Aye, I knew her. She was my daughter. After you were stolen, your mother died of a broken heart. I began to search for you, and during my search, I accidentally made tea with nightshade. As I lay dying, a forest fairy heard my gasps and took pity on me. She cured me. And after hearing my story, she gifted me by casting a spell that would make me a fairy, as well. And when I found you, I would not be just your grandmother, but also your fairy godmother."

Tears ran down Rapunzel's cheeks. "I am so happy. Could I ever feel any happier?"

Her god/grandmother chuckled. "I can't say, but who knows what the future will bring?"

"And will you always be near me?"

Her god/grandmother placed her hands on Rapunzel's face. "Always, my darling."

~~~~~

And so, Rapunzel's happily ever after truly began. Her children were healthy and grew to be a very good prince and princess. The salon continued to thrive. *King* Armel (he received his kingship from the council of kings after his second son was born) still rode out on quests, but was more content to stay home for longer periods of time with his family. It wasn't long before Rapunzel had more babies; two more boys and one more girl. Her life started off lonely and hopeless. Now she had a full life, where she also worked to help others, not only with their self-esteem, but also those who were in any kind of need. She was beloved by all who knew her. Perhaps there were those who felt jealous, but if they did, they kept it to themselves.

The day after the *Tenth Year Salon Celebration*, Rapunzel sat in her office going over the clientele list. She smiled as she remembered the first time Medusa came to the salon. "That was one nerve-wracking client," she said out loud.

Just then, Lady Abbi burst into the room. "Your Highness! Your Highness! You must come!"

"What is it?" she asked, feeling a sense of déjà vu.

"Just come!"

So, Rapunzel hurried out and followed Lady Abbi to the salon.

There, standing at the sign-in desk was Bigfoot.

"Oh my," Rapunzel whispered to herself. "Here we go again!"

END

A Baker's Guide to Fortune and Folly
Rachel Dib

Craig felt stupid.

For the past ten years, he'd spent his free time building a tower. Its construction had started off as a dare, of course. Most illogical endeavors did. He'd been at the tavern with his mates, and a few drinks in they were suddenly arguing about construction. Hugh, being the turd that he was, made a comment ("You just don't have a mind for building, Craig. Stick to your baking. That's what you're good at."), and the next thing he knew, Craig had agreed to build a tower.

Now, ten years later, the building was finished: a fifty-two-foot stone structure overlooking a flower-filled meadow. Sure, it was tucked away in the forest where not many people wanted to go, but it was not as if he could have found anywhere to build it inside the city. Not anywhere affordable, anyway.

The important part was that he'd completed the task. And it was well built too—except that he'd forgotten to add a door. Something Craig wished he'd realized before he'd dragged his friends out to see it.

"Nice job, Craig," Hugh sneered, slapping him on the back. "The only way to enter is to climb to that window all the way up there."

As his friends walked away, Craig tucked his hands into his pockets and stared up at his tower.

"All that work for nothing." Sighing, he walked a few paces back to the tree line and sat down at the base of an oak.

"Nice tower you have there."

Craig jumped. A woman had appeared at his side. He quickly glanced around, but didn't see anywhere from which she could have sprouted.

They say witches can appear from nowhere, he considered, eyeing her warily.

She looked about his mother's age, her graying, dark hair spilling down her back in a mess of tangled curls. She wore a long dress under a ragged cloak that was torn at the seam. Craig was about to cast aside the witch idea and pass her off as a local hag, but when he saw her face, he changed his mind. Her eyes were clear and sharp, her gaze cunning.

"Plan to live here, do you?" she asked.

Craig shook his head. "I just built it for...for fun."

"For fun, say you?" She tilted her head. "I suppose, then, you might have a mind to sell it?"

"Sell it?" Craig glanced back at the tower. *Ten years of my life belongs to that thing.*

"I can give you twice what it cost to build it, plus time, of course," the woman said.

Craig sighed. "There's no door."

"That is quite all right," she said evenly. "Part of its appeal, even. I like my privacy."

"But how would you—"

"Three times the building cost," the woman interrupted. "I am afraid I cannot go any higher."

"Three times the..." Craig shook his head. "Along with compensation for the time spent building it?"

She nodded. "Time is precious, is it not? You'll be paid for that as well."

Craig let out a heavy breath. "Fine. Yeah. If you're sure you really want it."

"Oh, I do. Truly." The woman grinned and pulled out a purse tucked beneath her cloak.

Though Craig walked away with a pocket full of gold, he did so with a guilty conscience.

As long as she's happy, right? he asked himself as he trod down the forest path toward the city. *That's all that really matters.*

Still, the transaction didn't sit well with him—until he joined his friends at the tavern. When they all stared at his pile of gold with a mixture of awe and respect, Craig filled with pride. No longer was his tower a failed endeavor. Now it was a shrewd business venture.

Craig generously bought the whole bar a round and then basked in everyone's praise.

~~~~

Craig didn't think about his tower again for fifteen years. With the money, he'd not only moved his wife and son into a bigger house, but he'd also bought his own bakery in the center of town. Within six months, he'd become a respected member of society.

He heard whispers of some trouble up at the castle. A kidnapping or some such calamity. But his rise to popularity had increased his business so much, he barely had time to dwell on the ill-fortunes of others. He and his family prospered, and all was well.

Until Jeremy, his son, grew up and refused to join the family business.

"I want to be a builder," he insisted. "I love architecture."

"Architecture?" Craig spat. "What is this architecture you speak of?"

"Exactly." Jeremy threw out his hands. "All of the buildings in this city are the same. They are boring. The new cathedral is the only structure with even an ounce of style."

"Not so," Craig said, crossing his arms. "I built a tower once. It was very original, too. And...stylish."

Jeremy lifted a brow. "*You* built a tower?"

"I did." Craig lifted his chin. "Selling it gave me my start. As well as your education," he added pointedly.

"Hmm. And where is this tower?"

"It's in the forest. Very private."

"Right," Jeremy replied with a click of his tongue.

"I'll show it to you," Craig said indignantly and promptly led his son into the forest.

He almost didn't remember the way. The path he'd used had become overgrown with bushes and brambles. But he slowly picked his way through, finally coming out into the meadow where the tower stood.

Jeremy glanced over the tower with a skeptical eye. "You built this?"

"I did."

"Where's the door?"

Craig winced. "I forgot to put one in. But there's a window."

"Yeah, all the way up there!" His son gestured near the roof of the tower.

"Well, the woman who purchased the tower said she was glad there wasn't a door." He shrugged. "She said it was part of the appeal."

"Hmm. Well, a doorless tower is pretty original, I suppose. If you can figure out a way inside." Jeremy pursed his lips. "Do you think she still lives here? Maybe she'll give us a tour. You know, for old times' sake."

"No, I don't!" Craig snapped, feeling suddenly uneasy. "In fact, I don't think she'd like us here at all. Odd sort, she was. You have to be odd to want a doorless tower."

"Rapunzel!" a woman's voice called.

Craig grabbed his son's arm and yanked him back into the trees.

"What are you—" Jeremy began, but Craig quickly shushed him.

"Just look, will you," he whispered, nodding toward the meadow.

A woman had appeared on the other side and was walking toward the tower. Though she was dressed a bit fancier, in a long red dress and shawl, Craig recognized her as the same woman who had purchased the tower so long ago. Especially since she still looked *exactly* the same.

She hasn't aged a day! He shook his head. *And my own dear mother already in the grave. It isn't natural.*

"Rapunzel!" she called out again as she halted before the tower. "Do let down your hair!"

A moment later, an undiscernible, thick, tangled mass fell from the window. The brown cord swung back and forth slightly, almost brushing the ground.

That's the strangest rope I've ever seen, Craig considered as the woman began hauling herself up the length of it. *Though she did call it hair...* He squinted and leaned forward. *I suppose it does look a bit like hair. Unsanitary, that is, letting hair knot so. Even I douse mine in a bit of water and give it a good brush now and again.*

When the woman had disappeared through the window, Craig nudged Jeremy. "Let's go afore she comes back. Something's not right here."

Jeremy shook his head. "The girl. That was the most beautiful girl I've ever seen."

Craig blinked. "Well, I won't say she wasn't pretty, but Jeremy, that woman is nearly three times your age. Maybe older. She doesn't seem to have aged much since I saw her last, anyhow. I have half a mind to call her a witch!"

"Not the old crone." Jeremy scowled. "The girl! The beauty that stood in the window! Rapunzel, she was called. A beautiful name for a maiden in distress!"

"I didn't see a girl, much less one in distress."

"Well, there was one," he said pointedly. "When called, she appeared like a specter, her face as pale as the moon but as beautiful as the stars. From the window she let down flowing locks that shimmered like gold in the afternoon sun."

Craig tilted his head. "What nonsense are you spouting, son? A specter as beautiful as the stars? Flowing locks? If there was a girl, a good haircut is what she'll be needing!"

Jeremy rolled his eyes. "It's not nonsense, Father. It's called poetry, and Rapunzel will love it!"

"I don't know if 'love' is the correct term," Craig muttered.

"All girls love poetry," he said matter-of-factly. "It's the only proper way to woo a lady."

"I see. Well, maybe you should work on your wording a bit. I've never known any woman who enjoyed being likened to a specter, for instance. But girl or not, we should be going. If the crone is a witch, she won't want to find us lurking about."

"But what if Rapunzel needs to be rescued?" Jeremy asked, wide-eyed. "We can't just leave her locked in a tower. She'll go mad!"

"Have you considered the fact she may already be mad? Why else would someone find herself locked in a doorless tower without so much as a brush? As much as you say girls love poetry, I can tell you with great confidence that they love perfect hair more. No sane girl would allow her locks to grow so long and become so matted. The witch might very well be her jailer."

His son shook his head. "You didn't see her face. It was angelic! No one so beautiful, so delicate, so perfect... As perfect as a newly bloomed rose—"

"Yes, the poetry again." Craig rubbed his brow. "Okay, son. Let's say she is a sane maiden locked in a tower. While I admire your audacity, how do you propose we rescue her?"

Jeremy paused and then began to pace a short distance. "Well, we'll wait until the crone has left."

"Which could be hours," he pointed out.

Jeremy ignored this point and continued. "And then we shall climb that tree there. You see the one closest to the window?"

"The one with the flimsy limbs?"

"Yes. We'll climb it and crawl through the window."

"Given it's still open and unlocked."

Jeremy ignored this point too. "And once inside, I'll rescue her!"

Craig nodded. "Right. Let's say you avoid breaking your neck and manage to get inside. What will you say to this Rapunzel once you've broken into her home? She may think you a thief."

"Well, I'll announce otherwise." Jeremy bent to one knee and held out an arm. "I'll say, 'Fair maiden of the doorless tower. From afar I spied you, and seeing your beauty, I knew I must rescue you from great torment!'"

"I see." Craig cleared his throat, attempting to keep a straight face. "And what if she says she doesn't need rescuing? What if she's happy where she is?"

"How could anyone—"

"I'm merely exploring all the possibilities," he cut in, holding up his hands.

Jeremy scratched his ear. "In that case, I'll ask her if she's sure. If she is, I'll leave." He shrugged.

"As simple as that, eh?" When his son nodded, Craig sighed. "All right then. But you still must wait until the witch leaves, and there is no knowing when that will be."

"Right now." He pointed to the tower.

Sure enough, the woman was climbing down the rope of hair. Once she had reached the ground, she glanced around her and then trotted off in the opposite direction of where Craig and Jeremy hid. When she was out of sight, Jeremy lunged toward the tower.

"Wait, son! You can't just—"

But Jeremy was already halfway there. Craig watched his son leap, grab hold of the hair, and begin shimmying up the rope.

"Changing the plan, I see," Craig grunted, jogging after him.

Thankfully, the hair still hung low enough for him to reach. "I'm too old for this," he growled as he began pulling himself up the wall.

When he had successfully followed his son through the window, he was surprised to see the room they'd entered was vacant—at least of any person. Ropes of knotted hair, on the other hand, lay strewn about, covering almost every inch of the floor.

Craig shuffled his feet, attempting to clear himself a space. Failing, he shook his head.

"Surely this cannot all belong to her," Jeremy muttered, glancing around. "At least not currently. Perhaps she sheds like a snake."

"I do no such thing!" a woman cried.

Startled, Craig looked up to see a slight, young woman standing in the doorway. This had to be Rapunzel. She seemed around the same age as Jeremy. And as he had articulated, she was pretty. Craig wasn't sure if her beauty was worth all the poetry his son had been spouting, but she was pretty, nonetheless. The hair though…

She eyed the two men narrowly. "Who are you and what are you doing in my home?"

As if taking that as his cue, Jeremy stepped forward. "Fair maiden, I—"

"Ugh." Rapunzel rolled her eyes. "Matilda is right. Boys are imbeciles. I mean, look at my hair." She tossed a matted rope of it over her shoulder. "Just tell me what you're doing here? No one was supposed to be able to find me. Are you from that newsletter that gets passed about? Because I don't do interviews."

"Um." Jeremy faltered.

Craig stepped forward. "Hi there. Rapunzel, is it? Sorry to disturb you. My son, here, just thought you were in trouble and decided to take it upon himself to rescue you."

"Rescue me?"

Craig nodded and motioned to the room. "Not many young ladies are found locked away in towers, you see. He thought you'd been stolen away or some such nonsense."

"Oh, I see." Rapunzel bit her lip. "I suppose I can see how my *situation* might be misconstrued."

"So, you're not in trouble, then?"

"No, I'm quite all right."

"You haven't been kidnapped by an evil witch who forces you to remain in this tower?" Craig pressed, just to cover all the bases.

The young woman chuckled. "Not in the traditional sense, no."

"Traditional sense?" Jeremy asked, his face brightening. "So, you are being held against your will in an *untraditional* sense, then?"

"Well, it isn't as if I *want* to be here," she replied. "Who wants to stay in a tower all day? I mean, I've gotten a lot of reading done, and my painting skills have greatly improved. But I am growing tired of reading and painting. I've asked Matilda—that's the witch who looks after me, since you mentioned it. Well, I've asked her for a piano but, no luck yet. She says it would be too hard to get through the window. If only the builder had remembered to put in a door."

Craig gulped, his cheeks flaming.

"So," she continued, "I suppose you *could* say I'm being held against my will. But, while my kidnapping is the official story, it's not actually the true story. My parents know where I am. They even come to visit me on occasion. They just hired Matilda to take care of me since she has special resources and has an easier time moving about unseen. But technically, my being here is completely legitimate."

"What do you mean by your kidnapping is the official story?" Jeremy asked. "Who stages a kidnaping?"

Rapunzel eyed them narrowly again. "Did you really not hear of Princess Rapunzel's kidnapping? Yes, it happened fifteen years ago, but has everyone truly forgotten about me?"

Noticing her lip was trembling slightly, Craig jumped in. "We have heard of it, Princess. We merely did not put two and two together. After all, we never expected to find the lost princess hidden here in the woods."

"I suppose not," she replied, glancing away. She seemed to take a moment to compose herself before looking back at them. "How did you find me, anyway? I was told no one would find this place."

"My father is the builder of this tower," Jeremy piped up.

Craig winced.

"*You* built this tower?" Rapunzel asked, eyeing him sharply.

"Yes, milady," Craig admitted grudgingly. "Though I built it upon a dare and had no idea what it would be used for when I sold it."

"Who builds a tower on a dare?" she asked.

"A poor baker down on his luck," he replied sullenly.

"Hmm. And was removing the door part of this bet?"

He shook his head with a sigh. "No. I simply forgot to add it. I did say I was a baker, did I not?"

She shrugged. "I suppose I considered doors basic building features. Pardon my mistake."

Craig gritted his teeth, but before he had a chance to respond, Jeremy had stepped forward.

"The question still remains, fair maiden. If you do not wish to reside in the tower, and no one commands you to stay, why not leave?"

"But I *am* commanded to stay," Rapunzel countered. "While my parents love me dearly, they do not wish their constituents to know of their daughter's..." She tugged at a lock of knotted hair. "Situation."

"Situation, milady?" Jeremy asked.

"My hair, obviously." She scowled. "It never stops growing. When it is cut, it grows even faster. Look around you. It's hardly a secret at this point."

"No one's hair stops growing," Jeremy pointed out. When the princess lifted a brow, he added, "True, this is a bit excessive, but surely it could be managed without you being hidden away."

Rapunzel shrugged. "Easier to hide me away. And hidden away, I shall remain. I couldn't bear to have everyone see me like this. Not even you can see the true extent of my fault."

"Surely someone as beautiful as yourself has no faults, milady, but merely a small blemish as all mortals have."

Pursing her lips, Rapunzel studied Jeremy for a moment before flicking her gaze to Craig. "Is he all right?"

"As well as he ever is, milady," Craig replied.

"So, he always talks like this?"

He shook his head. "No. Unfortunately, this is a recent change. He calls it poetry."

Rapunzel blinked. "Poetry?"

"Yes, milady," Jeremy broke in. "Poetry is considered quite fashionable. Perhaps locked aways as you've been, you haven't heard of it."

"Oh, I've heard of it," she replied. "Nothing akin to your verses, but I have heard of it."

As if taking this as a compliment, he puffed with pride. "Everything I speak is of my own creation, milady."

"No doubt." Rapunzel nodded, but Craig noticed her trying not to smirk.

For some reason, the princess's teasing annoyed Craig. Especially since Jeremy seemed completely oblivious to it. He took a step closer to the window and spoke up. "So, just to clarify, you don't wish to leave this tower?"

Rapunzel pulled at a rope of hair. "Not like this, no."

Craig sighed as a flicker of hope again lit in his son's eyes.

"Therefore, if we were to help you..." Jeremy hesitated, glancing over the heaps of hair. "Clean up a bit? You *would* want to leave?"

"I suppose so," she replied softly, as if suddenly shy. She shook her head. "But as I've said, it's not possible. Not like this."

Jeremy nodded, his gaze calculating. "If you don't mind my asking, when was the last time you cut your hair?"

Rapunzel shrugged. "I can't even remember. Years."

"So, you don't actually know the current growth rate following a cut?" he asked.

18

"No. I was but a child the last time. I believe my parents hewed it to my ears, and it grew to the floor within minutes."

"But did it stop or continue?" Jeremy pressed.

Rapunzel waved around the room. "Obviously, it continued."

"But did it continue on at a steady pace or did it slow?"

"I don't remember."

Jeremy nodded. "Then, with your permission, milady, I wish to conduct a series of experiments. We'll cut your hair as short as possible and try to calculate the speed your hair grows by studying the amount of growth that occurs within a certain time frame. Say an hour at first, but we can adjust the time restraints accordingly." He paused. "I may need an assistant."

Rapunzel didn't speak right away but eyed Jeremy with wary curiosity. Craig thought he detected a glint of newfound admiration in her eye.

Forget poetry, Craig considered. *If Jeremy wishes to win her over, he should stick with calculations!*

"An assistant?" she asked finally.

"Yes. Someone who knows more about hair itself." Jeremy faltered.

"He wants to make sure your hair comes out looking presentable in the end," Craig explained.

"Oh yes." Rapunzel nodded. "I suppose that is the overall goal, isn't it? I guess you can bring an assistant. Though only one."

"I have a cousin that should do."

"Briony?" Craig asked. When Jeremy affirmed his suspicion, he nodded. "Yes, she's very fond of hair."

Rapunzel seemed to relax slightly. "All right then. I will agree to your experimentation. It will give me something new to do, if nothing else. But you must promise to keep our operation a secret. I don't want word to get out that I'm here. You know, in case it doesn't work."

Jeremy nodded emphatically. "Of course, milady."

"And no more of this 'milady' nonsense. Call me Rapunzel."

"Yes, mi—Rapunzel," Jeremy replied in earnest. "When shall I return?"

"Same time tomorrow, I guess." Rapunzel shrugged. "Matilda is a habitual creature. If you return at the same time, you can climb up as soon as she leaves."

When everything had been settled, Craig led the way back out the window.

"There has to be a better way to do this," he grunted as he began his descent.

"There is," Rapunzel replied mildly. "Using the door. Oh, wait..."

"Ha. Ha. Ha." Craig scowled and rappelled down the tower.

~~~~~

Craig decided not to accompany Jeremy and Briony back to the tower. One visit had been enough for him. So, he wrote up some directions and sent them on their way.

His disinterest in the princess, however, did not stop Jeremy from regaling Craig on all things Rapunzel. Each night his son came straight to the bakery to inform him of everything they had tried that day.

"Our tests are going quite well," Jeremy said enthusiastically.

"That's nice."

"Yes! In fact, we've just about calculated the speed at which Rapunzel's hair grows. All we had to do was cut it and then allow it to grow for a full minute. Then we measured the amount of growth and divided that number by sixty, thereby discovering the amount of growth per second."

"Hmm."

"It's not a perfect science, of course," Jeremy continued. "Her hair seems to grow a different amount each time. Sometimes it's longer, sometimes shorter. But we've averaged the numbers and have made a qualified guess."

"How interesting."

"I know, right!"

The experiments continued until, finally, Jeremy arrived at the bakery one night with Rapunzel in tow. She stood shyly in the doorway, most of her hair piled atop her head in a messy bun. Her clothing looked a bit newer than when Craig had last seen her.

I suppose she went shopping first thing, he considered. *Next to hair, girls sure are particular about their clothes.*

"You don't mind if she stays the night, do you, Dad?" he asked. "Mom said to ask you."

"Er," Craig grunted, caught off guard. "Came down from your tower, did you?"

"Yes," Rapunzel replied, taking a hesitant step forward. "It seems as long as I cut my hair every time the clock strikes eight and two o'clock, I can more or less manage the length."

"Oh. That's nice, then."

She nodded. "I haven't told Mother and Father yet, though. So..."

"She's waiting for the right time," Jeremy added. "It's a delicate matter."

Craig scratched his neck. "I see."

"So, she can use the spare room?" he asked, his eyes pleading.

"I suppose she can for tonight," Craig replied gruffly. "But don't make a habit of it. She needs to tell her parents what she wishes to do. I mean, bloomin' onions, they're the king and queen! It's not as if she's hiding her escape from a pair of innkeepers."

"Of course!" Jeremy nodded, leading Rapunzel back toward the door. "As soon as she's ready!"

"As soon as she's ready," Craig grumbled, as the door closed behind them. He turned back to his ledger. "That'll be awhile. Might as well have asked if she could move in."

"Hopefully it does not come to that."

Craig jerked his head up to see the witch, Matilda, standing before him. He glanced at the door, then back to her. He swallowed. "I didn't hear you come in."

"Yes. I preferred it that way," Matilda replied. "Now, as you were saying, it very well could be a while before Rapunzel decides to tell her parents of her decision."

"You know about that, do you?"

"Good sir, I've known of your son's visits from the very first. Do you really think I didn't spot you two hiding in the thicket? You were wearing yellow, for goodness' sake." She shook her head. "I left your son to his experiments because I thought they might do some good. And they have."

"Oh."

"I never agreed with the decision to lock the princess away," Matilda continued with a flick of her hand. "What good does it do her to hide from the world? Much better to find a solution."

"I see."

"None of King Pacal's advisors could figure out what your son discovered in less than a week." Matilda let out a heavy sigh. "But now that a solution has been found, I see no reason to keep her in the tower."

"Of course."

"Which leads to your task."

Craig blinked. "Sorry, my what?"

"You put Rapunzel's escape into motion," Matilda said pointedly.

"Wait just a —"

"Now, you must persuade her to tell her parents," she continued. "And sooner than, 'when she's ready.'"

"Just how am I to do that?"

"I'm sure you can think of *something*. Now," she said, placing her hands down on the countertop, "do you have any of those blueberry tarts you're so famous for?"

Five minutes later, Craig watched Matilda slip out the door, a bag of blueberry tarts clutched to her chest. She'd gotten them for thirty percent off, too, having used a witch's discount that he hadn't known existed until then.

He blew out a puff of air and sat down. *Just how am I supposed to convince that princess to do anything? Girls that age are hard enough to talk to without having a royal title clinging to their name.*

Feeling defeated, Craig packed up and headed home.

~~~~~

As he and his wife prepared for bed, Craig confided his newfound duty to her. He'd expected to find some sympathy where the task was concerned, but Tess only shrugged.

"All you need to do is make her think it's her idea."

"How am I supposed to do that?" Craig scowled, taking his frustration out on his pillow. "She's made it pretty clear she's set on avoiding the issue."

Tess shrugged again. "You convince her otherwise."

"Again: how?"

She sighed. "By using the same method I do to get you to do anything: reverse psychology."

Craig blinked. "Reverse what?"

"Reverse psychology," she repeated. "It's the newest way to get what you want. Basically, you persuade someone to do something by telling them they don't want to do it. Simple."

"How is that simple?"

Tess threw back the covers. "Remember last week, when I wanted you to talk to Jeremy about his desire to become a builder?"

"Yes, and I *did* talk to him."

"You did." She nodded. "But only after I told you I should do it because he listens to me better. That's when you finally got off your butt and said you needed to do it because a son's life decisions needed to be discussed man-to-man."

Craig opened his mouth, but slowly closed it again without speaking. Tess lifted a knowing eyebrow and climbed into bed.

"Well, I'll have you know it was because of that conversation that all this Rapunzel business even came about," he growled, climbing in after her.

"And by the looks of it, that 'Rapunzel business' needed to happen," Tess retorted. "Just like you persuading her to talk to her parents needs to happen. So, figure it out, and soon. That girl was here for dinner, and she eats more than you and Jeremy put together. *And,* she's picky!"

Craig didn't sleep well that night. While the Rapunzel conundrum weighed heavily on his mind, he found himself more concerned with running through every conversation he'd had with Tess in the recent past. *Just how many times did she use this reverse psychology trick on me!* he marveled, as instance after instance seemed to bear traces of the mental manipulation.

After a night of tossing and turning, Craig rose groggy and ill-tempered to find Jeremy and Rapunzel breakfasting at the kitchen table.

He stopped in his tracks upon seeing the table littered with dishes. Most of them appeared barely touched, and apparently, all but a bowl of cereal belonged to Rapunzel.

One threatening glance from his wife told Craig he'd better start getting rid of the girl — and quick. Flinching, he took a seat across from the feasting princess.

No use having this conversation on an empty stomach, Craig considered. He reached toward a plate heaped with pancakes, but Rapunzel quickly batted it away.

"Oh, sorry. Not used to sharing," she said weakly. "I'm planning to eat those."

"I see," he replied flatly. "Might I ask what here you don't plan to eat?"

Rapunzel nodded to a bowl of grits.

Craig grimaced but pulled the bowl closer. *At least they're doused in butter.*

"So, Rapunzel," he announced, dipping his spoon into the gluey mixture, "about talking to your parents —"

"Oh, I don't believe I'm ready yet," she said quickly.

"Yes. I assumed as much and —"

"It's only that I don't think they'll approve of my leaving as I did," she continued. "With no written notice or anything."

"Right, well, I was going to say —"

"Mother and Father are sticklers for doing things in the proper decorum, you see." Rapunzel took a bite of a pancake, made a face, and set it back down. "You can have those if you want."

"Oh. Thanks."

Nodding, she reached for a slice of bacon. "They'll have expected me to write a five-paragraph essay detailing all the reasons why I should be allowed out. And you know, writing essays is nothing like creative writing. I don't mind writing creatively now and again — short stories, maybe the odd limerick."

Jeremy perked up.

"Please don't," she said quickly.

He sank back down, returning to his cereal.

"But I just *hate* writing essays." She shook her head and snapped the end of the bacon off with her teeth. "This is really good, Tess. See, I told you if you just cooked it a little longer, it would crisp to perfection."

Tess nodded politely, but then shot Craig another glower as soon as Rapunzel's back was turned.

Craig swallowed. *This reverse psychology thing is so much harder than Tess said it'd be. I can barely get a word in!*

"So, you see," Rapunzel continued, "I just don't think I'm mentally prepared yet for facing their condescension."

"Of course not." Craig nodded. "I just—"

"Though I suppose their disappointment will only deepen the longer I keep this from them," she pointed out. "That wouldn't do me any favors either."

"No, but—"

"And unless I plan to hide here for the foreseeable future, my parents will just find out from someone else that I left the tower, making the discovery ten times worse than if I'd just told them myself." Rapunzel bit her lip. "Then they might make me write a ten-paragraph essay!"

She shook her head, meeting Craig's eye. "You're right. I should probably tell them of my departure sooner rather than later."

"Right," he breathed as she pushed herself from the table.

"Jeremy, you shall accompany me to the castle," she said, motioning for him to stand. "You will need to explain your experiments to my parents. Hopefully, they consider an oral presentation as good as an essay. And if they don't, you can be my buffer."

"Glad to mi—Rapunzel," Jeremy replied happily.

"Thank you for your insight," she said, nodding at Craig. "I appreciate your candor." She turned to Tess. "And thank you for your hospitality. I hope I wasn't too much bother."

"Of course not, dear," Tess assured her.

As the two young people departed, Tess sank down in the chair beside Craig. "How can someone raised away from society for so long still be so spoiled?"

He shrugged and grabbed a slice of bacon. "I think it just goes along with being a princess."

"Hmm." She also selected a bacon slice. "I suppose I figured her unusual upbringing would have had some effect toward counteracting her princess nature."

Craig shrugged again and held up the bacon. "This really is good, by the way."

"I know," she replied tersely. "Little brat was right." She brushed off her fingers and rose from the table. "But hopefully she's back where she belongs now. Didn't I tell you reverse psychology was the key? You need to work on your technique a bit, but you did well for your first try."

~~~~~

When a week had passed and Craig hadn't heard any further news regarding the princess—or of his son, for that matter—he figured all had gone well at the castle.

Maybe they made him an earl. Or maybe a knight. He sighed. *Better than a builder.*

No sooner had this thought crossed his mind than the bakery door swung open, and his son strode in. He didn't look as if he'd been knighted or granted an earldom. If anything, he looked sad.

Craig waited for Jeremy to say something. When all he did was mope around to the back of the counter to rummage through the cream puffs, however, Craig knew he'd have to speak first.

He cleared his throat. "So, how's Rapunzel?"

A pained expression passed over Jeremy's features, but instead of answering, he merely stuffed a cream puff into his mouth.

"I see," Craig replied. "Well, don't eat all of those. The miller has ordered a dozen to be picked up this afternoon. I don't have time to make more."

Jeremy switched to strudel.

"Nope, those are spoken for too."

Groaning, Jeremy crumpled to the floor, his head in his hands. "I can't even eat away my sorrow."

"Hmm, and what sorrow might that be?"

He flicked his hand in a weak dismissal.

"Okay then." Craig started to turn away, but Jeremy lifted his head. "Rapunzel. My dearest Rapunzel. She left me for Thomas Joiner!"

He lifted a brow. "The carpenter's son?"

"It seems she's fond of well-made cabinetry. Oh Rapunzel, why!" Jeremy wailed.

The fact that cabinets impressed the princess struck Craig funny, and he turned away to hide his face.

"And what's worse is that I still have to see her every day," Jeremy moaned. "I was made one of the royal scientists."

Craig blinked. "Royal what?"

"Scientists," he replied. "They do experiments for King Pacal."

"Experiments like what you did to figure out Rapunzel's hair situation?"

Jeremy grunted noncommittally. "I can't really talk about it."

"I see." He crossed his arms. *Perhaps Jeremy procuring a court appointment isn't better than being a builder after all. Secret experimentation? Bah!* "Is this one of those placements you...aren't allowed to leave?"

Jeremy glanced up, suddenly alert. "I can leave whenever I wish, but why would I?"

"Because you seem miserable?" Craig pointed out before adding to himself, *And your job is a load of crock!*

His son shook his head. "Even so, I don't want to leave. I love my position. I think it's what I was made to do! Calculations. Experimentation. There's nothing better!"

"It's even better than building?" Craig pressed. "What about your dream of creating architecture? Have you given up on that, then?"

"Being a scientist is way better than that." He snorted. "What I do at the castle actually *means* something."

"I'm sure buildings mean something to the people that use them."

Jeremy shrugged. "Maybe. But like you proved, Dad, *anyone* can build a building. You must have a certain skillset to be a scientist."

"Right," Craig said flatly. Annoyed, he turned away and began gathering the ingredients to make a puff pastry.

Bull-headed boy, he inwardly growled. *If wanting to be a builder wasn't bad enough, now he's a scientist. Doing secret things! No good can come out of that. But what to do...*

Craig tilted his head as an idea came to him. "I suppose you just have to get over it, then."

Jeremy sat up a little straighter. "Get over what?"

"Over Rapunzel spurning you," he replied as he measured two cups of flour into a bowl. "Seems to me you gained a good job out of the deal. Maybe even your dream job. Why let a girl ruin the experience for you?"

He cast a furtive glance at Jeremy. He was happy to see his son looked stricken by the prospect. *Now, that's reverse psychology! He'll quit his job, chase the girl, and eventually return to normal life. Maybe even as a baker!*

"You know, you're right," Jeremy said, nodding slowly.

Craig about dropped the salt. "Wait, what?"

"You're right, Dad. I can't let Rapunzel ruin this opportunity for me. If she likes Thomas Joiner better than me, so be it." Jeremy pushed himself to his feet. "I love my job. That should be enough. Thanks for pointing out what truly matters."

"Right..."

Jeremy patted his father on the shoulder and headed toward the door. As he rounded the corner of the counter, he pointed to a tray of cinnamon rolls. "Are those reserved?"

"You can take one," Craig sighed.

Smiling, Jeremy selected a gooey roll and placed it in a bag. "And who knows," he added as he tugged open the front door, "Rapunzel could always change her mind." He winked and strode out.

Craig's shoulders sagged, a bitter wave of failure washing over him as he watched his son leave. He shook his head with a sigh. For the second time in fifteen years, Craig felt stupid.

END

Rapun Zel
Michelle Houston

I am Rapun Zel. I am the village weaver, werewolf, curse recipient, and blessed beyond abundance.

This is my story.

I have hardly any memories of my actual parents. I was around two when they died. I do remember my father's booming laugh, and I think I remember hearing my mother singing. That's it.

The story I've heard is that the neighbors woke up to my wailing. When they investigated, both my mom and dad had succumbed to the plague that was going around Mervellius that year. They notified the body wagon and the orphanage at the same time.

All I got to keep from my home was my name, Zelmantha.

The orphanage wasn't bad. Or rather I should say it was as good as it could be. Since there were no older kids, bullying was a minor issue. We had enough to eat, whether we liked it or not. Same with our monochrome clothes. There were enough beds that we only had to share with one or two other kids. And noise was always in abundant supply.

The thing we were lacking was security and love.

Everyone knew that the year your chin hit the top of the table, you would be taken on the adoption tour of the country. The matrons assured us they would only put us with good people, and if no one claimed us the government would take care of us at the older orphanages, where we would learn useful skills as we worked.

But with no one ever coming back from the tour, rumors grew and swarmed. The worst in my mind at the time was the stories of ogres adopting kids to eat them. Now, I know the worst were the stories of abusive adults.

Not that I had to deal with that, thankfully.

We traipsed from town to town, getting off of the wagons with the king's guardians at each stop. In our grey clothes we looked like a spreading puddle of dirty water amidst the colorful background of the towns' marketplaces. It didn't matter if the town was too small for a name or was so big we lost ourselves in it, we were set out on display. The king's decree was that all citizens come and see the orphan parade and pray about taking one of us. We all hoped to find someone to claim us, and in our innermost core, we dreamed of finding the parental love we had lost.

I don't remember much of the journey, other than the time Corey threw up on all of us after eating fish for the first time, and how uncomfortable it was to sleep in the wagons night after night. I do remember wishing I hadn't grown so fast, that I could stay in the safety of the orphanage.

But most of all, I remember the despair I felt as the tour dragged on and one by one my friends were chosen while the rest of us were consolidated into fewer and fewer wagons.

By the time we were nearing the end of the tour, I was feeling unwanted and unlovely. No one had picked me. One of our last stops was Nahwear, where we all lined up as usual and the whole village had to walk past.

Mama Rapun tells me I looked like a lonely puppy, with my jet-black hair hanging down to hide my expression, yet my dark eyes peeking through with forlorn hope like black garnets gleaming in a bed of cooled lava. Even though she had come with no intention of adopting a child, she couldn't let me go.

In my excitement, my first impression of Mama Rapun was of a short angel with warm, strong arms. I barely registered her face and was shocked the next day to discover how much we resembled each other. We both had darker coloring, dark hair, dark eyes. I vowed my eyes would learn to laugh like hers, my mouth would learn to pour out blessings like hers, so that we would be even more alike.

I thought my fate was secure, my path laid out.

I was now of the family Rapun. I had a new name. Rapun Zelmantha, or Rapun Zel for short.

The first six years passed uneventfully. Our small village accepted me, from the scruffy farmers who occasionally came to shop to the few merchants in our miniscule village center. Even the local baroness would just sniff at me when I barreled into her, all clumsy legs and arms and inattentive childhood play as I ran with the other youngsters.

Mama Rapun taught me her trade, weaving and sewing. She made all the rough cloth for the village and was a wonder at turning recalcitrant fibers from our sheep into yarn that could be knitted into warm garments. She was also a wonder at turning a recalcitrant, scared girl into a contented, confident young lady.

As she taught me how to spin the wool into yarn, she taught me how to spin love into all aspects of life. Her tedious lessons in weaving contained truths about the necessary presence of kindness and perseverance in all our actions. And as we danced the yarn in and out with our needles, I learned to see how her care for me tiptoed through all that she did.

We still had our spats. She was conservative; I was adventurous. She found joy in the repetitive mundane; I loved the joy of surprise or novelty.

I used to pour over our geography books, dreaming of other lands or excitedly tracing the maiden pilgrimage all girls had to make when they reached adulthood. Coming from Nahwear, my journey to Saint Mehter's congregation would take me across half our kingdom.

However, even when I was being spanked for going too far away from the village or yelling about my curfew, I never doubted her love for me. I was content.

One thing both Mama and I agreed on: you could never think too much or learn too much. Whenever a traveling scholar came to our village, both Mama and I would attend their performances and buy at least a little bit of their wares. Our rooms filled with books and pamphlets, and our conversations while weaving or knitting never got dull.

I remember after one scholar performed, I came back home laughing at the tales he had told of other countries. He claimed some countries didn't have our types of plants and animals. That the trees there couldn't pull up their roots and move when the soil got bad. I asked him if the trees killed animals to fertilize the bad soil, but he said they just died! Imagine! And even worse, he claimed that the dark aerial nests of the sky birds were just clouds with extra water in them. When these "rain clouds" got heavy enough, they caused rain. I tried asking questions, like how clear water could make a white cloud dark, or how heavy raindrops could just float in the air, but he was not one of the scholars who entertained questions. Mama was as skeptical as I was. Everyone knew rain came from the sky birds keeping their dark nests wet.

Anyway, my life changed when puberty changed me. A lot of girls had to stay inside for a day every moon cycle because they felt so bad. I had to stay inside because I turned into a wolf. A large, black-haired wolf with dark brown eyes and heavy fur.

But as Mama pointed out, at least I didn't have cramps.

The first time the change happened, I didn't even realize it. I woke up in bed feeling hot, and sleepily kicked the sheets off me before falling back asleep. The next morning, I couldn't understand why my nightgown sleeves were not on my arms or why there was so much black hair in my bed.

The second time it happened, I was so hot, I got up to open the window. Or tried to get up. I fell off the bed and got tangled in my sheets. My arms and legs weren't working properly and I got scared. I tried to call for Mama, but only loud, rough noises came out. Mama burst into my room, gaping at what she saw.

"Zel?" Her voice trembled, but she moved slowly toward me. "Do you understand me, Tib?" I could only whine in response, but she swept me up in her arms and hugged me close.

You had to admire the strength of a love that would put a hundred pounds of toothy panic close to her heart. She stayed with me all night.

The next day we delved into our books, looking for answers. Shifters, especially werewolves, weren't unknown in our part of the country, but they were very rare, and it wasn't considered in good taste to talk about that part of someone's private life. We found out that I was an average-strength werewolf. I kept my human mind and understanding, but I couldn't control when I transformed.

We had been living in two small rooms above Mama's shop in the middle of Nahwear. After suffering through a few more transformations, where I was so hot from all that fur, Mama dug into her savings and bought a rundown house at the edge of town.

It was a house that had long entranced my imagination. A good portion on one side was so water-damaged it was literally rotting away, with weeds growing on the roof and some bushes sprouting through holes in the floor. It was so unstable, Mama had forbidden me to go inside.

But the middle portion of the house still had a good roof and useable, if dirty, rooms. I wandered through them, excitedly dreaming of where we would put the chairs, my bed, our looms. Mama looked at the abandoned rat's nest in the corner and swatted down some of the bigger spiderwebs and determinedly kept her smile in place. Looking back, I think I heard a lot of calming, deep breaths coming from her while I wove visions over our new purchase.

But the far side of the house was a true hidden gem. It was a stone tower, the remnants of what once had been a church. It only had two rooms, one at the bottom with a high ceiling and one at the top, where the bells used to be hung. Covered with vines on the outside, the light shining through the small windows in the bottom room cast green diamonds along the walls. When we slipped up the stairs to the top, we gasped with amazement at the views from all sides. Sharp mountain crags, waving forests, lush sheep folds. There were more empty windows than walls, and a refreshing breeze poured through while the stone still radiated cooling waves despite the summer heat. Mama looked at me with a huge grin.

"Zel, this is yours. Your sanctuary every month."

I hugged her so tight she squeaked.

Mama called in many favors, cooked a huge meal, and had the village men tear down the rotted portion while putting in a new wall to enclose the middle portion. The village girls helped clear the inside of animals and dirt. Sadly, we also tore down all the vines climbing the grey stone tower.

My upstairs sanctuary lived up to its promise. No matter the outside temperature, the room remained cool with the wide windows and the cold stone floor. When it was time for my change, I would sleep up there. Many nights I spread out tummy first on that wonderful stone floor and let it soak the heat from me.

When I was eighteen, it was time for my maiden journey. The law of Mervellius required ladies, after three years of puberty, to make the pilgrimage to the congregation of Saint Mehter. This allowed the girls to explore other possible occupations besides marriage. Only after that trip could a woman marry. The king provided an armed escort twice a year so that no one worried about the girls' safety.

Since Nahwear is so close to our border, I had a longer trip than most to get to the congregation. I didn't mind. I loved seeing the different parts of our kingdom. After we left the mountains of my home, the land turned flat and treeless. There was so much sky to see, with birds of all colors and sizes flying back and forth. I wondered if something had driven all the trees away, but no one knew. It may have been the little furry mys with large eyes that crawled around everywhere. Though they were cute to look at, I did not enjoy them burrowing into my bed at night.

Then we traveled through an area of lakes and marshes. I got to see the houses and the people moving around on stilts, as they followed the migrating fish and reeds. My favorite houses were the ones with stork legs. They looked so funny bobbing along. Some of the people there told me the inside shook terribly and they had to pack everything away when the house moved. I was glad Mama's house stayed put.

But my favorite place was the city in the hills. The silver-green multi-story houses were all dome-shaped. I was never sure if I was looking at a hill or a building in the distance. And instead of curtains, long stemmed flowers grew up from chinks in the walls, covering the windows. The combination of color, beauty, and form was amazing.

When we finally reached the congregation of Saint Mehter, we were welcomed into their squat domiciles, which were half-hidden in the reddish ground. There were several large buildings, where the matrons and guests lived and worked. Above ground, a patchwork of greens showed the different crops tended by the matrons.

For three days we stayed there. The matrons showed us life in the congregation. We picked produce, dyed cloth, and cooked meals. We mended holes and laughed at our ineptitude. We had late night chat sessions and were inducted into all the rules that governed the place. It seemed to be a pleasant, though hard, life. But it wasn't mine. I missed Mama and my village.

Of course, we also visited the statue of Saint Mehter, supposedly made by one of her many children (if having twenty kids gives you hips that wide, count me out). Her kindness to women, maidens and orphans was told in story after story. Her demanding and busy life showed in her rough hands and bent back. But she had a smile I could trust. Two of the girls in our group decided to stay, preferring the congregation to the life they had at home. The rest of us left with our guards for the return trip.

We had dropped off all but myself and two other girls when the full moon rose. Mama and I had hoped I would be at home by then, but we had plans to handle the complication. I slept in my own tent, at the edge of camp, like usual. The girls knew I liked my privacy and sleep. I had never participated in any group gatherings after sundown, no matter how tempting their laughter was.

I had arranged the bedding to look like I was asleep in bed in case anyone looked in. I was under the cot, belly against the cool earth floor, while I waited to turn back and get rid of the hot fur.

Suddenly a flurry of dark grey sky birds and nests zoomed over our location. They were fighting, hurling their light curses with terrific bangs at each other. One curse missed its intended victim and plummeted to earth, hitting near our camp.

The guards were fine. As king's men, they all had powerful deflection spells woven into their clothing. We girls were not as fortunate.

The crashed curse scared everyone, but no one seemed hurt, so they all went to bed as the quarreling sky birds sped on toward another part of our kingdom. The remaining birds were quieter, simply keeping their nests good and moist, and soaking our camp in the process.

The next morning was an unpleasant surprise. And this is from someone who likes surprises.

The other two girls woke up with their hair about a foot longer and covered in sloughed body hair. Apparently, the curse caused all of their hair roots to permanently speed up, leading to longer tresses but also causing their arm and leg hair to go through several cycles of growth and shedding in one night.

If it sounds kind of gross, it is.

On the other hand, their mouse brown hair turned into a gorgeous shade of golden sunshine. As Mama says, there is always a blessing in every curse.

The curse affected me differently. Probably because I was in wolf form when it hit.

My hair did change color. I no longer had jet black hair or fur. It was now a light silver, almost white.

And my hair did not change length. Since I normally wore it braided, I was able to pretend it did grow, so the girls wouldn't suspect I was different.

Instead, my wolf fur grew. All night I was surrounded by an increasingly large pile of fur. I thought I would cook myself.

And when I changed back, a pile of wolf fur remained nested around me. I hid it in one of my bags.

In Mervellius, these things happen. Not to everyone, but anyone you ask will know of someone, however distant, who had a magical curse or blessing. You just deal with it.

So when I got home and tried to panic about the curse, Mama calmed me. She told me God never allows a curse without a blessing or a blessing without a curse. We just needed to look for it.

I cut my hair short, to make the color less noticeable so people wouldn't stare so much. And when my change happened the next month, Mama stayed with me, giving me cold water and combing the fur out as much as she could so I could lay on the cold stone floor.

I was still hot, but I wasn't cooking.

Afterward, Mama looked at the fur. There was more than the first time. My body must have saved up all the growth the other girls experienced in a month and shoved it on me in one day. There was about twenty to thirty feet of fur.

I was not happy.

Where is the blessing? I wondered.

What most people don't realize is that what we call animal fur is only the top layer. Most of the "hair" is actually really soft down underneath the top fur. The down keeps the animal warm.

Normally the down is so short you can't do much with it.

Mama pointed out that every month we would have yards of down. All in a beautiful light silver that we could dye into other colors as well.

So Mama and I did what we normally did with wool. We carded it, spun it, and wove it into blankets. Wonderfully warm, soft blankets. The coarser top fur turned into incredibly strong rope. Both sold out as soon as we could make them.

We were making twice as much money as usual. The only added expense was my eating. I was starving after all that growth. I would be weak and eat non-stop for two days. But again, no cramps! And I didn't have to worry about gaining weight!

We were doing so well that Mama was able to set aside some of the wool each month to weave for the poor. Our local baroness made sure nobody froze in the winter by keeping one of her barns open for the poor. Now we were able to provide additional comfort in the form of blankets and beds as well. Every time I saw an unfortunate individual wrap up and cuddle down in one of my blankets, I thanked God for my curse.

The other girls eventually found a blessing to their curse as well. They still had to sweep almost constantly, but they were able to go to the city a couple of times a month and sell their hair to wig makers. I've heard the price of wigs has dramatically dropped, and my fellow victims have extra money.

Only one thing marred my contentment.

Erik.

Erik was several years older than me. He was apprenticed to the local trader, so I saw him a lot as he ran errands around the town and picked up supplies from us. He was kind, tall, dark-haired, and totally handsome. Plus a killer smile, just slightly asymmetric, to make it zing right into my heart. I had been crushing on him for years, and now that I was back from my journey, I thought he was spending extra time in our shop.

Imagine my shock when I found out he proposed to another girl in a neighboring village.

She was everything I wasn't. Dark hair, light eyes, shy glances.

I was polite. I smiled. I made them a beautiful warm blanket to go on their bed for two. And I wanted to run away and never see their happiness again.

I had been stewing for six months. Six months during which the village seemed to close in, the work seemed to drag on, and none of the other boys looked interesting or were interested in me.

Ugh.

Life.

That was when the next traveling scholar, Leven Parr, came through.

He was young for a scholar. Probably only a little older than Erik. He was not handsome like Erik, but he was smart and kind and appreciated my questions. After the performance, he even sat down with me to show me some pictures of other countries and wonders. He talked of the fun and wonder of traveling. I felt like I smiled more in those few hours than I had for six months.

The day before he left town, he came to our shop.

"Zel, I have a letter for you."

"For me? How? Why?" I was totally at a loss as to who could be writing to me.

"Her name is Sora, Temal Sora. She said she was on the maiden journey with you and your friends. She told me what happened with the sky birds." His voice dropped as he leaned closer to me. "She also told me she had found a way to break the curse."

"What!" I grabbed the letter out of his hand and hurriedly read it. Sora told how she had let down all of her hair, shaved it all off, right at the skin, after getting frustrated with it one night. She said it never grew again. She no longer had head or body hair of any length. She was free.

My mind flooded with that thought. I could be free of the curse. Free to travel without worrying about a load of hair every month. Free of the heat and the exhaustion and the hunger. All I had to do was let down my hair forever.

My blank expression must have triggered inspiration in Parr. He leaned forward.

"Zel, I like you. You are pretty and smart. Would you like to travel with me? No ties, no dalliances, I promise. All proper behavior. But it would give us a chance to get to know each other better, and give you a chance to travel. I know you would like that."

If my mind was stalled before, it leapt into a chaotic turning of tangled thoughts now. Excitement, anticipation, dread, sorrow, all at once and together.

"I..I..I don't know," I finally managed to stutter.

He gave me a smile. "Don't worry. Think about it. I have to go through another couple of villages before I come back through this way." He scrunched up his eyes, doing some quick calculations in his thoughts. "I should be back in another three weeks. We'll talk then."

I nodded, my ability to hold a witty conversation, or any conversation, currently nonexistent.

I did think about it. And prayed about it. And talked to Mama about it.

Mama said I was old enough to make up my mind, that she would support me. She said she would always be here for me to come back to.

When I asked about the lack of wolf fur, she smiled.

"Zel, my Tib, we have saved quite a bit the last two years. I will be fine without it."

I thought about seeing new places.

I thought about the beauty of my home village.

I imagined the excitement I would feel at seeing the ocean.

I imagined missing the expressions of the poor people when they picked up one of my blankets, or the enthusiastic thanks I got when I made a custom piece for someone that lit up their life.

I thrilled at the thought of new and exciting people I would meet, and getting to know Parr better.

I sorrowed at missing the people who already loved me and cared for me.

I thought about never feeling the heat of fur, the accompanying hunger. Never sweeping up a pile of my own wool. Never carding it, dying it, weaving it, creating something beautiful with it to grace other people.

I weighed all my thoughts in the balance and made up my mind. I consulted with Mama and enjoyed her soft smile of pride and encouragement. And I waited for Parr.

It was actually closer to four weeks than three when he returned. I had gone through another change, and was presently weaving the wool, dyed a light rose for an expected baby, when he walked into the shop.

He stopped in the doorway and struck a dramatic pose with his hand in the air. "Maiden Rapun Zel! It is I, your handsome prince, here to rescue you from your tower and try to earn your fair hand."

I giggled at his playacting. "Leven Parr, it is good to see you again. Did your trip go well?"

Parr dropped his arm and his dramatics and came to where I was sitting. He leaned against the counter. "Very well, thank you. I have sold most of my parchment, all of my writing supplies, and several of my books. I will return to the capital to restock before heading east to the other side of the kingdom."

He paused and looked at me piercingly. "Have you decided? Will you let down your hair and come with me?"

I smiled and put out my hand to him, which he took softly. "Parr, thank you so much for your offer. After much thought, I am going to decline."

He looked a bit sad, but smiled back at me and squeezed my hand before letting go. "Oh well. Are you just declining traveling with me, or are you also declining to let down your hair?"

"Both. My hair is a bit of a curse, but it is also a blessing. I don't want to lose the blessing. And I have other blessings here as well that I don't want to lose. I am staying."

My voice got excited as I shared with him the rest of my plans. "However, I am going to start traveling more. Mama Rapun and I talked about it. I'll start traveling to open up new markets for our products, and to look for different fabrics that would work well for our people. If you give me your contact information, I'll try to arrange my trips to coincide with some of yours. It would be nice to see a familiar face in strange lands."

A slow smile bloomed over Parr's face. "Indeed it would, Zel. I look forward to it. Would you have time to share some tea with me tonight? I leave early tomorrow."

I enjoyed my time with Parr that evening. But I was surprised that I wasn't sad to see him go the next day. I was content again.

~~~~~

It has been a few years now. I travel for months at a time, bringing back bushels of my fur and samples of other fabrics.

We have hired another apprentice to help us with the sheep wool. Mama and I continue to be the only ones who work with the wolf wool. We sell some locally, we give some away, and we have found a large demand for it nationally.

Erik and his wife had a baby. She is the cutest thing. I get to babysit her at least once a week when I am home.

"Zel, hurry up, he's here!" Mama's voice bounces upstairs.

Remember how I said none of the other boys in the village were interested in me?

"Coming!" I finish applying my makeup and swish my way toward the door.

Boy was I wrong!

END

The Lost Princess
Kaitlyn Emery

Who could love a witch?

Ever since the first time I snuck a peak at the grimoire, I wondered if I had fated myself to a life of being seen as the villain, just like my captor.

My legs dangled from the roof's ledge like my sanity. The sloping tiles dug into my back, their warmth soaking into my body as I watched the sky change colors. The sun crept further and further into its resting place behind the wall of jagged rocks that ripped through the landscape, cutting me off from the outside world.

The barrier used to make me feel safe. Now it was a cage, and I was the butterfly whose wings had been torn from its body. Trapped and flightless. No way to soar beyond my prison.

I sat up, pushing my heavy braids off my shoulder, judging the distance between the watchtower roof and the ground. I was six the first time I contemplated jumping from the watchtower. I knew it would kill me, but at least I would finally be free...

I longed for a mother's love and human connection—two things Romilda never provided. She loved her power more than she could ever love me. I couldn't remember a time when she cared. Magic met my needs growing up. Even as a toddler, back when I thought she was my mother, there was no genuine love or affection. Romilda would leave me for weeks at a time, sobbing and crying, awaiting her return. When I was old enough to climb to the tower's window, I would watch for her. Always waiting.

Those were my earliest memories. Loneliness. Fear. Waiting.

I snapped my fingers over and over, using the flame flickering on the tips with every snap to lull me into a trance.

A dark head of hair popped up from the ledge where my legs hung. The look on the twelve-year-old's face could only be described as resigned frustration. "Jewel's being a baby. She's tired, and whiny, and doesn't like when you are out on the roof. She says it scares her. And she's annoying me. Can't you come put her to bed already?"

I sighed, flopping back against the roof tiles and letting the dancing flame fizzle out. The stars were just starting to appear in a sky of pinks and orange. "The only one I hear whining is you, Wish."

She shoved my legs, making me shift my weight and return to a seated position. Wish's scrunched nose and stuck out tongue were not an attractive greeting.

"All right, all right," I huffed. "Move out of my way."

Wish scurried back out of sight and down, through the tower window. I scooted to the edge of the roof, grasped the unfriendly gargoyle standing at attention, and swung myself over the edge and into the same window.

"Hurry up!" Wish cried over her shoulder as she descended the spiral staircase two steps at a time.

Romilda resented Wish, the inconvenient child with the long, dark waves. But I loved the girl who was the reason I didn't jump from this tower twelve years ago. I still contemplated whether that made her my savior or my jailer, but at the end of the day, I continued to draw breath because of Wish.

I could remember Wish's arrival into my world like it was yesterday. Romilda had been home when I stood on the edge of the windowsill, despair driving me to that moment. We had had another fight. Romilda had been gone longer than usual that time, and as soon as she returned, she retreated to her lair. I begged her to take me down with her so I didn't have to be alone again. The answer was the same every time.

No.

I couldn't take it anymore, so there I stood, on the windowsill ledge, counting down my demise at the tender age of six.

That was when I witnessed something I'd never seen before. Walking through the barrier toward the cottage was a stranger. No one came in or out of the barrier, ever, except Romilda. But on that day, an old woman, wrapped in a cloak, skulked across the field at dusk toward my home.

This was the most exciting thing to ever happen in the monotonous life I lived, so I climbed from the windowsill and snuck down the tower stairs. I heard whispers before I could see the light of the cottage hearth illuminating the old woman's figure outside the front door. A basket was slung over her arm.

"I told you never to come here!" Romilda's tone was sharp and pointed, like a sword thrust into someone's chest.

"I know, I know, but look! I placed a sleeping spell to quiet her, but I can't keep the awful thing! Can't you add the little rat to your collection? The noise is horrible!"

"I already have one I don't need," Romilda retorted. "Why would I want another?"

"It's not a collection if you only have one," the other woman offered.

Romilda snorted, lifting the corner of the blanket draped over the basket. "How did you acquire her in the first place?"

I could see the other woman shiver in disgust. "It was another thieving flesh bag! A farmer, and he sought to steal from me!"

"Peasants are such vile creatures!" Romilda agreed, seeming to forget for the moment that she was angry at the other woman for violating our home with her presence. "What did he steal, Golga?"

"He wanted to steal a wish from my well, but he was unsuccessful. He begged and groveled—something about his crops, but I didn't pay attention. He had to pay, Romilda! Had to! I can't have rodents scurrying all over and taking whatever they fancy! I remembered what you did when that horrible villager shot your stag to feed his wife and child during the famine. I cast him out and took his child as punishment!"

"Hush, you horrid fool!" Romilda cried, quickly placing her hand over the woman's mouth, glancing around to see if anyone had heard her.

I shrunk deeper into the shadows. As Romilda scanned the darkness, I hoped her sharp eyes couldn't pierce through the shadows hiding me. I held my breath and imagined all the horrible things she could turn me into. But, after a moment, Romilda seemed satisfied her secret was safe. She turned back to Golga and narrowed her eyes, voice menacing. "I have what I need from the first one. I don't need another one to anchor the spell."

"Your talisman will be healthier if she has a plaything. That will strengthen the magic. Please, Romilda, I wanted to punish the flesh bag, not myself in the process! This child's shrieks are horrible. Horrible! I'll make you a trade."

Romilda's eyes lit up at this idea. "What sort of trade?"

"A valuable one."

The two women began to haggle over the price for taking in the other witch's captive while I snuck back to my room and hid under the covers, afraid Romilda would know I'd heard her secret.

What was I to Romilda? She said she had what she needed from me. What had I given her? What made me, a rat, useful? What was my purpose? And what was a talisman?

I dreamed that night of a man bouncing me on his knee and a woman, with hair as red and wild as my own, gently caressing my face. I had dreamed of them before, but that night I knew these dreams were a glimmer of the life I had before my capture.

I never again saw Romilda as my mother.

The next morning, Wish was deposited into my care. She was thin and fussy, but she gave me purpose. And when Romilda left, I was no longer alone. That was Wish's purpose. To keep my will to live going for whatever reason Romilda needed me.

I still toyed with the idea of taking my life, from time to time. Especially in those moments of self-reflection when I felt like I was becoming Romilda in my pursuit of magic. But I knew I couldn't leave the girls, even though the feeling of freeing myself from this bondage never left.

Jewel's pathetic wailing pulled me from my reminiscing. Leaving this life was not my current priority. Taming the raging emotions of a five-year-old was.

"Whatever is the matter, you silly thing?" I asked the screaming toddler. Wish stuck her fingers in her ears, glaring at Jewel's outbursts like daggers taking aim.

"Fawn!" Jewel cried, throwing herself at me and clinging to my skirts. "You came back!"

"Jewel, what have we talked about?" I brushed golden strands off her damp cheek and tucked them behind her ear.

Jewel's lip quivered slightly. "That you won't leave me."

"That's right! How could I ever leave such a face?" I pulled the five-year-old into my lap and hugged her like I would never let go. I tried to be patient with her in these moments, remembering how I felt when Romilda would leave me alone.

Wish snorted. "I sure could!"

"Fawn! Wish is being mean!" Jewel wailed, bursting back into tears.

I narrowed my eyes at Wish. "She's just teasing. We would never leave our girl. Sometimes I just need time to think by myself."

Jewel snuggled against my chest, rubbing her eyes with her fists.

"Clearly someone is tired. I think it's time we get you girls off to bed."

"Aw, man!" Wish groaned. "Why do you have to be such a baby, Jewel?"

"Because she is a baby," I said, defending her. "Now come on, Wish." I carried Jewel off to the bedroom, Wish dragging her feet in defiance behind me.

I playfully plopped the fussy girl onto her pillow and grabbed a hairbrush. "All right, Jewel, you're a big girl. There's nothing to cry about. Let's fix your hair for bed." I sat down on the mattress, humming softly, working my brush through the thick golden locks that tumbled down her back.

"Tell us a story, Fawn?" Jewel asked with a yawn.

I felt drained from another long day of caring for the two girls—breaking up petty squabbles, tending to the chickens and the milk cow—but Jewel could always tug at my heart. She was still so naive and unfettered by this dreary life we led. Stories were the one thing that could change from day to day.

I glanced over at Wish to see her propped on her pillow, waiting for the story she knew would come. I forced a smile for them, resigned to my fate.

"There are many types of magic in this world," I began. "As many types as there are people. Some you feel deep in your bones. Others can be dug up from the ground and used to produce powerful potions. And some can be found within a single strand of hair."

Magic was as familiar to the girls as air. Our home was filled with it. Cupboards that never ran empty, washbasins that always maintained crystal clear water, and candles that never grew smaller with use were just a few examples. Romilda studied magic obsessively and would spend hours in the lair, brewing new potions to take with her when she left.

I learned a long time ago to stop asking Romilda to teach me magic. She feared magic as much as she craved it. If I were to learn her ways, I could rival her power and, by default, her control. The only way to gain knowledge, I learned, was to take it.

"Does my hair have magic?" Jewel cried, clapping her hands in delight. She preferred stories that included her.

"Why not? Anything is possible in a story," I replied, tucking her under the covers and kissing her cheek. I would never let the girls near the forbidden lair, afraid Romilda would catch them, or their souls become as tainted as my own by practicing magic. After all, witches never had happy endings in the stories.

"Hair that glows pure as a drop of sunlight," I continued, running my fingers through Jewel's blond strands, "has great powers indeed!"

"Tell me!" Jewel clapped eagerly.

I smiled. "With a flick of your magic hair, you bring life into the world. Wherever your hair touches, jewels grow. Beautiful jewels fit for a princess!"

I wove my fingers through the air, my story coming to life like drawings in a picture book. Sparkling gems tumbled from the long golden curls of the character resembling Jewel.

Mesmerized, Jewel's eyelids grew heavy as she smiled and snuggled back into her pillow, watching the narrative. "I love my power."

"What about me?" Wish asked.

I manipulated my powers through my fingers again, adding a character that resembled Wish to the narrative. I moved to her bed and sat behind her, removing the double braids that ran down her back.

Romilda had three rules, the first of which was that no knife could ever touch our hair. This rule started before I could remember, when I was a child and my auburn curls seemed to take on a life of their own. Over the years I developed quite the talent for plaiting, winding, and piling my wild curls onto my head and down my back so they didn't drag on the ground behind me.

Romilda always said my hair was a side effect of growing up in close proximity to the magic infusing our small world and feeding its growth. I believed her until the day I realized neither of the younger girls' hair grew like mine. It was yet another mystery surrounding the world in which I was trapped.

"Your hair," I began, "dark as night, would enchant anyone who looked upon you with your beauty. Your every whim would be met simply with a bat of your eyelids and a toss of your hair. Humanity would fall at your feet and worship you as the queen you are."

Wish smirked at the hordes of vague figures that bowed before her in a wave, their faces on the ground. "And my first decree as queen would be chocolates for every meal!"

"What a notable first decree, your majesty," I said with a flick of my hand. Gobs of candylike images sprang from my palms like confetti. Wish laid down and I pulled the blankets up over her, tucked her in, and placed a kiss on her forehead.

"And what about yours, Fawn?" Wish asked, as Jewel's deep breathing signaled she had fallen asleep.

I rose from the bed, approaching the mirror that helped me resituate the flaming locks struggling to escape their coiled piles. "Mine would help heal broken hearts," I replied, raising my hand and motioning for the images to retreat back into the palm from which they had sprung. As all of the images rushed back into my glowing palm, I slowly closed my fist. Just like that, the magic vanished from the room.

Silence fell between us as I brushed through the unbridled mane that cascaded over my shoulders, down my back, and fell into a pool of red tendrils on the floor beside me. I scooped up the hair and loosely tied it in layers with a ribbon to keep it from tangling in my sleep, wishing I had the power to mend the shattered pieces of my heart.

"Thank you, for always taking care of us, Fawn," Wish whispered.

"I will always make sure nothing bad happens to the two of you, Wish," I promised, the same as I did when I first held her in my arms. The same way I promised baby Jewel when she suddenly appeared in our lives. Yet another child who did not belong to Romilda.

I was the child of a man seeking food for his starving family. Wish was the child of a man pursuing a wish to save his family during drought. And Jewel, I could only deduce, was the child of someone who sought a jewel and instead lost their greatest treasure.

If I could only be brave like the heroes I read about in books. I wanted to be free from this place so badly, but no one came. Not even a prince, like the one who resided in my dreams. Life had taught me those were just fantasies, and I was neither brave, nor worth rescuing.

"Goodnight. Don't forget the lights," Wish murmured as she pulled the covers over her head.

"Goodnight," I responded, rubbing the tips of my fingers together, letting the power build, before snapping them, sending a pulse through the room that snuffed out every candle.

~~~~~

I grabbed the heather broom from the corner and swept the stone floor for the second time today. I checked on the vegetable stew simmering in the large cauldron hanging over the fireplace. I plucked a few more spices from the dried herbs hanging from the rafters and added them, just for good measure, before dusting my hands off on my apron.

I could hear the girls outside, giggling and carrying on. Jewel had already collected the eggs from beneath the chickens, and Wish had milked the dairy cow earlier in the morning. Everything was done, except the one unwashed cup sitting on the table that someone must have left. I waved my hand over its lip and spoke a quick incantation, refilling the vessel so I didn't feel the need to wash it.

I went to the bookshelves and paged through one of the many stories I had reread at least a dozen times. I could recite its familiar tale by heart, making the idea of rereading it unappealing. Books were a luxury Romilda had begrudgingly given into when I was younger. She always said stories were dangerous, holding their own kind of power. I suppose Romilda had decided stories were a lesser kind of evil, since they didn't pose a threat to her magic.

Books opened my eyes to the world beyond my enclosure. I wanted to be a warrior or a dragon tamer. A legend. Maybe even a princess. Anything but a captive within this prison. But instead of being one of those great and noble things, I was still just a girl, living locked away on the edge of nowhere. And now, out of desperation, I was becoming the very thing I hated. A witch. Just like Romilda.

I peeked out the front door, overhung with flowering vines. "Wish, would you look after your sister, please?"

Wish looked up from playing. She already knew where I was going. "I'll keep a lookout," she said hesitantly, always fearful Romilda would return when I was doing exactly what she had forbidden me to do.

Rule one: Never let a knife touch my hair. Rule two: No use of magic by anyone other than herself. And rule three: No one, under any circumstance, could enter her lair.

There was only one of those rules I had never broken.

I'd tried to be happy living as a victim of Romilda's whim. I really did. I tried to be everything she wanted, to be happy and content for the sake of the girls, and to follow the rules. But I couldn't. Not for a long time.

The entrance to the lair was outside the back of the cottage, the double doors leading down beneath the earth chained with a lock. It was the only place within the barrier to which we were denied access. I was thirteen when being forbidden from entering the lair had driven me to the point of insanity and I decided I had to know Romilda's secrets.

I closed my eyes, drawing my hands before the lock and whispering the incantation I had memorized from years of watching Romilda from the shadows. Power tingled from my heart, down my arms and through my fingertips, as I let my hands move in an almost rhythmic dance. The lock gave way beneath my glowing tendrils of power, and I quickly pulled back the chains before descending into the depths of Romilda's world.

Deerskin hides, with maps of the surrounding forest inscribed upon them, hung on the walls beside bookshelves. The shelves held pages written in a script I couldn't read, skulls of different creatures, numerous jars of various sizes holding gemstones, potions, and tinctures, and tomes on herbalism and plant identification.

Barrels of collected rainwater stood at the base of the stairs where mistletoe, yew, spruce, and holly were clustered together like curtains hanging from the ceiling to dry. A worktable sat to the right-hand side, cluttered with a mortar and pestle, scales, and other miscellaneous tools. In the center of the lair's chaotic mess stood a large, black cauldron.

I probably should've felt trepidation being in the one place I was forbidden, but I'd now spent several years within these walls honing my skills and gaining control of my surroundings. Romilda couldn't be bothered when one of the girls had an anxiety attack, let alone any other crisis, and at times, those needs felt more terrifying than anything Romilda could have done to me. Stories about knights and princesses may have held the power to inspire my spirit, but not the power to improve our daily lives. Having that power seemed worth the risk.

The item of most use in my pursuits sat on a small pedestal beside the large brewing cauldron. It was a grimoire, something I came to view as my textbook on magic. It had instructions on how to create magical objects like talismans and amulets, how to perform magical spells, charms and divination, information on rituals, the preparation of magical tools, and lists of ingredients and their magical counterparts. But the most useful part of the grimoire were the hundreds of handwritten notes scribbled throughout by Romilda over the decades, guiding me in my pursuit of magic.

It was almost like having her as a teacher. Without the incurred wrath.

Being self-taught came with its challenges. Over the years I had experienced a lot of trial and error, as well as results. Nothing that couldn't be covered up and hidden from Romilda, but there were close calls I thought for sure would give away what I'd been doing. Being underestimated by Romilda had its advantages. She'd never once suspected what I had been up to all these years.

I walked over to the potion shelves, pushing tinctures and specimen jars out of my way to reveal a hidden container I had been working on for weeks. I just needed to add one last ingredient and it would finally be complete.

Digging the roots I had collected and dried earlier in the week out of my pocket, I took them over to the mortar and pestle and began to grind them down into a powder. As I worked the roots into a dust, I thought about the one lock in Romilda's lair that I couldn't open.

When I first discovered the hidden chest beneath the floorboards, I found its lock was enchanted by a powerful spell. One I couldn't counter. After months and months of denied access, I searched for other means to open it.

Whatever was inside the chest had to be important. I hoped it contained the answers to questions long weighing on my brain. Why did Romilda and Golga call me a talisman all those years ago? What was I anchoring? Try as I might, I had never found the answers in my magical pursuits.

The root was finally ready. I held my breath as I added it to the rest of my mix before closing the lid and shaking all the ingredients together. Holding the clear glass up to my face, I waited, staring down the magical creation and hoping it would work.

Nothing.

I wanted to pull my hair out. It was exhausting having to interpret the information in the grimoire on my own. Whenever I made a mistake, I had to retrace my steps to determine where I went wrong. Sometimes I lacked the knowledge to discover my error.

All that work, wasted! Weeks of carefully preparing each ingredient. I set the jar on the table and slumped to the ground, drawing my knees up to my chest.

I couldn't be any of the things I wanted in life. My only option for self-improvement was to be a witch, and I couldn't even be a very good one. How much longer could I live like this? Every day felt like a heavier burden.

Over a year ago, I thought I had come across a way to bring down the barrier outside our prison. The knowledge weighed on my mind every night as I lay in bed tossing and turning. But where would we go? How would I find food and shelter for us? The woman I thought was my mother had turned out to be my abductor, so who could I trust in this strange world full of dragons, ruffians, and other witches with more experience than me?

Why couldn't I be like the heroes in my books? Maybe because unlike them I lived in relative safety and security. It was a prison, certainly, but one that left me with no physical needs. Out beyond the barrier would be different. How many times had Romilda told us we couldn't leave with her because we would never survive the world beyond and the dangers it held? Here I could care for the girls, but out there I was likely to get us all killed.

A high-pitched hiss startled me onto my feet. My jar bubbled and popped, the dry ingredients inside it whirling around before settling in the bottom of the jar and glowing like phosphorescent purple dust.

I stood frozen, taking a moment to process the fact that my potion had worked.

And then I screeched.

I had done it! I shouldn't have given up so easily. One of the rules of the grimoire was that magic took patience. I always seemed to forget that teaching.

I clutched the jar close to my chest. This was it! I felt deliriously lightheaded with excitement. Rushing over to the pile of furs in the corner, I ripped the pelts away from the trap door in the floor. I lifted the heavy wooden frame and dragged it out of my way before reaching into the dark hole and hauling the heavy chest from its depths.

Eagerly I began to dump the potion onto the solid metal lock, watching in delight as the purple powder ate away at the metal. Within moments, the lock fell to the ground, releasing its hold with a loud thud.

This was the moment of truth! What had Romilda been hiding away all this time? Maybe it was a potion for mass destruction. Or some sort of powerful amulet. I held my breath as I opened the chest. What could Romilda possibly need to hide so carefully in an already protected lair?

Papers.

I felt a sense of disappointment as I sifted through the contents of the chest. Old, brittle papers and a satchel. I was disheartened. All this time concocting in my mind what was inside this chest, and it turned out to be nothing. How disappointing.

I carefully unfolded one of the pieces of paper. A reward poster? Why were there reward posters in here? I unfolded another, the same as the first, both indicating a search for a lost princess.

Why would Romilda have these?

Beneath the reward posters was a map. Circled on the map was a small kingdom. I wasn't the best map reader, having never been able to put what I learned to the test, but I knew from Romilda's other maps where our barrier was in reference to the rest of the world. The circled castle was some distance from our home, nestled between the sunlit forest and the North Sea in a land called Lumiria.

Something in the pit of my stomach felt sick, reminding me of the moment I learned I had been stolen from a family that loved me. I'd felt this dread before.

Maybe it was better not knowing Romilda's secrets? I could close the chest and pretend I never found it.

I sat for a moment, contemplating all my options. But in my heart, I knew I couldn't unsee this. I needed the truth.

I shoved the papers aside and pulled out the satchel. Reaching inside, my fingers met cool metal. I already knew what it was before I pulled it out.

A locket.

Vines were engraved into the gold with crusted jewels placed like flower petals along the vines. The light caught on them, casting prisms against the walls. It was the most beautiful piece of jewelry I had ever seen.

I held my breath, fingers trembling, as I opened the clasp. Staring at me on one side was a portrait of a baby. She had full lips and blond curly whisps encircling her face. Around her neck was the very locket in my hands. But the most startling revelation was that I knew the blue eyes staring up at me. It was a perfect likeness.

On the other side of the locket was a man and a woman, lovingly holding one another as they seemingly gazed at the picture of their child on the opposite side. Atop their heads were a pair of crowns and fur capes draped off their shoulders.

I felt sick.

I closed the locket, tucking it into my apron pocket, and rummaged through the rest of the satchel. There was a proclamation describing the deep pain felt by the king and queen of Lumiria over the abduction of their child. A little girl known as Aurelia, the golden princess. They would spare no expense in the search for their child. Any information that could lead to her return would be handsomely rewarded.

At the bottom of the proclamation was an image of the child. The same image of the child in the locket. The same face I had come to love five years ago...

The sound of footsteps pounding down the stairway instantly sent dread down my spine.

Wish flew into the room and surveyed the situation with wild, frightened eyes. "Romilda is here!"

The blood in my veins seemed to freeze. Romilda would kill me! There was no doubt in my mind what she would do if she found me here, especially if she knew I had learned this secret. I had to move quickly.

"You have to stall, Wish. You have to!" I cried, shoving her back up the stairs. "Don't let her catch you down here! Get Jewel. And be calm!"

I shoved the chest back into its hiding place. Everything had to look like it did the last time Romilda was down here—the lock! I had disintegrated the lock! What if she came down here to get into the chest and found what I had done? How could I have been so stupid and not think about that in my plans to open it?

Time was running out. I had to hope she wouldn't look for the chest before I had time to figure out a plan. I rushed to scoop up the tools I had been using and shoved them back in place.

My heart pounded in my ears as I left the lair, taking the stairs three at a time. I tried to close the doors as quietly as possible, but my hands were shaking. I heard Romilda's voice.

It took longer than normal to lock the lair, but I finally did. I heard Romilda asking about me and went to rush toward her before realizing I still had the locket in my pocket!

I looked around wildly for somewhere to hide it, but the sparkle of the jewels made it difficult to conceal. The voices were drawing closer. I was running out of time.

I dove for one of the flowerbeds nearest to me, yanking a plant from the ground by its roots and digging into the dirt with my nails. Sweat beaded my upper lip. I shoved the locket into the ground before placing the plant back over it and scooping dirt into place.

"Fawn, there you are."

I had done it.

I schooled my features to calmness as I finished the final pats needed to hold the plant in place. My life, and the girls', depended on my ability to sell the normalcy of the moment. I stood up, dusting off my hands. "I'm so sorry, Mother, I must've been lost in tending the plants. I didn't hear you were home!"

Wish and Jewel stood behind the irritated Romilda. Wish's greatest survival instinct was her ability to seem completely disinterested in life, no matter what was going on.

My eyes locked with Jewel's. The image of the loving parents gazing at their child haunted me. If I didn't want to get caught, I had to ignore her.

As I focused on Romilda, I realized she had a basket hanging from her arm. "How was your trip, Mother? You must be tired; can I take that for you?"

As I approached her, Romilda studied my face intently. "It's unlike you not to greet me, child."

"I'm so sorry, Mother. How can I make it up to you?"

"Fawn made us stew, Mother!" Jewel cried, stepping between the two of us and diverting Romilda's attention.

"How thoughtful of her, my pet," Romilda replied, breaking her visual interrogation.

I could feel the tension in my shoulders ease as Jewel intentionally drew Romilda's attention from me. Jewel was the only one capable of distracting her, and somehow at the tender age of five, she already knew it.

"I brought some supplies back with me for you to put away, Fawn." Romilda's voice snapped my wandering brain into the moment.

"Of course, Mother, let me take that for you."

I quickly took the basket before leading everyone into the cottage. As I unloaded it, I focused on keeping calm and participating in conversation with Romilda and the girls as normally as I could. I knew if I could just get through dinner, Romilda would seek her lair for the rest of the night.

"Come to the table, girls," Romilda called. "It's time to sit down and eat as a family."

Family. I wanted to spit in the stew. She had no right to use that word.

"Where did you go this time, Mother?" Jewel asked as we sat to the meal. "You were gone an awfully long time."

Wish silently ate her food, glancing in my direction.

"I know, darling." Romilda smiled. "Mother hates leaving you so long, but I can't help it. Besides," she turned toward me, "doesn't Fawn take good care of you while I'm away?"

Jewel nodded emphatically. "Of course she does! Fawn always takes care of us."

"How long will you be staying this time, Mother?" Wish asked timidly, keeping her gaze locked on her stew. She had grown up knowing it was better for her to be barely seen, and never heard, when it came to Romilda.

Romilda's annoyance oozed from her body. "Don't be pouty, girl. I have a busy life which benefits you. If I didn't leave to take care of things, you wouldn't have a roof over your head."

Lies. Magic took care of us. Romilda could be gone a year and we'd never know the difference. I had decided years ago she left because she craved the attention that enhanced youth, power, and beauty afforded her. Not because she needed to.

"Will you be staying with us for a while, Mother?" I asked the nearly identical question. I was more likely to receive an answer than Wish.

"I leave tomorrow. This is just a short stay to restock some of the items I need from the lair."

Her answer brought me relief, but also dread at the mention of the lair. Never had I been so fearful that she could discover I had broken one of the forbidden rules.

"Can we go with you this time, Mother?" Jewel asked.

Perhaps it was natural for Jewel to want to be loved by the witch who stole her, same as it had been for me once upon a time, but knowing what Romilda stole from Jewel made the child's desire for love and acceptance from her abductor grate on me.

"Oh darling, why would you want to come with me? Our home is so lovely, and the world outside so ugly. So much chaos and carnage. Wars fought over land. Fields and crops drying up and giving no yield. It's not a very nice place. Nothing like our home, so cozy and hidden from harm."

I had heard those words so many times over the course of my life; they were the reason I was afraid to leave this cage. But everything Romilda ever told us was a lie. So why did I believe her when she insisted the world beyond the barrier was full of so many horrible things?

"Can we not help them?"

I'd stopped asking questions like that over the years, but Jewel was still young enough to hope.

"Why would we help those who steal from us, child?"

Something inside me snapped. It wasn't courage I was feeling, but something stronger and more volatile.

I once believed maybe my parents deserved what happened to them, same as Wish's. After all, they did try to steal from powerful witches. But now I knew the hypocrisy of Romilda's offense when she herself had stolen a child.

Romilda shook her head, finishing the last of her stew. "People exploit power for their own advancement. They war over lands and commodities, spilling blood for their own gain. My power would be a weapon in the wrong hands."

"Well..." Jewel murmured. "Is there anything you can do to stop it?"

Romilda arched one eyebrow. "Assuming I had that kind of power, why would I, my pet?"

Jewel scrunched her blond brows together in confusion. "Because people are hungry and hurting."

Romilda chuckled, easing the growing tension in the air. She seemed to find Jewel's distress amusing. "My dear, your heart bleeds too much for others. People will use that to take advantage of you. That is why you must remain here where I can keep you and your sisters safe. It brings me great comfort knowing no harm may come to you here, under my protection, and Fawn's care. Now hush, darling. Eat your stew. Mother doesn't want to hear any more questions. I have work to do."

As Romilda left the table, we continued to eat in silence, except for the occasional scraping of the silverware. Wish looked nervously at me as she heard the lair doors open from behind the cottage. I held my breath, waiting for a shriek and Romilda to storm back up the stairs and descend upon me in a fury. But her wrath never came.

I breathed a sigh of relief. It appeared, for the moment, that my secret was still safe. Another benefit of being underestimated.

As I cleaned up the evening meal and worked to get everyone to bed, I played the information I had uncovered earlier over and over in my mind.

It had never made sense to me why Jewel was treated differently.

Now I knew.

Jewel was the one child Romilda sought, instead of a child she was saddled with. Romilda was a powerful sorceress, but she didn't have the power that came with a throne until she stole the crown jewel, and rightful heir, of the kingdom.

Romilda was incapable of love. We were all pawns in her game. My best guess was Romilda was raising Jewel as her own, like a pig fattened for slaughter, so she could one day place the child on her rightful throne and become her regent. But Romilda would never relinquish power. In the pit of my churning stomach, I knew she would kill Jewel when she came of age, just as easily as she would a pig. Because when it came down to it, that's really all we were to her. Or rather rats, as Golga had called us twelve years ago.

I lay awake in bed, thinking through my options. Romilda might have instilled in me how cruel the world beyond the barrier was, but nothing could be as cruel as the spider's web she had us trapped in. One by one, she would consume us.

I didn't know much about life beyond the barrier, but I did know one thing. Wish and Jewel were the only things worth living and fighting for, and I wouldn't let Romilda destroy my only reason for being. I had promised Wish I would protect them. Now I needed to fulfill that promise.

It was time to leave our prison. And we were never coming back.

I rolled over in bed, looking across the room at Wish's sleeping form. I couldn't do this alone. I needed the one person who always had my back. The person who kept me alive and sane.

I propped myself up on my elbow. "Wish, are you awake?"

With a groan, Wish rolled over to face me. "Yes." She sounded irritated, but not groggy.

I rose, my feet padded softly across the floor, and I crawled into bed beside her, placing my mouth close to her ear.

"We have to leave here. Tomorrow. If we don't, we're all in danger."

~~~~~

"But Fawn, Mother says you can't cut your hair!" Jewel cried, her eyes wide and frightened.

"She's not our mother, Jewel!" Wish snapped, skipping a rock across the pond.

None of this plan was going smoothly. Ever since Romilda had left the day before, everyone was on edge.

I set the knife in my hand down along the bank, encouraging Jewel to come sit with me.

"My sweet, sweet Jewel. Do you trust me?"

Jewel's eyes glazed with tears and her body trembled. "Yes, Fawn. I love you!" She threw herself against me and wrapped her arms around my neck. I felt the fear radiating through her body. It mirrored my own emotions. I wished the girls had a real hero to save them, but I was all they had. I needed to be strong.

"How about a story, Fawn?" Wish offered, sitting down beside me and putting her hand on my knee. "Maybe Jewel won't be so scared if she has a story."

I knew what Wish was implying. It was the same thing she had said the night I told her my plan.

I pulled Jewel down into my lap, slowly rocking her.

"I love stories," Jewel said, her lip quivering.

I didn't want to tell her. Not with so much unknown ahead of her. The less she could tell people we encountered, the better. But maybe Wish was right. Maybe telling her something would help. "Okay, how about I tell you a new story? One you've never heard?"

"What's it called?" Jewel asked.

"It's called The Lost Princess, and it's about a little girl with beautiful blond curls and bright blue eyes."

Jewel smiled. "Like me!"

"Yes, exactly like you," I said, stroking the curls spilling down her back like a waterfall of sunlight. "And this child was a princess, dearly loved by her parents, the king and queen of a beautiful kingdom."

"Why did the king and queen lose their princess?"

"An evil witch snuck into the castle, stealing their daughter, and hiding her deep in the woods where no one would find her."

"How awful!"

"It was awful, but the little princess had something to remember her beloved parents by." Digging in my pocket, I pulled out the golden locket, its stones dazzling in the sunlight.

Jewel gasped in awe. "How pretty!"

"It is, isn't it?" I whispered, placing the locket over her head, and letting it rest against her chest. She would have been a beautiful princess, sweet and adored by all her subjects.

"Is it mine?" Jewel asked, opening the clasp, and gazing at the portrait of her parents.

A lump formed in my throat. I would probably never find my parents, or Wish's, but at least we could reunite Jewel with hers. "Yes. And that's why we must leave, so we can return the lost princess to her parents. Can you keep her locket safe for me?"

Jewel looked up from the portrait, visibly unsure.

I cupped her soft, pink cheek in my hand. "I need you to be brave, Jewel. Can you be brave?"

"Fawn and I will be with you the whole time," Wish said to encourage her.

Jewel looked back down at the locket, her little thumb caressing the portrait. "Am I the lost princess?"

I bit my lower lip. I wanted to lie to protect her, but I also didn't want to be Romilda, who had lied to us our entire lives.

"Yes."

Jewel looked up at me, blue eyes swimming in tears. "That's why Wish said Romilda's not my mother."

"She's not, Jewel," Wish insisted. "But you have a mother out there who loves you, and Fawn is going to make sure you get to see her."

Jewel sat quietly for a long time, staring at the likeness of her parents.

"You won't leave me, will you Fawn?" The tremble in Jewel's voice made my heart ache. This was so much for her to process, and I didn't know what the future held.

"I need you to be brave, Jewel." It seemed wrong to ask her to be something I wasn't myself. "And we have to keep this a secret until we get to the castle. Can you do that for me?"

Jewel nodded, clutching the locket in her hands.

I forced a smile. "Good girl. Now, before we leave, we must get ready, and I'm going to have to cut my hair."

"But why?"

Because it was time to break all the rules. But a five-year-old wouldn't understand why. "My hair would be too hard to run away with." Not to mention the abnormally long flaming locks were an easy identifier if Romilda came looking for us.

Jewel glanced toward the knife. "She'll be mad, though, and hurt you."

"We will never see her again," Wish assured her. "Fawn's going to cover our tracks with magic and take us deep into the forest. Romilda will never be able to hurt us."

"Will your magic break the barrier, Fawn?"

I hoped so. I had spent all morning pouring over the grimoire, looking for spells that might work. "I promise, I'll find a way out, Jewel."

The child nodded. "Okay. You can cut your hair."

I smiled, lifting Jewel out of my lap and approaching the water's edge with the blade in my hand. It was time to free myself of the hair that had weighed me down most of my life. I looked at my reflection in the water and grabbed a fistful of my hair, poising the knife.

The second the blade met my locks, a loud crack ricocheted throughout the barrier, reverberating across the waters.

"Fawn, look!" Wish cried, pointing to the amber stones cutting us off from the rest of the world. Right through the center of one of the stones ran a crack, fracture lines spidering across its glass-like surface.

I looked down at the handful of hair in my hand, severed from my head.

I have what I need from the first one. I don't need another to anchor the spell.

It couldn't be…

With fevered desperation, I hacked at my hair, watching it fall to the ground in a heaping pile. With every cut of the knife, the barrier fractured more, the spider lines growing and deepening. Holding the last chunk of untouched hair in my hand, I slashed it, separating its connection to me.

A deafening sound vibrated through the air as the barrier shattered into a cloud of amber smoke. I stood up, staring in silent disbelief. Through the dissipating smoke I could see a forest as far as my vision reached.

"Your hair, Fawn," Wish stuttered. "It… It…"

"It was magic!" Jewel cried. "Just like your story!"

I looked down at the limp pile of hair littering the ground. I couldn't remember feeling this weightless. My hair had been like a millstone around my neck since I was a child.

Romilda had made me the bailiff of our imprisonment. It made so much sense now. All the emphasis on maintaining my hair, the meticulous care, and the nightly rituals. She had made me a talisman. Spells were always stronger when tied to a living being. That was why she had kept me all those years. No peasant would ever steal from her again because I was the key to her fortress.

Not anymore.

"Fawn?" Wish's voice pierced the dark thoughts swirling in my mind. "Are you okay?"

I didn't have an answer. "Wish, take Jewel and pack anything you want to keep."

"Where are you going?"

"To make sure we survive," I said over my shoulder.

Without waiting for Wish to respond, I raced to the lair, throwing open the doors and tearing through every shelf. I didn't want to hide anymore. Let Romilda know I had been down there.

I dug the map out of the hidden chest, packed potions and herbs that could be beneficial on our journey into satchels, and took the pouch of precious stones and coins that Romilda kept on the shelf. I knew from my books that coins were a valuable form of trade in the world.

I paused for a moment, second guessing myself as my anger and fear warred within my soul. I couldn't remember a life where all our needs weren't met magically by the enchantments of the cottage. How was I supposed to provide for the girls? How would I keep them safe? I knew nothing of the world outside except what I had read in books.

No! I wouldn't let Romilda cause me to doubt myself anymore. I shrieked, my tumultuous emotions bubbling over like a cauldron, and yanked over one of the cases filled with specimen jars. The glass shattered across the ground, liquids pooling on the floor of Romilda's once spotless lair.

I looked over at Romilda's revered spell book and walked toward it, the shards beneath my boots crunching. I lifted the grimoire from its stand, flipping through the pages. There was so much knowledge held within these pages. So much more I hadn't learned or tried. I was confident that within these pages, I could find the means to survive.

Determined, I tucked the book inside the satchel with the map that would lead us to the kingdom of Lumiria and headed back up the stairwell. I feared a world without Wish and Jewel more than I feared anything beyond the tree line.

I rummaged through the cupboards in the cottage and packed provisions for our trip, letting my thoughts roam to all the things I wanted to do after we escaped from here. I wanted to go to a marketplace and haggle over something. Maybe I could open my own shop and sell tinctures and poultices I had learned to make from my magic. I wanted to do anything but remain a prisoner in this cage.

I looked forward to seeing a castle for the first time and smelling salty sea air. I had read about those things but never experienced them personally. Maybe I could befriend a dragon or defeat a knight in combat?

"What if she comes after us?" Wish asked. I hadn't heard her enter the room.

"We will have a head start, and Romilda underestimates us. We will go to the king and queen and show them the locket as proof of who Jewel is. We can do this, Wish."

"I know, I'm just scared…"

I tucked the last provisions in my pack. "Me too."

"We're ready." Jewel came up beside Wish, ragdoll tucked in the crook of her arm.

I readjusted Jewel's cloak and pulled the hood up over her curls before giving her a reassuring smile. "Then let's go."

Shouldering the provisions, I took Jewel's hand in mine. Together, the three of us walked out of the cottage, past the gardens, the barn, and the tower, and came to the edge of the only world we had ever known.

The tree line felt ominous as I pulled out the grimoire, flipped through the pages, and came across a spell that would mask our tracks. As I spoke the incantation, I felt the power seeping from my body into the ground and merging at our feet. Shame washed over me.

"Are you okay, Fawn?"

I closed the book. "You probably think I'm just like her now… a witch. I'm sorry I'm not the hero you were hoping for."

A hand touched my shoulder. "No one was coming to rescue us, Fawn." It was Wish, pack on the ground and eyes begging me to feel her love and admiration. "You are nothing like Romilda. You're using your magic to keep us safe. Not imprison us."

I felt Jewel tuck her hand back into mine and looked down at her. Big blue eyes, trusting and full of love, gazed up at me. "Let's go, Fawn."

I brushed back a tear from the corner of my eye. I wasn't a princess, like I had hoped. And I probably wouldn't be a dragon tamer or a knight. I was just a witch, and not a very good one. But in their eyes, I was so much more. Maybe, just maybe, even a witch could become the hero of her own story. If I would let myself.

I straightened my back, staring down the dark forest beyond the destroyed barrier. "Let's go."

I held both girls' hands in mine before taking my first step toward freedom. It was time to take back my wings and fly.

END

Operation Breakout
Stoney M. Setzer

"Gillis! Hit the wall, now!" Sarge commanded.

The sound of running footsteps was followed by the thunder of the dining area wall exploding. Gillis had done his job, crashing through and making a hole big enough for us to run through. Operation Breakout was underway.

Offering up a quick prayer, I followed the sounds of my cohorts to find the opening and hustle through it. Getting outside the building was the easy part. Now we had to fight for our freedom as the guards regrouped. At least we could use our newfound abilities — the ones we got here — against them.

Maybe Sarge should have called it Operation Bedlam. Chaos erupted all around me, partially because of me, but of course I couldn't see it. Thanks to our captors, I hadn't been able to see anything in weeks. I could hear it, though — from the panicked shouts of the guards to the crackling of the flames to the whistling of the projectiles I hurled through the air.

All the experiments we had suffered through had endowed each of us with a superhuman ability at the cost of a disability. Some combinations had no bearing on each other. Villanueva had acromegaly now, but that didn't impede his newfound power of firestarting.

Unfortunately for me, blindness and telekinesis didn't mix well. My other four senses were heightened, but that only helped so much. There were a lot of metal objects around me — I could tell by a certain smell I had never noticed when I was still sighted — so I knew I had plenty of stuff to throw. By my amplified hearing, I could also distinguish and pinpoint the voices of my comrades and our enemies, helping me aim my makeshift missiles.

Unfortunately, I couldn't see what I was throwing, nor could I see what anybody else was doing. With my mind, I picked up an object that I estimated must have weighed twenty pounds and started to launch it...

"Mays! No!" Sarge cried. "Don't throw the propane tank that way! That's where Villanueva's aiming!"

I heard him, but I had already thrown it by the time the words sank in. *Please, God, no! No no no...*

KA-BOOM!

A wave of heat and pressure slammed me backward. I hit my head against something hard and blacked out.

~~~~~

I have no idea how long I was unconscious, but it must have been a long time. Long enough for all the chaos around me to be replaced by silence. Dead silence, the kind that seems almost deafening.

Rubble and debris were on top of me, but I found I wasn't pinned down. With a little effort, I was able to free myself and get back on my feet. Pain buffeted me from head to toe, but nothing seemed to be broken. Even if I had broken every bone in my body, that would have been the least of my concerns.

"Sarge!" I shouted. "Villanueva! Gillis! Where are you?" I knew our enemies would hear me if they were still around, but that was a chance I was willing to take.

Anyway, it didn't matter. I called the names of everybody in our squadron, multiple times, hearing only the echo of my own voice in return. If anybody was still there, I would have heard them with my heightened hearing. Apparently, all our enemies had been wiped out too, but there was no consolation in that. People like Dr. Lockhart and Dr. Balelo deserved to die, but not Sarge, not Villanueva or Gillis or any of the rest of us...

Everybody's dead, I thought in horror. *They're all dead, and it's all my fault. Instead of helping us all escape, I killed them. If it wasn't for me, they'd still be alive. I blew it. I shouldn't have ever tried to help because I'm nothing but a screw-up.*

Frantically, I groped through the debris, not really knowing what I was looking for. What I found was a piece of PVC pipe, long enough to make for a serviceable walking stick. At least I could use it to make my way out of there.

Thanks to my screw-up, nobody else had survived our breakout attempt. I didn't deserve to make it, but if I didn't, it would be like they had all died in vain.

I had enough on my conscience without that. I thought about my prayer before I went charging through the hole in the wall. *God, why did You let me live? After the way I failed, why leave me here to live with that?*

~~~~~

Even without my eyesight, I could discern certain details to help me navigate. I found a set of railroad tracks, and I could tell from the growth around them that they hadn't borne a train in years. Taking a few steps in either direction, I intuited that they ran east to west. I don't really know how I knew that, but I did, as if the experiments had equipped me with some kind of internal compass in addition to telekinesis. My squadron had been in Memphis when we were abducted, and I had heard that accent in some of our captors' voices, especially the guards. Based on that, I went east, figuring I could at least stay in Tennessee and be in somewhat familiar territory. Maybe the tracks would take me to Chattanooga. I had a cousin out there who might be able to help me if I could get that far.

Yeah, help me contact the National Guard so they can come lock me up for wiping out my whole squadron. Not even Cousin Mike could save me from Uncle Sam. But I'll worry about that if I get that far.

I walked a long time without encountering any signs of human life. That made sense for the first couple of hours—nighttime, based on the sounds of owls hooting and crickets chirping. Now, birds were chirping, and I could feel the sun's rays directly on my face as I continued east, but I had yet to hear any sounds that could have been made by people, even though it seemed like there was plenty of open area around the tracks. No talking, no cars, nothing.

Maybe I was just out in the middle of nowhere, or maybe there had been another pandemic, and everyone was too terrified of infection to step outdoors to see what I was doing. Without being able to see, there was no way to know for sure...

Then I heard her scream.

I froze in my tracks, listening intently. A woman's voice, not a child's. Somewhere in the general vicinity, but still at a distance. A mile away, by my estimation.

Another scream. Definitely a mile off, and *up*—several stories above ground level. Whoever she was, she was in anguish. Instinct took over, and I ran, sweeping my walking stick back and forth before me in rapid arcs as I hurried down the tracks.

The sound of the breeze changed, suggesting that I had passed from the countryside and entered a town. Wind makes a different noise blowing through buildings than it does through trees. Still no sounds of people out and about. Either I was right about a pandemic, or I was in a ghost town of sorts, abandoned as the local economy died and people left in search of a living.

So if this place was abandoned, then who was screaming, and why?

As best I could, I tried to estimate the source. Maybe a hundred more yards ahead and then to my right. By the time I had covered the hundred yards, she verified my estimate by screaming a third time. Now she was three blocks to the right, and five stories up. At least the first part would be easy.

I stepped off the railroad tracks and pressed on, still sweeping with my stick. The asphalt was uneven, suggesting cracks carved by age. Such rough terrain forced me to slow down a little, but I pressed on as quickly as I dared.

She had time to scream three more times before I found myself directly beneath the source. I reached out and felt a brick wall—old, sturdy, but cracked and weathered. Maybe a century old, give or take a decade. Probing further, I discovered a windowsill and then a handrail leading upward. Whatever this place used to be, she must be on the fifth floor.

Self-doubt cut through me like a knife. Who was I kidding? Powers or not, I was a blind man, five stories below her. What could I do?

Besides that, I wasn't a hero. Too much blood on my hands. Since all these changes had been forced on me, I felt more like a monster than a man. Whoever she was, whatever was making her scream, she was better off without me getting involved...

One more scream, full of agony and terror, broke those thoughts like so much glass. If I did nothing, then by my inaction I would have a hand in whatever fate awaited her. I couldn't handle that.

"Hang on, I'm coming to help you!" I shouted.

Bad idea. I could actually smell the watchdogs before I heard them barking — two Dobermans, unless I missed my guess. Coming from inside the building, but from the ground floor, giving me precious little time to react. At least they both came from the same direction so I wouldn't have to divide my focus.

They burst through the door a few feet to my right. I thrust my arm toward them, imagining them floating six feet above the ground. Almost instantaneously, their vicious snarls gave way to frightened yelps and whimpers as my power levitated them into the air. Concentrating, I visualized a bubble around them, carrying them miles away, to the outer limits of my telekinetic range. Within seconds, they were too far away for me to hear them, but mentally I still took care to deposit them safely on the ground.

"Number Sixty-One, is that you?" a voice called from overhead, sounding as if it came from roughly the same place as the screams. A man's voice, but with a pronounced lisp — a voice I had hoped I would never hear again outside of my nightmares — Dr. Balelo. Somebody had survived the doomed escape attempt, and of all people it had to be him. "Who else could have taken care of my guard dogs so easily? Incredible!"

I froze. Being called Sixty-One again struck a particular nerve. That had been my test subject number during the experiments. Nightmarish memories spewed up like a geyser in my mind — some from before the tinkering that cost me my eyesight, some after. Hypodermic needles containing who knew what, jabbed into my arm over and over again. Provisions that were as tough as leather and tasted like it too. Myriad foul smells, all co-mingled into one horrid stench. The agonized screams of the others, so loud I could scarcely hear my own cries — and of course, the pain. Pain like no words can capture.

And then of course, our ill-fated attempt to fight back and escape.

Successful for me in the sense that I was still alive, but at a higher cost than I had ever wanted to pay. We didn't have a real plan, and between my power and Villanueva's, things got sloppy. Fatally sloppy. Until now, I had thought all the scientists and most of my fellow conscripts were dead, but I should have known better. If I had survived, then maybe I wasn't the only one...

Run! If they've got that lady, you can't help her! Get out of here!
No! You can't leave her at their mercy, knowing what they're capable of!

Only a moment of indecision, but it was too much. More than enough time for the decision to be made for me.

From above came the sound of something flying through the air, followed by a crack like that of a whip. It struck me squarely in the solar plexus, knocking the wind out of me and my feet out from under me. As soon as I landed on my back, four tendrils of some kind wrapped around my wrists and ankles. Vise grips—no hope of breaking free.

Catching my breath, I tried to focus on what exactly had me. The tendrils felt like many fibers on my skin, thousands all together. A distinctive smell caught my nose, one I hadn't smelled in ages, sort of a lavender scent...

Was I smelling a woman's shampoo? Were these tendrils made of hair? Who was attacking me anyway, Rapunzel?

As I struggled, I heard a woman sobbing from above me. "Please, I don't want to do this! Don't make me!"

"Silence, Ninety-Four!" Balelo commanded. "Don't you realize that this is the perfect test for your new abilities?"

That was the way all our captors thought. I may have had a hand in a lot of deaths when we tried to escape, but in my case it had been unintentional. Our tormentors simply hadn't cared. They pushed their subjects to the outer limits, both physically and psychologically. All that mattered to them was their goal—developing the human race's supposedly latent powers.

So much for thinking I had escaped all that.

"Reel in him! Bring him up here!"

The ground slipped away as the tentacles pulled me upward. My walking stick fell from my grasp and clattered on the sidewalk below, but that was the least of my worries. I didn't know how many of them were up here, but even one was too many.

Come on, concentrate! Your life and hers depend on it! Better off dead than at their mercy again!

Maybe I'm fighting this the wrong way...

Focusing my telekinetic powers, I worked on prying the viselike locks of hair off of my wrists. I got my right hand free first, then my left...

Not my best idea. Suspended by my ankles, I swung backward and upside down, slamming into the building's brick wall. Although I was already blind, the impact plunged me into a different kind of darkness...

~~~~~

"Well, well, you weren't out long," the familiar voice lisped as I regained consciousness. "Either you didn't hit that wall quite as hard as I thought, or else you gained a lot of resiliency from your treatments."

"Treatments!" I snapped, then winced as my head throbbed. "I lost my eyesight, who knows how many people lost their lives, and you have the gall to call them treatments?"

"Clearly the blow did nothing to affect your memory. Would you happen to remember who I am?"

"Balelo...but that's not what we called you behind your back."

"Very good. I'm impressed, Sixty-One."

"Did you ever know my name?"

Balelo's laugh dripped with condescension. "I never worried too much about introductions to lab rats, no matter the species."

I reached out with my remaining senses, trying to explore my surroundings. My power didn't require eyesight, but it was only useful if I knew what was around for me to potentially manipulate. Right now, telekinesis without vision seemed about as useful as a shovel without a handle.

Other than a general musty smell, nothing in this room seemed to have any particular aroma. I was still bound, so I couldn't really touch anything, taking that sense off the table—other than being able to discern that I was still bound by restraints made of hair. As for my heightened sense of taste, don't get me started on how unhelpful that could be in a situation like this.

That left me to rely on my hearing. Listening carefully, I could pick up on the sounds of breathing. Besides me and Balelo, there was a weeping woman, gasping and sobbing. She must have been the one whose screams drew me here in the first place. Other than the three of us, there was no movement, which meant no sound, making it impossible to tell what else might be in here. For all I could tell, this room might have plenty of potential weapons, or none at all.

"Where are we?" I asked. "What is this place?"

"We are in what used to be a county health department building, but I understand it hasn't been used in that capacity for years. The Organization bought it and the properties around it years ago for use as a remote facility. About a week ago, a few of us had an inkling you were planning something. We decided to each take one test subject and relocate to separate remote facilities like this one, just in case. We maintained communication, so I heard about your escape attempt. Fortuitously, you survived and found your way here."

The quiet and the desolation made more sense in light of that explanation. Somehow, I had blindly wandered upon a test facility—run by my former captors, no less. Either I had the worst luck on the planet, or else a higher power had drawn me here for a purpose. But what purpose could God have for a screw-up like me, who had already blown it once?

"Who is she?" I demanded.

"She is Test Subject Ninety-Four. I'm sorry, but I'm afraid that I can't give you her phone number." Balelo snickered at his own joke. "How do you like her hair, Sixty-One?"

Test Subject Ninety-Four. She was just another human lab rat in his eyes, and I was experiencing the results first-hand. She definitely didn't sound like a willing participant, any more than we had been. What if I could win her trust and get her to work with me? Then we could both escape...

...Yeah, just as long as it doesn't work out like it did back at the labs. No matter how far I ran, I still couldn't escape my guilt. Like a demented Jiminy Cricket in reverse, it accused me of my past failures rather than trying to point me in the right direction. For the umpteenth time, I tried to ignore it, knowing I couldn't do it for long.

I turned my head as best I could toward what seemed to be her general direction. "My name's Bart. Bart Mays. What's yours?" No response. It crossed my mind that she might not be able to hear me at all. If the experiments had cost me my sight, maybe they had affected her hearing. "What's your name?" I asked again, this time a little more loudly.

At last she spoke. "Not telling you," she sputtered between her tears.

"Why not?" I asked, doing my best to sound non-threatening.

A loud, wet sniffle. "I don't have to tell you anything. And if you know this man, you're probably bad news, too."

"Guilt by association," Balelo sneered. "Maybe you would have been better off not letting on that we know each other."

Ignoring him, I asked, "How long have you been this man's prisoner? That's how I know him. I used to be his prisoner."

"So you say."

Growing desperate, I tried another tactic. "Is this your hair that I'm wrapped up in? Has he been experimenting on you?"

"It looks like the hair part would be pretty obvious. Don't patronize me."

She didn't realize that I was blind. Maybe I needed to run with that. "So, what are you, anyway? Blonde, brunette, redhead? You don't sound old enough for it to be gray or white yet, but if this snake has been experimenting on you, I suppose anything is possible. Or is it maybe one of those dye shades that looks like something from a crayon box?"

Her hesitation in replying indicated that I had caught her off guard. "You're not funny. Don't play games with me."

"Who's playing? I'm blind...thanks to this rat and others like him. I haven't been able to see a thing since they got through with me."

That got her attention. "So they experimented on you, too?" she asked hesitantly. I could still hear the despair in her voice, but something else was there as well. Not hope, exactly, but close. Sometimes it helped just knowing that you weren't alone.

"Yeah, they did. And Balelo was in on it. He's a monster, I tell you, him and all his colleagues."

"That may be true, Sixty-One," Balelo said, "but don't you think that you should tell this young lady the whole truth about yourself? About what kind of a monster you are?"

Her hair tightened around my limbs as her body tensed. "What does he mean by that?" she demanded.

I only hesitated for a moment, but that was all the time that Balelo needed. "Oh, this guy is responsible for dozens of deaths. When he escaped from our facility, he left a trail of bodies behind him. Not only my colleagues, but also the people who were trying to escape with him. And yet he has the nerve to call me a monster?"

"If I'm a monster, it's only because you turned me into one!" Fury burned within me, and I thrashed against my bonds, to no avail. It had been the same way back at the labs. Experimenting on us wasn't enough. They had tried to turn us against each other as well, fearing what might happen if we tried to work together. Fears that were realized when a mere half-dozen of us were finally able to unite against them.

Now Balelo was trying to pit her against me. I couldn't allow that. As badly as I wanted to fight my way out of this, I needed some help, and she was my only hope.

"Is he telling the truth?" she asked. "Have you really killed people?"

The temptation to lie was overwhelming, but I knew all of my credibility with her would be shot if I did. "Yes, but accidentally. We were trying to escape, and I was trying to use the powers I got through their experiments. So was somebody else, a guy named Villanueva. Unfortunately, since I can't see anymore, it—well, backfired."

"How?"

"I'm telekinetic. He was a firestarter. He was trying to ignite the same objects that I was trying to hurl around. We wound up with fireballs flying, flames spreading..."

"That's enough," she said. "I get the picture."

"So I ran. I've been on the road since yesterday. And then I came here, wherever this place is..."

"And you heard her screaming and came rushing over here," Balelo scoffed. "But by your own admission, you're not cut out to be anybody's savior."

I wanted to rail back at him, but I couldn't bring myself to do it. His accusation was far too accurate, cutting right down to the core of my being. Unbidden, the memories of their dying screams came back to me— Sarge, Villanueva, Gillis, all of them. I had never believed in ghosts before, but their memories certainly haunted me.

Balelo was right. I was a failure. Who did I think I was to try this again?

She began to weep loudly, the kind of crying that gets so intense it leaves the person shuddering and gasping for breath. That sound did something to me, as if it flipped some kind of a switch deep within my psyche. What would be worse, trying to save her and failing, or not trying at all? One way might lead to disaster, but the other way was guaranteed to leave her in this plight.

I let my head drop as if in a gesture of defeat, but inwardly I doubled my efforts. Focusing my attention as best I could over her loud sobs, I tried to send out feelers with my mind. If my telekinesis could be used like another set of hands to move things, then maybe it could also be used to probe my surroundings, like someone feeling around in the dark. There had to be something I could use...

...And there it was, some kind of very solid object. I concentrated, imagining it in my hands, running my fingers along every inch of it. Hard, lightweight, metal, with a blade and a sharp point. A letter opener, as near as I could tell. Potentially useful, but it would be better if that wasn't the only thing I put into play.

The letter opener wasn't on the floor but rather on a surface a few feet higher—the right height for a desk. Surely that wasn't the only thing sitting there. Probing further, I felt ink pens, computer paraphernalia, a coffee mug, and a stack of papers underneath a smooth rock that must have been a paperweight of some sort. Plenty of items that could be weaponized with a little creativity on my part.

But it wouldn't do to have everything coming from the same direction. It would be better if I could find a variety of items from all directions...

Like back at the lab? Back when all the chaos became the telekinetic version of friendly fire?

"So they gave you powers, too?" she asked between sobs. "Took your sight, but gave you powers?"

"That's right. So what's your name?"

"Luna. My name is Luna. And by the way, it's brown."

"Excuse me?"

"My hair. It's brown. Brown with some red highlights. I'd just had it done before all this, believe it or not." The grip she held on my wrists and ankles was finally loosening—not much, but just enough for me to notice.

"All right. Thank you for that." I was doing my best to keep a lid on my emotions. My hopes depended on it. "How did you end up here, Luna?"

"I...I was trying to earn some extra money, and I saw a flyer saying that this research lab was going to pay participants to be part of a study. I signed up, and they sent me to this empty waiting room. I heard the air conditioner kicking on. Then I smelled this weird, sweet aroma, and suddenly I got sleepy—really sleepy. Next thing I knew, I was waking up tied down to this table, and..." She started crying again.

"Sounds about right," I said. "They gassed us too, a whole squadron of us at a National Guard base."

"You can stop now, Sixty-One," Balelo interrupted. "She's staying here, and so are you, now. We can finally get Project Pandora back on track..."

I heard something flying through the air. It took me a minute to realize it was a lock of her hair, but not headed for me this time. There was a loud crack, like a whip, followed by Balelo yelping in pain.

"He's on the floor, on his knees!" Luna shouted. She released my wrists and ankles completely now. "Ten feet to your left!"

Focusing my power, I flung everything I could find on the desk in that direction. Not all at once, but one item at a time, trying to time my salvos so he would still be reeling from one hit when the next one came. I heard him crying out in pain, but I had no way of knowing if I was doing much good or not.

"That letter opener got him in the Achilles tendon!" she reported. "Still alive, but we can get away from him if you'll help me!"

"Help you?"

"Yeah." Luna sounded as if she was crying again. "You can't see, and I can't walk. Thanks to him."

I stood there for a minute, stunned. Why hadn't I considered that? Every power had come at a price. My telekinesis in exchange for my sight. Villanueva's firestarting had come with acromegaly, and so on. The exchanges always seemed random but were always present. Paraplegia didn't seem to be a fitting tradeoff for weaponized hair, but I shouldn't have been as surprised as I was.

More than ever, I realized I hadn't thought this out well at all, but it was too late to turn back now. "I've never tried to use my telekinesis on myself before. I don't know if I can levitate both of us at the same time."

"So we're stuck?"

"Not necessarily. How about the same way you got me up here?"

"What, my hair?"

"If it was long enough to reach me on the sidewalk, wouldn't it be long enough to get back down there?"

"You forget one nagging little detail," Luna said. "I'm still attached to it."

"Not a problem. Do you know anything about rappelling?"

Although I couldn't see her face, I heard the realization in her voice. "I've always wanted to try it!"

A few moments later, we had a strand of her hair secured to anchor us and were easing ourselves out of the window. I braced my feet against the wall and held Luna in my arms while she handled her hair like a rope. She was petite, maybe even underweight. For this mode of escape, it helped.

I pushed off, and we slid down several feet. When my feet planted again, I asked, "Got the hang of it?"

"Got it." Her voice was full of gratitude and affection, and in my mind's eye I could see her grinning from ear to ear at me.

"All right, let's keep it going."

"Or you could get to the ground a little quicker!" Balelo's voice growled from overhead. "Ninety-Four, I think it's time you got a haircut!"

Luna screamed at about the same time her hair started to give way. I had to think fast. "What good are we to your precious experiments if you let us fall to our deaths?" I challenged.

"What good are you if I let you escape? You can both be replaced, and any cord can be cut." I heard a distinctive sawing sound, and immediately we dropped several inches. Luna gasped, and I felt the panic in her tiny frame.

"Don't make it easy on him! You've got more hair than this, right?" I cried. I telekinetically probed at the window we had just exited.

I heard another lock of Luna's hair whip through the air even as our current one snapped. It kept us from falling, but we wouldn't have long if I couldn't do something about Balelo.

Just as he started on the newest lock of hair, I finally got my telekinetic "hands" on him. Concentrating with all my might, I plucked him out of the window and had him floating above us, above the pavement below. He cursed loudly.

"What are you doing? Let me go!"

"Really? You want me to drop you?" I'll admit it, I enjoyed the chance to taunt him.

"No!"

"Okay, then be careful what you ask for. A lab rat like me might just take you literally. Since you don't want to be dropped, it might be time for you to give up the barber business, wouldn't you think?"

"All right, fine!" Balelo gasped. "I won't cut any more! I don't want to fall!"

"Fair enough," I said with a smirk. "All right, Luna, if you think your hair is still tied securely, let's finish this off."

Keeping my captive suspended in mid-air while continuing to rappel and hold on to Luna wasn't an easy task, as it divided my attention, but somehow, I managed.

"Thank you," Luna said as soon as my feet touched the pavement.

"What about me?" Balelo screeched. "I demand that you put me down at once!"

"Not so fast. We demand some answers first. Why have you been doing all these experiments on people against their will?"

"We were trying to tap into latent human abilities. You just think we're the bad guys. Trust me, there's something far worse out there. Our goal was to build up a force to fight against them!"

"With a blind man and a paralyzed girl?" Luna retorted.

"Those side effects weren't supposed to happen. We were trying to get the abilities without the side effects!"

I wasn't sure if I believed him, but I couldn't dismiss it out of hand either. The idea of something out there worse than Balelo was profoundly disturbing, but I kept my game face up. "You said there are others like us out there?"

"Yes, scattered across several top secret locations. I don't know them all. Now put me down!"

"Sure," I replied. "Just not here." Focusing my efforts, I sent Balelo as far away as I could, the same way I did with the dogs, with the bubble. Only maybe I gave him a slightly bumpier landing. With any luck, maybe he would find himself reunited with those Dobermans — and maybe they didn't like him very much.

"Thank you again," Luna repeated, this time planting a small kiss on my cheek. "I think there's a wheelchair in front of the hospital doors — fifty yards to your right."

I reached out, found it, and pulled it over. Wheeled objects were so much easier to manipulate. Gently, and with her direction, I set her down in the chair. "What about your hair?"

"That's one nice thing about it, I can pretty much make it style itself." I heard soft rustling all around me. "There we are, did-it-itself braids."

I shook my head. "Amazing."

"Thanks." She paused, and when she spoke again I heard the concern and uncertainty in her voice. "Do you think Balelo was telling the truth? About something worse being out there?"

"I don't know. But even if he is, we will face that when the time comes."

"Together?" she asked.

"Yes, together."

"All right, now where do we go?"

I shrugged my shoulders. "Beats me. Anywhere but here."

Luna paused again as if in deep thought. "Where were you heading before you heard me screaming?"

"I had thought about Chattanooga, but like I said..."

She chuckled. "Anywhere but here. All right, then, let's go."

So off we went. Luna was my eyes, and I was her legs. Neither of us had any idea what the future held for us, but at least now we knew we didn't have to face it alone.

END

Blood Gold
Etta-Tamara Wilson

The pale light of an early summer morning washed over the jewel box of a garden, dew sparkling like diamonds studding the soil. The dark velvet earth hid a wealth of ivory turnips and potatoes, golden carrots pushing ferns above the surface to frame plants in numerous varieties of jade. Each was adorned with fruits in shades of sapphire, amethyst, and ruby. The prize of the garden, however, occupied its own bed: a dense collection of short round plants, the celadon leaves displaying ruffled crimson edges and a blood-red stem. The delicate leaves were tender and sweet, and better yet, addictive and extremely rare. Margaret guarded them jealously, glorying in the fact that she was the only one capable of meeting the growing demand for such greens. Access was power, after all.

She shivered in the cool air and drew her shawl close as she bent to examine the plants. Another harvest was close. Another couple of days and she could take several layers of the tender leaves without harming the plants. That would give her enough time to find the best customer for them... or more precisely, the person who would pay the most. She eased an outer leaf to one side for a better look, but her view was interrupted by her hair as the thick braid escaped its pins and swung into the way. Her hair was a shade or two lighter than the blood-tinged morning light, the rope of ancient gold reflecting hints of ruby fire onto the rusted edges of the lettuce. She jerked her head in annoyance, flipping her braid back over her shoulder, and froze.

So too did the small boy perched in her plum tree, his fingers brushing the ripe fruit hanging from the tip of an overhead branch. His disheveled clothing, stained with dirt and worse for wear from his climb, and eyes the size of melons gave him the look of a storm-tossed owl.

"What do you think you're doing?"

At her indignant screech, the boy startled and overbalanced, arms cartwheeling as he tilted backward and dropped out of the tree. Luckily, the branch wasn't that high up. He uttered a breathless noise when he hit, but scrambled to his feet and darted for the gate out of the stone-walled garden. Unfortunately for him, the narrow pathways slowed him down, so she reached the gate first. She slammed the door shut and turned to face the boy, enjoying the sight of the lad wilting in on himself. She noted the worn patches on his clothing, as well as the stains of various colors dotting his shirt. Her plums weren't his only prize that morning.

"Were the fruits tasty?" At the child's tentative nod, she crossed her arms. "I'm glad you're satisfied. How do you intend to pay for them? They aren't free."

The boy paled, his mouth working silently for a moment. He patted his pockets and looked at her miserably, holding up their contents: a few smooth stones from the river, some cracked nuts from the forest, and a misshapen ring of green glass. She plucked the glass from his palm, ignoring his crestfallen expression. It was the handle of some sort of glass bottle, the broken edges worn smooth. "Well, it *is* pretty." The boy nodded, his eyes fixed on the dirt at his feet. "Not worth the cost of the plums, though, much less the other fruits you ate. Do you have anything else?" At the boy's panicked expression, she clenched her fingers around the glass. "I thought not."

"Do you know what the punishment for theft is? If you're lucky, it's a couple of lashes and a few hours in the stocks. If the judge is in a bad mood, though, you could get a branding or even lose a finger." She nodded at the boy's sudden wide-eyed expression. "Or… you could work for me for a while, and I *might* consider not telling the sheriff. But only if you do a satisfactory job. Does that sound reasonable to you?" The boy sniffed and nodded, rubbing his nose on his sleeve. "Good."

She snatched a basket from the hook next to the door and shoved it into the boy's chest. "Carry this. We're headed to the market." She clicked open the latch and shoved the gate open, then paused, looking back at the boy. "Oh, and I'm keeping the glass."

~~~~

The pair rounded the corner and entered the square, emerging in the center of the market. It was early yet. The booths were well-stocked, the tabletops littered with goods, barely visible through the jars and packages. A small number of people, young men and women dressed in faded clothing, bustled around the area collecting the goods they'd been dispatched to retrieve for their masters. She ignored them and peered around the crowd to judge the goods on offer. Still plenty of quality wares left, that she could see. Pleased, she steered the boy to an uncrowded table.

Later in the season, she'd be stocking a booth with her own wares, the ripened produce pulling in crowds from around the marketplace, away from her competitors. Not just local buyers, either. The last few years, she'd attracted wealthy patrons from surrounding towns, ones who tended to overpay. She might even need help manning the table this year, with the size of the upcoming harvest she had in her garden. She eyed the boy, who was staring at a jar on the table, face close as he tried to see inside it. Maybe she should keep him until then. It wasn't like he'd be able to complain about it.

"Hello, Mistress." Brother James, a priest from the local abbey smiled at them, the expression crinkling his sunburnt face. His light brown hair was cut in an unattractive bowl shape and was the same shade as his eyes and the dusty robes he wore. He looked like he was made intact from a massive lump of clay, she thought. He smiled down at the boy, who was still absorbed by the row of jars lined up in front of him. "Well, who is this?"

"A boy I'm employing for a while. He's working in exchange for goods." Margaret decided to leave it suitably vague. The abbey tended to get obnoxious about how people treated the poor, so it was best to keep the details secret.

The priest raised an eyebrow. "I assume there's a story there, but since you seem disinclined to share, I'll just remind you that it's how you treat others that affect how others treat you. Be kind." He stared at her for a moment, trying to enforce his point, then turned to the boy. "I see you're interested in the jar. Do you know what it is?"

The boy contemplated the jar. It contained a dark amber liquid behind its cloudy glass walls. "...Honey?"

The priest nodded. "Clever boy. The jar is filled with the bounty of the Father's most industrious earthly creatures." He reached for an already open jar. "Would you like to try some?" He grinned at the boy's enthusiastic nod and retrieved a piece of a small loaf from a basket on the table, smeared it with a thick layer of honey, and handed it to the child. "Here you go, lad." The boy promptly tried to shove the entire piece into his mouth at one time, causing the priest to chuckle.

"Steady there, boy. No one is going to take it away." He handed Margaret her own piece. "Here, Mistress. This batch is from the lavender fields last fall."

It tasted like liquid sunshine and would make a grand treat for winter. She added a jar to her usual order of candles and goat's milk soaps. The priest nodded and gave the boy another chunk of honeyed bread, then wrapped up the order in a thin cloth wrapping. He passed the bundle to the now-sticky boy to put in the basket, accepted payment, and watched silently as the woman pulled the child toward a distant table.

The boy looked longingly back over his shoulder at the booth as they moved away. Margaret moved them quickly out of earshot of the abbey's table before leaning close to his ear. "Don't dawdle. You have a lot of work to do before your debt is clear." She jerked her head toward the nearest table, sending the boy scrambling.

The booth was positioned in front of the town bakery, filled with racks of baked goods. Stacks of steaming leaves stood on one end of the table, their rich, yeasty smell warring with the more delicate sweet scents drifting from the baskets of hand pies spread across the rest of the table.

The golden crusts of the pies were pierced in myriad patterns, the slits hinting at the jewel-toned fruit fillings. She could see a wide variety, from the ruby glow of strawberry and cherry filling, to the deep amethyst of plums, and even the amber glow of spiced pear from last fall. From the scent of it, she was fairly sure that one basket in the middle, filled with pies cut with star-shaped slits the color of the night sky, might be filled with spiced raisins.

A nudge at her side made her look down. The boy was staring wide-eyed at the table, clutching the basket for dear life. She pushed him back, putting room between him and the table full of temptation. He was here to work. She doubted the bakers would be as willing to hand out free samples as the priest was. Both of them jumped at the sound of a deep laugh.

"Quite a sight, isn't it?" A man approached from the other end of the table, a lidded basket pinned under his arm. The boy held his basket up, trying to hide behind it, then nodded. The man grinned. "It's enough to make a man think he's found a king's table."

"Yes, but I bet it's also worth a prince's ransom," Margaret replied, shaking her head. "It's not in the budget." She grasped a pair of loaves from the racks, handed the baker a few coppers, and nudged the boy to steer him away. The boy's shoulders slumped and his eyes drifted to stare at the ground. The man frowned.

"Well, that seems like a shame, Mistress. Everyone should have a treat now and then." He shifted back on his heels and tapped his chin. He was well-dressed, wearing clothing of finer cloth then she'd ever seen in the village. His tunic was the color of sapphires, with boots and pants in the dark brown of newly turned earth. This was *not* a local. Margaret shifted her gaze to his belt, looking for a way to identify him. Painted on the upper flap of an impressively large belt pouch, its leather sides stretched close to bursting and the imprint of coins visible at close range, was a badge of a gray stone tower. The tower was surrounded by thorn-covered vines, a single red rose in full bloom hovering above it. The man was from the castle down by the lake.

"I got it!" The man brightened and smiled at her, raising his eyebrows. "Please let me treat you both. No lad should have to go without just because his family has to live with tight purse-strings." He looked hopeful. The boy turned to stare at her with matching pleading eyes.

Grabbing the boy had turned out to be a fabulous decision. She'd not gotten this much free stuff in years. She was definitely keeping him for a while, perhaps even through harvest and into winter. She smiled at the man and placed her hand on the boy's shoulder in what she hoped read as a maternal gesture. The boy just looked confused. "I'm sure he'd be as grateful as I am for the offer, sir. It's not often we get a treat, especially not one from such a kind gentleman." She squeezed his shoulder in warning. The boy squeaked, then nodded vigorously.

"Excellent. Which one would you like, lad?" He waved a hand at the pies on the table. The child stared at them in indecision, overwhelmed by the sudden wealth of options. "Too much to decide, eh? Why don't we go with a tried-and-true quality, then?" The man pointed to one of the pies marked with several sets of pointed leaf shapes, each pair joined at one end. A deep garnet filling showed through the cut-outs, and the rich scent of cherries drifted from them. The boy nodded in delight, shifting the basket to get a better look.

"Does that choice work for you as well, mistress?" At her nod, the man set his basket on the table and purchased a pair of the pies. He traded one to the boy for the basket he held. The boy tore into it, crumbs flying everywhere and dark filling staining his mouth and hands. The man chuckled, turning to face the woman. "Let me take those, Mistress." He held out the basket to take the bread. Margaret took a cloth from the basket and wrapped the loaves, then dropped it into the waiting basket. He placed the bundle onto the table next to his own, then handed her the other pie.

"Thank you, m'lord...?" She hesitated, fishing for an introduction. Her hope was rewarded.

"Gregory Fisher, Mistress. Lately assistant to the steward of Thorne Castle." He bowed at the waist.

She bobbed a quick curtsy, "My name is Margaret Wood. It's a pleasure to meet you. It's a long way from the castle to this market, sir. What brought you to this town?"

He gave a faint smile, gaze darting to her hair for a moment, then away. "We've discovered that the local markets don't have what we need. So now we're having to go farther afield for it. We're very selective about what we seek." He shifted his feet, eyes scanning the market. He practically radiated discomfort. It was strange, but no matter. An opportunity was an opportunity.

"If quality is what you seek, sir, then you came to the right market. Just on the wrong day." At his raised eyebrow, she smiled. "None of my product is ripe yet. Another week or so and you would have been able to purchase the best sweet lettuce in the district. I'm the only one in the village capable of producing sweet lettuce at this time of season. Ask anyone." She gave him a self-satisfied smile and nibbled on her pastry.

"That does sound like something we would be interested in, but I don't think we're in the market for that just yet," he said, looking conflicted. He turned, looking for his next destination. She had to hook him fast.

"If you need proof of quality, just ask the mayor. He's a long-standing client of good character." Well, not exactly *good* character, but for cheaper lettuce, he'd sing her praises to anyone who asked. It paid to have the only product in town.

"I'll do that, mistress." He removed another pair of coppers from his pouch, and twisted the clasp shut. "If it turns out the cook is interested, we'll get in touch with you." He smiled at her and handed the coins to the baker. "Another pair of pies for my friends here, thank you." He patted the boy on the shoulder and handed him back the basket, then turned and strode away from the table. She watched him go in frustration. Another possible missed sale. It could have been a profitable one, too.

A throat clearing caught her attention. The baker raised an eyebrow and held out the pies. She glowered and snatched the pies, slipping them into the wrappings around the bread loaves. She glanced up at the whine from the boy. "Consider this a fee to service your debt. And stop whining, you already got one." She stuffed the bundle back into the basket. "Those had better still be there later." She grabbed him by the arm and hauled him around, pushing him in the direction of another table. "Time to get back to work. And don't get any ideas. No more snacks today."

Neither of them noticed the man, hidden in the shadows of the butcher's shop, watching them work their way around the marketplace.

~~~~~

Margaret had to admit, the baker made delicious pies. Finishing off the first pie, she was eyeing the second one when the staccato knock echoed through her home. She scowled and got to her feet, accompanied by the sharp screech of the chair's feet against the rough floor. Orders were made on market days, not the day after, especially not shortly after sunrise. She jerked the front door open, ready to tear a strip out of the hide of the visitor, but stopped short. The young man standing there was smartly dressed in a tunic of fine sapphire wool, with the same badge as Master Fisher had worn sewn to its middle. She gaped at the sight, turning red when the man raised an eyebrow. She composed herself and cleared her throat. "Can I help you?"

"Is this the house of …" he looked down at the scroll in his hand. "Mistress Margaret Wood? The purveyor of specialty vegetables?"

She straightened her spine. "Yes, I am she. How can I help you?"

He flicked the end of the scroll toward her. "An order for you, from the palace. I'm to wait for a confirmation." He watched her open the scroll, her forehead creasing as she examined the text. "Do you need any sort of explanation?" From his tone, it was clear he doubted her ability to read and understand it. She resisted the urge to stick out her tongue at the insolent courier. He was just a servant, after all. She'd have it addressed later.

Mistress Wood,

My assistant has alerted me to the high quality and abundant variety of your vegetables. I was most pleased to hear that you have in stock a number of sweet lettuces. The lady of the castle has always been partial to dishes of sweet greens, and I've had dismal luck trying to grow some in the castle gardens. I would like to extend an offer to you to come tour the castle, in addition to a request of an order of the best quality greens that you can supply within the week. Please pass along your reply to the invitation, as well as your required costs of the order, to the messenger. Thank you for your consideration.

In anticipation,
Simon Granger
Head Cook, Thorne Castle

She could barely contain her excitement. An order for a noble? This was the key to a much better paid level of customer. She had already promised her best to the mayor, but she could switch him to the lower-quality heads. The oaf wouldn't even be able to tell the difference. The real question was, how much to charge the castle? She considered charging them four times more than the mayor paid, but she wasn't sure what the household had heard about her prices. She decided to play it safe. The woman turned to a table near the window and prepared a short note, sealing the folded page before handing it to the messenger.

"I accept," she said, nodding. "They'll have the order requested within the time allotted for the price within the note." It was more then twice her usual price, but they didn't need to know that. If they accepted, she could always figure out a way to raise the price as time went on.

The messenger tucked the note into his pouch. "I'll pass along the response. Have a good evening, Mistress." He turned and strolled down the path toward a horse she could now see was tied to the gate. The gelding was stripping the grass away from the bottom of the wall and eyeing the flowers in the field across the road. She shut the door on the sight, her mind already moving on to the busy week ahead. She had plants to pamper, and several customers to disappoint.

~~~~~

It was a sign of a good castle when even the entrance for deliveries was fancy-looking. Margaret admired the door to the servants' entrance for several moments, working up the nerve to pull the bell cords. Most people were content to leave the door seen only by the lower classes in a plain state, but the caretakers of the castle had painted it a beautiful deep blue, with delicate silver and gold tracing. It went well with the wrought-iron hardware and whitewashed plaster of the castle walls. She admired the door but was certain that she wouldn't see this sight again. No, next time, she was coming in the front door. Blowing her anxiety out in a deep sigh, she shifted her basket of goods to her left arm and gave the cord a strong yank. Deep within, a dull bong sounded. Only silence greeted her.

Just as she began to panic, soft footsteps approached the other side of the door. It creaked open to reveal a girl standing there. The slight figure was dressed in a stark gray dress, high-waisted, with a hem that brushed the floor and tight sleeves ending at the wrists. She had a starched white hood wrapped tightly around her head. Every strand of her hair was hidden by the cap, giving the girl an ageless appearance. She leaned her head to one side in curiosity. "May I help you?" Her voice was young. Likely a teenager.

Margaret held up her basket. "My name is Mistress Wood. I'm here to deliver an order, and I've got an invitation to take a tour."

"You do?" The girl raised an eyebrow. "That's unusual." She turned to the side and gestured back down the hallway behind her. "I suppose you should come in. We'll take that to the kitchen. Maybe they'll know what to do from there." Margaret took a few steps inside and waited as the girl shut and locked the heavy door. It wasn't painted on this side, the surface stained a simple dark brown. The trio of locks was unusual, but the area had developed a problem with bandits recently. Smart of them to be safe.

The two women hurried down the dimly lit hall, past rows of plain wooden doors studding whitewashed plaster walls. At the end, a glowing archway led to the kitchen. The cavernous room was washed in warm golden light, the glow of tiers of candles in bronze and tin holders reflected by scores of copper pots lined up on the enormous, scarred oak table occupying the center of the room. To one side sat the stove, the wide body radiating heat. It reminded her of a sleeping dragon, dreaming of doing battle with armies of copper-plated foes. Two men stood in the space between, deep in discussion. The younger one frowned and rubbed his hand over his face, turning to glance at the women as they entered. Margaret realized with a start that the younger man was Gregory Fisher, the assistant she'd met in the market. He stared at her for a moment in confusion, then his expression cleared and he sighed, beckoning them closer.

"Mistress Wood, I'm glad to see you again. May I introduce you to Master Granger, the head cook." He gestured to the older man he'd been arguing with. The cook dipped his head at her.

"Greetings, Mistress. I was glad to get your note. I have your payment ready in my office. Is that the delivery?" He nodded at the basket she was holding. At her nod, he took it and carefully examined the contents, exclaiming at the various fruits and vegetables within. He pulled out the bundle of lettuce to inspect it carefully. "Beautiful. Looks just like the ones we were trying to grow. How did you manage to get them to grow successfully?"

"It's all about location. My garden has the best soil in the area. I'm the only local capable of growing these."

"We'll have to keep that in mind, then. Locating good sources of products is very important to the castle." He placed the produce into the cooling cabinet to keep for later. He waved a hand at the hallway on the other wall. "With that out of the way, would you like your tour? If we're lucky, there might even be time for a surprise along the way. We'll end with a visit to my office for your payment."

"That sounds lovely, thank you." Margaret followed the cook out of the room, missing both the questioning look the maid gave the assistant, and his resulting head shake and sigh.

~~~~~

Much to her delight, the bulk of the tour involved the public areas of the castle, which were as elaborately decorated as the outside. Gold and silver filigree and roses were everywhere. They veered through a darkened hallway away from the throne room and past a small room, the walls covered in white sheets. She tried to stop and look into the room, but the cook hurried her on to a small stairwell.

"I wanted to see that one. Why was the room like that?"

He shook his head. "The room is being remodeled. It used to be a mirrored hall, but our lady isn't much a fan of those anymore." They stopped at the head of the stairs and he peeked through a nearby door for a moment, brightening quickly. "Speaking of the lady, it looks like it's time for that surprise I mentioned." He opened the door wide and motioned her through. Inside was the largest library she'd ever seen, the shelves stretching upward several floors, the sounds of her footsteps muffled by thick carpets under her feet and numerous sets of massive drapes shrouding the windows.

"Hello."

Margaret jumped and spun in place at the unfamiliar voice. At the far end of the room, seated in a large, overstuffed chair next to an enormous stone fireplace, sat a woman. She wore a dress of sapphire blue wool, edged with fine white lace and tied with golden cords. A coverlet of snowy knitted lace, delicate as a spider's web, covered her lap. A cap similar to the one the maid wore covered her head, but this one was made of fine linen and edged with lace. The lady in the chair set the book she was holding on her lap and beckoned to them.

"Come closer and introduce our guest. It's not often we get visitors." She smiled at the cook. He bowed at the waist.

"My Lady, let me introduce you to Margaret Wood, the best purveyor of quality vegetables in this district. She brought us some of her lettuces for your dinner tonight. Mistress Wood, this is Princess Reine de Glace, the Lady of Thorne Castle."

Margaret curtsied and immediately wished she'd worn her festival dress for this trip. It looked fancier. The princess nodded at her.

"I'm pleased to hear that. It's been so long since I had a quality salad. I look forward to learning your secret for obtaining those greens." She squinted, staring at her hair. "You have beautiful hair, Mistress Wood. I've never seen that color outside of portraits. What's it called?" She glanced at the cook.

"Blood Gold, my Lady. Several trendsetters in the capital have been trying to imitate it with rinses, but without much luck."

Margaret glanced at the princess. Her cap obscured her hair, so she couldn't tell what color she had. She had dark eyebrows, though, so she assumed the princess likely had dark hair originally. Whether it still was that color was up for debate, however, as the lady's face showed age lines.

"Ah. It's a stroke of luck you have it naturally, then. I assume it's natural and not a wash, correct?" At Margaret's nod, the princess smiled. "Very good. I hope you're enjoying the tour." She turned toward the cook. "I approve. Be sure to treat our guest well, and give her a nice snack before she goes, all right?" The cook nodded. "I'll let you get back to it, then. I'm glad to have met you, Mistress Wood, and I look forward to sampling your products. Have a lovely afternoon." She nodded at the younger woman and lifted her book again.

The cook placed a hand on the dazzled visitor and steered her back through the door.

"That was a stroke of luck. Lady Reine rarely approves of visitors." He grinned at her, eyes shining. "Looks like we're keeping you. Let's get you back to the office for your reward." He guided her through the servant's hallway to a small locked office. She seated herself while he retrieved a pouch from a cabinet across the room. Seating himself at the other side of a small table, he handed her the pouch. "I think you'll find the required fee all there."

She opened it and inspected the coins. It was indeed all there. Next time, considering what she saw today, she was raising the price. "It is indeed. Of course, this was the 'new customer' price, so future crops will be more. Savings can be obtained by creating a standing order, however." She raised her eyebrows at the cook. He smiled back at her.

"I'm sure we'll be able to arrange something, depending on how my lady likes the salad." He set two glasses on the table and uncorked a glass bottle of a dark amber liquid. The smell of rich spices filled the small room. "Since we're going into a business relationship, indulge my curiosity. How did you become the only one able to successfully grow that lettuce?"

"Those greens grow like weeds in my garden. The land itself is blessed. The previous owner was persuaded to sell some of the soil once, but the lettuce doesn't grow anywhere else. It was a good thing I managed to get the place, as they didn't want to sell any of the plants themselves."

"Really? Why not?"

She shrugged. "The excuse they gave? They said the place was cursed. Apparently, it was involved in some family tragedy several decades ago. Some lost child or something. They were always ripping out the plants, but they just grew back. Personally, I think they just wanted to keep the lettuce for themselves."

"Good thing you have it now, then." The cook poured a generous amount into both glasses and offered her one. "A toast. To blessed lettuces, lovely hair, and successful approvals."

Lovely hair? She shook off the weird comment and accepted the glass. "To success." She drained the glass and set it back on the table. The cook smiled at her enthusiasm, sipping at his own glass.

"So, if my lady likes your greens, how long would it take for your plants to be ready for harvest?"

Negotiations went quickly. Eventually, they agreed on a delivery of the best greens once a week. It was a tight schedule and would mean shorting several other clients, but as they also agreed to pay almost twice what they paid for this shipment, she was fine with that. A six-fold profit was worth the trouble. The alcohol was starting to get to her, however. Her head was spinning. Time to head home. She waited for the cook to write up the agreement and tried to clear the fog away. She tried to examine the promissory note he slid across the table, but the words were fuzzy and trying to read was making her head hurt.

Oh well, she could clearly see the price agreed on and the date at the end, so she signed it and pushed it away. Struggling to her feet, she was alarmed to see the room darken and tilt sickeningly. She would have hit the floor if the cook hadn't caught her on the way down. Margaret blinked at him in confusion.

"Sorry, Mistress. But we don't get approvals very often."

The room vanished in a spice-scented darkness.

~~~~~

The air smelled stale and damp, like water stuck in a cave for too long. Margaret struggled to open her eyes or move, but something wrapped around her body tightened its grip. Fear spiked through her. Where was she? A faint scuffling sound to her right made her freeze, her heart quivering in her chest. Eternity dragged on as she waited for whatever was there to reveal itself, but only silence met her.

Clamping down on her jangling nerves, she cracked open her leaden eyelids and peered desperately into the darkness. After a moment, the fog lifted, revealing a dimly lit storeroom. To her left sat a table, a chipped bowl in the center of the scarred workspace. A trio of leather-wrapped bundles sat beside the bowl, along with a jug that seemed to be the source of the water smell. A small glass-topped lantern sat on the other side of the bowl, the flame inside burning low, the dim red light casting long shadows on the walls and ceiling. The contrast of light and dark reminded her of the abbey's passion plays. She shivered.

The scuffling sound returned, and she rotated her head to find it. No luck, it was behind her. She tried to swivel at the waist, but a rough band tightened around her chest. She squinted downward in the gloom. She was strapped to a thick wooden chair by wide leather straps around her chest and legs, her arms similarly bound to the chair's strong arms. She was also dressed only in her shift. A hint of red beyond her hem caught her eye, and she sighed. They'd taken her boots as well. She frowned at her scarlet-clad toes as she tried to remember what happened. The last thing she recalled was sitting down to have a drink with the cook. Nothing she'd seen in the castle looked like this room, however. Where had she been taken?

The scuffling sound rounded her chair in a series of halting steps. She jumped slightly, nerves clattering like the bone wind chimes in her garden, then breathed a sigh of relief. The small round face, topped with messy hair and the large brown eyes of a fawn, was familiar. The boy who had stolen her plums. She would be okay.

"Hello there. Can you undo these, please?" She jerked her right arm, tugging the leather strap tight for a moment. The boy's gaze dropped to the strap, then back up to her face. His expression remained blank, void of understanding. She clamped down on her impatience. "Come on, boy. Undo the strap."

Nothing. Maybe he needed motivation?

"If you let me out, I'll forgive the theft of the fruit. No more debt. You can even have more if you want. Just unlatch the straps." She waggled her right hand again. The boy stared at her blankly for a moment, then narrowed his eyes. He hurried toward the chair. "That's right, remove the... wait, what are you...?"

The boy had reached the chair, but instead of reaching for the straps, he'd turned toward the table. Margaret squirmed in her restraints as he grabbed one of the leather bundles. The straps groaned in protest but didn't budge. She glared at the boy as he fiddled with the ties on what appeared to be a small sack. His arm disappeared into the opening for a moment.

"When you're done there, untie me. Immediately."

The boy ignored her, his face scrunched up in concentration as he rooted around. His face suddenly relaxed and he gave a wordless cry of joy. He removed his arm from the sack and opened his hand, revealing the little lump of polished glass she'd taken from him the week before. The leather ties she'd looped through the hole in the glass dragged across the tabletop as he dropped the sack and turned away.

"You aren't supposed to be in here." A voice, made of gravel and wood smoke, came from behind her. She startled and tried to twist to see the speaker. Still no use. The boy's head darted up, his hands pulling into his chest. "Go on. You have chores, don't you?" The boy nodded in response, then looped the ties over his head and hurried around the chair, disappearing from view. A heavy wooden thud was followed by a hard click, then the slow sound of heavy footsteps. A tall but quite thin man strode into view. Clad in rough garments in shades of dusty brown and faded grey, the man's face could very well have been carved of the same stone as the walls of the dim cell, all cracks and uneven surfaces. His eyes were so deep-set that they disappeared in the faint light. He moved around the room to retrieve a stool and place it next to the left arm of her chair, seating himself on it and giving her a wide grin. The expression and his eyes gave him a skeletal appearance. Her veins froze.

"Sorry about the boy. That scamp gets into all sorts of places he shouldn't." He twisted the knob on the lantern, increasing the flame. It didn't improve the sight. His eyes glinted like ruby fire reflecting off obsidian chips. He smiled at her again, but it never reached those cold eyes. He grabbed her chin, using his grasp to twist her head to one side. "That is such lovely hair."

"... thank you?"

The man nodded absently and turned, unrolling the larger bundle. He extracted a wide leather strap and a thick mass of cloth. "I was delayed. I was supposed to be underway well before now. Letting you wake up like this is just unprofessional. You have my apologies. I'll do this quickly." He attached one side of the strap to a hook next to her head.

She shrank as far from it as she could get in her condition. "Let me go! Please, I won't tell anyone!"

He patted her hand, then pulled her roughly back into position and shoved the cloth bundle between her teeth when she gasped. The strap was flipped across her mouth and slipped onto a hook on the other side of her head. Peeling open the cover of the last leather bundle on the table, the man revealed a row of gleaming knives. He mused in consideration a moment, before smiling and removing one from its well-worn pocket, reaching for the basin with his other hand. "So, shall we begin?"

~~~~~

Despite the lateness of the hour and the coolness of the evening air flowing through the wide-open windows, the palace was stifling from the shear mass of bodies crammed into the hall. The jewel-encrusted finery adorning the partygoers glinted like stars in the light of the constellation of candles in rose-shaped votives of silver and crystal. The holders hung from the ceiling on golden vines, each one suspended from arches made of the branches of gilded trees carved into the pillars of the enormous ballroom. In one corner of the room, the polished gray slate floor erupted upward into a sand-lined rock grotto. A number of the younger or more inebriated partygoers danced around in the clear water that filled the folly. One dodged backward to avoid getting splashed, only to wave his heavily embroidered sleeve through the flame of one of the candles perched on some of the higher rocks around the edges of the pool. A flare of light bloomed on his arm as the teenager flailed in panic. Luckily for him, a quick plunge through the water that trickled from a pipe in the wall and babbled down the rocks into the grotto limited the damage.

Despite this excitement, the bulk of the attention of the crowd was directed to the hostess of the ball, the legendary Lady Reine de Glace, the Princess of Thorns. She was the person to imitate in society, her every action admired and copied for decades. In the years since her husband had abdicated the throne due to the recurrence of his blindness, she'd dedicated herself to controlling the path of fashion. At her own event, she didn't disappoint. She was clad from head to toe in a deep emerald silk gown, embroidered in silver and gold vines and studded with pearls and miniature roses carved of pink quartz. A wide collar of emeralds, interspersed with pearls and beads of gold and rose-colored quartz, circled her neck. Shoes of gold cloth peeked out under the hem. The real conversation starter, however, was her wig.

The princess had started the trend of wearing elaborate wigs many years before. The best one, by widespread agreement, was from a winter ball two years ago: an ebony wig, with silver ribbons woven through it and a working clockwork automaton of a pair of gold songbirds embedded in it. The wig this evening, however, was elegant but simple. It was a deep shade of gold with a faint scarlet tint to it, arranged in a riot of curls, held in place with green silk ribbons and golden pins. The princess was surrounded by admirers.

"Oh, this? Yes, it's new. It's a one-of-a-kind item gifted to me by a local merchant as a thank you gift when I bought her farm. The color is called Blood Gold, I believe..."

END

Down the Fire Escape
Kathleen Bird

Just another couple of clicks, and I'll be done! Annaliese's fingers practically flew across the keyboard as she finished the last couple of sentences in her discussion post response. *Yes, I agree with what Samuel said...blah, blah, blah.* She wrote enough to hit the required word count, without putting too much thought into it, before finally clicking submit and clamshelling her laptop with a satisfying soft slam. "Now, it's time to move on to other things," she said to the practically empty apartment.

Moving out of her study room and into the kitchen was a welcome break from the rest of her daily routine. During the day, she spent most of her time in the apartment's second bedroom, which functioned as both a study and an exercise room. Which really just meant a bookshelf overflowing with historical romance novels, a desk to hold her laptop and various school supplies, and the stationary bike she'd brought with her from her old room at home. It might not be the most effective use of space, but it worked for her.

The rest of her apartment looked less...disjointed. In fact, it looked as though an interior designer had been behind most of the purchases. Which was actually the case, since Mother had picked out almost everything. Annaliese had contributed her specifications for cookware and baking supplies, as she'd developed quite an extensive culinary repertoire over the years. One benefit to being homeschooled meant she'd had plenty of time to explore her various interests. So, the cozy feel of the kitchen was a safe space for her after a somewhat exhausting day. Nothing had quite seemed to go right, from her first paper of the day failing to submit, to the final discussion board turning out to be far more confusing than she'd first thought.

I'm ready for this whole day to just be over. Or, well pretty much over. There were still a few things she was looking forward to about today.

She turned on the kitchen radio, which was tuned into the local pop station...granted it was the one that played music from the last decade as opposed to the last year; but that was what she liked anyway. Peppy music drifted into her tiny space and began to ease the tension from her body. Annaliese took another deep breath and just enjoyed the moment before proceeding to her next task.

Once she'd sufficiently savored the calm, she began pulling out ingredients and materials from the various cabinets in her kitchen. One small pot. Milk. Sugar. Black tea. Cardamom. Cloves. Fresh ginger root, which she sliced quickly before setting aside. All the necessary ingredients for a hot cup of chai. She carefully measured out her water and added her spices, letting them come to a boil before adding her milk. The whole process was soothing, as it required very little thinking on her part. And as long as she did it right, the result was perfect every time. As the tea turned the delicious shade of brown that meant it was finished, she carefully poured it into her mug via a strainer. The whole kitchen smelled pleasantly of spices.

Now she could turn her attention to the window seat and the city scene below it.

She tugged at the end of her braid as she nervously glanced at the clock. It was almost 4 o'clock, and she was running out of time. Annaliese forced herself to grip the sides of her mug tighter, allowing the warmth to penetrate her hands and calm her nerves at the sudden reminder of how little time she had left before she had to focus on her next task. *He always walks by about now.* Another quick glance at the clock before she turned her attention back to staring out the window beside her.

People watching was her absolute favorite pastime, even more than bingeing reruns of *The Great British Baking Show* on Netflix. Every day when she finished her online classes, she made a fresh cup of chai and snuggled down on her window seat to stare at the people passing by on the streets below. And there was a certain someone she especially enjoyed seeing every day.

Maybe I should get my hair cut, she thought distractedly as she played with the blond strands escaping from her formerly neat braid. It had gotten rather out of control since she moved away from home. Now it fell all the way to her waist. *But Mother insists it looks better long like this.* She sighed and pushed the dilemma aside for another day. Her gaze drifted back to the sidewalk, and suddenly she felt like all the air had been sucked from her lungs.

"He's here," she whispered, pressing one hand to the chill glass as though it might magically pass through and reach him. In the midst of the crowds going about their business, there was the most handsome man she'd ever seen in her life. Every day around this time, he approached the corner her apartment building stood on. She took in his brown jacket and ripped jeans, the tousled brown hair that fell slightly over his eyes, and the sunglasses that he always wore, rain or shine. He carried a worn satchel slung over his shoulder and held a to-go cup, presumably filled with coffee, in his left hand. And of course, the unique accessory that had attracted her attention in the first place: a white cane that tapped the sidewalk in front of him.

"Meooow!" Her dreamy state of contentment was interrupted by an impatient request from Princess, her fluffy Persian cat companion, who had suddenly decided to grace her with her presence.

"I'll feed you in a minute," Annaliese said sternly. "Mother's going to call any time now, so just let me enjoy my freedom for a few more measly seconds." The lack of understanding in the feline's eyes just underscored how ridiculous it was to try to have a conversation with Princess.

Is he gone? She frantically turned back to the window and searched the crowds for her mystery man. *He's still waiting for the stoplight to change,* she thought with a sigh of relief as she finally located him. Soon he'd cross the street and disappear from view until tomorrow afternoon. Every day she wondered where he was going, what he was doing in the city, did he have a girlfriend...the questions were endless. But what really astounded her was how brave he must be to walk around the city by himself when he was, you know, blind.

She, on the other hand, had been living in the city for almost six months now, but she still barely left her apartment. It was easy enough to have her groceries delivered, and all her classes so far had been available online. Mother had been determined that she could (and *should*) do all her college classes from the comfort and safety of their home in the country, but Annaliese desperately wanted to get away and out on her own. So, she moved to the city and found her own apartment at the top of an older high-rise that hosted beautiful architecture. But there had been one condition for Mother's assistance with the rent: every day she had to be ready to answer her phone and talk to her mother. And of course, Mother didn't believe in cell phones, so she'd had to install a landline as soon as she moved in. Since her mother had a fascination with schedules and routines, it was easy enough to adjust her schedule to accommodate the phone calls that came at approximately 4 o'clock every day. Particularly since she had yet to work up the courage to explore much beyond the four walls of her apartment building.

"Meooow!" Princess leapt up on the window seat beside her and stared at her, bright blue eyes filled with accusation.

"Sorry!" She took one last look out the window, glanced at the clock, and then carried her mug to the counter. Grabbing both Princess's wet food and the can opener from her drawer, she quickly cut off the lid and dumped the food unceremoniously into the bowl.

Ring! Ring! Ring!

Still carrying the food dish in one hand, she grabbed up the wireless phone and hit the answer button. "Mother?"

"Of course it's me, dear! Who else has your number?"

"Well, um...no one but the telemarketers, I guess."

Princess was rubbing anxiously against her legs, so she carefully set the bowl on the ground. Another quick look out the window told her the rain was starting, as tiny droplets started to impact the windowpanes.

"How were classes today, darling?"

"Um...fine, I guess." She edged her way around her cat, now completely focused on inhaling her dinner, so she could plant herself back on the window seat. *He's probably gone by now anyway.*

"Just fine? Is something wrong, dear?"

"No, um...nothing's wrong..." Unconsciously, she'd been searching the streets to see if that familiar brown jacket was still visible. And it was, in fact!

But what she saw wasn't the familiar scene. Mystery man was still on the corner closest to her apartment building, but he'd dropped his cane and his coffee and was struggling with an assailant to keep hold of his satchel. He was being mugged!

What kind of jerk robs a blind guy?

And unfortunately, the rain had sent most of the pedestrians scrambling for cover. It was just the two men and the cars passing by too fast to care.

"Annaliese, are you even listening to me? You know I expect an actual *conversation* during these phone calls!"

She flinched at her mother's angry tone. "I'm...I'm sorry, Mother. I'm just...just a little distracted today." *Isn't anyone going to help him?* She felt the panic rising up in her chest and threatening to strangle her. The thief had finally gotten the satchel and was now running down the street in the opposite direction. Her mystery man was clearly yelling at him, but there was nothing he could do to prevent the villain from getting away.

"This is why I was so worried about you moving away! This level of distraction is only going to keep you from your studies. What if you lose your scholarship, dear? How will you manage to pay for school then?"

"Get a loan, I guess," she mumbled, but her mind was still completely focused on the tragedy happening on the sidewalk below her. Unfortunately, the white cane had rolled away from its master. He was frantically searching for it, scrambling on his knees to feel for it. *Seriously, is no one else seeing this? Why isn't anyone helping him?* "Why aren't I helping him?" she whispered, so softly she thought no one could hear. Unfortunately, she was wrong.

"Help who, dear?" Her mother's tone was distinctly more angry than concerned.

"Oh, um...I was looking out the window while we were talking..."

"Goodness, so sorry to be boring you," Mother interrupted tersely, sarcasm dripping with every word.

"No, it's not that! It's just um...there was this guy, and he just got robbed. Maybe I should call the police or something, to report it, you know?"

"Not at all!" she said harshly. "You should stay out of it. Do you even know this man?"

"Well, no not exactly…"

"Then why bother interfering? The thief will be long gone by now anyway."

"Well, maybe I should go down and help him…"

"Help him with what?"

She sensed the tension coming from the other end of the phone line. *I should drop this.* But a voice inside her was screaming to press on, almost like it was a wave of water ready to burst over the dam. She pressed her hand against the glass again, the chill bringing her back to a grounded reality.

"Never mind, Mother. I'm sorry to have sidetracked our conversation."

"Apology accepted, dear. You know I just want you to be safe, right?"

"Yes, of course," Annaliese whispered, still watching as her mystery man struggled to pick himself up from the ground. He still hadn't managed to find his cane, and he was completely drenched from head to toe as the rain continued pouring down on him. Now he was clearly trying to reorient himself as he turned his head back and forth. He was also limping as he attempted to stand and take a few steps. *Perhaps the thief was a little rougher on him than I saw?*

"So, let's try telling me about your day again. Or would you prefer to hear about mine?"

"Um, why don't you start?" she said distractedly as she watched him finally stop searching for his cane. Instead, he froze, perhaps listening to tell which direction the traffic was coming from? Then he slowly started backing up toward her building until he disappeared from sight. Annaliese held her breath, but he didn't reappear. *Where did he go?* Her heart felt like it might burst with worry for this complete stranger who didn't even realize what an important part of her day he was.

Her mother was still droning on about her client's ridiculous taste in wallpaper, so she could focus her attention on the unfolding scene below her. Or rather the sudden end to said scene's visibility. *What if he's hurt? Did he go inside the apartment building or something? Is he trying to get help?*

"Don't you agree, dear?"

"Hmmm?"

"I don't like having to repeat myself, Annaliese," Mother said sternly. "I asked if you agreed?"

She hovered near the window, torn apart with indecision, and tried desperately to remember what Mother had been talking about.

"I'm sorry, Mother. I'm afraid I didn't catch what you were saying," she finally admitted and then braced herself for the onslaught she knew was coming.

"What have I told you about paying attention? You mustn't let yourself daydream when you're in the middle of a conversation. I mean, how else are you supposed to carry on a conversation? I'm very disappointed in you today, Annaliese. You know, I expect much better from you."

Surprisingly, she was able to tune out most of her mother's diatribe by pressing her nose to the cold glass and trying to stare directly downward. Of course, she still couldn't see anything, with a fire escape in the way, and the glass fogged up with her breath.

"Is there anything you have to say to me?" There was a deliberate pause on the other end of the line meant for her to fill with an apology.

But something stopped her. *What do I really have to be sorry about?* she thought suddenly. *I haven't done anything wrong, other than perhaps be a little rude. But I'm genuinely concerned about this guy! What if I'm the only one who saw what happened? What if that guy is passed out by the building or something?*

"Annaliese," her mother's voice once again interrupted her thoughts. "I said, is there anything you have to say to me?"

"Yes, actually," she said and took a deep breath before plunging ahead. "Mother, I have to go."

"Is this about that man who got mugged? I told you, it's not safe to go and help him! Let someone else do it."

"But what if there isn't anybody else? What if I'm the only one who can?"

"There's always someone else, dear. I promise you, someone else will take care of him."

"But what if *I* want to take care of him?" she blurted without thinking, and then blushed immediately at the implication of her words.

"I thought you said you don't know him!"

"Well, I don't. But…"

"Then why on earth would you want to take care of him?"

She didn't have a great answer to that. *All I know is that I* **do** *want to take care of him.* "I don't know, Mother. But I'm going to help him because I think that's the right thing to do." She paused, and surprisingly her mother didn't immediately fill the space. *She must be in shock that I'm talking back to her.* "Oh, and I also think I'm going to cut my hair," she said hurriedly before rushing to the kitchen and slamming the phone down into its cradle.

Immediately the sound of ringing mixed with loud "meowing" filled the apartment as Princess objected to all the rushing about. But she blocked out the sounds, grabbed her slip-on shoes from beside the door, and rushed out into the hallway.

A hand-written sign with **OUT OF ORDER** in black permanent marker was taped to the elevator door. Groaning, she paused to evaluate her options. With the elevator out of commission, her next best option was probably the stairwell at the end of the hallway. Quickly slipping her shoes on, she ran to the hallway and banged open the crash bar, grateful for her exercise routine...minimal as it was. She made it down one flight of stairs before she ran into a problem.

"Well, hey, Annaliese! Don't often see you outside your place!" It was her neighbor, who'd told her his name was Jacko (even though that couldn't possibly be true).

The large man was holding one end of a sofa, which was currently wedged in an impossible position that managed to block all access to the remainder of the stairwell.

"Sorry, 'bout this," he said sheepishly, as he motioned vaguely at the couch. "My brother found this down at the thrift store, ya know, and he had to have it. Didn't think ta measure or nothing before he bought it!" He gave another man she couldn't see, but was presumably at the other end of the couch, a glare for emphasis, and she heard some sort of a response in a language she didn't recognize.

She bounced on her toes and tried to think about how else she could get downstairs. The longer it took, the more she imagined that poor man unconscious on the sidewalk in the cold rain, getting colder and colder the longer she was delayed. Without another word to Jacko, she spun around and headed back upstairs.

Once she was back in her apartment, still filled with the angry sounds of Princess's meowing and her incessantly ringing phone, she headed to the only other option available to her: the fire escape outside her window. Quickly, she pulled all the pillows off the window seat and tossed them onto the floor. One managed to hit the cat, which only resulted in even angrier protestations. With the way now cleared, she climbed up and pressed the button that unlocked the window. With a gentle push, it swung outward. She was pelted with the not-so-gentle rain, now spewing into her apartment with a vengeance. Mortified at the thought of getting wet, Princess finally vanished into the bedroom, with a few more angry yowls on her way out.

I can do this, she thought. "I can do this," she repeated as she flung both feet out the window and sat precariously on its ledge before dropping to the metal landing below her. The wind howled, and she wrapped her arms around herself, clutching her thin pink sweater close. Coupled with her bright blue leggings dotted with smiling sloths, they were definitely *not* meant for rainy weather like this. Loose blond strands of hair whipped into her face, and she brushed them out of the way angrily. *I have to get moving!* Carefully, she slid her feet one step at a time toward the metal stairs that snaked their way down to the ground. With each step, the wind threatened to unseat her as her shoes, which unfortunately lacked any kind of tread whatsoever, failed to find traction on the slick metal. But one by one, she made her way down each step and each landing, until she reached the final step.

She could finally see her mystery man, who was in fact seated with his back pressed against the building directly below the fire escape. His abandoned coffee cup had rolled away until it landed in a puddle, spilling coffee all over the sidewalk, now mingled with the water. Since it was hard to see anything distinctly with all this rain, she couldn't tell if he was injured or unconscious or even breathing.

Just hang in there a little longer! The last leg of this fire escape adventure was releasing the sliding ladder to allow her to drop down to the sidewalk. She fiddled with the lock far longer than she wanted until it finally released. Unfortunately, to get a better position, she had climbed onto the ladder *before* unlocking it. With a scream, she felt the ladder sliding down with her holding tightly to the sides. Her braid caught in the mechanism for a split second, but the weight of both her and the ladder ripped it free from its elastic and left it spilling over her shoulders wildly. She tumbled the final few feet from the ladder to the ground, landing in a puddle that completed her drenched look. Wet hair attacked her vision, and she desperately wished she'd already gotten that haircut.

"Who's there?" a curious masculine voice demanded.

Annaliese hurried to her feet and tried in vain to straighten her clothes and fix her wild hair. *What am I doing? The man is **blind**. What does he care what I look like?* She looked down to see her mystery man turned toward her, his unseeing eyes on full display as he searched for the source of the sounds he'd obviously heard. *At least he didn't have to see my pathetic rescue attempt.*

"Um, are you okay?"

"By the sounds of that commotion, I feel like I should be asking you that," the young man replied with a smile.

"Oh, yeah," she said awkwardly as she continued to try to brush hair out of her eyes. She took a few steps toward him and offered her hand to help him up. Then immediately blushed when he couldn't see her silent offer.

"I'm Taylor, by the way," he said politely, but she could see the laughter he was trying to suppress.

"Annaliese," she muttered, as she stepped away from him to rescue his cane before it rolled into the street. Now feeling like she could at least be *somewhat* helpful, she returned to his side and held the cane out to him, letting it gently touch his arm so he could grab it himself.

"Hey, thanks! It was gonna be a long walk home without this guy." He pulled himself up to his feet and straightened his wet clothing. Before he could take off in the opposite direction, she let out a choked gasp and grabbed his sleeve. His face turned down at her hand on his arm curiously.

"S-s-sorry," she stuttered as she released the fabric and blushed. *Thankfully, he can't see that either.* "Um, I saw what happened. With the mugger."

"Yeah," the young man said with a sigh. "It's a bummer about my satchel. It had my computer with all my lyrics on it."

"Lyrics?"

"Yeah, for my band. I write all our lyrics, and I was super close to getting this new song banged out. Oh well, second try's the charm, am I right?" He smiled at her, and she felt warmth inside despite the drizzling rain that still fell on both of them.

"Did you want to…um…come inside for a bit? To warm up or wait for the rain to stop or call the police or something?" The words tumbled out in a disorderly fashion, but he seemed to get the gist.

"Sure, how can I say no to an offer like that? My cell was in my bag, so I should probably call my sister and let her know I'll be home late."

She wasn't sure how to lead him back to her apartment, but he offered her an elbow, which she gratefully took. *Don't think about how strong his arm feels,* she thought as she pushed open the lobby door. They made their way up the stairs slowly, and thankfully Jacko had managed to maneuver the couch out while she'd been climbing down the fire escape. Her door was still open, and the curtains flapped in the breeze.

"Be careful, the floor's a little slick from the rain," she cautioned as she released his arm and rushed to the window.

"Did you leave your window open in the middle of a storm?"

"Well, yes. I had to climb down the fire escape to reach you."

"My lady in shining armor," Taylor quipped with a laugh. "Glad you were watching out for me."

He remained standing where she'd left him, and she suddenly realized he had no idea where any of her furniture was. Groaning at her ineptness, she guided him to a chair farthest from the window and thus the driest. At that point, her phone started ringing again.

"Better answer that. I'll just sit here dripping water on your furniture."

Annaliese grabbed the phone off the cradle and was ready to snap a reply when all she heard was sobbing.

"Mother?"

"Annaliese? Darling, I was so worried when you hung up and then didn't answer me! Whatever were you doing?"

Guilt gripped her at the sound of her mother's frantic voice. She hadn't really thought about how her actions would appear to her mother, whose mind would immediately be filled with worst case scenarios.

"Climbing out the fire escape," she said quietly.

"You were **what**?"

She took a deep breath before plunging ahead. "Mother, I appreciate that you're worried about me. Really. I know it shows how much you love me. But I can't just stay hidden away in my apartment all the time where it's safe. Sometimes I've got to do what I know is right!"

There was no response except for a few quiet sniffles. She was shivering, both from the cold and the fear that she'd hurt her mother's feelings.

"I know, Annaliese." Mother's voice finally came over the line. "You've always tried to do the right thing, even when it was hard for you. That's why I worry so much about you, I guess. But I know that you aren't a princess who can be locked away in a tower. You're my daughter, and I'm proud of you. I just want you to be safe."

This much emotional truth from her mother was incredibly unexpected, and she felt the tears bubbling up inside her. "I love you, Mother."

"I love you too, Annaliese."

There was a pause as both women took in the change in their relationship that had just transpired.

Finally, she broke the silence. "Mother, I've got to go now, okay? I'll call you back later."

Her mother said her polite good-byes, and she gently placed the phone back on its holder. She was shocked at the seemingly sudden change in her mother's tone, but she also felt quite proud of herself for doing what she felt was right.

"Everything all right there?"

She jumped at the masculine voice. *I almost forgot he was still here!* The blush that had barely left her cheeks returned with a vengeance. "Yeah. Yeah, everything's all right." She glanced around the now quiet apartment, vaguely wondering if Princess would make an appearance now that the normal equilibrium had been restored. "Can I make you some tea?"

"Really more of a coffee guy, if you've got it."

She laughed. "Sorry, I'm a strictly tea girl myself. But trust me, I can make a tea drinker out of you too."

He chuckled in response. And as the rain finally came to a stop and the sun started to peek through her window again, Annaliese found herself making two fresh cups of chai for herself and an unexpected new friend.

Two weeks later, Annaliese danced around her apartment as her favorite song blared on the radio. Princess glared judgmentally from her place on the window seat, and the moment was suddenly interrupted by a series of knocks on the door. She rushed to open it and revealed Taylor standing on her welcome mat with the same old brown jacket, but a brand-new satchel and a bright orange thermos.

"I came armed with my own coffee, today," he joked as his cane led the way into her apartment with its cheerful tapping.

She rushed over to switch off the radio and give her cat one last pat on the head. "Give me just a 'sec, and I'll be ready to head out." Her purse and jacket were already lying on the chair, so she swept them up and slipped her shoes on. A tinny jangling melody sounded, forcing her to dig quickly through her purse to find her newly purchased smartphone.

"Mom's FaceTiming," she called over her shoulder as she pushed *accept*. Her mother's smiling face with her always professional appearance came on the screen. "So, what do you think?" she asked as she flipped her head to show off her blonde bob that stopped just as it hit her chin.

"Annaliese, I love it! Really. It turned out great."

"I think so too, Mrs. Richardson," Taylor said as he photobombed in the background. She playfully punched him in the arm when he got close enough. "Hey, I always think you look great!" he said defensively.

She rolled her eyes as her mother laughed. "Are you two headed out for dinner?"

"Yeah, Taylor's taking me to try a Thai place he really likes."

"That sounds delicious!"

"If it looks good, I'll be sure to send a picture."

"Oh, it'll look good. I promise," Taylor quipped. The two women laughed.

"Well, I won't keep you, then. Love you, Annaliese."

"Love you too, Mom," she said earnestly. They exchanged a final smile before ending the call, and she dropped her phone unceremoniously back into her purse.

"I'm starving! Let's get out of here," her boyfriend said dramatically. She laughed as she grabbed his arm and pulled him out the door.

"Well, then we'd better be on our way!" she said as she locked the door behind them.

END

Tower To Tower
Michelle L. Levigne

"What happened to the two of you?" Zared, lord of the enchanted castle, paused halfway out of his saddle in the castle's courtyard.

"Please don't tell me Fang is back." Ashlyn, lady of the enchanted castle, looked around with some trepidation. "He's been beating up on both of you, hasn't he?"

Fang was a peculiarly long-lived bunny who hadn't quite finished transforming into a vampire. This tended to make him bad-tempered. As he had been Ashlyn's companion and partner in escapades that irritated King Ruprick in her youth, he was a regular visitor to the enchanted castle. Usually when he needed help with regularly occurring difficulties.

"Not that at all, Mother." 'Na, who preferred to be called that rather than her full name of Belladonna, exchanged glances with Ambrose.

During the four days her parents were away dealing with another magical emergency, a problem had manifested within the walls of the castle itself. Ambrose had taken time from his service to Prince Ruprick to visit and had seen the problem first-hand He had more bruises than she did, from constantly putting himself between her and the troublemakers.

"It's the library," 'Na said, once her parents had dismounted and the housekeeping breezes took their baggage upstairs and led the horses away to the stables.

"It's the newest wagonload of books," Ambrose added. "They're being bullied by the older books."

"How?" Ashlyn said, stopping short and looking around. "We always put the new books in a separate room until they acclimate ... oh, of course. The older books are jealous because the new books got a new room. What are they doing?"

In silent agreement, the four headed through the main floor of the castle, toward the library. Just in the eight months since 'Na's troublesome seventeenth birthday, when she had met Ambrose, the castle had added another room to the library. Her parents had brought at least a wagonload of books home with them after each of the last six magical rescue missions.

"At night," 'Na said, "they're jumping off the shelves and flopping their way into the new room and knocking the new books off their shelves. And of course, they're getting damaged by the falling and flopping, and somehow that's my fault. At least, that's the impression I get when I find time to do mending. And they aren't happy if they have to wait more than an hour for mending what they inflicted on themselves."

"I hate to say this …" Zared looked around as they stepped into the main library. The temporarily quiescent books loomed over them. He hunched his shoulders. "I think we may have come to our limit of how many books this castle can hold."

'Na realized her father anticipated an avalanche of books to come pelting them in reaction to his words. But none came. She couldn't imagine the residents of the library feared her father's anger or even her mother's. So did their quiet reaction mean they agreed? That struck her as rather greedy and selfish. What right did the books have to refuse other books the rescue and care they had found in the enchanted castle?

"No, I don't think that's it," Ambrose said after a few seconds of no reaction. "A few have snapped at me on my last two visits. I'm afraid the books are upset because 'Na is spending time with me. They used to have most of her attention, her only friends."

"Other than the housekeeping breezes and the other bookish girls I chat with in the magic mirror web," 'Na corrected him. It paid to be scrupulously honest when dealing with magic books. Even if she was complaining about their rude behavior.

"Other than them. Now …" He shrugged, and raised his head to look around the library, as if he expected a rain of books.

"What are we going to do?" Ashlyn murmured. "I refuse to immure my daughter in this place at the whim of books that have grown temperamental because their former owners were idiots. She has a right to the same adventures her father and I enjoy. And more romance than what can be dug up in poems and purple prose," she added, raising her voice and aiming a reproving glare at that nook in the library where the poetry and syrupy sweet tales resided.

'Na nearly laughed when Ambrose flushed dark pink and couldn't look at her.

Zared chuckled. "We've had threats of this before. The library problem will eventually resolve itself, even if it means cannibalistic fights at the dark of the moon." He raised his voice. "We could clear some shelves by getting rid of duplicates."

That raised some thumping and hissing of pages as the four left the library.

"Here's an idea," he said, after they had trod the corridor in thoughtful silence and paused at the door of the dining room. "Find someone to help you wrangle the books. You two are ready to go out on missions now, so you can't be here three-quarters of the time like you used to, especially at the dark of the moon when the books are most irritable."

"The only beings I know who love books more than 'Na are dragons, and the books aren't ready to allow one within one hundred paces of the castle," Ashlyn said.

"Hmm, true ..."

"Perhaps someone with the soul of a dragon?" Ambrose suggested. They stepped into the dining room and took their places at the long table groaning with food.

"Fiercer than that. A librarian," Zared said with a chuckle.

"They're a dying breed," Ashlyn said. "That's why we're in the predicament we are. Hardly anyone is passionate about books anymore."

"Hmm, maybe not," 'Na said, as a name popped into her mind. Just as she started to smile, a few details chopped through the growing beanstalk of her idea. "Zella won't go for it. She's quite cozy in her tower. Granted, there's always some idiot third or fourth-born prince on a quest, who comes to interrupt her reading and can't believe she doesn't need to be rescued, but ... well, we'd have to offer her a lot to get her to pack up all her books and come here."

"Zella? Which one of your friends is this?" her mother asked.

"She's Granny Pepper's tower-sitter."

"Granny Pepper? As in Granny Pepper's Potions? My mother loves her seasoning line," Ambrose added. Then he frowned. "I thought she had her headquarters in Outer Gonmolia."

"That's just the billing address, for the sake of style. Nobody would believe all those exotic potions and liquid spells are shipped out of a castle in Wunsaponnathyme." 'Na muffled a snicker when Ambrose's mouth fell open slightly and he shook his head.

"Zella's tower is on the northern border of Fafaraway. That's where Granny started her business. When it got too big, she had to move operations to have more room. Before that, Zella's great-grandmother was her goddaughter and apprentice, and had an accident with a concentrated hair growth potion. It turned into a curse while they were trying to fix it, so it attaches to whoever occupies the tower. She started a quite profitable business making and selling wigs for sorcerers' apprentices and dragon hunters who had industrial accidents." She paused to serve herself from one of the many platters slowly floating up and down the table.

"So, they kept the tower, to keep the curse and the business going. They've passed the business, mother to daughter, to Zella. Other than those pesky princes trying to prove they're heroes, the setup is perfect."

"There's that tower out back that no one is using," Zared pointed out. "If she wants to keep the wig business going, I'm sure we could find a comparable spell to help her. And I dare anyone to try to rescue Zella from the enchanted castle."

"After the debacle on our wedding day?" Ashlyn chuckled. She raised her goblet and he tapped it with his goblet, so the crystal bowls chimed. "I should hope no one would ever be so foolish to try again."

"What happened on their wedding day?" Ambrose whispered to 'Na.

"Three princes tried to rescue Mother. When they started fighting each other for the privilege, the castle woke up and defended her. The magic wardrobe was highly offended anyone would break in while Mother was getting dressed."

"I wish I had been here to see it." He exchanged grins with her.

"Eyesallova preserved the images. She loves to show them on their anniversary every year."

"Who is Eyesallova?"

"Oh, she's our central magic mirror. We'll need to talk to her anyway, to contact Zella."

~~~~~

After dinner, 'Na led Ambrose to the solarium. Magic mirrors used for communication fed off of light. Sunlight was twenty times as powerful as torch or lantern light, and moonlight was preferable to flame. The dome of the room was all glass. A massive mirror on a crystal stand sat on a wheeled cart on a track, allowing it to turn to follow the course of the sun throughout the day.

"Eyesallova, this is my friend, Ambrose," she announced.

"Yes, pleased to meet you. Gossamer, the mirror assigned to Ruprick's castle, says you have a good head on your shoulders," a shimmering, chiming sort of voice answered. Ripples of green and blue light moved across the mirror's surface.

"Thank you. I am honored to meet you, Eyesallova," Ambrose said, after a slight pause, and he bowed to the mirror.

"Would it be too much trouble to have a call put through to Zella at Granny Pepper's tower?" 'Na asked.

"Not at all. Showing off your suitor, are you?" Eyesallova chuckled.

"Bragging is cruel and rude." 'Na winked at Ambrose, who flushed red, and led him over to a bench facing the mirror. She explained why she needed to talk to Zella.

Silence fell over the room. 'Na waited for the ripples to move across the mirror's surface, becoming multicolored sparkles that would resolve into Zella's face.

She counted to fifty. Then to fifty again.

"I'm sorry, there seems to be some difficulty," Eyesallova announced.

"What kind of difficulty?"

"As odd as it seems, there is some legal action pending. The new owner of the castle where the trunk connection resides has been wrangling with the deed, claiming it gives him control over the mirrors in the web serviced out of the castle. Plus, there seems to be some legal blockages focused on Zella's tower."

"How does that interfere with the magic mirror web?" Ambrose asked. "The mirrors aren't tied to physical locations. I mean, they are, in one sense, but the magic web that connects them isn't a physical thing." He frowned and shook his head. "Is it?"

"I'm getting different stories every time I request an explanation," Eyesallova said. "There are all sorts of legal documents. One claims Zella is an illegal occupant. Another is trying to break the godmother clause supporting her residency. There are three demands that Granny Pepper's tax history be investigated, and several documents claim Zella is being held prisoner." She snorted. "Three lower-level mirrors believe some prince is trying to take over the wig business for personal reasons. He's been cursed by dozens of victims of his lies and schemes, to the point the standard nose-growing curse has overloaded and broken. Now he's losing his hair and the cosmetic spells are fighting each other."

"That sounds serious despite being so ridiculous," Ambrose said. "If we can't talk to your friend, then perhaps we should go to her tower and see what we can do to help."

If Eyesallova wasn't right there, watching and probably recording for posterity, 'Na would have kissed Ambrose.

Her parents agreed with his assessment. Before dawn the next morning, they set off. They carried the bag of provision, which cut down on luggage, since it produced all the food, clothing, and weapons they would ever need. With no baggage horse, they could travel as swiftly as couriers. 'Na carried a medium-sized hand mirror attached to a stand on the front of her saddle, so Eyesallova could accompany them. Her connection to the magic mirror web through the enchanted castle meant they could work around the current blockages affecting Zella's tower.

~~~~~

They stopped for a late lunch, then twenty minutes after climbing back into the saddle, they encountered a group of travelers in King Ruprick's livery. They were all haggard, flinching every time a stick broke or a bird tweeted, and looking over their shoulders.

"I'm sorry," Ambrose said, and turned his horse to block the trail.

'Na tried not to feel irritated. She understood why he had to inquire what they were doing. Relations between the enchanted castle and King Ruprick were prickly at best, since Prince Ruprick had failed to win her as a bride. If the king learned Ambrose had ignored fellow servants out here in the enchanted forest, he might curtail future visits.

She conferred with Eyesallova on progress breaking the blockage in the mirror web and didn't hear Ambrose's conversation with the servants. The mirror reported that more legal briefings now laid claim to Granny Pepper's inventory in the tower. 'Na didn't quite understand some of the terms. She made a note to ask the mirror later to access the lexicons in the castle's library, just as Ruprick's servants went on their way.

"We're doomed," Ambrose said, and tried to smile.

"What are they running away from?" she asked.

"Poor Ruprick is out here, escorting his overbearing cousin from Nuyorck, Prince Rumpton, on a quest. Rumpton claims he has to rescue his true love from a tower."

"Do I want to know why their servants ran away?"

"They're terrified by a new magical practice called real estate, an allegedly peaceful conquest of estates and even towns and countries, to gain what has always been won through battle and bravery and solving challenges. Just parchment and gold and lots of trickery, and wording that changes thanks to spells woven into the contracts."

'Na shuddered at the explanation. A man who won acclaim with muscle and swordplay was much easier to read than one who relied on tangled words written in enchanted ink on spelled parchment.

"Rumpton talks of nothing else, every chance he gets." Ambrose shuddered, and 'Na swore he went several shades paler. "It's all fancy words that make no sense, all convoluted and repetitive. Several lords and ladies of the court actually fell asleep during the welcoming feast, face-down in their squab in orange sauce, he carried on so long and tediously, talking about his passion. Ruprick snored so ferociously, he got sauce and a tiny drumstick up his nose."

"That sounds rather horrific."

"You should have heard him boasting. He doubled his father's kingdom in five years' time through real estate. He calls it peaceful conquest, but it sounds like dark magic to me, driving men insane, if not to the poorhouse. He starts out by paying to use property adjoining the borders of his father's kingdom, and then hauls the owners into court, claiming they didn't live up to the terms of the contract. All sorts of clauses and penalties show up that the owners claim they never saw when they signed the contract. Every time he wins, the property is turned over to him. Then he adds it to his father's kingdom, moving the borders outward again and again. The braggart complained that no one wants to do business with him, and he takes his victims to court for slandering him when they protest."

"That sounds heinous. I think I feel sorry for Ruprick."

"My guess is that the king sent him out to bore Rumpton until he leaves and keep him from practicing real estate on the kingdom." Ambrose shuddered. "There's no telling where those two are ahead of us. I don't suppose you have any spells to fold roads so we can bypass them?"

"No, sorry. I will make a note to pack some on our next quest."

That earned a nearly normal smile from Ambrose.

It faded far too soon. Far too soon, they heard a familiar jolly, yet oddly trembling voice call out from the shadows of the trail ahead of them.

"Hello! Fancy meeting you out here."

'Na reminded herself she felt sorry for Ruprick as they drew close enough to the princes to make out details.

"Is there something wrong with Rumpton's hair?" she whispered.

"Not that I know of. Why?"

"There seems to be ... several different visions of his hair. One is like hay and flying in every direction, an odd shade of orange."

"I don't see it." Ambrose chuckled. "Probably some sort of cosmetic spell at work. You're so thoroughly drenched in magic, you're immune to spells that fool the rest of us. I envy you."

"No, you should pity me. There's something horrific about that dry, ugly tangle. Like something died on top of his head and it won't blow away no matter how hard it tries."

Now he laughed. She felt sorry for Ambrose, because he had to fight to compose his face and stop laughing before the prince cousins got close enough to hear. She hurried to apologize to Eyesallova and put the mirror out of sight, so the two princes wouldn't try to confiscate her to help in Rumpton's quest, as part of royal privilege.

'Na tried not to judge people too quickly upon meeting them, but Rumpton irritated her. He very clearly classified her as unworthy of attention. Whether because of her simple, sturdy traveling clothes, or that she wore trousers and rode astride instead of side-saddle, or that Ruprick emphasized that Ambrose was courting her. Rumpton's overly generous lip curled up as he looked her over, head-to-toe twice, then looked away. Dismissed and relegated to the servant class.

He frowned in offended confusion when Ruprick added that she was the daughter of Lady Ashlyn and Lord Zared of the enchanted castle. *Why,* his expression clearly shouted, *is she consorting with a servant?*

'Na decided his awful hair and the need for cosmetic spells came from a curse. She promised herself she would find a counter-spell to reveal his true face to the world.

"Forgive my curiosity, Lady Belladonna," Rumpton said. She loathed the fact he used her full name, and his snooty tone that clearly said he *wasn't* asking forgiveness. "What is the true name of the castle? It's hard to research deeds and ownership history without the proper name."

"Why do you need to research the deeds?" A prickle raced up her back, warning of impending danger. This had something to do with his dark art of real estate, she feared.

"Oh, it's just a hobby of mine. I find it fascinating, discovering who owns what or who doesn't own something when they think they do."

"The enchanted castle owns itself," Ambrose said. "With all the magical items stored there to prevent unpleasant accidents, it's alive in some aspects. It has a history of reacting badly when people try to claim ownership over it."

"It's like a cat, I suppose," Ruprick offered. He didn't look at his cousin, much like he didn't look at his father, whenever possible. "You know, no one really owns cats. They own their people, in a lot of ways."

"Yes, how clever of you, Cousin." Rumpton's upper lip curled. 'Na wondered how he could speak clearly with his lip like that. "I was just curious ... but that is several items down on my list of tasks for this visit. I'm in a quandary over a tenant who won't vacate property that I'm sure belongs to me. Until she does, I can't do a proper search of the occupancy spells woven into the building. There's a godmother clause involved. To make matters more difficult, I'm afraid I've fallen in love with her, and there's a curse to untangle before we can have our happily-ever-after. It's all so sloppy. A lesser man would be embarrassed, but ah, well, the things we do for love, yes?" He spread his arms, gesturing around the otherwise empty clearing. "And to make matters worse, someone has made off with all our servants. How lucky that you two showed up, to assist us."

'Na suddenly wished she hadn't enjoyed her lunch quite so much. What were the odds that Rumpton was involved in the whole ugly mess trying to evict Zella from Granny Pepper's tower?

"Yes, you will join us, won't you?" Ruprick had a sorrowful puppy expression she found hard to resist, as she truly did feel sorry for him.

In all honesty, 'Na thought Ruprick wasn't quite as much an idiot as he had first appeared. Possibly she had changed a bit herself, since their disastrous encounter on her seventeenth birthday. She had also seen Ruprick in better circumstances when she visited the palace and admired how he tried to stand up to his father, difficult for even a confident, grounded person. King Ruprick was an unnatural force of nature, and Ruprick had been trained to let people push him into a jelly mold. They kept shoving him around and wouldn't let him settle and solidify. Despite them, he was learning to stand up for himself, and decide who to like and dislike, trust and distrust. 'Na decided better to trust the maturing jelly she knew than the suave, greedy interloper she didn't.

There was no way to avoid having the two princes as traveling companions. If Rumpton was headed for Zella's tower to try to evict her, 'Na owed her bookish friend a warning and help. Better to stick close to the source of the problem and learn his battle strategy. The wise course of action was to agree and find a private spot to confer with Eyesallova once they had made camp for the night.

Her admiration for Ambrose's self-control and fortitude increased as the afternoon stretched on and Rumpton did all the talking. About real estate. Until 'Na thought her brain would liquefy and escape out her ears. She couldn't tune out his irritating, pompous voice, repeating himself ad infinitum. Between the throbbing in her temples and the base of her skull, she felt somewhat nauseous by sunset, when they could finally stop. Through all the repetition, though, some things did come clear.

Rumpton contradicted himself. Repeatedly. He wanted to rescue the maiden trapped in the tower. He complained about the godmother clause in the tower occupancy spell that prevented him evicting her, now that the land under the tower belonged to his father's kingdom.

Bottom line: "evict" and "rescue" could not apply to the same person.

After dinner, Rumpton commandeered Ambrose's help in dictating a massive pile of legal documentation. First, registering complaints against the vanished servants. Then orders to initiate legal action and fire them. He seemed to love saying, "You're fired," again and again. He also intended to warn the six surrounding kingdoms to ensure other nobility didn't employ those servants. When was the pompous egotist going to run out of breath or at least get a sore throat, and go to sleep? She needed to consult with Eyesallova.

He ignored Ruprick, so she engaged the hapless younger prince in conversation, hoping to be ignored as well. Ruprick was piteously grateful for the attention and asked if she would look at a book he had in his saddlebag. He referred to it as a prince manual. He wanted her opinion on what was smart and what was balderdash. Each chapter contained tales of princes facing challenges, many of which they failed, and ended with a series of questions to generate learning by the good or bad examples. 'Na made note of the team of authors and the scholarly monastery that had produced the book. Her parents liked to donate portions of their growing treasure to worthy causes. An endeavor to teach princes common sense and courtesy was highly worthy. She could see her parents funding a massive copying project to get this book into the hands of every prince and knight errant throughout the world. It would save curse-breakers like her parents thousands of hours of frustration every year.

Finally, Rumpton wound down in his complaints. Before he drifted off to sleep, he gave 'Na a momentary start, when he asked where she had obtained the bag of provision. It had provided their dinner and enough blankets for a comfortable camp. Her answer that it belonged to the enchanted castle didn't satisfy him. He speculated on whether the treasury in his father's palace might contain the original bag of provision, meaning all other bags of provision might violate copyright, whatever that was. He was still mumbling about royalties and intellectual property when he fell asleep. He snored loudly enough to rattle the leaves overhead.

"He's the one causing all the trouble," Eyesallova said, as soon as 'Na took her far enough away from the camp to have a private conversation.

With the noise of Rumpton's snores, she could have spoken to the mirror on the other side of the campfire, and he wouldn't have heard her.

But Ruprick might have, and she couldn't risk that.

"I've been busy consulting with other mirrors in the web, and we've finally found a way around the piles of legal documents high enough to fill three moats and smother the monsters living in them," the magic mirror continued. "We have a plan to tangle him with the contracts and legal magic he's been using against Zella and the tower."

"What do we need to do?" 'Na could hardly speak for the relief stealing her breath. She hoped she would have a front row seat to the humiliation and frustration the mirrors would inflict on Rumpton, turning his own weapons against him.

And if she never heard about real estate and contracts and copyright ever again, it would be too soon.

Before she and Ambrose could implement the first step in the plan, Ruprick proved he had been absorbing the lessons from the prince manual.

'Na's ability to speak to animals meant, unfortunately, she also understood them when they talked, and talked, and talked, without any sense or usefulness. Her parents had brought her with them on disenchantment missions since she was very young, to teach her how to ignore the meaningless chatter of animals that didn't have the sense to know everyone could hear them. Then when she mastered that skill, they taught her how to hear the animals that had something important to say.

She woke the next morning to the sound of a voice in sorrowful song, coming from the brook flowing by their campsite. When she followed the song, she found Ruprick ahead of her, displaying surprising stealth talent.

"Where are you?" he whispered, creeping up to the brook. "May I be of any service?"

"Oh, no, I don't think so," a very wet, chirpy voice responded. A warty little frog jumped up on the bank. "Thank you very much for asking, though."

Warts didn't belong on frogs. Her clear voice and good manners marked her as a princess who had been slapped with a curse, most likely meant to punish someone else. Probably her parents.

"I don't suppose you're under an enchantment, are you?" Ruprick knelt and bent down to rest on his elbows so they were nearly eye-to-eye. "You see, I was supposed to be given the ability to understand animals and other gifts when I was christened. My father has this tendency to irritate everyone. All the magical folk got offended before the ceremony and left, so ..." He shrugged. "If I can understand you, then you're the one with magic, not me."

Well, Ruprick was full of surprises. The largest being that he didn't whine about being robbed by his father's bullying and stupidity.

"I'm not much good as a hero, but I can listen. You were crying. It helps to talk about it. Sometimes. Would you like to try?"

"Oh, yes, thank you," the frog chirped, and burst into tears.

'Na left when Ruprick pulled out a silk handkerchief, picked up the frog and dabbed at her tears.

He proved he had quite a bit of common sense and consideration when he crept into camp an hour later. Rumpton was still snoring, making the ground shake. 'Na had finally been able to share Eyesallova's plan with Ambrose and had just finished telling him about Ruprick and the frog princess.

Ruprick stopped on the edge of the clearing and beckoned for 'Na and Ambrose to follow him. They crept out of the camp, fearing Rumpton would wake up now and start shouting for his breakfast. 'Na took the bag of provision with her in case he decided to follow up on his sleep-talking about copyright infringement and royal privilege.

She noticed Ruprick wasn't wearing his jacket or cloak, and soon saw they were wrapped around a petite, very wet, slightly green-tinted girl with fading sparkles of magic swirling around her.

"You kissed her, didn't you?" Ambrose asked.

Prince and princess blushed. He, very red with spots, and she, a lovely mint shade. They both grinned and nodded.

"You do know what that means, don't you?"

"Do you think my father will give us a hard time?" Ruprick tucked the cloak closer around her. "Because I'm half-resolved to just take off from here and never see home again. There are still a few layers of spells to remove to completely rescue Phibbia, but it's a good start and she's ..." He shrugged and blushed darker. "She's simply wonderful."

"I think you need to get on your horse and take her home right now and tell that old tyrant you two are getting married before sunset," 'Na said. "I won't waste time explaining all the codicils of magic and breaking spells and ensuring all the attendant blessings are applied before the magic fades, but ... I think you two will be very happy, and very good for each other."

'Na took Phibbia aside, got her dried off and provided her a decent wardrobe from the bag of provision. Ambrose and Ruprick saddled his horse. 'Na filled the saddlebags with food to last them on the journey, and then they rode off. The two new sweethearts looked rather romantic, riding away into the sunrise. Ruprick even looked heroic, with Phibbia riding pillion behind him, her tiny arms wrapped around his waist. He sat up straighter and looked less pudgy and pale, and there was a new, determined set to his jaw.

'Na told Ambrose what Ruprick had said about losing his christening gifts because of his father. "I wouldn't be surprised if those magic gifts were bestowed after all, just kept hidden, waiting for him to grow up. I think being determined to defy that old tyrant triggered some of them. Maybe all."

Ambrose agreed. Chances were good the christening gifts had been hidden to ensure the king didn't benefit from them. The prince needed to learn some hard lessons, to ensure he didn't grow up to be like his father.

Rumpton woke up a short time later and told them not to serve breakfast until after he had his bath. He headed for the brook, turning to shout, "You're fired! You're all fired!" over his shoulder every ten steps.

"Do you think there's some sort of insanity spell settling on him?" 'Na asked. "He speaks more gibberish, the longer we have to listen to him."

"Maybe we're the ones going insane," Ambrose returned.

'Na had to press both hands over her mouth to muffle her laughter.

Rumpton finally realized Ruprick was missing after breakfast, when he shouted for his cousin to write down everything he had been saying.

"Well, either the enchanted forest is in a bad mood again and it ate him… or he found another enchanted princess and took her to the king to get his blessing to marry her." Ambrose spoke in a tone somewhere between exasperated and bored, as if Ruprick did this did often.

"If she doesn't have a kingdom to bring with her, Ru is an idiot. As usual," Rumpton grumbled. "Who's going to take notes on my new strategy for mergers?"

Ambrose's story of the forest eating Ruprick proved helpful later. When he said they had to be silent for the next ten hours as they navigated this stretch of forest, or none of them would get through alive, Rumpton shut up. He busied himself writing down all his plans. This necessitated frequent stops to chase down the pages he dropped while trying to dry the ink before he put them in his saddlebags.

"Now's the time," Ambrose said, during the second stop.

The next phase of Eyesallova's plan necessitated 'Na sneaking away and racing through the forest to reach Zella's tower first. She made sure she kissed Ambrose with enough intensity to convey how much she appreciated him metaphorically falling on his sword. He would stay to distract and slow Rumpton, and endure more maniacal lectures on real estate. If the prince ever noticed she was missing, Ambrose would simply say the forest had eaten her. She turned her horse off the trail to go around Rumpton, riding until she could no longer hear his muttering, then headed back onto the trail. She vowed that next time, she would definitely pack a road-folding spell.

~~~~~

Eyesallova tested the mirror web every hour or so, but there was no connection with Zella's mirror, Primp, even when the top of the tower came into view.

"With all the legal foolery, isn't there something to stop idiots like

Rumpton from interfering with the mirror web?" 'Na grumbled. She paused on the edge of the clearing a bowshot deep around the base of the tower.

Like all good enchanted towers, it had no visible doors, no windows until the fourth story, and a good repulsion spell that prevented the growth of vines handy for climbing on the slick, greenish-gray surface.

"Believe me," Eyesallova responded, coming as close as her shimmery voice could come to a snarl, "we're looking into it."

"Hello?" A familiar female voice came from overhead. "I'm sorry, you need to step closer to the funnel for me to hear you. If you're here about the new order, I told you it won't be ready until the new moon. My hair only grows so fast. Quality over quantity."

'Na tipped her head back and studied the thick canopy of leaves until she found a pale green gourd two trees to her right, hanging just out of reach. It was hollow and a sparkle of magic lined the interior. She assumed the gourd was part of a sound transference system.

"Sorry, not here for an order. I'm here to warn you about Rumpton who can't make up his mind if he's going to rescue you or evict you."

"Oh, gads, not him again. I've been pestered too much by useless princes who want to make a name for themselves by rescuing me. I don't need rescuing!" The gourd vibrated visibly with the force of Zella's volume. "I'm perfectly happy. My books keep my mind healthy and brushing my hair gives me plenty of exercise. Do you know how many steps you can get in, brushing one hundred strokes morning and evening, when your hair is three stories long?"

"Yes, you've told me." 'Na shuddered.

"I have?"

"Yes, but I'm hoping I can persuade you there's more to life than solitude and earning enough money for new books."

Zella laughed. "You can try."

A thump and the painfully familiar sound of a cascade of magical books leaping off several shelves came through the gourd.

"Ah, sorry. I keep forgetting you have the same problem I do, with magical books having a snit."

"Having — 'Na? Is that you? What are you doing here?"

'Na laughed. "Yes, it's me. Sorry about irritating the books."

"Actually, you didn't. They're my early warning system. That idiot is two hours away. The books don't like him."

"They have good taste. Look, could I come up? I'm here about your problem with the mirror web, too. And a proposal that could solve a lot of problems."

"What problem with the mirror web?"

"The girl likes her solitude a little too much," Eyesallova muttered.

111

"How can she not notice that nobody is getting through the web?"

"I'm not going to have to climb your hair, am I?" 'Na asked.

"That's just part of the discouragement illusion." Zella chuckled a little louder. "Walk four times around the tower counterclockwise, turn yourself counterclockwise three times, and then walk clockwise until you find the green door."

'Na tied up her horse, and in less than ten minutes the green door appeared. It opened into a box that rose to the top of the tower on a friendly breeze and deposited her into a comfortable room lined with bookshelves and plenty of enormous cushions for sprawling to read in comfort. Zella kept her hair out of the way by braiding it, then hanging it on several magical padded hooks that floated behind her. She greeted 'Na with a hug exuberant enough to make the braid swing around and nearly clobber both of them.

She laughed and apologized, and they settled on the cushions. "Now, what new version of his land-grabbing tale is the idiot telling this moon?"

'Na related how she and Ambrose had met up with the princes and Eyesallova had devised a plan with the other administrative mirrors of the mirror web. That necessitated backtracking to explain about the blockage of Zella's mirror. Then she had to explain the whole reason for contacting her in the first place: the increasing temper tantrums of the magical books in the enchanted castle's library that felt neglected now that she was spending more time with Ambrose. A second shelf of books leaped up, giving warning of Rumpton's proximity, by the time she finished.

'Na was quite impressed with how Zella had turned the testiness of the magical books to her benefit. She wondered if they should do something like that at the enchanted castle. A warning would be helpful, when it came to overbearing repeat customers who never seemed to learn their lesson, no matter how many times spells and curses and testy enchantments bit various portions of their anatomy.

According to a mirror in Rumpton's palace, his plan was to build a nest or "park" of towers for wizards to settle and work together, sharing research and resources, with a regular patrol of guards protecting their solitude. He would essentially control who approached them for assistance and advice, and who could buy their spells and magical devices. The residue from the potions Granny Pepper had been brewing for decades made this clearing the perfect location to anchor the first cluster of towers.

"Now are you going to tell us your plan?" 'Na asked Eyesallova.

"Let him take over," the mirror said, almost purring. "Or at least think he's going to take over. There are so many codicils to the spells woven through the tower and the hair growth curse. Thanks to all those princes who wouldn't take 'no thanks, I don't need or want rescuing' for an answer, everything is wound up like a gigantic rat trap. They'll tangle irretrievably with all his cosmetic spells, no matter how many scribes and legal web spinners he gets involved."

"Sweet revenge, but ..." Zella sighed, then caught herself and grinned. "Actually, I do like the job offer ... would the change of location stop all those princes from trying to rescue me?"

'Na's nasty grin was all the answer she needed to give. Zella and Eyesallova burst out in equally nasty laughter.

~~~~~

The first step in the plan was for 'Na and Zella to awaken Primp, the magic mirror. She was properly infuriated to learn a sleeping spell had kept her from realizing that communication with other mirrors had stopped. They removed her from the wall and inserted a much gaudier but unoccupied mirror in her place. She and Eyesallova were settled outside, within a camouflage spell. While 'Na and Zella packed up the library, the mirrors arranged for transporting the contents of the tower. Eyesallova contacted a drover team that specialized in traveling through the corridor dimensions. They needed to have everything out before Rumpton arrived. Fortunately, Granny Pepper had left detailed plans for rapid escape. A spiral chute woven of the hair from four generations would provide swift descent the moment Zella signed the contract.

The plan was to make Rumpton sign a very different contract than the one he brought her. The mirror network had provided a copy of the contract, thanks to Rumpton's magic mirror, Silver. His constant lectures about real estate and his nasty, greedy glee at robbing people through quasi-legal means irritated her to the point she was ready to crack. Anything she could do to knock him down a few pegs made her happy.

Zella needed to distract him so the mirrors could sew several dozen codicils in her favor into the contract. At the same time, they needed to remove the ones to tangle her and her offspring, their hair and profits, and anyone who used those hair products, into service to Rumpton and his heirs for posterity. Eyesallova's plan depended on his greed and vanity to blind him to the changes before he signed the contract.

Then Rumpton and Ambrose arrived, at dusk, and there was no more time to fuss with details. The drovers, hidden inside another camouflage spell, were nearly done loading the books and Granny Pepper's inventory. The real estate prince never hesitated for a moment when Zella responded to his shout and threw down a ladder of hair for him to climb up. She refused to tell him about the airlift box. Let the man sweat a little before he stumbled into the trap he so richly deserved.

'Na tested the smoothness of the ride of the chute, to escape out one window while Rumpton struggled up on the opposite side of the tower. She landed in a pile of several bags of Zella's clothes, bounced to her feet, and hurried across the clearing to the mirrors' hiding place. Ambrose was just coming around the tower. His face lit up as soon as their gazes met, and he hurried to join her inside the camouflage spell. They had time to get comfortable before Rumpton finally tumbled with very little dignity through the window.

"He should spend more time outdoors and less time sitting at his desk, scheming to cheat people of their homes and livelihood," Primp muttered. Images appeared on her and Eyesallova's surfaces, showing the scene in the tower room from two angles.

Rumpton unrolled a thick scroll of contract, with multiple layers of parchment, and glowing X's in the spots where Zella needed to sign.

"Is that going to be a problem?" 'Na whispered, gesturing at the layers.

"The grafting spell will take care of that," Eyesallova assured her.

"Please tell me you found a way to give him everything he deserves," Ambrose said.

"We won't know until the last signature. Oh, good girl. Prolong the torment."

In the mirror, Zella flipped through the multiple layers of the contract and dragged her finger down the left-hand margin, reading each line. Veins pulsed in Rumpton's temples and the hinge of his jaw, then a large vein down the center of his forehead, the longer it took for her to get through the contract. Then Zella ran her finger under several lines, apparently reading them aloud.

"What is she saying?" Ambrose said.

"All hair grown in the tower," Eyesallova said. "Oh, this is going to be good!"

Zella pulled out a straight razor. Rumpton's eyes bulged and he took a step back.

"What is she doing?" Fortunately, the camouflage spell prevented Ambrose's yelp being heard from outside.

Zella flourished the razor. Rumpton turned so pale, the line on his neck where the base coat of his makeup stopped became visible. She yanked up a massive handful of her hair, long streamers of chestnut with highlights of navy, and skimmed the razor over the side of her head, cutting her hair off at the roots. 'Na held her breath as her friend swiped, turned, and laid down the handful. Those strands burst free of the leg-thick braid. The magic hooks holding up her hair released, dropping their burden over the contract.

She gathered up more. Swipe and turn and lay down the handful. In mere moments, the deed was done, her head was pale and smooth and bare, and long streamers buried the contract.

"Good girl," Eyesallova muttered. Dark blue and green light spiraled across both mirrors. Matching flashes of dark blue and green light seeped through the hair covering the contract.

Rumpton stared at Zella, his mouth hanging open. Fury battled with his astonishment. He wasn't looking at the contract while mirror magic trimmed away his trickery and sewed in the new clauses to benefit Zella.

"Clever," Ambrose said. "If she agrees that all the hair grown in the tower is his, she can't leave as long as she's wearing hair that belongs to him, and as long as he keeps her there, the hair that keeps growing is his. He's lost his source. I wonder if he's going to refuse to go ahead with the deal."

"Move," 'Na muttered. "Before he finds a way to — yes!" She blushed hot when her voice rang from the walls of the camouflage spell.

In the mirror, Zella swept aside her shorn hair, picked up the contract, and flipped through the pages, scrawling her signature in eight places on one page, six on the next, ten on the one after that, signing and flipping and dipping in the inkwell and scrawling.

Less than a minute later, the deed was done. Rumpton let out a shout of triumph and snatched up the contract. He flipped through it, signing on the lines under her signature, twice as quickly as she had.

"You really should learn to read contracts more carefully before you sign," he cried, his voice so loud with triumph it rang from the tower window. He scrawled his name on the last line, then dipped his signet ring in a puddle of spilled ink and slammed the imprint onto the line next to his name. "Done! And with this magic ink, irreversible and incontestable!"

Rumpton's jawline sagged, his eyes went puffy, and his skin turned blotchy red and gray. His nose elongated, splitting into three branches that went in ten directions. His eyebrows resembled caterpillars and pox marks ran from temple to jaw line.

"The hair curse is settling in and overriding the other cosmetic spells." Eyesallova sounded primly amused. "Ah, there it goes."

Rumpton's defects twisted and melted until he was once again the chiseled, tanned image of princely perfection. The faded, tangled, dry twists of hair fell out, clinging to his shoulder epaulets. He slapped his hands on his bald head, then a moment later a grin spread across his face. Thick, gleaming golden curls sprang up from his scalp. Rumpton raced over to the mirror that had taken Primp's place and turned from side to side, studying his hair.

Zella wrapped a scarf around her naked head and dove out the window and down the hair chute. 'Na led Ambrose back around the tower to meet her. She rolled out the bottom of the chute and reached up, yanking on the anchor strand. The tunnel unraveled from the bottom up, disintegrating in a sparkle of silver magic.

"Technically, he only has rights to the hair inside the tower, so he can't accuse me of stealing or destroying his property, but ..." Zella fluttered her lashes in a thoroughly unconvincing look of innocence.

The yelling from the top of the tower didn't start until the drovers had already left the clearing. Rumpton's voice carried far in the cooling night air. Eyesallova showed images of him tearing up and down the stairs, from one level to another, searching for Zella and shouting, "Girl, where are you? Come back here. Where did you go? Where is the door? How do I get out of here? Why is my hair growing so fast?"

'Na opened the bag of provision and set out dinner for the three of them and the driver of the last wagon, which Zella would ride in. Perhaps it wasn't nice, but they quite enjoyed dining and watching the prince's frantic racing up and down through the tower. Quite frankly, 'Na didn't think Rumpton had that much stamina. Every time he got back to the top floor, he snatched up Zella's razor and trimmed off the arm's length of tangled curls that had grown since his last stop there. Every time he shaved his head, the hair came back a different color.

"Read the contract!" Zella shouted. Multiple times.

They were nearly done with their dinner before Rumpton calmed down enough to hear her and come to the window and look out.

'Na and Ambrose hid.

"Read the contract and specify your conditions. Nothing is finalized until you read and sign and fill in the blanks," Zella said.

"Where is the door?" Rumpton leaned out the window, letting his hair fall out, so it hung past the sill. It grew downward three more bricks while Zella explained. He had to specify how fast he wanted his hair to grow and the color and texture. Right now, with no supervision, his hair changed with every slice of the razor. She recommended he not use the razor, as it was enchanted. Ordinary scissors didn't cause a magical reaction.

Access to the door out of the tower would come when he fulfilled all the conditions. Rumpton's mouth dropped open wider with every detail.

"None of that was in the contract I gave you," he snarled.

"No, but it was in the modified contract we both signed. You need to be careful to read contracts before you sign them," Zella responded. She didn't even try to look innocent.

Rumpton didn't see. His hair now covered his eyes. Snarling, he staggered backward into the room. The mirror showed him fumbling for the razor, to swipe it over his head again. He dug through the growing pile of shorn hair in five different colors, seeking the contract.

"We need to flee now," Ambrose said.

"Agreed." Zella turned to the driver of her wagon. He grinned, revealing pointed teeth nearly matched by his pointed ears, and helped her up into the seat, then climbed up beside her. "Let's go. The sooner I get the books settled in their new home, the happier everyone will be."

~~~~~

Rumpton didn't finish signing the contract and filling in the many and detailed specifications with multiple choices until nearly four moons later. His constantly growing hair kept getting in his eyes, making him trip and often knock himself unconscious. Headaches and bruises seemed to slow his thinking ability.

To compound that, he broke seven mirrors before he realized he didn't have access to the mirror web. The attendant bad luck activated several codicils tied into the habitation requirement of the contract. He found no doors out of the tower. Rumpton's attempts to leave before the contract was defined and fulfilled activated a penalty clause. The shutters closed when he tried to braid his hair into a ladder to climb out. His temper tantrum on discovering all Granny Pepper's potions were gone activated more spells and codicils and penalties.

Prince Ruprick and Princess Phibbia returned from their honeymoon with stories of a vicious, hairy creature haunting a tower. No one could agree if the creature was an enchanted princess or the monster keeping her prisoner. More princes went to the tower every moon, hoping to make a heroic name for themselves, and came away broken in mind and heart, and generating fear in anyone who heard of the dreaded new dark magical art called real estate.

END

The Safe Tower
Beka Gremikova

Zombies, zombies, zombies. Nearly everywhere Zeke turned, the world was *dripping* with zombies.

Readjusting his grip on his ax, he scanned the immediate vicinity. No Singers, with their bulging eyes, sharp teeth, twisted human features, and magical songs that pinned you to the spot, haunted the surrounding plain. Nothing but crispy, yellowed grass stretched before him, framed by clusters of dark woodland on both sides.

He frowned. He hadn't run into any Singers for almost an entire day. He was about due for an ambush.

And his rapunzel stash... He doublechecked the dried dark, leafy lettuce strands tucked into the pouch at his waist. Just a few twisted leaves remained.

He gritted his teeth. He'd never liked the stuff that once grew so plentifully across the Sithian Empire, but consuming it limited the Singers' powers over you. Much better to swallow something that tasted like puke than hand your brain to a zombie on a silver platter.

Too bad the very thing that helped him had also caused the apocalypse. The rapunzel blight had been devastating for Sithe, poisoning any who consumed the affected plants and turning them into flesh-hungry Singers.

Even the Sithian Court, the empire's seat of power, hadn't escaped the chaos—though they'd tried. Zeke shuddered, shoving away the images trying to invade his mind. *Leave it behind. Think of Simon. Think of safety.*

The letter he carried close to his chest seemed to burn through his tunic into his skin. It'd been one of the last letters ever delivered before the entire Sithian Post had disbanded—shortly before the Court itself had met its bloody end.

> Zeke,
> *There really is a land where the blight never hit—the country of Kiltra. We can seek refugee status with its queen and live in true safety. It lies beyond the southern borders of Sithe, across the desert and the Kiltran Mountain range. If you make it here in one piece, I promise I'll shut up about all the scratchy noises you make while you write.*

Get here soon, Inkblot.
Simon

Soon was a relative term. The roads were even more treacherous now that most of the Voicers, whose magical songs could stop Singers in their tracks, had been killed. Travelling was left to the desperate and foolhardy.

Zeke trudged forward. *Desperate? Yes. Foolhardy? Definitely.* He had to reach his brother. He had to hope for a better life ahead of them, especially after Simon had left his home and family, risking his life to seek out a safer land.

And that place existed! Zeke expelled a weary breath. But getting there was turning out more complicated than he'd anticipated. He'd tried joining a travelling combat team, but they hadn't wanted a scrawny scribe-turned-warrior. *Just an extra mouth to feed. Too big of a risk.*

When he'd even offered his brother's letter as incentive, they'd merely taken the information and left him behind.

Would he even get to Simon? Without a team to look out for him, his chances seemed slim. Why bother even to hope, even to dare—

Except, if he didn't hope, didn't dare... he'd crack completely. He gave himself a mental shake. *Search for Singers, you dolt! Or you will end up dead!*

He looked around again. Were those shadows shifting amongst the trees? He quickened his pace.

Up ahead, a spire peeked through the treetops, the peak stabbing at the sky.

His heart leapt. A Safe Tower.

Except it was probably empty. Despite their security, he didn't enjoy sleeping in abandoned towers, surrounded by scraps of clothes, food, and weapons left by their doomed owners. Constantly reminded that his own journey might meet a dismal end.

Then, from the direction of the tower, he heard a woman's loud, clear voice start to sing. She tossed the words out with the force of a thousand nightingales, and, though he couldn't understand the lyrics, her song brimmed with hurt and longing, tickling his soul with the familiar heady, tingling sensation of magic.

This singer... was a Voicer. And what was more, she sounded *kind*. The words floated gently through the air like soft summer clouds.

He caught his breath.

Keep walking, his doubt whispered. *She'd most likely just turn you away, too.*

Or maybe, just maybe, she'd welcome a scribe-turned-ax-wielding-warrior. He lengthened his stride, following the lilting notes, keeping one eye on the possible creatures lurking amidst the trees.

Half an hour later, he reached his destination. Like every Safe Tower, it boasted thorn bushes that curved right to the top, jagged and sharp. Singers couldn't climb the thorn-wrapped walls without disintegrating from the thorns' poison.

He forced himself not to look all the way up. Not to ogle the height. Sucking in a deep breath, he pulled on his worn leather gloves and leapt onto the thorn ladder. The long, thin spears tore into his legs and arms and ripped his already ragged clothing. Blood seeped through his trousers.

He sighed. It'd be nice to keep at least *one* of his two pairs of pants clean. It made things feel a tad less apocalyptic.

Slowly, he swung himself up the tower wall. The thorns seemed to enjoy poking him, and by the time he was halfway up, their poison had him itchier than a fly-swarmed cow.

During his uncomfortable ascent, the singer continued her melody, seemingly unaware of his encroachment. As he neared the top, he glimpsed a woman sitting by the open window, one arm dangling while she fiddled absentmindedly with a strand of bright blue-green hair that would have belonged in the Royal Elven Brigade. She looked like a mermaid sunning herself on a rock.

A thorn stabbed his palm through a hole in his glove.

"Towers damn it!" he hissed.

The singing stopped. The woman peered down at him, eyes wide.

He cleared his throat. "I beg your pardon." A flush crept up his neck at her baleful stare, as though he had not only interrupted her rhythm but ruined her entire day. He scrabbled for something appeasing to say, increasingly aware of the growing distance between himself and the ground. "Ni—nice hair," he managed. "It's... green." Then he could have hit himself. *This* was what happened when you stuck a former aristocrat into an apocalypse—he'd lost all sense of court decorum.

She gave a deep, troubled sigh. "It's teal, actually." She tucked a strand of it behind her pointed ear, her fingers brushing multiple silver piercings. The elf tilted her head, frowning. "You seek shelter for the night?"

He nodded.

"Where did you come from?"

He waved behind him, then regretted letting go of the thorns. He pressed himself closer to the wall, his head spinning. "The Sithian Court."

"Ahhhh, *that's* why you sound like a noble, but look like you've taken fashion advice from a tree." Her lips trembled, and he realized she was trying not to laugh.

For all its faults, he'd enjoyed the Court's tendency toward vibrant, flashy colours. "I'll have you know, this style was once popular—"

She snorted. "Some things lose popularity for a *reason*."

He glowered, scrambling for a comeback. "Is this how you greet *all* your guests? Or just me?"

Her gaze dropped, and her hand flew back to her ear, rubbing against her piercings. "Forgive me," she mumbled. "I've forgotten how to talk with people. We don't have guests anymore." She stared past him, gaze unfocussed. "I shouldn't even let *you* in here, but..." A silver flush crept over her cheeks. "I've grown tired of singing to only the birds."

An opening. "You have a beautiful voice," he offered.

She rolled her eyes. "Of course I do."

Towers curse it! Had the art of flirting died along with the rest of the land? Not that he'd ever been adept at it to begin with...

Then she coughed, rubbing the back of her neck, the silver in her cheeks deepening. "I... suppose that sounds a tad full of myself. What I meant was, most elves have beautiful voices. I'm not that special."

"Many wield weapons to fight the monsters, too." He tilted his head toward his own ax, tucked in the safety of its holster. "Does that make the work they do any less important?" As soon as the words tumbled out, he pressed his mouth shut, hoping he hadn't sounded too condescending.

Her lips pursed, and she shook her head, the bones woven into her braids clicking against each other. "You're an odd one, Axman." But she smiled, her eyes crinkling at the corners.

His shoulders slumped in relief. "Why thank you, Mermaid. And you can call me Zeke, if you wish." He bowed his head—and stared down at the ground far below, swirling in hues of green, yellow, and brown.

Towers damn it.

His voice came out breathy and higher-pitched than he wanted. "Please—may I—come in?"

She hesitated a moment before she nodded, stepping back for him to scramble up and tumble onto the floor. He gasped for breath, pressing his cheek against the cool cobblestones.

She knelt beside him, not too close, but near enough to be comforting. "Deep breaths. My name's Kaya, by the way."

A few deep breaths later, he could sit up. Embarrassment fizzled through him. "I—I've climbed lots of towers," he began, crossing his arms, "it's just... I try not to look down."

"You needn't explain your fears to me, Axman." She patted his shoulder. "Fears are natural in this world." She bit her lip. "It's how we react to them that can turn... unnatural."

"Well, thank you for letting me impose." He rubbed his chest, wishing his heart would stop thundering.

The shadow across her face slipped away, and another smile flitted about her lips. "It's been a pleasure—so far." She dipped her head, hiding her face behind her hair.

His cheeks warmed, and he quickly looked around. A tower of pillows stood against the wall, their stitches worn and frayed. Supply sacks lay strewn over the floor. "Anyone else live here, Mermaid?" Would they welcome him as she had, or feed him to the Singers?

Immediately the smile playing about her mouth tightened into a frown. "Yes."

He rubbed the back of his neck. "Are they... friendly toward strangers?"

Her eyelids lowered.

His stomach tightened. Another sleepless night, then, craning every sense for the hint of Singers. He edged reluctantly toward the window. Beyond, greys and pinks tinged the sky, and the ground loomed below in foggy darkness.

"No!" The word burst from her, and she reached out as though to snag his sleeve. "Please—please don't leave," she whispered. The pleading in her voice tugged at him, even as memories surged.

I'll come with you, Simon!

No, Zeke. I don't even know where I'm going. Stay here at Court until I send word. Mother and Father would never forgive me if you died, too.

He blinked through the mental sludge threatening to overwhelm him. Watching Simon leave, not knowing if he'd ever see him alive again, had been the worst day of his life. "But this other person you live with— surely they'll mind?"

Kaya's lips parted.

Rustling echoed behind him, and boots thumped against the floor. A smooth, lilting voice cut in. "I certainly *do* mind."

Zeke whirled, drawing his ax. Kaya grabbed his arm, her fingers clenched into his worn coat.

Before him, a short woman dressed in a black tunic and leggings straightened, crossing her arms. Her grey-streaked golden hair tumbled down her back in bone-beaded braids. A sword hung at her side. Her ears were round, and she flushed a bright, wrathful red. "I mind, very much."

Kaya's grip on Zeke tightened. "Lavina," she murmured, eyes wide and beseeching. "*Please*—I need—"

Lavina brandished her sword, and Zeke lowered his ax between them. "Why'd you let a stranger up here?" she hissed at Kaya. "You *know* it's dangerous! How do we know he's not allied with the Singers?"

Kaya stiffened.

A shiver ran down Zeke's back. He'd heard of people bartering with Singers, exchanging friends or family for safe passage through their territory. Straightening, he cast Lavina his most disgusted look. "I find those deals repulsive."

"Most of us did, once," she growled. "But even the most upstanding citizens have turned to rot." Her fingers trembled around her sword hilt, and she pointed her blade at Zeke's chest. "No more strangers." She edged closer to him, pushing him back toward the window and the plummeting drop.

His heart thundered. But he raised his ax, pressing it against Lavina's blade, his gaze locking with hers. He didn't want to attack a person, but if he had to fight for his life...

Kaya's hand leapt to his shoulder, tugging him back slightly. "But Lavina, what about the harvest?" With her eyes lowered and her shoulders hunched, she reminded Zeke of a submissive dragon.

Lavina blinked. "What?"

Kaya cleared her throat, her eyes flicking to Zeke. "Our *rapun—*"

"Hush!" Lavina hissed, though her brow furrowed.

The corners of Kaya's mouth lifted, but that was the only hint Zeke caught of a smile. "You said the harvest would be too large for just us two. *And* the rains will arrive soon." Kaya coughed meaningfully.

"Towers *curse* it," Lavina muttered.

"*And* it'll be impossible to find anyone else in such a short timeframe," Kaya continued, glancing out the window. "So few... humans come by this way." She reached out, clasping Lavina's hand. "*Alula*," she murmured. "We need him." Her eyes dropped again. "To survive. To stay... *safe*."

That one word seemed to fall like a spell. Lavina's weapon slid away from Zeke's. She brushed past him, wrapping her arms around the elf. "Yes. Safe." She breathed it like a prayer, with a frenzied note to her voice that shot chills through Zeke's limbs. He'd heard that same tone in the Sithian nobles not long before the Court completely crumbled.

Lavina turned to Zeke, her nose wrinkled. "Fine. You may stay. But in return, you must help us with our harvest before you leave."

Zeke's heart sank. The rains wouldn't come for another three months. His journey had already stretched on too long. What if Simon gave up hope of Zeke ever arriving?

But what was his alternative? Getting murdered? His throat closed, but he managed a nod.

Kaya closed her eyes, her shoulders slumping as she let out a sigh.

Though Lavina no longer aimed a weapon at him, Zeke couldn't relax. He might have escaped an ambush, but now he was trapped in a tower with strangers for three months. He slumped against the wall, aware of Lavina's assessment of his every step, of her willingness to strike at any wrong move.

So much for being a *Safe* Tower.

~~~~~

That night, he huddled under a thin blanket. A ragged curtain hung down the middle of the room, separating him from the women. The window shutters were bolted, but a breeze seeped between the cracks, carrying with it the Singers' high, whispering voices as they wandered the plain below.

He lay shivering, fighting his exhaustion. Not quite able to sleep with a murderous woman on the other side of a tattered, over-large rag.

The curtain fluttered.

He wiped sweaty palms against his trousers. Had he summoned the beast?

A teal-haired head poked through, gleaming in the light of the lantern he kept by his bedroll. Kaya pushed the curtain aside.

"You still awake?" Seeing that he was, she slipped onto his side of the chamber, the curtain falling closed behind her.

He sat up, wrapping the blanket around himself. "What about Lavina?"

"She's a deep sleeper." Kaya rubbed her puffy, purple-rimmed eyes. "Tires herself out during the day. Sleeps like a log at night."

"She really was going to kill me, wasn't she?" he murmured. It wouldn't have been the first time a stranger turned against him, but he'd always thought there was an unspoken code amongst those who sought refuge in the Safe Towers.

Kaya dropped next to him, wrapping her arms around her knees. "Lavina isn't one to be crossed. She loves—and hates—fiercely." Her lips trembled. "She's kept me safe for a long time. From *everyone.*" She plucked at a loose strand of embroidery on her skirts. "You're the first one who's stayed in this tower in, oh... seven years."

Zeke felt like he'd been sprung on by seven Singers at once. "*Seven years?*" he hissed. "You've been locked up in here for *seven years*? What about Kiltra?" He tore the letter from his pocket, holding it out to her. Surely Lavina would jump at the chance at a better life, a truly safe place— an entire continent rather than a tiny island that was being slowly consumed.

But Kaya didn't touch the piece of paper. Her shoulders seemed to droop, and silver crept into her skin. Her fingers leapt to her ear, pinching at her piercings. "We've *tried* to get to Kiltra." She blinked rapidly. "We were rapunzel farmers, though none of us liked to eat it ourselves. Lavina was our neighbour, like a second mother to me." She hiccupped, laughing softly. Tears shimmered in her eyes. "When the blight broke out, we tried to get to Kiltra, to escape. But some of our companions..." She sucked in a deep breath. "They traded my parents to the Singers in exchange for safe passage." She swiped her sleeve over her nose.

Zeke's stomach twisted. A picture of his own parents crept into his mind: their smiles spattered with blood; their teeth sharp and flashing; their fingers curved into claws. Their bodies contorted, their minds overtaken by a single desire: *hunger*. "I'm so sorry," he whispered.

She nodded, staring at the barred window. "Lavina whisked me back here to my family's ancestral tower, and we've never left except to gather food and harvest our rapunzel supply." Her voice dropped. "Here, we're..."

"Safe?"

This time, the word fell less like a spell and more like an ax.

She flinched. "Maybe. For now. But..." She kept pinching her ear, gnawing at her bottom lip. "But it's come at a cost." Her voice cracked. "You may be the first person to stay in the tower, but you're not the first to try. When we got here, travellers asked for our help all the time. Lavina always refused. She even pushed people out the window." She covered her face with her hands. "And I did nothing. I was terrified that if I spoke up, if I intervened... she'd push me out, too."

His throat closed. "That's horrible."

"I was hoping she'd changed, that maybe now she wanted company like I did... that she wouldn't try to hurt you. I'm sorry. I was... desperate." She bowed her head, expelling a ragged breath. "She wasn't always this way. But after my parents, and so many years up here with just the two of us..." Sighing, she rested her head against the wall. "Lavina needs to get out of here, but this place has so many memories. I think it's the only thing keeping her sane."

"And what about you?" he asked. "Do *you* need to get out of here?" He peered closely at her worn face, then the restless fingers now tapping against the stones.

She didn't answer.

He had to say it anyway. Just so she had the option, should she need it. "Mermaid, I know we haven't known each other long, but..." When the silence stretched, he almost lost his nerve. He rubbed a hand over his face, fingers tangling in his thin, scraggly beard. But Kaya deserved a chance at a better, safer life if she wanted it.

He couldn't abandon her to wither away here or get eaten by Singers as they slowly consumed every Sithian territory. The longer they lingered, the lower their chances at surviving.

Perhaps he could help save this *one* life.

He sucked in another deep breath. "I—if you'd like to come with me when I leave, I'd be happy to have a travelling companion."

Something like a strangled laugh snarled in her throat. "You—you surely don't *mean* that? We're—we're practically strangers!"

"Who are currently sharing each other's deepest, darkest secrets," he pointed out.

She flushed a deep, sparkling silver. "That's what happens when you're starved for company," she muttered.

"Besides, by the time I leave, we won't be complete strangers. You'll have known me for at least three months," he continued.

"Which, by apocalyptic measure, is practically forever, I suppose."

Was she being earnest or sarcastic? Had he bungled everything? He sighed inwardly. "Please don't fret over it, Mermaid. It's not a marriage proposal, or anything untoward. I'm suggesting partnership. If you *want* to leave, we can help each other."

Her eyelids flickered, and she leaned closer to him. "Thank you for the offer." Their shoulders brushed. "I just... I can't leave Lavina. And she won't... she won't want to leave."

He wanted to yell in frustration, but instead he patted Kaya gently on the back. "Perhaps she'll change her mind," he said mildly. "If she does, the offer's there."

Kaya stared up at the ceiling. "Thank you, Axman." She blinked rapidly. "Will you—will you promise not to leave before end of harvest?"

His chest constricted at the hopelessness in her voice. As much as he wanted to reach his brother, he couldn't leave Kaya as things stood. "I promise, Mermaid."

She gave him a trembling smile. "I'll hold you to it."

~~~~~

They sat together a little while longer, and it struck Zeke just how much sadness Kaya carried from Lavina's protective possessiveness. The words tumbled out of her, and with her openness, he found himself sharing everything: his favorite memories with Simon, his longing to reunite with his brother and continue his work as a scribe. When she finally wandered to bed, he snuggled into his blanket, frowning into the gold-tinged darkness, feeling oddly light of heart but down in spirit. By the time he finally drifted close to sleep, daylight peeked through the cracks in the shutters. Voices floated through the cool morning air.

"I'll check on the rapunzel," Lavina said with a grunt, as if she were pulling on her boots.

"Are you taking him with you?" Kaya asked, voice low.

A pause, in which Zeke tensed and prayed that he wouldn't be stuck with Lavina the entire day. "Not until the harvest is ready. I hate to leave him with you, Kaya-girl, but I don't want him knowing where our supply is until absolutely necessary." Lavina sighed. "If *anything* happens, leave him to the Singers. You have your dagger?"

Zeke could hear the smile in Kaya's voice. "Do *you* have your sword?"

"Never leave without it." Lavina thumped across the tower, stopping at the edge of Zeke's bedroll. He squeezed his eyes shut tighter. "Behave yourself, *sir*," she muttered over him, "or I'll toss you off this tower and eat your brains for breakfast."

When she was gone, he rolled out of bed. "Well, I'm awake *now*."

Across the room, Kaya lay atop the tower of pillows, staring at the ceiling. "Be glad she didn't follow through with it," she murmured.

"Believe me, I'm grateful." He clambered to his feet, stretching.

Kaya jumped down from her perch, landing in a crouch. Her braids swung around her hips as she straightened, adjusting her sword belt. "Ready for gathering duty?" Her eyes started to sparkle, and her smile grew long and mischievous. "Maybe we can find some Singers to fight, too."

She seemed even more at ease with him after their conversations the night before.

"To certain death we go," he quipped.

She full-out grinned. "Don't worry, I'll protect you." And she leapt out the window.

His mind buzzed; it took him a few moments before he could follow. The thorns bristled in the chill breeze, and he narrowly avoided getting stabbed in the eye. By the time he'd levered himself out the window, Kaya was halfway down the tower.

Stomach sloshing, he inched after her.

"You all right?" she asked when he reached the bottom, cradling his stomach.

He peeled off his gloves, stuffing them in his belt. "It's *much* easier climbing up than down."

"Here. This will settle your stomach—and it's nice against the zombies, too." She tossed him a bundle, and he unwrapped it to find a dark green, crinkled rapunzel leaf.

Grimacing, he stuffed it in his mouth, chewing through the bitterness. "You guys *really* have an entire harvest of this?"

"*Maybe*. Stick around, and you'll see." Kaya hurried away from the tower, beckoning him to follow her through the thin, straggly trees.

~~~~~

Zeke settled back against a tree trunk and sighed. After foraging all morning, they'd collected a variety of mushrooms and weeds. His stomach growled, and he nibbled on one of the plants, swallowing it despite the grainy texture.

He offered a handful to Kaya. "Want some?"

She stood guard, gaze flicking from tree to tree. "Sure." She took the dry green stalk, chewing on it absentmindedly.

He got to his feet. "Your turn. I'll guard."

She nodded. They moved on to a new spot, Kaya inspecting whatever caught her eye, while Zeke kept his concentration on the dark, tangled woods around them. Sunlight filtered through the leaves, burning off whatever fog remained. Squirrels leapt from branch to branch, and birds chirped, flicking here and there amongst the foliage.

With the animals so lively, he doubted there'd be Singers in the area. Tension eased from his body, and he shook out his limbs.

"It's actually... pretty beautiful around here," he murmured. The scene made him think of those described by his favourite poets: quiet glades, dappled light..."

Kaya grunted. "For now."

He blinked. "What do you mean?"

Her lips thinned. "That's how the Singers in this territory get you — they lull you into false security." She nodded to a nearby tree.

Zeke squinted — and went cold.

A narrow face with bulging, light green eyes peeked out at them. Teeth flashed in the shadows, but the monster didn't move. A mouse scurried across the grass in front of it, but its gaze never wavered from Zeke and Kaya.

"They know to wait," Kaya whispered. "They're part of the scenery, like the trees. The animals don't even care anymore." She shivered and stood, facing the zombie as it licked its lips.

"Are... are they *all* like that around here?" Zeke's skin prickled. "How have you survived this long?"

Kaya drew her dagger, its blade glinting. "By going out only when I have to."

"How much longer do you think you can do that?"

She glanced at him sharply, but there was a hint of wildness to her eyes that reminded him of Lavina. Of the Sithian Court on the verge of collapse. A growing paranoia, a growing fear that soon, the world would never feel welcome again. "I... I don't know." Her shoulders slumped. "I *hate* sitting here, waiting to die, when there's someplace —" She bit down on her lower lip, trapping the rest of the words.

"Then *don't*. You could come with me, help me find my brother." He hoped he didn't sound as desperate as he felt.

She shook her head. "I can't! The tower... is my *home*. And Lavina... How could I leave her, after everything she's done for me?"

"And how could she keep you from the possibility of a better life?" he shot back.

Kaya pierced him with a glare, her nostrils flaring, before quickly turning back to the zombie. The creature tilted its head, as if deciding whether to take them both on. Zeke slid his ax out of its holster, hefting it in his hands.

Planting her feet, Kaya clutched the hilt of her dagger. "She's all I have left, Zeke. I can't lose her, too."

"But what if staying means you lose more?" He swung his weapon at the zombie, who hissed and retreated deeper into the trees, its lips curled. "What if you lose any hope for a future at all?"

"What makes you think I haven't already lost that?"

"Because you let me up the tower," he said quietly. "There's part of you clinging to it, Mermaid."

She'd opened her mouth to protest when the zombie's high, reedy cry floated through the air. Zeke felt its magic gnawing at his limbs, trying to freeze his feet in place so it could catch him. But with the rapunzel safely in his stomach, the Singer's call had no effect.

His jaw clenched. His fingers tightened around the ax handle. He was *sick* of zombies. He darted forward.

Hissing, the zombie lunged, fangs bared.

Another song rippled through the forest: soaring, spitting like sparks. Clear, cool, and full of longing. Its power surged behind Zeke, propelling him closer to the monster, then shooting past him to wrap around the zombie's limbs.

The zombie froze, unable to move, its bulging green eyes wide.

Zeke swung, shutting his eyes at the last moment. Not daring to look past the grotesque features of the monster to the remnant of the human.

His blade hit something solid. A cry gurgled out. Blood spattered his face and clothes.

The song died away, and he turned to see Kaya, her cheeks flushed a bright, shining silver.

So *that* was a Voicer in action.

"That... was intense," he breathed.

She ducked her head, scratching at the tip of her ear. "You did rather well yourself." She nodded to his bloodied ax, which he quickly wiped against the grass.

"There are lots of Singers on the way to Kiltra, if you're bored." He gave her a slight shrug, to show her she could take it as a joke if she wished. But the idea crept through him with the same shivering sensation he'd once felt while jotting down the bards' epic ballads.

The silver in her skin heightened before she scowled at him. "Don't tempt me." But as they headed out of the forest, she glanced back and sighed wistfully.

~~~~~

That night, the curtain fluttered again. Barefoot, Kaya quietly slipped back into his side of the chamber. "I—I hope you don't mind," she whispered, dragging her toe over the floor. "It's just nice to have real conversations."

Sitting up, he tugged his blanket around his shoulders and fought back a yawn. After so long travelling by himself, he didn't mind at all. It was nice to have someone enjoy his company, rather than leave him in the dirt or want to push him out a window. "You and Lavina don't talk much?"

She settled beside him, crossing her legs. "Not really. She hates talking about the past—and certainly never the future."

The future that loomed, uncertain except, it seemed, for the certainty of death.

They sat in silence, listening to the moaning of the wind that carried the low, hissing words of the Singers. Kaya shivered, and he offered to share his blanket. She grabbed one end, wrapping it around herself, and scooted close to him, her shoulder pressed against his.

"Your brother you're going to meet... is he a scribe, too?" Kaya asked.

Zeke laughed softly. "No. Simon's a carpenter. He helped furnish the Court."

She raised her brows. "I thought you were nobility."

"Merchant nobility, not by blood. Our family earned noble status through their trades." His eyes stung. "Simon built me the bookshelves in my study." He pictured those shelves, a comforting dark walnut, stuffed with scrolls and books and vibrant, colourful ink bottles. Did he even know how to hold a quill properly anymore? How to avoid smearing ink across a written page? He held up his hand, staring at the rough calloused on his palm, the scars from so many battles that zigzagged across his skin.

"I'd love to learn a trade someday." Kaya's gentle voice eased him from his troubled thoughts.

Grateful for the distraction, he asked, "What would you want to learn?"

"Archery. Though does that count as a trade?"

"It'd certainly be helpful against the zombies," he murmured thoughtfully.

"Oh, I don't want to learn it just for that." She drew her knees up to her chin. "I want to learn how to shoot an arrow from horseback and join the Royal Elven Brigade." She sifted her fingers through her hair. "That's why I dye my hair, too—the ladies always have such colorful pigments."

"So I've heard."

She continued dreamily, "My parents wanted to join the Brigade, but we didn't own any horses. One of the caravans we met before they... well, it was full of Brigade elves. Even though they were on the run, they still practiced the show. I watched them rehearse..." She smiled into the flickering gloom, as though she could see the dance of elf, horse, and bow in the shadows. "It was beautiful. I wish—"

"Wish you could see it again?" he asked quietly.

Her fingers knotted together in her lap. "I can't, and that's that."

He sighed. "Listen, I don't want to sound like I'm pestering. I... I just hate the idea of leaving you behind in a few months."

"Then you'll understand why I can't just *leave* Lavina. Even if I want to." She rubbed her fists into her eyes.

"Even if it ends up costing your life?"

"What's my life, after I just watched Lavina push all those people out the window?" She hunched forward, forehead pressed against her knees.

Heat pierced him. "You were a *child*! Lavina had all the power, and she used it for evil. That shouldn't be *your* burden to bear. *You're* worth fighting for. *You're* worth saving!" He had to fight to keep his voice low and level.

For a moment, she didn't say anything. Then came a whispered, "I can't accept it, but thank you anyway, Axman."

~~~~~

The days passed in a blur of foraging and nightly conversations, where he learned that Kaya loved mint tea, sunny days, and comedic ballads where the heroes bumbled about like idiots until they stumbled into a happy end. Lavina continued to zealously guard the location of the rapunzel crop, and when she was around, he and Kaya kept their distance from each other.

Then one morning he woke to Lavina crouching by his bedroll. He started, heart thundering. Gloomy grey light crept through the window, hinting toward the change in seasons that approached. In just a month, the rains would drench the plains and forests of Sithe, rotting any rapunzel that hadn't yet been collected.

"Harvesttime," Lavina said, tapping one of his boots. "Time to earn your keep."

His ears burned, but he scrambled to his feet, taking the piece of dried rapunzel that Kaya threw to him. He followed the women out of the tower. Once he reached the ground, Lavina wrapped a dark cloth around his eyes.

"Just. In. Case," she muttered, tying it tightly around his skull. She grabbed him by the ear, towing him forward.

Pain lanced through his head. He stumbled, stretching out his arms for balance.

A cool, roughened hand took his, squeezing his fingers. Kaya.

Lavina's breath hissed, and her fingertips tore into his ear.

Kaya quickly dropped his hand.

Their journey continued in silence except for the thud of their boots and their gasping breaths. At one point, Lavina stopped completely, swearing under her breath.

Kaya had drifted closer to Zeke again. He could feel her arms pumping close to his, her presence comforting and friendly compared to that of the woman hauling him along.

Her breath caught, and she grabbed his hand. "A caravan!"

"We'll go around," Lavina snapped. She groaned. "The *long way*."

"But what if—"

"Absolutely not! One stranger is enough—and more than I ever wanted." She yanked Zeke around, setting off in a different direction.

He staggered over an upturned root and nearly fell flat on his face. So much for trying to be a dashing hero. *He* would be the lucky one to get out of the tower alive. He tried to regain his footing, straining his senses for any hint of Singers.

A few times, Kaya cursed and muttered to Lavina, and then they'd switch their route again, probably avoiding swarms of the creatures.

Finally, Lavina lurched to a halt, stripping the blindfold from his face. He blinked through the haze of light, then stared.

Towering trees guarded a large, makeshift garden, where wild rapunzel sunned its broad, wrinkled leaves. Most of the plants were fully grown, but a few merely boasted vivid teal flowers instead of dark green leaves.

He clutched at his chest, crinkling the letter tucked in his pocket. An entire year's worth of rapunzel. Right there. No wonder Lavina protected it so viciously.

"H-how?" he sputtered.

Lavina didn't answer. She thrust a sack into his hands. "Get to work. Kaya, you keep first watch. We'll rotate when we get tired." She turned away, striding into the thicket of plants.

Kaya lingered near, lowering her voice. "Lavina found this last year. I think it used to be an elven rapunzel farm, like my family's." She pointed through the trees, where Zeke glimpsed a rotting pile of wood that vaguely resembled a house. Squirrels dashed over the roof, collecting acorns that peppered the beams.

"I wonder how many more of these there might be," he murmured.

"Trying to plan a route for when you leave?" She was fiddling with her piercings.

He wished he could reassure her, but he couldn't hide the truth. Wouldn't hide the truth. "I wish I didn't have to go—"

"You don't," she breathed, then flushed when he stared at her. She ducked her head, though he could tell from the flick of her ears she was still listening for enemies. "Maybe—I could convince Lavina to let you stay—"

He snorted softly. "Lavina's as likely to do that as leave."

Kaya flinched. "That's not fair."

"Kaya." He plucked a leaf and stuffed it into the bag. "I can't stay. I want to see my brother again." He glanced across the garden, but Lavina was wrestling a particularly large clump of rapunzel. "And I want you to leave with me."

Kaya's lips thinned. "I guess we're stuck, aren't we?" Her voice cracked. She turned abruptly, spine rigid. "I'm going to check the area." She stalked off toward the farmhouse.

Great. He ripped a plant out by its roots, grinding his teeth.

He couldn't keep doing this. If he couldn't convince Kaya, he had to try to get Lavina to see reason. For both her and Kaya's sakes. Taking a deep breath, he wandered closer to her. "Lavina, we need to talk."

"I didn't keep you around for talk." She jammed a bunch of leaves into her sack, glaring at him.

"Please, just hear me out. I'm headed to—"

"—the land without zombies, yes, yes," Lavina interrupted. "You and every other fool out there."

His cheeks heated. "My brother isn't a fool!" he hissed. "And he *got there*! He's truly safe, in an entire nation unaffected by the blight or the Singers. If you and Kaya came with me, we could get there, before—" He swallowed. Before their tower stood empty, with nothing but tattered pillows and rotten food sacks piled against the walls. Kaya and Lavina had been lucky to survive for *seven* years so far—but eventually that luck would run out.

"We're not leaving," Lavina said coldly. "Kaya-girl and I, as long as we stick together, we'll be all right. That tower is *our home*."

"The tower won't work forever. Surely you heard what happened at the Sithian Court."

Her entire body stiffened. *"That won't happen."*

"You can't guarantee that!" he hissed. "You can't guarantee *anything*!"

The Sithian Court had tried to survive in its armoured fortress, too— but then the paranoia set in. Nobles had turned against each other in a bloodbath, and the survivors had scattered across the capital city, picked off by Singers that roamed the streets.

"And *you* can?" she spat, straightening. "You little spit of a boy, who trespasses in *my* tower, and tries to tell me how to raise my own daughter?"

His cheeks heated. Maybe he was just a spit of a boy. Maybe he really didn't know anything—but he knew that Lavina's love was poisonous, blighted by paranoia and control. He'd seen *that* often enough in Court, where nobles clawed at each other with passion and venom both.

"You can't keep using her love for you to keep her here!"

"So she can perish with every other idiot who tries to get to Kiltra? *Never*!" Lavina snarled. "I—"

A piercing shriek split the air.

Zeke's hackles rose. His heart thundered. That *sound*—it'd come from the farmhouse.

He spun, Lavina forgotten, and ran toward the ruined building. The house and trees around it erupted with movement, the shadows flickering to reveal an entire colony of Singers. Kaya emerged from the doorway, her lips parted in an attempt to sing, but she was too busy fending off the monsters.

She staggered forward, falling to her hands and knees.

Before Zeke could think, his ax was in his hands. "Forward, Mermaid!" he shouted as one of the creatures leapt into the air, its face split with a ravenous grin.

She pulled herself over the grass, closer to him, and he tossed his ax.

It sailed over her, colliding with the zombie midair. There was a sickening crunch, a shriek, and the Singer tumbled to the earth, blood splattering. His ax landed in the grass with a thud. Kaya snatched it, lurching to her feet to face the oncoming horde.

Lavina appeared beside them, her sword drawn, her lips white. "Get out of here, Kaya!"

Kaya stared at her. "*What*?"

"Run! Leave us!"

"You can't be serious! I've fought zombies before!" Kaya's nostrils flared.

"There are too many this time!" Lavina clutched at Kaya, her eyes wider and more desperate than Zeke had ever seen. "Get back to the tower, *please*!" She grabbed the ax from Kaya's hands and thrust it toward Zeke.

His heart twisted as he gripped his weapon once more. As much as he sympathized with Lavina, there *were* too many zombies—too many for Kaya to possibly escape. They circled like a pack of wild dogs, their long, curved teeth bared and flashing in the gloomy light. Lavina's protective instinct would merely get them *all* killed.

"Mermaid!" he yelled, and Kaya tore her gaze from Lavina to meet his.

What? she mouthed, and he saw the hopelessness there, the uncertainty. Lavina yanked Kaya back, pulling her toward the edge of the garden.

"*Sing!*" he screamed and plunged into the throng.

For a moment, all he could hear were the hissing voices of the Singers, their melodic magic snatching at his limbs. Then Kaya's smooth, clear voice soared above the fray. Though her song couldn't stop all the creatures—they were far too numerous for that—she'd make his work a lot easier.

Lavina shot him a murderous glare, but Zeke didn't care. Kaya was their best chance at getting out of here alive.

He tore through the Singers, slashing and stabbing, while Kaya's song wove through the air. He almost fancied he could see the strands of her magic wrapping around the zombies' legs, pinning them in place.

He didn't look too closely at the creatures' mangled features. In the past he'd dared, only to find the remnants of old friends in the broken, jagged skin. Familiar green eyes without the glint of recognition—just the sheen of ravenous hunger.

He hadn't slept for weeks afterward.

He banished the memories and focussed on fighting, hacking at whatever Singer veered too close to his blade. He glimpsed Lavina darting back and forth, her sword flashing.

The monsters were *everywhere*—worse than rabbits. He narrowly avoided one's plunging fangs. He rolled away from another's grasping fingers.

Kaya, song wavering, scrambled for the safety of a tree.

He didn't see the moving shadow in the branches overhead until too late. His warning cry went unheeded. The monster sprang down, colliding with Kaya and knocking her to the grass. Its fangs sank into her side before she knocked it away, stabbing it with her dagger.

She lurched to her feet, still singing, though her voice was weaker now.

He whirled, ax flying, zombies dropping around him. Crimson stained the rapunzel leaves, and he slid across the wet grass.

Finally, they stood alone in a field of corpses. He rushed toward Kaya, but Lavina beat him to her, tearing strips off her tunic to wrap Kaya's wound.

His heart thundered. "Is it bad?" He knelt by Kaya, who gave him a watery smile.

"I'll live," she murmured. "Don't fret about it, Axman." Her fingers curled around his.

"*Do* fret about it, *Axman*," Lavina snapped. She smacked their hands, her eyes flashing. "You nearly killed her!"

"If she hadn't done what she did, we'd *all* be dead!" he retorted. "*Including* her! You can't protect her from every bad thing in the world—sometimes, she'll have to fight them!"

"Stop, both of you!" Kaya struggled to her feet, holding her bandage. "This is not the place!"

She was right, of course. Zeke swallowed the rest of his ire. When Lavina moved to blindfold him again, he raised his ax. "Not this time, lady. If we get swarmed again—"

"I'll feed you to them," she snarled.

~~~~~

The atmosphere in the tower that evening made Zeke feel like he'd been surrounded by Singers again. Lavina stripped him of any rapunzel he carried, then ordered him to help her bind Kaya's wounds. He did so quietly, fingers shaking, and he noticed that Lavina seemed grimly satisfied at his discomfort.

Doubt crept in. What if he really shouldn't have encouraged Kaya to help them? Perhaps she might have escaped...

The notion haunted him throughout the rest of the day, gnawing at his thoughts. He kept to his side of the chamber, hoping to avoid Lavina's further ire while she stayed by Kaya. When Lavina finally fell asleep, long after the moon had risen, he tossed and turned on his bedroll.

"You're fretting, Axman," Kaya rasped, poking her head through the curtain.

He sat up, dragging his fingers through his tangled hair. "What are you—"

She waved away his concern. "I'll be fine." She shuffled in, leaning against the wall beside him. "I'm more concerned that you're wallowing in guilt right now."

"Perhaps a bit," he admitted, pressing the heels of his hands into his eyes. "How did you know?"

"Because I understand the feeling," she said softly. "It's part of the reason I've stayed with Lavina. The idea that if I left her, I'd be guilty of disloyalty." She wiped at her eyes. "But I can't keep living like this. I—I *want* to try to get to that place again, Zeke. I want to go with you, to have a future." She cleared her throat. "And you... you've encouraged me to fight for that future." She slid to the floor, her hand splayed mere inches from his.

Was she saying...?

Heart in his throat, he stretched his hand to her, his fingers spread in a silent, open invitation.

He fancied he heard her gulp... and then her fingers slid between his, their callouses rubbing against each other.

Was that her pulse thundering, or his? Or did it even matter?

"So you don't hate me, then?" he asked.

She snorted. "You can't control everything. You didn't know what was going to happen. And it was my decision to stay. Your encouragement just told me that I was needed." She turned her face toward him, eyes gleaming. "And that feeling... I can't even describe how happy it makes me."

"As happy as *this* makes me?" He held up their joined hands, pressing a gentle kiss against her fingers.

Her eyes widened, and silver streaked across her cheeks. She buried her face in his shoulder. "It's nothing." But her voice cracked a little.

"Sure, Mermaid."

"Shut up, Axman."

Somehow, Zeke got a few hours' sleep, despite the war of giddiness and guilt raging in his mind. By the time sunlight filtered through his eyelids, he felt like he'd faced off a thousand Singers in his dreams.

Lavina stood by his bedroll again, scowling down at him. "Hope you had a lovely final evening."

He blinked blearily. "Pardon me?"

She lifted her chin. "You're no longer needed. Or wanted. Get out." Her fingers danced along the hilt of her sword, rubbing the well-worn pommel.

He scrambled out of the bedroll. "Might I — might I say goodbye?"

"Absolutely not. Kaya and you mean nothing to each other. You're strangers." Lavina's gaze hardened. "That's all you'll ever be. You're going to leave us *alone*."

"Lavina?" Kaya's voice floated from the other side of the curtain. She flipped it open, rubbing her eyes, yawning. Her hair was a rumpled, tangled mess. "You're up already?"

"*Someone* should check to see what we can salvage from the garden." Kaya's shoulders hunched slightly. "I'll help," she said quietly, turning back to her side of the room.

"You're staying here," Lavina said stiffly.

Kaya stilled, fingers clutching the edge of the curtain. "Excuse me?"

Lavina straightened to her full height. "No more venturing out of the tower for you. I'll forage from now on."

"What about — what about Zeke?"

"*He* — " Lavina jerked her chin toward him. "*He* is leaving. Right now."

Kaya's jaw dropped. "But — but harvest isn't complete! There's still a full month — "

"*What harvest?*" Lavina snapped. "If we can salvage *anything*, it'll be enough for me to handle alone. We don't need *him* any longer."

"Yes, we do!" Kaya spun, catching the woman's arm. Her eyes were wide and pleading. "Please, *alula!*"

"He's a risk I'm no longer willing to take," Lavina said coldly.

"*Why*? Because he *wants* me to have a better life?"

Lavina's eyes widened. "How *dare* you!" she hissed. "I've sheltered and protected you for *seven years*, you ungrateful brat. I've been your *mother*, sister, friend — "

"This isn't about protecting *me*!" Kaya shouted, and her words echoed off the walls. "This is about protecting *yourself*! You'd rather lock me up where you'll always have me, than let me even *try* to get to Kiltra!" Her eyes were wild, and her fingers snagged in her piercings, *click click clicking* until Zeke's ears rang with that tiny sound. "How are you any better than the Singers themselves?"

Lavina shrank back, her lips curling, her face completely white. She whirled on Zeke, teeth bared. "*You!* Before you, she was *safe!* She didn't want to leave, until *you* filled her head with hopeless *nonsense!*" Her eyes shimmered, and her entire body shook.

Zeke raised his hands. "Lavina, please, listen—"

Dimly, he heard Kaya crying frantically, "*Alula*, I'm sorry, I shouldn't have said—"

But Lavina didn't listen. Instead, her hands snatched at his tunic and *pushed*. Over and over. Caught off guard, he didn't have the chance to regain his footing before the next push came. There was a flurry of movement, and he glimpsed Kaya snatching at him, her lips rounded in horror.

His calves bumped against a ledge. A breeze ruffled the back of his shirt.

And then he was tumbling through open air, the tower a dizzying blur above him.

"*No!*" Kaya's shriek tore through the wind howling in his ears. He flung out his arms, catching at the thorn ladder. Ravenous, they ripped into his hands. Pain pierced his head, and blood spurted across his cheek. His vision in one eye blurred.

His own strangled scream joined Kaya's cries, but his fingers tightened around the thorn curtain. Then, fumbling for footholds, he stumbled down the rest of the wall, collapsing once he reached the ground.

He stared up at the sky roiling with crimson and blue. His body felt stiff, and his heart thundered in his ears. Something thumped nearby, and footsteps ran up to him.

"Towers damn it!" Kaya's fingers flew over his body, checking his injuries. "Axman..." She gave a strangled sob.

Warmth filled him. "I told you it was easier going up than down," he croaked.

"*Not funny!*"

He tried to smile at her, to reassure her it was indeed funny, but her face blurred into smears of darkness and blood. Her voice faded, and he fell into a dream of thorns that wrapped around his body, smothering him completely.

~~~~~

A soft breeze stirred Zeke's cheek, cool and brisk as the coming rains. He groaned, blinking until he realized he was in a tiny tent. A bandage had been wrapped around his head, covering one eye. He shifted, wincing as his entire body protested the movement.

The tent flap fluttered, and Kaya flew inside. Her cheeks were flushed, her tunic and trousers bloody. Her hair stuck out in all directions.

"You're awake!" she cried, falling to her knees beside him.

"Wh-where are we?"

"Currently camped in the middle of... somewhere."

"H-how...?" He gingerly touched his bandage, then winced at the spike of agony and hastily lowered his hand.

Kaya gave a one-shouldered shrug. "Tracked down that caravan from before and traded some rapunzel for help. Got someone to help me tend you and carry you here."

A shudder rippled through him. "And Lavina?" he whispered.

Kaya sucked in a deep breath. "She's... back at the tower. She made her choice. And I've made mine." She lifted her chin. "She will not apologize, and neither will I." She took his hand, squeezing his fingers. "Thank you."

He blinked at her through his one good eye. "For what, Mermaid?"

"For fighting for my future." A deep silver flush crept over her face.

Slowly, with her help, he sat up. Through the heady rush of her arm around him, he tried to focus on the practical side of things. They couldn't get *too* lost in the moment. Not yet. "We still might end up dead out there."

She gently rested her head on his shoulder. "Or we might find a way out of this zombie-infested kingdom."

She was missing the point.

"Or get maimed."

"Or get married." She brushed her lips against his cheek.

His face heated. "Or be zombie food," he persisted, glowering at her.

"Should we give out weapons as wedding favors?" she mused. Then she smiled at him, as serene as a mermaid sunning herself on a rock. "I understand what I'm getting into, Axman. But I also understand what I'm leaving behind."

His heart swelled. "I—I can't give you much," he choked out. "Even... even if we reach my brother. I'm just a scribe."

She shrugged. "And I'm just an elven peasant."

"A *magical* elven peasant."

She clucked her tongue. *"Many wield weapons to fight the monsters, too. Does that make the work they do any less important?"*

"I wish you wouldn't quote me to myself," he muttered.

"You walked right into it. How could I resist?"

Probably the same way he couldn't resist that long, teasing grin. He sighed. "You win. For now."

"Good. Otherwise, I'd be an *annoyed* magical elven peasant."

~~~~~

It took a month for them both to heal completely from their

wounds—a month of running from place to place, trying to avoid the Singers wandering the forests and plains.

Weeks later, blood-spattered and spent, they reached another Safe Tower, this one on the edge of a desert. The rainy season had come, and droplets soaked into the dry, brittle grass beneath their feet. In the distance, the Kiltran Mountains loomed.

Zeke clambered up the thorn-wrapped tower wall, Kaya covering him in case he slipped. He edged around the thorns, careful to avoid their spikes. When he reached the top, the tower was empty.

Kaya staggered in after him. Her face was dirt-streaked, her eyes puffy, and her roots were starting to show. She dragged her fingers through her hair, releasing a long sigh as she collapsed on the stone flags.

Gingerly, he settled beside her. She dropped her head against his shoulder, pressing a tiny kiss on his coat. His heart swelled at the small reminder that they were here, they were alive, and they'd make it through together.

He rested his hand on her knee. His fingertips rubbed over blood and dirt and what he suspected were splattered zombie brains. "Think we can finally sleep now?" He'd never felt fully comfortable all those weeks they'd spent on the ground.

She nodded, but when he made to move, she wrapped her hands around his arm. "Not just yet," she whispered. "Let's sit a bit longer."

"All right."

They sat listening to the thundering of the rains, Kaya tucked against his chest, until the trembling in her fingers had faded, until her raspy, uneven breaths had turned rhythmic and regular. He laid her out on the floor, rolling up his jacket to jam under her head.

"Good night, Mermaid," he murmured to her before settling down to sleep a few feet away.

Shadows fell upon shadows in the abandoned tower. Had the people before them reached their destination, or had they been caught and killed? Would *they* make it? Or had he challenged Lavina over Kaya's freedom, only to lead her adopted daughter to doom? He ran his hands over his face.

Only time would tell.

He slept fitfully.

~~~~~

The next day, he didn't stir until late morning. Something soft cradled his head, and after a bleary moment, he realized it was his coat. Beside him, Kaya sat cross-legged, braiding her hair into long plaits, the teal mixing with her natural walnut brown.

"Morning, Axman." She bent down, planting a kiss on him.

He froze, shocked by the sweetness after the tumult of the past few weeks. He sat up, cradling her face as she deepened the kiss, wrapping her arms around his neck. When they finally parted, he asked raggedly, "What was *that* for?"

Her eyes glistened. "For still being alive when I woke up." She ran her thumbs across his battle-scarred cheeks, her gaze flicking to his wounded eye.

He buried his face in her neck to hide his giddy grin. "I hope to be alive for you many more mornings."

Her hands, now trapped against his chest, curled into his shirt. "I won't make you promise," she said, voice low, "because we mortals don't control life and death. But as much as it's in my power, Axman, I'm going to hold you to it."

He raised his head to brush another kiss across her lips. "Please do."

END

Starchild
Abigail Falanga

Drift

"Extreme quarantine measures in place. Do not approach. Violators of quarantine zone will be fired upon. Do not approach. Extreme quarantine measures in place. Do not approach..."

Automated words repeated, over and over. Impersonal. Harsh. Clanging over sounds of screams.

Her screams.

The rush of feet pounding on metal flooring. Her mother's tears wetting her hair. Her father clasping her. Something wrenching her away. Reaching her hands back toward them.

The airlock of the light cruiser slamming shut. Shooting away from the Citadel, blackness on every side.

Those words repeat again and again until the coms are too far out of range to receive the signal:

"Extreme quarantine measures in place. Do not approach. Violators of quarantine zone will be fired upon. Do not approach."

Zell couldn't remember much of her Life Before, but she could remember *that*. That moment. That last moment with her parents before she was torn away and locked in the cruiser, a universe of blackness and emptiness between them. That smell of tears and hot metal and her father's sweat and her mother's perfume and something else that she had finally decided was blood, after ruling out several thousand other scents stored in the cruiser's database. And always, *always*, that blaring announcement:

"Extreme quarantine measures in place. Do not approach. Violators of quarantine zone will be fired upon. Do not approach."

Why?

Why only that memory, when surely there had been many happy moments with her parents on the Citadel?

It wasn't fair.

Zell sighed and cracked her eyes open. She couldn't pretend to be asleep anymore. Wakefulness made her limbs restless and That Memory drove away normal dreams and made her breaths short and uneven. Slipping out from under soft blankets, she set her feet on a thick, welcoming carpet and blinked out the port at the same exact view that met her every morning: a distant starfield, the corner of the Forest Nebula, and a whole lot of black. It never changed. Even if someday about ten years from now the cruiser reached the Ungel Station, it would still be the same exact view. The universe was so vast that going very fast got you basically nowhere.

Nanny had responded to her movements by gradually, almost imperceptibly, increasing light and warmth as she sat there feeling sorry for herself. Now it hummed a gentle wake-up as she raked fingers through her hair and yawned.

"Good morning, Zell," it said in its usual friendly tone. "Are you ready for breakfast, or would you like to exercise first?"

Of course, Nanny didn't always have a friendly tone. It could be sharp when it pleased, sending tiny corrective jolts through her when she got out of line.

How else was a ship's computer supposed to train a little girl who had no one else to look after her?

"Breakfast."

"Put on something warm! I have a treat for you."

Zell slid on a robe and shuffled to the table. "What's the occasion?"

"It's the fifth anniversary of your journey aboard the cruiser!"

"Oh, yippee." That explained The Memory coming back.

A hatch in the wall slid open and a bowl piled high with ice cream spun out in front of her — cherry and vanilla-flavored simulated frozen cream-like stuff from the nutrient stores. Her favorite.

Zell put a spoonful in her mouth and let the sweetness melt over her tongue, turning ashy and sour as it mixed with loneliness and grief.

Five years.

It wasn't always this bad. But...

Five long, featureless, lonely years.

She looked around the space. Small living quarters with the bed, facilities, room for garments, table. Larger room beyond filled with books and toys and a gravity-controlled exercise area. Control center in the bow.

Lavish, comfortable, even luxurious... Even though it still felt like a prison sometimes.

"Nanny?"

No response.

The ship's computer, which she'd nicknamed "Nanny" almost her first day, didn't interact with her except during instructional times or unless she needed something like meals or repairs.

Zell sighed. "Nanny, bring up my parents."

A hologram wavered into view. Her father and mother, smiling and laughing, asking how she was, if she'd read anything interesting.

She finished her ice cream talking with them, almost forgetting they were nothing but simulations programmed to give responses according to personality and history records. Then she reached out to touch her mother's arm—and her fingers fell through nothing but light and air.

Contact

Zero-G tennis never failed to take her mind off things.

Surrounded by a multicolored holographic tennis court, with her favorite artificial opponents (the closest things she had to friends), she could spend hours drifting around the exercise area, propelled by simulated micro-rockets and the back-force of her own racket swings.

Zell had lost track of time (and half a dozen balls) when an alarm went off later that day, bringing her abruptly back to reality. The tennis game froze, and she pushed herself back into the common room.

"Nanny, what's that?"

The computer didn't respond, so Zell scampered into the control module, with its huge ports and banks of shiny toggles and buttons and plopped into the pilot's chair. She wasn't much of a pilot, but she knew what everything did. She punched in a command.

Information popped up on the port screen: "Proximity alert. errant-class patrol vessel within sensor range."

Zell's breath hitched. Another vessel? But... there *were* no other vessels! No one ever came out this far.

Another bleeping alarm she'd never heard before, and more words appeared on the screen: "Errant-class patrol vessel hailing. Response requested."

Heart pounding, Zell reached for the coms control, then snatched her hand back, then with sudden decisiveness slammed her shaking hand onto the button.

They knew she was there. They knew she wasn't just a piece of space junk. They knew now that something alive—

The radio crackled and hummed. "Hello, pilot," a broken, distant-sounding voice said. "Your vehicle is unknown. Please identify."

"Um..." Zell squeaked. She cleared her throat and went on stronger, though still with a waver in her voice: "This is the light cruiser *Tower* bound for Station Ungel."

"Wow."

Any thought she might have still had that this was an unmanned patrol drone left her at that word. It sounded warm. Astounded even, and masculine, and young.

"At your current speed and trajectory," he went on after a moment, "you won't reach Station Ungel for another three standard years, *Tower*."

"Yes, I'm aware. It's taken me five years to get *here*, so actually I'm more than halfway to my destination, thank you very much."

"But... Why?"

"Why not?" Zell flared.

"Just wondering why you don't use portals."

"Humans don't have portal technology. This light cruiser is intended for long-term travel—the *Citadel*, which I came from, is a generational ship. Just who are you, anyway? Why do you want to know? What do you care?"

A gentle laugh. "I apologize, *Tower*. This is Kings-son Solstice—it's my job to keep an eye out for trouble and help anyone in need. I picked up a signal from your cruiser yesterday and had to check it out. Sounded like singing."

"I can't believe you heard that," Zell said softly.

"Once a signal goes out, it never stops. And there's nothing out here, so of course I noticed. It was beautiful."

Zell's cheeks felt hot, and she pressed her cold fingers into them. "Thanks."

Static.

"You still there, Solstice?"

"Yes. What's your name, *Tower*?"

Don't talk to strangers.

Who had told her that? Goth-L? Nanny? Maybe even her mother, since there weren't any strangers out here for Goth-L to worry about. Didn't matter, though; she'd already told this stranger more than enough.

"I'm Zell Rampion."

"It was pleasant encountering you, Zell Rampion. I should go now."

"I suppose..."

"Unless you need anything?"

People? Room to move around? Something other than emptiness to stare at? Someone *real* to talk to?

"No. No—I'm fine. Thank you, Solstice."

"May your voyages be safe, *Tower*."

Static.

Another blip, and then the port screen was clear.

The blackness felt emptier than ever.

Child

A familiar buzz and the computer interface announced: "Incoming request from Goth-L drone."

Zell finished the sentence she'd been trying to read for the last twenty minutes, dropped a bookmark in place, and slouched to the controls.

A press of the finger and the friendliest voice she encountered in her daily existence intoned: "Zell, engage docking procedures."

This part was more instinctual than most of the controls. Zell slid a hand into a compartment that always felt cold but today seemed icy, then closed her eyes and waited until the mechanism responded.

Open. Reach. Take. Pull, she commanded the tendril-like grapplers and interlocking doors. *Contain. Close.*

It wasn't really a command, of course. Goth-L had walked her through the airlock controls the first few times and explained the series of minor adjustments of the complex mechanisms responding to real-time changes and emergencies. Not instinct. Just a skill that one learned and got very good at. Piloting the cruiser would be even more complicated; perhaps someday Goth-L would teach her that as well.

The airlock, aft beyond the common room, opened sufficiently for an oblong chest to slide through and come to rest in its slot. It was the non-propulsive part of the Goth-L drone—the heart remained in the docking bay outside—which gathered usable gases and minerals from the nebula's outer reaches and interfaced with components within the cruiser.

Including with Zell.

The Goth-L hologram materialized in a crystalline cloud of light fragments unlike any other hologram. It was always in the form of a beautiful old woman with long, silvery hair. Today, for some reason, it wore diaphanous brown-and-purple robes; her appearance was supposed to reflect Zell's mood or needs, though she could never understand how.

"Greetings, starchild." The hologram smiled warmly, the only thing capable of anything remotely like real conversation, rather than the ultimately predictable AIs that made up her "friends." "What news do you have?"

Zell considered mentioning the encounter with Solstice, but decided not. Goth-L could be overprotective, and she'd rather just talk. "Nothing much."

"And here I thought it was the fifth anniversary of your journey on the *Tower*! You call that nothing much?"

Oh yeah. "Doesn't exactly feel like something worth celebrating."

"Oh, Zell..." Goth-L sighed with realistic sympathy and settled on the sofa, patting the cushion beside her. "I know you feel lonely out here sometimes. But you're safe and comfortable and happy, on your way to new friends and a new life."

"I miss my parents."

"But you can talk to their holograms any time you like!"

Zell blinked away the sudden warmth of tears and slouched over to curl up beside Goth-L on the couch. "It's not the same. I can't touch them! Sometimes it seems like I can't even remember them."

The hologram laughed. "Well, of course you can't. It was five years ago that you last saw them."

"I was twelve." Zell shot her a glare. "You're supposed to remember things from before you were twelve! Like, what your apartment looked like, or if you liked ice cream, or whether you had any pets, or your first crush, or the feel of the carpet in your room. And I don't remember any of that! All I remember is that Mom smelled like jasmine and musk and Dad smelled like blood and sweat."

"That is a phenomenon of memory wherein childhood formational experiences are replaced by more essential long-term memories, made all the more pronounced in your case by an extreme change in living conditions and—"

"Tell me," she interrupted before this could become an instructional lecture. "Tell me *why* I had to leave. What happened?"

The hologram froze, like there was a glitch in the machine. Then Goth-L sighed, shoulders slumping a little. "I suppose now is as good a time as any—you're old enough."

She settled back, reached out, and ran a hand through Zell's hair. It was a gentle, comforting gesture that usually only felt a little warm. Today, the energy field tingled as if there was almost pressure, like fingers tangled in the strands. Zell shivered and yet didn't pull away; Goth-L sometimes took offense at that.

"The *Citadel* is a place full of all kinds of people," Goth-L recited in the singsong she always used when telling stories. "Your parents worked in the scientific laboratories studying bio-astronomic phenomenology and how multigenerational space travel affects biology. So, they were among the first to notice the emergence of a new virus that threatened to overrun the *Citadel*'s population. They recognized that its spread would be rapid and devastating, and they resolved to do what they could to alleviate it and if possible, find a cure. But they knew all too well that before this could happen, many people would likely die. They determined to save their daughter in the only way they could; by sending her off on her own to the nearest space station, though it was not the *Citadel*'s destination. Ungel Station is not human, yet they knew that a child would find refuge and a future there, whether among aliens or with the human diaspora." Her voice softened. "Your parents sent you away knowing they would likely never see you again, but they saved you from great illness or death as best they could."

"That's why the quarantine..."

"Yes."

"But what about—" Zell sniffed and rubbed her eyes, then left her head down and continued, mumbling into her sleeve: "What about everyone else? What happened on the *Citadel* after?"

"We have no way of knowing. We're outside of transmission range."

"I hope they're all right..."

"*You're* safe and that's all that matters, right?"

Zell shook her head. "Maybe to you, but you're just a drone." She glanced up, just in time to catch an irritated line form between the hologram's eyebrows.

Goth-L laughed it off. "You're too compassionate for your own good, starchild."

"I'd rather be that, than not."

"Of course," said Goth-L, and bent forward to wrap her in an embrace that was warm and weightless like steam in a shower.

Connect

Two days later, the alarm bleeped again.

Zell's heart did a strange leap and she hurtled to the controls to answer.

"Hailing *Tower*," Solstice said through static. "Tower, are you there?"

"Yes." Zell swallowed a lump. "Yes, I'm here, Solstice."

Silence, and she wondered if she scared him off. Or if maybe she was in trouble and she should've told Goth-L after all.

"Good to hear your voice, Zell Rampion."

"Good to hear your smile." She squeaked and slapped a hand over her mouth. What a ridiculous thing to say!

"Haven't caught any songs from you lately, *Tower*. Have you stopped singing?"

"Just... felt a little silly knowing someone was listening, I guess."

"Don't. This corner of the galaxy could use some beauty."

There was a sigh in his voice.

"Really?" She settled into the pilot's seat and pulled her knee up.

"The Forest Nebula has been flaring lately. It's a mess — causes major disruptions to vessels passing through, isn't good for lifeforms, affects people's minds. That's why I'm still around. I've been assigned to beat it back where I can, assist disabled vehicles, keep things peaceful."

"So... you'll be close enough to — to talk?"

"Yes, *Tower*, at least for a while." He paused. "And... I'd like it if you sing sometimes."

Zell grinned, though she was the only one to see it. "Maybe I will, then."

"Good. Oh, speaking of assisting disabled vehicles, are you sure your guidance systems are functional? If you're headed to the Ungel Station, your trajectory is off by nearly seven degrees."

"Must be to compensate for an obstruction or something. My ship's computer and my drone are in charge of steering."

"Understood. I—" Static. A moment later: "Just received a call. I'll talk to you later, Zell."

"Okay."

The communications line went dead, but instead of emptiness, Zell felt a surge of warmth and leaned back in the seat, smiling out the viewports.

~~~~~

Conversations with Kings-son Solstice became a regular thing. Some days, there was nothing. But on those days, Zell turned on open coms and simply sang whatever caught her fancy from old movies or older books. Other days, Solstice called and they chatted for hours — about his homeworld and its beauties and culture, which seemed so foreign yet also recognizable and comfortable, about the books she read and what little she remembered of her previous life, about simple things like the beauty of the stars or complex things like dreams and truth.

It was more like having a friend than anything Zell could remember.

"You said the nebula was messing with people's minds," she finally said one day. "Does that include things like — like memory?"

"Yes, sometimes. Why?"

"I don't remember much of anything before being here, on the *Tower*."

"Oh. That's more extreme than almost any other case I've encountered."

"It's just snatches of things, like the way the light came in across the city, the sound of the catwalks, the laboratory. Strange things. I've been thinking about it, and most of my memories of my parents and our life together are from holograms and records."

"That must be disorienting."

Zell was quiet for a moment. "Good word for it. Goth-L says it's simply that one doesn't often remember much from one's childhood, and I thought maybe it was the nebula. But I wonder if there's something more. But..."

"Yeah?"

"Goth-L says there was a virus that threatened the *Citadel* and that's why my parents sent me away, and that matches my memory. I just wondered... You have portal technology on your vessel, right? Do you think—maybe... Could you go and check on them perhaps?"

Solstice was silent long enough to make her very worried he'd gone. But then— "Send me the coordinates."

Truth

Days slipped by—so many that Zell began to wonder if something had happened to Solstice, or if going against orders had gotten him reassigned, or if her request had been too presumptuous and he no longer wished to speak with her. She only understood the basic principles of portal travel; she couldn't tell how long or what complications might be involved in going the distance it had taken her five years to travel at sub-light speeds.

Goth-L came and refused, politely, to talk further about the *Citadel*. Zell tried to ask in a roundabout way about the Kings-sons and the patrols they did, but Goth-L said she knew nothing about the jurisdictional ways of this remote reach of space.

Then she suggested a stack of new study material about civics and political theory, from Hammurabi down, and left again.

So, Zell continued to sing over the open coms, hoping.

The holograms had never really felt like true companionship, though she had been able to pretend. Now, they felt as empty and lifeless as the example characters in algebra word problems.

But she sang, and she hoped.

~~~~~

The familiar buzz sounded and Zell pushed aside the book she'd been reading, puzzled. It was too soon for Goth-L to be back. Normally, she only visited with materials every week or so. What...?

"*Tower,* are you there?"

It was Solstice!

Zell clasped her hands over her mouth as if she could contain the sob of relief. Then she summoned a readout and display on the screen. An errant-class vessel!

She hit the button. "Yes, I'm here."

"Open your port." There was a grin in his voice, quickly replaced by formality. "I wish to dock and request permission to board."

"Of course! I mean — permission granted. Come aboard, Kingsson."

She brought the vessel in and then swung around as the airlock doors opened with a reluctant clunk — it was their first time in five years, after all.

"Strange docking system," came his voice, clear and without the intervening static of the radio. "Those tentacles looked almost alive. Though I know little of human technology so—"

Zell was barely listening, for her heart was pounding in her ears like a thousand drums. He was actually here! They would look each other in the eye! She was nervous because this was the first living contact in ages — right? There was no other reason... Or, was it that, maybe — ?

She jumped up, tugging her shirt straight and pushing back her hair, and rushed into the common room. It was a mess. She should've —

He was right there.

Her breath completely deserted her, though her heart seemed to pound all the harder.

He was right there! Tall and straight but with a jaunty tilt to his perfectly sculpted shoulders, soft topaz skin smooth across his chiseled features, straight sapphire hair tied back in an intricate knot. A grin lifted his perfect mouth, as teasing and assured as she'd imagined.

Zell let out her breath in a huff of relief and smiled, for she only then realized that she'd fallen in love with a voice and it was a mercy he had the looks to make it worthwhile.

"Hi," she choked out.

"Zell Rampion, it is a great pleasure to meet face to face," he said with an unusual bow, hands clasped at his heart then raised to his forehead. "You are more beautiful than your songs made the sky."

Several things that needed to be said tangled with a laugh, and then finally Zell whispered, "Can I touch you?"

Solstice's eyebrows drew together, but he put out a hand to her, palm up, beckoning.

She reached and, hesitant, uncertain, almost afraid, laid her hand in his.

It did not pass through, but met flesh to warm, living, soft flesh.

Zell choked as tears slid from her control and down her cheeks. "You're real!"

"Of course." He smiled, even as concern filled his eyes. "I felt it was time we met and talked in person."

"It's been so long..." The words came out as a sob.

Her other hand found its way to his shoulder covered in the thick protective fabric of his uniform, then up to where his neck and jaw met, then down to the solid reality of his chest. Then she snatched it back and collapsed into tears.

This was *not* how she'd wanted to meet anyone for the first time.

He pulled her closer into an embrace as warm and real as she could hope for, as solid as the chair or table. And she didn't resist.

"This is embarrassing." Zell sniffled after a moment, laughing away the rest of her tears. "I'm sorry."

"Five years is a long time."

"Very." She pushed away, shrugging to straighten herself out and glanced through the airlock. "But I'm starting to think I had it good! Your whole vessel doesn't look much bigger than my control room."

"I don't need more. It's quick and responsive and provides

everything I could want. I'll show you, once you feel up to it. Are you all right now?"

Zell nodded.

Solstice drew a breath and straightened, his demeanor almost businesslike again, and gestured to the couch. "We should sit. As much as I would like to talk and—and simply get to know you in person, Zell, there is something we must discuss about the task you entrusted to me."

"Yes?" She had been on the point of sitting, but jumped up again. "The *Citadel*! Did you find it? Is it still quarantined? My parents—"

"I found it. Not without effort, for it was not where the coordinates said it should be. There was no quarantine in place, and when I asked the governors about it, they said that viruses and illnesses arise all the time but there has never been any on the dangerous scale you described."

"And..." Zell's voice was barely audible. "My parents?"

"There was great trouble in making them understand who I searched for," Solstice said, slowly, as if he chose his words with care. "They would not allow me to board. After much effort, I at last was able to ascertain that there were many scientists aboard and even some by the name of Rampion. They didn't seem able to tell me more. The one name they did recognize was," he paused, "Goth-L."

Zell sat down. "But—Goth-L is just a drone. Why would anyone know a *drone* by name?"

"They did not recognize it as a drone, but as a woman. Very wealthy, and much feared, and so old she seemed like a legend. But she disappeared some years ago, together with her cruiser."

"I don't understand. I remember—"

"You remember nothing, starchild!" The new voice rang out clear and strong and shivering with more than computer rage.

Zell leapt up and snatched at Solstice's hand, her pulse racing.

The Goth-L hologram took shape before them, straight and strong and clad in armor. She looked furious. "What's this? Conspiring with strangers and aliens behind my back? You'll regret this, girl!"

Solstice stepped forward, stern and commanding. "Are you the representative of Madame Gothel? As a Kings-son, I demand an explanation for—"

"Be silent! I'll deal with you later." Goth-L sneered. "And you'll get your explanation. Because you are nothing, girl, do you hear me? Nothing! Your 'parents' as you call them created you as an experiment, mixed your blood with substances found in the nebula, made you of stardust and DNA. And you! Always running away, always rebelling. You were supposed to provide the building blocks of a new me and instead, look at me! Nothing but a few bits left of my body, housed in a drone, only able to communicate through an enhanced hologram, and obliged to skitter about in space collecting stuff to build you and make you into what you were always meant to be—my starchild!"

Zell gasped and recoiled, wanting to fight back, to argue. Yet unable, for memories returned in harsh snatches. Memories of her parents by blood and deed, treating her as nothing more than a specimen, mistreating her as less than human. Of moments snatched away from them, in her room on the carpet, playing with books and junk that served as toys—then on catwalks high in the *Citadel*, making friends with other children. Of Gothel, an old, old woman with metal parts keeping her hideously alive. Of shouts and screams and her father's blood.

Why did she still think of him as her father? Why did she still love them?

The final memory, rewriting the old one—a drone with Gothel's voice, dragging her away with force that finally made her pass out from the pain.

"Leave her alone!" Solstice was shouting. "You have no right to her!"

"Right!" Goth-L screamed. "I have every right! She is mine, to do with as I please." A cruel smile marred her mouth. "And I please to cast her away."

An electric charge crackled through the ship as the airlock doors began to break.

"I have no need of her anymore—I have taken all I need and now even this pathetic light cruiser has outlived its usefulness. For now I have your errant-class vessel!" The hologram blinked and for an instant she looked as kindly as ever. "Don't fear, though, for I will have mercy. The starchild I cast away, and she will live very well on stardust and the milk of the nebula. The Kings-son, so reliant on the sensors and controls of his pretty little vessel, I cast into blindness and immobility, trapped on a crippled cruiser."

With a final shudder and earsplitting explosion, the vessel broke free from the *Tower*. Solstice collapsed, choking on the void. Zell reached for him, shrieking.

But before she could touch him, something seized her by the hair and pulled her free of the cruiser, just as the airlock slammed shut.

The Goth-L drone released her, then shot into the errant-class vessel, settling into the controls.

Something shimmered and wavered in the void. A portal!

And suddenly, Zell was alone in the vastness of space.

The green of the Forest Nebula was the only thing near. Green from her hair danced in the corners of her vision where tears didn't cloud it.

The *Tower* had been blown who-knew-where by the back-blast from the portal. She couldn't follow — she didn't know how!

Wait.

How was she alive?

And... green from her *hair*?

Zell twisted and would have gasped if there had been air. Her hair — miles and miles of it — flowed out from her as verdant and shining as the stuff of the nebula. It moved at her command; it moved *her* as she wished.

She was not human.

She was a starchild.

Sundered

Time had no meaning, at first.

After what seemed ages, Zell began to tell how time passed by looking at the way the stars shone and small particles moved.

And then time flowed in a steady dance of its own that she learned to move with, as months slipped by and then years.

Two years.

She found her way into the Forest Nebula and then began to know a joy unlike any she had ever suspected could exist. There were creatures there not unlike her, and yet very unlike. For she was still human in a strange way. She found she could eat of the strange gases and radiation, and her sleep was deeper and sweeter than ever before. And she learned to let go of the father and mother she had loved but who never loved her, of the life on the *Citadel* when she had been happy, of her old affection for Nanny and the cruiser and especially Goth-L.

But not of Solstice.

And she was miserable.

At first, she hoped to follow the *Tower* and find Solstice, or perhaps track down the errant-class vessel and bring Goth-L the vengeance she deserved. But she could not travel that fast.

The Ungel Station was far beyond her reach, and the *Citadel* even further.

So at last she gave up. Gradually she moved through the nebula and toward — something. This was her life now. Alone. Forever the only one of her kind, alone in the black.

There came a time when Zell found radio signals and something almost like sound waves, which she recognized by a feeling like intuition. Shaping them was different than using breath and vocal cords; but after much trying, she soon began to work them into song and send them out again, beautiful and new. This brought her joy.

But in a way, it served to highlight the loneliness. She was the only one to hear them and feel them. The other creatures like her were yet more unlike her in that they either noticed and fled from the songs or did not notice at all.

So, she created songs for herself, and herself alone.

This was all her life now.

~~~~~

A new radio wave.

Zell caught it and regarded it from several angles. These things were everywhere once she knew how to look for them, but they weren't always usable at first without a little tweaking.

She twisted and turned it and —

Caught her hand away as her auditory nerve recognized something about it.

A voice?

Solstice's voice?

Impossible.

But what if...?

Swiftly, Zell shaped the radio wave into a snatch of song like she used to sing in the old days, and then sent it back in the direction it came.

She had not long to wait.

Some weeks later, something broke the black, coming toward her. The light cruiser! Hobbling and slow, but her old *Tower*!

With an odd tightness in her throat, Zell rushed toward it, meeting it partway. Her hair wrapped around it as she found the port screens and tried to peer inside. The shielding wouldn't allow it.

The airlock!

Zell found the airlock and commanded her hair to reach within and manipulate the controls in the old way.

It opened, rusty and broken, and she slipped inside.

Only then did the horror of what she might find hit her. What if he was dead? What if—

"Zell?"

The sound filled her ears and her head as she dropped to the deck in the sudden drag of artificial gravity, coughing from oxygen her lungs had grown accustomed to doing without.

"Zell!" Warm hands found her, pulled her up, arms wrapped around her in a frenzied embrace. "I can't believe it! It's you—it's really you! You survived! When I heard your songs, I couldn't believe it; but I followed them anyway—there was nothing else. I couldn't see anything else—the ship couldn't—But here you are! Alive! Against all hope!"

"Solstice." She found her voice, rough and harsh after so long. "Solstice, dear one... Are you well?"

"I am now. With you here, I have all I would ever need."

She let him pull her up and her hair lifted her until their lips met in a kiss that seemed to set everything right. Except everything *wasn't* right.

"Nevertheless," she laughed a little, "I *can* fix this ship now!"

Zell stepped into the control room, now littered and dirty, and closed her eyes. She commanded her hair into every part of the broken ship, repairing and strengthening. The systems buzzed and came alive.

"Navigations," Solstice said, close beside her, awe in his voice. "Sensors. Fuel. Directional control... All systems are online! I can't believe it."

"I've learned many things. Can you get us anywhere now?"

He dropped into the pilot's seat and manipulated a few controls. "Yes. Star system, not far from here. It should only take... three years or so."

A laugh burst from Zell, clear and strong as if she had had the use of laughter this whole time. "Three years? What's that now that we have found each other again!"

Solstice grinned up at her, then pulled her down into his arms again so their tears mingled as they kissed.

Joined

They hadn't really finished kissing when an alarm buzzed. Solstice bumped the button with his elbow.

Static, then: "Kings-son Solstice? Kings-son Solstice — is that you? Please respond."

"Yes?" He jerked upright and leaned close to the coms. "Who is this?"

"Solstice! It is good to hear your voice. This is Kings-son Commander Vrast. You were nearly given up for dead, until a patrol ship picked up your errant-class along with a vicious cyborg. We made her talk. She told where to look for you, but we wouldn't have found you if it hadn't been for that song beacon you sent out. Send coordinates and we'll pick you up."

Zell punched the button, then turned back to look deep into Solstice's eyes, laughing for joy like that which she had found in making the songs but so full and whole it was beyond mere happiness.

"Well," he said. "How would you like to visit my world, Zell Rampion?"

END

Deserted
Cortney Manning

Heat pressed against the bare skin of my back and arms like a shroud.

I tried to pry my eyes open, but specks of sand cut with every blink. At first, only darkness met my gaze. Panic thudded from my chest into my overheated veins until I realized the shadow of a massive rock darkened my face.

Painfully, I lifted one hand to finger the scarred outcropping of black and gray gneiss. The muscles in my arm tingled in protest.

How long have I been here?

I rolled onto my back in a field of sand and squinted against the sun's angry glare.

And where is here?

Shoving against the shifting sand, I forced myself to sit. Nausea rolled through my stomach, and I realized my throat felt impossibly dry. I needed water, yet nothing but yellow sand and mounds of rock met my hungry gaze.

Searing heat pressed against my feet, and I pulled them closer, into the shrinking shade of the outcropping at my side.

"H-hello?" I croaked, my voice impossibly small and broken in the expansive sea of sand.

I wrapped my arms around my knees, hugging them close and wondering if I had any tears within me to cry. A gust of wind blasted dust across my vision, and I tilted my face back toward the sky.

Above me, the heavens were bluer than a robin's egg, brushed with the smallest tufts of pure-white clouds.

There was more in this world than sand and heat.

Shards of memory spun across my mind, centered on a square of blue sky.

"More, child. I expect more the next time I return, or there will be consequences," growls my captor.

I nod, forcing myself to focus on the cerulean expanse outlined by my windowframe of stone. Breathing in and breathing out, I envision the world beneath that sky, a world I've never seen.

My nails dug into my palms, and I struggled upward on unsteady feet. The world awaited me now.

Sunlight beat against my honey-toned skin as I rose above the outcropping's shrinking shadow. My head felt impossibly light, and uneven strands of hair brushed my jaw.

The tears I'd wondered if I possessed sprang unbidden to my eyes, but I blinked them back, desperate to conserve the little water I had within me.

Slowly, I lifted a hand to my shorn hair and choked back a sob at the overwhelming wave of loss that washed against me.

I took a step but staggered, completely off-balance. A stab of pain lanced through my skull, and I felt dried blood when I touched the back of my head with my hand.

A glance back at the outcropping revealed a matching red-brown stain.

I suppose that's why I don't know who I am... I don't know who I am?

Panic fluttered through my stomach, and dizziness gnawed at my brain. I stretched my arms outward for balance, gritted my teeth, and inched my way across the desert sand, striving to ignore the empty void in my mind. With each step, the burning heat against my feet grew fainter, leaving nothing but numbness in my joints and skin.

Somewhere beyond this endless expanse of yellow-brown dust, a wide-open world waited for me. I had only to reach it.

Time passed, I'm certain. The shadow at my feet shrank and grew again, but the dunes I struggled to climb did not end.

My tongue felt large and useless in my grime-filled mouth. The gray-brown rags cast around my body provided little protection against the sun's oppressive waves. Countless times I stumbled, collapsing to my knees in the always shifting sand.

Just as often, I turned my gaze to the azure heavens, clinging to their promise of a distant world like a lifeline in a raging sea.

Gradually I became aware of a change in the sky's tint. From sapphire to indigo it shifted, and, at my back, the sun's weight felt lighter. For a moment I paused, turning back to observe its brilliant defeat, sinking beyond the horizon and slashing the sky with vivid hues of mustard, rust, and ruby, like streaks of blood staining the wide expanse of a wall.

My knees quivered, and a shiver racked my shoulders. Without the sun's harsh glare, what kind of world would I face now?

A long pair of shadows circled across the sands at my feet. I craned my neck around to find the source of the movement. High above and to the west, I spied two large creatures, their wings flapping lazily against the faintest drafts of wind. Biting down the panic that soured my mouth, I turned back to the east and forced my feet onward, even faster than before.

As the sun disappeared, so did the heat. Its presence was leached from the desert as quickly as the light, and a bitter chill crept into my bones.

All at once, I could not shake the feeling that I was being watched. The gray light of dusk cast deep shadows, and my gaze flitted nervously between drifting sands and mounds of rock.

I crept slowly past a dark knoll. The hair on my neck stood on end, and the faint sound of breathing met my ears.

A dry scream escaped my throat, and I leapt to the side as a maned beast pounced forward. Heart thudding, I scrambled up the side of the outcropping. A blood-curdling roar scraped against my ears, and my hands shook as I grappled for purchase on the stone.

Wind rushed past my frame, swishing my short hair and ragged clothes around my face and body. I flinched, awaiting the searing pain of fangs and claws ripping into my flesh.

The impact never came.

Instead, I heard an animal's shriek and feathers pounding against the air.

Loosening my tensed muscles, I peered over my shoulder.

Two beasts circled each other on the sand, their heads level with my bare feet, a full man's height above the ground.

One, its head framed in a brown mane, snarled, revealing sharpened fangs. My skin tingled at the thought of those teeth ripping me open. I'd heard of such beasts before: a lion, youthful, wild, and as hungry as me.

The other stood between the hunter and me. Gold-white wings spread ten feet or more out from its back, and its silken tail brushed against my heels. Its red-gold hackles rose, and a deep growl emanated from its throat.

I swallowed and shifted as high as I could on the outcropping of rock.

Then the lion pounced, and the creatures moved too quickly for my eyes to follow. Feathers, fur, and dust flashed through the air, and growls and grunts crashed against my ears.

Claws slashed against the winged creature's muzzle, and it released an agonized howl.

"No," I gasped.

Then another form swooped down from the sky, as dark and silent as a shadow. Black fur and feathers pounded into the lion's side, shoving it several feet backward.

I held my breath as the lion spun around, sides heaving with exertion. For a moment, I thought he would attack again, but the black beast spread out its wings, inching closer.

At last, the lion surrendered, slinking back into the growing night.

Then the winged creature spun around. I froze, but it ignored me, approaching its white-gold companion instead. The lighter beast had dropped to the sand, breathing heavily.

A faint whimper drifted up to my ears, tugging at an inexplicable joy deep within my chest.

The black beast bent downward and licked the claw marks on its companion's muzzle. Then it spun back, and its silver eyes pierced my soul.

I knew those eyes.

"Dusk?" I whispered.

The creature's wings fluttered gently, and I carefully slipped down from my rocky sanctuary.

A memory tickled the back of my mind, and I frowned, squinting at the two forms in the sand below. I knew these beasts. They were...

I rubbed my brow the moment my feet touched the ground and struggled against the empty expanse within my mind.

They were... sky-hounds.

Dusk released a nervous whine and his massive head nudged my hand. Sucking a breath in between my teeth, I opened my palm, slowly rubbing my fingers against his smooth fur.

Somehow, I knew I had nothing to fear from this beast. He was mine, and I was his. We had chosen each other long ago.

And I had chosen Dawn as well.

I rushed to her side where she lay in the sand with blood coating her snout.

"Oh," I whispered, gingerly reaching for her face. Sorrow and regret welled within me, and I longed to help her as she had helped me against the lion.

The moment my fingers touched her fur, a familiar sensation tingled across my skin. I almost drew back, but curiosity and instinct held my hand in place, and I began to hum.

The tune was simple but soothing, and with every note, the tingle in my hands grew into a pulse. Blue-black fog curled between my fingers and washed against her wound. Before my eyes, the claw marks shrank and disappeared until not a scratch remained.

I blinked, unable to comprehend the sight, but Dawn rolled up from her side and knocked against me, covering my face in wet kisses. Giddy laughter rocked my frame, and I wrapped my arms around her golden neck.

"My precious girl," I murmured as other fragments of memory landed in my mind like pieces of a broken jug.

"More, child! I need more," my tormentor demands.

My fingers and arms ache with exertion as I bend over the table full of jars, humming all the while to keep my mind off the pain.

The owner of the voice drops a rough and heavy hand on the top of my head, pressing my face closer to the jars where my blue-black magic pools.

"No!" I jerked my head backward and fell against Dusk. His snout gently snuffled against the short strands of my hair. "Who am I?" I moaned, gazing between my hands and the sky-hounds beside me.

Their inquisitive stares provided no answer.

I pushed myself up from the sand and stood, my head level with their wings. Instinctively I reached backward, rubbing a pair of scars on my own back.

Something had been taken from me years ago, along with my freedom. Something more than a head-full of hair.

I shook my head, focusing on the present for I knew I could not unravel my past. A shiver wracked my limbs, and I leaned into the heat of Dusk's long fur. Something knocked against my elbow, and I noticed a leather satchel beneath his wings.

A growl rattled my stomach, and I wondered if any food could be found inside. My fingers trembled as I unhooked its clasp and peered within the bag.

Something golden glinted there.

A pair of sky-hound pups roll over the worn and patched fabric of my skirt. "Do you like them?"

I look up from Dusk and Dawn's antics into the bluest eyes I have ever seen, eyes that remind me of the sky.

"Like them?" I whisper reverently. "Aurelius, I love them!"

A brilliant smile reveals his white teeth and simple pleasure. A blush heats my cheeks, and I stare back down at the creatures in my lap. Dawn stands on my knee, sniffing the air until Dusk pounces on her from behind.

Both Aurelius and I reach out to catch them, and our hands touch.

I've known the feeling of magic pulsing through my fingertips for as long as I can remember. It's thrilling but draining at the same time, and beneath my mistress's watchful eye, it can be painful, too.

But this feeling, this tingling in my skin, is unlike anything I've felt before.

And Aurelius feels it, too; I'm certain. It's like a magnetic pull between his skin and mine. The blue-black aura of my magic dances outward, twining around the golden light that emanates from him.

I blink up at his face, suddenly quite near to mine. His breath warms my skin, and his eyes are more brilliant than the skies beyond my window.

That is when I realize he would give me the world if I let him.

The golden feathers of his wings brush my arm, wings like the ones I had been denied. I draw backward, shame curdling in my gut.

"Wait!"

I angle my body away from him, but he sets the two sky-hounds aside to kneel beside me.

"You are just as much a Fee as I am, darling."

I flinch at the word of endearment, knowing I do not deserve it. "I am a slave, Aurelius, and it's time you realize that and stop wasting so many hours in this forsaken tower."

His hand cups my cheek, and I cannot bring myself to pull away.

"How can my time be wasted when I am with you?" His gentle touch ignites the hope within me that I dare not cherish: the hope that I might one day be the Fee he sees me as instead of the slave I am, trapped within my mistress's lonely tower.

"Here, I have something for you."

My eyes widen as he draws the golden chain of a necklace over his head. A pendant of twisted gold wires dances at the end of its length. I shake my head vigorously.

"You've already given me so much."

His gilded curls bob in the sunlight when he chuckles. "I only wish I could give you more." Gently, his fingers unclasp the necklace and slip it beneath the long and heavy braids of my blue-black hair. The orb-shaped pendant rests warmly against my chest, holding all the power of his love, a love I scarcely dare to trust.

I staggered back from the satchel and sank to the cold sand, willing the spinning of my head to stop. Then I drew Aurelius's necklace from the bag.

An ache expanded in my chest at the realization that, for a time, I had not been alone, yet now – now I was.

A gentle whine sounded in Dawn's throat, and I glanced between her and the chain in my hand. Determination welled in my breast.

No, I was not alone. Dawn and Dusk were with me now, and this Aurelius was out there somewhere. He had to be.

The metal in my palm heated beneath my grip, and my breaths came quicker as I focused on the pendant, struggling to remember where to find the Fee who had given me such treasure.

Despite the chill air, beads of sweat formed on my brow. A faint wind fluttered the hair at my neck and swung the pendant before my eyes. All at once, I felt the familiar prick of magic escaping my fingers, spooling loose a tendril of blue-black fog that wrapped around the chain, spinning the pendant round and round until more magic spilled down: an intertwined thread of black and gold.

My heart thudded as I recognized the color of Aurelius's magic reacting to mine. My mind focused on him. His deep blue eyes. The way one side of his mouth always lifted higher when he smiled. His deep voice. The feel of his warm palm touching mine.

The thread of gold and black shot forward like a star shooting across the night sky, blazing a path through the dimly lit desert ahead. I tightened my grip on the chain and the magic pulsing through it until I felt a connection, distant, but solid. A magnetic tug.

"I'm coming Aurelius."

My feet broke into a desperate sprint across the sand, and I ignored the pain of unseen rocks pounding against my toes. At first, I noticed nothing, not even the full moon overhead.

But then my ears recognized the sound of paws padding beside me to the left and the right. Despite my sudden departure, Dawn and Dusk had loyally remained at my side, their wings dragging through the sand behind them.

Wings.

At once, I stopped and spun toward Dusk. The moon framed his head and lit the curiosity in his silver eyes.

"I have no wings." I gestured toward my bare back, wondering how much the creature understood. "Can you carry me? Bring me to Aurelius?"

At the familiar name, Dusk spread out his wings, and I crept around them before climbing on the sky-hound's back. His fur felt softer than silk against my legs, and I leaned my body close to his head and gripped his neck.

"I'm ready," I whispered, and he understood.

Dust swooshed into the air around us as his massive wings flapped soundly. For a moment, I knew nothing but the rush of air roaring against my ears.

Then we were flying high above the desert floor.

I had expected to be afraid, soaring so high above the earth, but I leaned back, marveling at the motion I felt. Dawn swooped beside us, and I threw back my head to stare at the stars.

My mistress's tower had been high, but this… flight was freedom.

After a moment, I focused back on the pendant in my grip. The black and gold thread of magic still tugged at my hand. Dusk seemed to sense the magic, too, for his flight carried us directly in its trail.

Beneath us, our shadows sped across countless dunes like fish through an ocean. Several times, I caught my head nodding with exhaustion, but I clung tighter to Dusk, for no one could survive a fall from such heights.

Gradually, the sky began to lighten again, and more outcroppings broke the surface of the desert sands. As the sun broke across the horizon, I realized that mountains cut across the sky, blocking portions of the glorious sunrise with their own majestic proportions.

The sun's light painted the landscape purple and pink as we approached the mountains, and I shivered at the sight of snow capping their heights. However, Dusk and Dawn flew between the peaks, low enough to avoid the worst of the chill but high enough to pass though the stony range.

On the other side of the mountains, forests covered the rocky slopes, and after a lush plateau, a massive ocean reflected the fiery glow of the rising sun.

Beneath me, the flapping of Dusk's wings seemed to slow, and his breath came in heavy pants.

I leaned close to his ear and called out, "Let's find a place to land."

Again, Dusk seemed to understand my words, and we glided downward. Blinking against the brilliant sunlight, I took in the plateau beneath us.

Much of it was green and lush: fields laced with silver-blue streams and rivers. However, just ahead, a city rose. Orange-brown huts and villas were neatly arranged and topped with open balconies, leafy vines, and heavily scented tropical flowers.

Dusk dropped to the hard-packed clay of a road at the outskirts of a market with multileveled wooden booths and colorful canopies. I slid off Dusk's back, and Dawn dipped to the ground beside us. My legs quivered beneath my weight, and I stumbled with my sky-hounds toward a square pool of water, sinking my face to its cool surface in my eagerness to quench my thirst.

After dunking my head in the water, I cupped my hands and shoveled more in my mouth, not caring that Dusk and Dawn slurped from the same pool to my left.

Something struck my bare foot, and I swiveled around, water glistening as sharply as diamonds as it dripped from my face.

"The pool's for the sheep, slave." My hand jerked instinctively to the twin scars on my back as a large form loomed over me, its voice deep and raspy.

Mistress Ornelia, my mind screamed as I stared at the ogre who had kicked me. Her skin was ashen and cracked like stone, but her clothing was wool, not silk, like that of the ogre who had owned my all my life.

This ogre growled and stomped around me, but I remained frozen for several moments, struggling to convince myself that Mistress Ornelia was not nearby.

Mistress Ornelia. My heart thudded with memories of her harsh voice, sharp nails, and heavy hands. My nostrils could nearly perceive the stench of her breath, hot at my neck as I poured all my magic and strength into the jars and potions she sold.

"Attention. *Attention!*" The voice of a loud crier filled the air, dragging me away from my thoughts and back to the market beyond the pool. Humans and ogres paused beside their booths, and several Fee hovered in the air at the edge of raised platforms. I gazed at their brown and tan feathers, wishing I could join them in the sky above.

"A message from the king!" My head swiveled toward the booming voice, and I saw a brilliant pair of orange wings and a blue uniform covering the crier's warm brown skin. "Our dear prince is missing, and the king will pay a handsome reward for anyone with news that aids in the recovery of Prince Aurelius."

My heart stuttered in my chest, and I staggered to my feet. "Aurelius," I whispered, glancing desperately around me. I reached for the arm of a human woman. "Did he say Aurelius?"

A look of disgust crossed the woman's features, and she jerked her arm from my grip. "Of course – that *is* the prince's name."

I gripped the chain in my hand more tightly, struggling to understand. Around me, I heard the voices of others muttering in shock and worry.

"The prince is missing?"

"What will we do without our prince?"

"Where can Aurelius be?"

"Who has seen him?"

"I have." The words escaped my mouth without a thought, and I felt a number of eyes turn toward me.

"*You* have seen the prince?" Disbelief dripped in the man's statement, and I shrank back toward the pool, clutching my arms around my gut. The gold pendant bounced against my hip.

"Y-yes."

"Then where is he?" the woman with him demanded, crossing her arms.

"Run!" Aurelius yells, and I duck as a branch of thorns swings toward us. His wing slams against me, shoving me to safety and lifting him upward.

Ornelia's cackle fills my ears as several thorny vines shoot toward him.

The sound of shattering pottery meets my ears, and I shudder at the sight of my repurposed magic filling the tower like a black fog. I cough at the stench of the herbs Ornelia always blends in with my magic.

She stands at the other end of the tower room, a hideous smirk twisting her gray skin.

"You thought you could escape me and my tower? Foolish child."

She waves her hands, and the black fog spirals around her, solidifying into more thorny branches that grow and writhe around the room. Several thorny vines wrap around Aurelius above me, tightening around his limbs no matter how he struggles.

"Let him go," I cry, rushing toward my mistress, fists raised.

Then her vines are around my wrists and long hair, slinging me backward.

"Why should I, slave? He is my prisoner now, too, just as much as you are."

"I am no one's prisoner, Ornelia, and she is not your slave, not anymore."

I cringe at Aurelius's words, wishing he would escape instead of defying the powerful ogre for my sake.

Harsh laughter scrapes against my ears, making me flinch.

"And by whose authority do you speak, Fee?" Ornelia treads along the edge of the room, her gaze taunting and terrible. "These are my *thorns that bind you."*

Gold light emanates from Aurelius's skin. "I am Aurelius, prince of Feeia."

"A prince?" Ornelia cast a speculative glance at me. "I'm shocked that my slave has garnered such regal attention, yet prince though you may be, you are just as trapped as her. I could sell you for quite a ransom, but I still have no reason to release my slave."

I blink as brilliant light shoots out from Aurelius's form. "You do not have the power to keep me here, ogre."

Then Ornelia's arm is around my waist, and I feel a cold stone knife pressed against my throat. Above us, the vines have fallen back from Aurelius, but he stops mid-dive at the sight of her grip on me.

"Yet I have the power to take her life."

"Let her go."

"Why should I?" Ornelia's saliva sprays against my cheek.

Aurelius folds his wings and sinks to the floor before us. "Because I will take her place."

"No," I whimper, not daring to shake my head with the knife still pressed to my throat.

"Let her go, alive and unharmed, and I will take her place as your prisoner."

I feel Ornelia's solid chest against my back. She holds her breath, as though deep in thought, while I meet Aurelius's cerulean gaze, begging him with my eyes to change his mind.

Instead, he extends his arms, magic dimmed, allowing Ornelia's vines to twine around him once more.

"Very well. I will remove your wings as I did hers, and you will be my slave." Ornelia motions for her thorns to tighten around Aurelius, and then she drops her hold on me.

"Aurelius!" I cry, reaching for him.

"Not so fast." Ornelia grips my braids, stopping me short. "I'll be needing a bit more of your magic first."

I hear the slice of her knife before I realize what is happening. Suddenly my head feels lighter than it has in years, and short hair brushes against my chin. I gasp at the shock and the loss of a part of me that has grown with every year of torture and every session of pouring out my magic for her use.

A growl sounds beyond me. Ornelia flings the braids before her, releasing the black fog of my magic like a shield against Aurelius's golden light that pulses forward again.

"You said you would not harm her!"

"I said I would send her away, and now, I shall." The fog emanating from my shorn braids thickens, and my ears pop. I see a row of thorns slicing at Aurelius's beautiful eyes. Then I feel my own body propelling through empty space, first frigid then hot, until something strikes my head, and the world turns black.

"He's in the tower," I whispered to the market crowd. "Ornelia's tower."

"She's mad," a Fee scoffed above me.

The ogre shepherdess from before poked my back with a jagged fingernail. "What do you expect from a wingless Fee?"

"A slave?" The human woman gasped, and the man with her tugged her quickly away, as if I could contaminate her with my shame.

The Fee from above landed in the dirt behind me, and I had to turn to meet his eyes. He was young and wore a horrified expression on his face.

"I've heard of Fee who are enslaved, who were desperate enough to sell their wings and freedom to serve another, but I've never actually *seen* something so pitiful myself before."

A curious Fee child leaned forward, eager to gaze at me, but her mother dragged her quickly away. I felt the eyes of many gawking at me, and I instinctively swiveled my wingless back toward the pool of water.

"What made you give up your wings?" Aurelius asks, his voice softer than the clouds drifting across the starry sky outside my window. Still, my body tenses, and I dig my nails into the windowsill we lean against.

"You don't have to tell me," he murmurs.

I squeeze my eyes tight against the tears that form. How can he always be so understanding and kind to a slave like me? "I didn't give them up. They were taken from me after my parents struck a deal with Ornelia. My mother was ill and needed healing. My father loved her deeply and wanted her well more than he wanted anything else in the world, even more than a child."

Aurelius's warm hand presses against mine, and I force myself not to pull away. "I'm sorry."

"Don't be." I force a grim laugh. "After all, I'm not completely unwanted. Ornelia has made quite a success of her potion business with the extra boost my magic provides"

I do not need to open my eyes to feel Aurelius's intense stare, the one he wears when he is solving a puzzle or inventing intricate metal-works in his mind. I touch the necklace he gifted me, the one with the carefully twisted strands of gold that he wove together himself. "Yet she treats you so cruelly. You deserve more than that."

I drop the necklace, feeling it thud hollowly against my chest. "I deserve nothing, Aurelius. I am a slave."

"Look at me." His calloused fingers press into my arms, and I blink my eyes open to find myself face to face with his perfect features. I begin to turn my head away, but he presses his brow to mine, and I cannot tear my gaze from his cerulean eyes, eyes that reflect the multitude of stars above. "Everyone deserves love."

My heart thudded heavily against my chest, and my hand reached back to catch against the edge of the pool as I sank onto the tile. Dawn's wet nose nudged my elbow, and I glanced around me. The staring crowd had departed, concerned with more pressing worries than an addled slave. After all, Prince Aurelius was missing.

Gritting my teeth, I lifted his necklace in my hand once more, forcing every ounce of my magic into its chain. Again, the black thread inched downward, teasing out the gold of Aurelius's magic built into his creation.

A prince, an artist, and an inventor.

A hopeless smile tugged at my lips. I did not deserve him.

Nor did he deserve my fate. My fingers tightened on the chain, and the gold and black thread of magic shot out once more, delineating my path.

My head swiveled from side to side, but no one else seemed to perceive the magic. This was my journey to make, and I doubted anyone else would follow.

"Except for you." I smiled down at my sky-hounds. Already, Dusk and Dawn had risen from the packed dirt to stand eagerly at my feet. This time I gestured to Dawn and climbed atop her back. Within moments, we were in the sky again, flying north.

We passed high above the city. Many other Fee flitted about from structure to structure, going about their lives. At the heart of the city rose the palace. Its crystalline walls reflected the sun and sky in a brilliant glare that I could not bring myself to gaze upon for long.

Beyond the palace were more structures – homes, gardens, bathhouses, and theatres. A part of me longed to explore this world I had never seen, but then guilt tightened around my frame like a noose. While I flew free above this lovely city, Aurelius himself was trapped in my mistress's tower.

My mind whirled with dark possibilities. Was he still alive? The last I saw, he and Ornelia had been engaged in a battle of light and darkness, his golden magic against the black fog of my usurped magic. If she had defeated him, then had she also clipped his beautiful wings?

Stinging wind drew moisture to my eyes, and I struggled against my anxious fears. I could not predict the unknown. All I could do was hope for the best and urge Dawn onward, toward my prison.

I noticed its shadow before I saw the tower itself with its rusty bricks and sloping roof.

Massive thorns twined around the structure, making it impossible for Dawn to approach my little window.

After circling several times, we landed at the base instead. Powerful scents filled the air – the herbs Ornelia always added to her jars and something else, like lightning from a storm. Glancing at the clear skies, I shivered, unsure what I would find in my tower. I found Ornelia's door easily – the one she used to enter the looming tower every time she visited. The door had always been bolted on the outside with a lock, a bar, and an ogre charm, but now it stood open, revealing a dark passage within.

Green grass bent beneath my bare feet as I stepped closer, heart pounding. Nothing else stirred, and not even birdsong met my ears. I squinted inside but could see very little. At last, I lifted my foot and passed over the threshold.

Creaking sounded behind me, and Dusk barked as the thorns near the door shot forward, twining across the doorway and blocking my skyhounds' path. My blood felt cold in my veins as I realized I would not be able to escape the same way I had entered.

Once more, I was trapped in my tower.

Sweat formed on my face, and my pulse pounded, but I forced myself to breathe as evenly as possible. It did not matter if the exit was blocked. I had come to find Aurelius; it did not matter what became of me.

Cautiously, I felt my way forward in the darkness. Gradually, my eyes adjusted to the lack of light, and I made out the hoist Ornelia used to draw herself from the base of the tower to my chambers above. Bracing my feet against its wooden planks, I hefted the rope and began drawing myself upward.

My progress was slow. Sweat dripped down the twin scars on my back and pooled on the few strips of fabric wound around my body. My arms ached, and my palms burned. Several times, my grip slipped, and I feared I would plummet back to the base of the tower.

I forced my hands to keep moving until I noticed the pain no more. I focused on the walls around me instead of glancing up or down.

At last, I reached my chamber.

Shorn hair and broken thorns lay scattered on the wooden floor.

My eyes took in the signs of struggle – toppled tables and magic-scarred floors – but Ornelia and Aurelius were not in sight.

"Aurelius?" I called, my voice weak in the empty room.

A blast rocked the tower, and a cloud of dust, both black and gold, burst from the loft above.

I wiped my sweaty palms on the fabric at my hips before slipping Aurelius's necklace back over my head and stepping forward.

Instantly, the thorns and hair at my feet sprang to life. Like snakes, they slithered forward to wrap around my feet.

I kicked back and tried to leap above them, but they only grew, digging into my skin. A cry of pain escaped my lips as a thorn scraped across my back and wrapped tightly around my arms. I felt blood drip down my skin.

The hair I had missed bound me in place, and I could not move without thorns stabbing into my flesh.

For some time, I struggled anyway, but every twist and turn served only to tighten my bonds and deepen my wounds.

I was trapped.

Alone in my tower again.

A sob nearly escaped my lips, but I forced it down as I had every night for years after I had realized I could not escape my prison.

I was a slave.

It was my fate to live and die in this cell.

Slave.

"I'm a slave, Aurelius!" I tear myself from his embrace and pull back the braids of my hair to reveal the long scars on my back where silver wings once grew. "Don't you understand? I deserve nothing, least of all your love."

"But it is my love, and I can give it where I choose."

Tears prick my eyes at his declaration. One of his hands cups my elbow, and the other gently lifts my chin until I stare into his eyes again.

"Do you believe me when I tell you I love you?"

I swallow, then bob my head in a small nod.

"And do you care about me?"

His face is quite close now, and I feel his warm breath on my skin. My gaze darts desperately between his eyes. I long to lie, but I cannot. Instead, I nod again. His hand on my arm inches upward across my skin, and then his touch twines around my waist, warming me, supporting me.

"Then please don't push me away."

"I don't want to," I murmur, and my gaze darts down to his lips. My heart thuds, and his breaths come faster. His mouth is just a breath from mine. My lashes flutter downward of their own accord.

Then my hand reaches up to splay across his chest. "This is not right, Aurelius. You could have anyone in the world. I am no one."

"You, Persinette, are the Fee I choose to love."

My eyelids flung open, and my chest heaved against my restraints.

Persinette. That was my name.

I was someone.

My fingers tightened into fists.

Ornelia had robbed me of my childhood, my home, and my freedom, but Aurelius had taught me one thing I could never let myself forget again.

I could be more than a slave in a tower.

Another crash sounded above, and I felt the throb of magic pounding in my veins. I began humming, focusing on nothing but the power within me, my power as a Fee. Like a flame, I fanned the magic until it ignited like an inferno. At once, the thorny vines on my wrists snapped, and I felt the dead strands of hair slip back down to the ground.

I moved forward, ready to climb to the loft, but then I noticed: the ladder had been blasted into splinters during the battle.

I bit my lip and stared around me as more blasts of magic surged from above. A faint glint in the corner caught my eye. It was the spot where Aurelius and I had stood, just before Ornelia returned.

Aurelius's lips press against mine gently, and my magic thrums in my veins. For a moment, I still hesitate, but then I throw my arms about his neck and kiss him soundly in return.

"Persy," he whispers after a time, pressing his brow against mine. I meet his gaze, my breathing light and fast.

"Yes?"

"I have something for you, a way to leave this tower."

Part of my mind urges me to turn away, to rush up to my loft and forget his promises and the hope they bring. But I refuse to remain a slave any longer. "What is it?" I ask.

He smiles, one side of his mouth lifting higher than the other, and then he draws back to dig in his satchel. I sway a little, unbalanced in the wake of his embrace.

"Here." Starlight and candle flame glint off the silver wires. Like the necklace he gave me and all his other work, the metal threads interlace and twine together to form a strong and intricate design.

"Are those..." my jaw drops, and I can barely speak, but I force myself to finish, "wings?"

He nods, and I feel his cerulean gaze on me as I lift my fingers to carefully touch the delicate frame.

"How... how do they work?"

His grin widens, and he turns the silver wires so I can see a simple harness of threaded metal. "You slip your arms through here, and fasten it there, and then you can summon your magic to power them."

"Do you really think it will work?"

He places the wings in my hands.

"There's only one way to find out."

I draw the metal frame closer when a roar sounds from the hoist, and I know we have not been careful enough.

Mistress Ornelia has found us.

I bent over the metal frame and lifted it from the floor. Despite having been ripped from my hands by thorns and knocked to the ground, they seem completely undamaged. After a steadying breath, I slipped my arms into the harness, just as Aurelius had showed me. The fit was perfect. He truly had made them just for me.

The thought sent a frisson of heat from my heart into my veins, and I focused it into my magic. Blue-black fog pooled around me, billowing outward. In the strength of my outpouring of magic, I felt my shortened hair grow several inches, as it sometimes had when summoning large quantities of magic for Ornelia's jars.

This time, I would use my own strength instead of pouring it away. I gestured with my fingers toward my wings, and the cloud of magic floated backward and then forward until the wings began pumping, and I was rising, several feet above the floor.

For a moment, I lost focus and dipped lower, but I steadied myself quickly and rose to the level of the loft.

There I saw both Aurelius and Ornelia, locked in a stalemate. Her thorny vines twined around them both, while several golden threads of light held her back from Aurelius's bloodied face.

I bit back a horrified sob at the sight. Where his cerulean eyes had been, I saw only cuts and blood, but in all this time, he had not surrendered. Blood and sweat plastered his shirt to his chest, and the golden feathers of his wings pounded through the air, forcing back Ornelia's thorns.

Yet one thin vine slithered across the floor toward Aurelius's feet like a snake.

"Look out!" I cried.

"Persy?" The sight of Aurelius's injured face swiveling toward me nearly broke my heart before the vine snapped around his ankle, pinning him with thorns.

"Stay back, child," Ornelia growled. "This quarrel is between me and him. I let you go, so *go*. He is my prize. You have no power here."

"But I do," I murmured, watching the blue-black threads of magic feeding her thorns. For years, Ornelia had controlled me and my magic, but Aurelius had swept into my life and uncovered a secret Ornelia had not wanted me to learn. "I may not have my wings, but I am more than a slave. I am a Fee, and I have the freedom to choose love over fear."

I lifted my hands and gestured toward the magic fueling her thorns. At first it resisted. I felt the enchantments and enhancements she had worked in with her herbs and incantations.

But at its core, this magic was *mine*, and I intended to reclaim it. I felt its roots and branches, even the thorns digging into Aurelius's veins.

And he felt it, too, I was certain. His golden magic surged forward, meeting mine and twining with it. Together, we ripped apart the vines and thorns. Like sawdust, they floated away.

"No!" Ornelia shouted, stumbling after the fading thorns. In her haste, she tripped, plunging from the loft onto the thorns in the tower room below. A blast of gold and black rocked through the tower, and I felt it crumbling.

Then Aurelius's arms were around me, and we were flying amid a rain of shingles and dust.

When I opened my eyes again, the tower had crumbled, taking Mistress Ornelia with it in its fall.

We did not speak. I simply felt my wings in the air, and Aurelius's golden warmth.

Dusk and Dawn barked below, and we gradually drifted down to the grass beside them.

Though my feet touched the ground again, I did not release my hold on Aurelius's strong arms.

"Is it over?" I whispered, not daring to look him in the face.

"It is."

I released a shaky breath. "Thank you, for everything."

"And thank you for coming back." His palm pressed lightly on my jaw, tilting my head back. I swallowed, forcing myself to gaze on his wounds.

I gasped.

"Your eyes–"

"Your magic healed me." His cerulean stare was only intensified by the faint lines of scars where his wounds had been just moments before. "Your magic has always been powerful, Persy, that's why Ornelia was so desperate to keep you here as her slave and as her source of income."

My head turned toward the collapsed structure of the tower, and I shivered, unsure how to feel. "But now she's gone."

Aurelius's hands rubbed against my bare arms, warming me. "You're free."

I shook my head, scarcely believing.

"What will I do now?" I gazed at the crumbled remains of the tower that had been both home and prison all my life. "Where will I go?"

"Come with me," Aurelius offered.

My mind scrambled back to the city and its marketplace where the people had mocked me. Did I dare return?

I turned slowly, staring first at the ruins and then at my love, his cerulean eyes no longer perfect, but so full of promise, just like the world I had always hoped to explore.

I placed my hand in his and twined our fingers together. "Where will *we* go?"

The feathers of his wings ruffled as he spread them wide. "Let's start with the sky."

END

Fairy Cursed
Lindsi McIntyre

Fairies give curses, not gifts.

Lea shivered despite the summer heat still clinging to the night air. Grandmother's old warning hadn't helped Mother. And it wouldn't do any good to remember it now. Not tonight.

Not when Lea was so close to fulfilling her promise.

Long green grass blew in the wind, tickling her nose. Lying on the hill, Lea had a perfect view into the tiny valley below. At its center, Lord Byron's manor glowed from within as candlelight showcased his wealth to the incoming guests.

Practically every well-to-do man and woman in the country had been invited to the Lord's eldest daughter's coming out party. Lea would never have a better chance to sneak in.

Bring her back.

Mother's last words. The promise Lea had to keep. It was the only thing that had kept her going through the years of living alone on the streets of Anchor. Rapunzel was in there somewhere, and Lea was going to find her.

Ever so slowly, Lea lifted herself into a crouch and slipped down the side of the hill to her waiting horse.

~~~~~

Lords, ladies, and the title-less wealthy mingled beneath the light of a massive crystal chandelier inside Byron Manor's ballroom. Black-and-white-clad maids wove in and out of the crowd unseen, carrying treat-covered trays with expert dexterity.

Lea paused beside one of the massive gold-lined windows just long enough to take in the scene, then slipped back into the shadows. The light would make it impossible to see outside unless someone pressed themselves directly against glass, but she still ducked beneath each opening, just to be safe. A guard leaned against a pillar up ahead, boredom painted across his face. It didn't look like he'd be moving any time soon. With each step carefully measured, Lea began to sneak past him.

He sneezed.

She froze.

Her heart marched double time inside her chest. If he turned his head, even a fraction, he'd spot her and ruin everything.

The man rubbed at his face, then abruptly turned away, heading in the opposite direction of her target. Lea let out a soundless sigh and crept onward.

The night was deep and moonless, but Lea had no trouble seeing the path before her. She'd never had trouble seeing in the dark.

As she rounded the corner, a short tower at the back of the manor rose black against the starlit sky. The structure was a leftover remnant from the time when lords needed such things to fight off invading armies. Nowadays, it should have acted as a statement piece used to house important guests.

Instead, all of the doors on the outside of that particular section of the manor were sealed off with bricks.

That *had* to be it.

The closer she got to the tower, the darker the world became. It was as if Lord Byron were trying to hide the tower itself in the shadows. Every window in that wing on the ground floor had been shuttered and every tree had been cleared away to make the only window in the tower itself impossible to reach.

Well, impossible for anyone who couldn't climb walls.

Lea couldn't help the smile that tugged at her lips as she reached the base of the tower and studied the large rocks that made up its surface. Finding handholds in that was child's play for someone like her. Even on such a dark night.

The stone dug into her calloused palms and scraped against the soles of her boots as she climbed. She reached the window and pulled her torso up onto the ledge. Easy. Lea lifted her eyes.

A pair of blue eyes stared out into the night on the other side of the glass. Every muscle tensed in shock at her sudden discovery. Lea jumped instinctively and lost her balance. With a hiss, she fought to regain her position even as her hands slipped against the stone and nearly sent her plunging back to the ground.

She managed to hold on despite the pain from her torn skin. Her stomach settled, though her heart kept pounding as she took deep shuddering breaths. The face wasn't that of a guard, but of a girl. The wide blue eyes sparked with recognition beneath a crop of short blond hair.

"Lea," Rapunzel said, her little voice muffled behind the glass separating them.

Lea's throat tightened around a lump of emotion. She'd done it. She'd found her little sister. "Hang on, Rapunzel. I'm coming in."

The window opened outward but had been sealed shut using a simple iron bar bolted into the base with four screws. To open it, the bar had to be removed. With a grunt, Lea leveraged herself higher onto the ledge, grabbed the bar to use as a handhold and pulled out her dagger.

The edge of the steel slipped a few times before it caught in the groove of the screw. Through ragged breaths, Lea turned the blade. The screw inched out of its hole, then fell to the sill with a soft clink.

A curse escaped as Lea turned to the next one. The agonizingly slow process left her muscles screaming but eventually the last screw slipped free of its resting place.

The bar fell to the sill with a deafening clank, taking her with it. Lea cursed again as she fought to keep it from making any more noise and simultaneously keep herself from falling. With what was left of her strength she kicked against the wall, grabbed the window's edge to open it, and pulled herself inside.

Lea collapsed on the ground, gasping for air. Rapunzel crouched beside her, worry crinkling her brow. As soon as her muscles steadied, Lea pulled her sister into a hug.

"Rapunzel. Rapunzel. Thank God you're here."

Rapunzel stiffened, then slowly wrapped her arms around Lea.

After a second, Lea pulled back and studied the sister she hadn't seen in years. The little girl before her was taller than the six-year-old who'd been snatched away from their drunk of a father before he'd been killed, but her eyes were the same shade of forget-me-not blue and her nose still turned up at the end in the cutest of ways. But the smattering of freckles along her nose had faded from being kept locked up. And her smile was gone.

Lea stood, pulling Rapunzel up with her. "Come on, we're leaving."

Her sister's eyes sparkled for a moment, but then she hung her head. "I can't. I'll get in trouble."

Lea wanted to break Lionel Byron's big fat nose. "No, you won't. I promise." When Rapunzel didn't look up, she gently took hold of her shoulders. "Hey, have I ever broken a promise?"

Her sister peeked up at Lea through the ragged ends of hair that fell over her eyes. "No."

Lea smiled despite the anger churning in her chest. That hair was the cause of all of this. From a distance it looked like average dark blond hair. Up close, however, its true nature was revealed. The "gift" of Mother's fairy godmother, strands of pure gold growing out of her sister's head. There was no way the fairy hadn't known the fate waiting to trap Rapunzel. A lifetime of being chased and held captive by greedy sleazebags for financial gain.

Lea fought to keep her anger hidden. "That's right. And I'm not gonna start now. So, let's get going."

Footsteps and yelling echoed through the thick wooden door on the other side of the room. Rapunzel gasped and stepped away, clutching at her chest. With a growl, Lea sprinted to the door. Someone must have heard the commotion with the bar and spotted the open window. With a grunt, she shoved the wardrobe until it tipped over and blocked the only other way into the room.

She thought she'd have more time, but even the best of plans faced drawbacks. It was now or never. She dashed back to her sister. "Okay, Rapunzel. Do you remember when you were little and I used to carry you on my back?"

Rapunzel nodded.

"Good." Lea pulled her toward the window. "'Cause I need you to be real brave right now while I carry you down with me."

Somehow, Rapunzel's fear-filled eyes got even bigger. "I'll fall."

Lea shook her head. "You just have to hold on tight." The lock in the door clicked and someone rattled the knob. When that failed to move the wooden obstruction, they slammed into it, shaking the wardrobe on the floor. Men shouted on the other side. "Please, Rapunzel. You have to trust me."

She watched the lines of fear crossing her sister's face settle into determination.

"Okay."

"That's my girl." Lea knelt to let Rapunzel climb onto her back. She was heavier than she'd been at six. Maybe too heavy, but Lea didn't have a choice. They were getting out of the tower one way or another.

At first Rapunzel's skinny arms and legs held on with only the minimal required force, but as Lea stepped up onto the windowsill, they tightened. Lea grunted as bony limbs dug into her neck and stomach. She didn't tell her sister to loosen her grip, though.

Better for Rapunzel to hang on too tightly than drop thirty-five feet to the ground below.

Lea grunted as she grabbed onto the wall beside the window and started down. The stone dug into the torn skin of her fingers. Rapunzel's legs dug into her waist. Each handhold was a struggle. Each step down a fight. But Lea persisted. The banging at the door continued until finally a crack echoed through the window into the night above. Rushed footsteps preceded a man's head in the opening. His eyes locked on hers and he cursed loudly.

"They're getting away. Get outside. Hurry."

Lea sped up their descent. The guards would need to run all the way down the tower's stairs and to the nearest unblocked doorway. If Lea could get them down and away before that happened—

The man at the window swung his leg over the side. Of all the rotten luck. Of course, he would climb down after them instead of following the others. He began closing the gap between them far too fast.

Finally, the ground came close enough for Lea to drop safely, but there was no time to catch her breath. She slid Rapunzel from her back and took hold of her hand. They just had to make it to the tree line where she'd stashed her horse. The man might be a fast climber, but he'd never be able to keep up with a horse on foot.

The two girls raced away from the prison. Lea heard the man drop to the ground. His steps thundered across the grass behind them as he gave chase. With a quick look back, Lea saw he'd nearly halved their lead in just those few moments. She pulled her sister along, desperate for more speed. Rapunzel did her best to keep up, but it was no use. Her shorter legs just couldn't outpace a full-grown man. She stumbled, only avoiding a face full of dirt thanks to Lea's firm grip.

Through heavy breaths, Lea turned and pulled Rapunzel behind her in a protective stance. "Stand back," she whispered. Rapunzel scrambled a few steps away, terror twisting her lips into a horrible frown.

The man slowed as he drew closer, a half-smile pulling at his lips. "Decide to give up, did we?"

Lea pulled out her dagger. Its razor-sharp edge danced with starlight.

The man chuckled. "Come on, now. I don't want to hurt you. Just hand over the girl and leave."

"Underestimating me is a good way to die." There was no malice in her words. No censure. It was just a fact. One she'd learned scraping by in back alleys when bigger people thought they could steal from her and get away with it.

The man's eyes narrowed. "You're the one underestimating here." He pulled the dagger resting against his hip from its sheath. "But if you're bound and determined to make this a fight, then I'm happy to oblige."

He leapt forward, probably hoping she'd be taken by surprise. Unfortunately for him, her eyes could track even the slightest movements. She deftly sidestepped his strike and brought her blade down on his wrist. He yelled, weapon falling from his injured hand. Lea followed up her attack with a kick to his overextended knee. A crack rewarded her effort. As he stumbled, she caught him in the jaw with a swift upward kick that sent his head back with a snap.

He collapsed in a heap. And just like that, the fight was over.

Rapunzel stared at her with awe. Lea smiled.

Fairies give curses, not gifts.

There was truth in those words. If anyone had ever found out about the magic emeralds that served as Lea's irises, they'd have gouged her eyes out the first chance they got. She'd been in just as much danger as Rapunzel. More so, in some respects.

But Lea had turned her curse into a gift with her own blood, sweat and tears. Scrounging in alleys, she'd learned how to fight. She'd discovered that her eyes were amazing at tracking movement using light.

Even in the pitch black of a moonless night. Her emerald eyes had been meant as a burden, but she'd turned them into a blessing. A blessing that would now help save her sister.

She held out her hand to Rapunzel. "Time to go home."

~~~~~

Lea leaned her head against the boulder behind her and smiled. Their short foray into town had been profitable in more ways than one. They now had enough food to last them long enough to get to the cabin they'd soon call home.

But more importantly, she'd learned through the rumor mill that Lord Byron had been arrested for not paying his taxes. He'd apparently spent far too much money on his daughter's party, borrowing more than he could repay, likely banking on a certain magical girl's hair to pay it all off. Rapunzel's absence had devastated the man who had no real skills or talents of his own. It seemed, despite being born into wealth and kidnapping a child to fortify that wealth, he never bothered to learn how to make any of his own.

Served him right.

Rapunzel sat beside her on the ancient remains of a fallen oak tree, hair dyed brown beneath the old cap Lea had her wear. It was only a temporary disguise. Once she taught Rapunzel how to fight and she got a bit older, Lea planned to let her sister decide what she wanted to do with her hair.

Rapunzel's bright blue eyes scanned their surroundings as if she'd never get enough of the sights. Three years of isolation was a long time to catch up on. But now, with the biggest threat to their secrets locked away, they had all the time in the world.

END

The Princess of Callanway Broch
Meaghan Elizabeth Ward

The shadow of the towering broch chased after me as I clambered down the narrow path cut in the hill. My feet found the smooth, steady stones with ease as I gathered my basket snug against my hip and tucked an icy hand under my faded wool arisaid.

Sell the rampion roots. Get home before she knows you've been gone. My eyes darted again to the sky, to the clouds rimmed in red and darkening blue. If my luck held, I'd have just enough time to get home before dark.

Still, I quickened my pace as I neared the village. The stone cottages were dark creases along the winding path to the water's edge. Dying light lined their thatched roofs with gold.

"Rhapona? Is that you, lass?" A man stood before the door of the cottage I passed, hand frozen upon the door latch. Shaw. His was the second house down the path.

Often in the mornings, as the sun rose over Callanway, I watched the men leave their homes for the fields or the shore. Shaw was always easiest to spot, because he first turned to the broch and waved — a habit I suspected he kept whether he saw me at my tower window or not — before continuing down the hill with his faded blonde head bowed.

I often thought him sad. He was certainly alone, with his wife gone and no family to speak of. Yet when I was a child, he'd always had a trinket or a kind smile for me and a soft word for my ma. And so, when he waved or smiled, I made a point to wave or smile back.

"Evening, Shaw." I pulled aside on the path.

Shaw's lips quirked upward despite the weary slant of his shoulders. His soft eyes crinkled at the corners as they settled on my basket. "And what are you selling tonight, lass?"

"Rampion root — for anyone in the market who will take it."

"I'll take it. Tonight is not a night for you to be at the market. You should be home. Why such urgency?"

"Ma has used all her wool. She'll want more for weaving, and there is no coin."

I wanted to ask why he'd keep me from the market, but the truth was, I was glad of it. Spring may have been upon us, but there was a chill in the air that bit into my bones, and I was uncertain how long Ma would sleep.

"How is your màthair?"

185

I wrapped the rampion in a numb fist and passed them to him, not meeting his eyes. "She is not well today."

He cradled the roots against his belly. "Your màthair has not been well for many years now. How long will you continue to lie to yourself, lass?" He ducked his head, forcing me to meet his eye. "The offer of the wool merchant's widow still stands. Your màthair may stay with her with enough wool to keep her happy until the end of her days. You wouldnae have to live in the tower. You could do whatever you desired."

A cold ache tightened in my stomach. I knew Shaw and the others meant well, but if Ma was no longer mine to care for, and I no longer lived in the broch, what would I do? Where would I go? Would I live alone in an empty cottage like Shaw, abandoned to a faded life? "I dinnae know what I desire."

"That cannae be true. I've seen you, looking out across the water with those sea-troubled eyes."

It wasn't a lie. When I looked past the shore and across the ocean, I knew only that I wanted things — be it place or truth or dream — that I could not name. My gaze strayed down the road even then. I scanned the sea absentmindedly for a grey-headed selkie to surface or a sleek-necked kelpie to thrust its head from the surf, but in the back of my mind, a question rose in the silence between Shaw and me, and I did not know how to give it voice.

I was pulling at the fragmented words in my mind when I spotted a shadow on the path. A man on horseback rode our way, his face lifted to the tower and the last of the light.

I did not know him.

Shaw stiffened.

"Who is that?" I asked.

The stranger saw us before Shaw could answer. He spurred his mount closer.

His face was red and chapped, giving him a boyish appearance, but though he was still young, his cheeks were hollowed and his keen features were that of a man. He might have been handsome if he smiled.

He reined his shaggy bay alongside us.

"What brings you here, stranger?" There was a growl and bite to Shaw's tone I had never heard before, but the stranger did not even blink.

"I have a question. None here have answered me as of yet, but perhaps you might be so kind. Rumors have reached me." He nodded toward the broch. "Rumors of that tower."

I drew in a sharp breath.

"That tower is cursed," Shaw said quickly. "A stranger like you would do best to keep that in mind."

"It is this curse that I wish to know of."

He looked at the broch again, so long and hard I could not possibly know what he was thinking. I didn't know what to think myself. Callanway had boasted of few visitors over the years — none had pried into our lives or ever asked after my tower home — but the unspoken rule remained. Callanway's secrets were ours to keep, and ours alone, whether we understood the whole of them or not.

"Word has spread," he continued, "of a dark figure in the window — of a song on the air. What do you know of this?"

Shaw lifted his chin. "That broch has been abandoned for many years. No one lives there but ghosts, and nothing sings but the wind."

The stranger turned his dark gaze on me. "Is that so?"

A gust of wind tore between us, churning my skirts and stealing my breath.

A warm hand brushed my spine. Shaw stood behind me, his hidden gesture drawing me back to the present.

"No one lives there," I said. My voice didn't even shake.

"Someone must. I've seen many brochs across the countryside — all crumbling and in ruins. Not one whole, and not one with a window."

"I understand you are a stranger and not familiar with our ways, but it would be wise to not voice such things," Shaw said. "Indeed, some might see it as an omen — an omen of death — to speak of things you've seen or heard that are not really there."

"I'll keep that in mind," the stranger finally said. He clicked his tongue and turned his mount back toward the market, but before he went, he spared one last inscrutable look at the tower, then he nodded in our direction. "Evening."

Shaw and I did not reply. Silence sat heavy between us until he vanished beyond a fold of the path.

Questions clawed up my throat, but it was Shaw who spoke first. "Best go home, Rhapona. I'll bring you the wool when our stranger has gone." His gaze strayed fleetingly from the road to me. "Until then, stay there. Stay safe."

~~~~~

A dark pull swelled in the pit of my stomach — a feeling that might have been curiosity, or merely cold exhaustion — as I crested the hill to the broch. The wind throbbed in my ears. It burned my cheeks and fingers and toes. My grip on the basket tightened as I rounded the broom shrubs crowding the tower base. Their yellow blooms gave way to dried climbing vines the same honeyed tone as my hair.

I paused for a moment, staring up at the three-story broch, imagining it through the stranger's eyes. The ancient, grey-green rock changed to stone that was strong and new, and the black-eyed window stared, indifferently out of place, across the village and sea cliffs and unrolling moor.

Still... I could not remember a time when the tower wasn't there, wasn't mine.

My eyes darted back toward the village, then I ducked my head and continued on. Unlike most brochs, the entrance lay off to the side, cut into the hill and hidden by the bog myrtle. A fresh, lemony scent rose in the air as I brushed past the leaves to the low doorway and threw my weight against the rusty hinges.

I felt my way through the tunnel to the ground chambers where the fire had fallen to embers. I discarded my basket on the way to the hearth and strained to hear any signs of Ma stirring in the upper chamber, but all was still as I stoked the fire and added more peat.

When I stood, my toes banged against the stack of dirty supper dishes still waiting to be scrubbed. I sucked in a breath.

On the floor above, Ma cried out.

I skipped to the stairs and pounded up them two at a time. I spotted her as soon as I stepped onto the second-floor chamber. She stood a few steps from our straw mattress. The lantern she kept with her at all times trembled in her fist. The precious tallow candle inside flickered, casting more shadow than light.

"Zelia?" she called.

"I'm here, Ma. It's Rhapona."

I didn't know who Zelia was. I doubted Ma even knew herself. I slid the lantern from her fist. My other hand reached for her forehead. "You're still warm. Come. Lie back down."

Ma pulled my hand away and wrapped my fingers in her own. "You're cold to the bone, lass. Where have you been?"

"What do you mean? I've been here, Ma."

I wondered if she believed me. Either way, I was glad she could not see me holding my breath as I guided her back to the mattress and resettled her under the blankets and furs.

Her hands fidgeted over the covers. "Rhapona — lass — bring me a bit of wool and my drop spindle, at least. I must do something."

"You must rest first, Ma. I'll fetch some fresh bog myrtle and make you some tea. How does that sound?"

I laid the lantern upon the floor beside her and moved to stand, but Ma's breath hiccupped and she snatched at my sleeve. "Wait. Stay."

"I won't be but a minute."

"No. Stay," she said again. "Stay here with me. Promise?"

"Always, Ma," I lied.

"You won't go for the bog myrtle?"

"I won't go." At least not now. "I swear."

I combed my fingers through her sweaty hair like she used to do with me when I felt ill. Restlessly, she turned her head against my hand and murmured what might have been words or a name.

"Rest," I whispered. "Just rest."

Ma's skin was clammy and sallow. The candlelight caught on the gaunt hollows of her face and the paper-thin lines gathered around her brows, eyes, and lips.

That dark feeling rose in my chest again, but this time, it was most definitely fear. When had our roles first reversed? When did I start caring for her and hiding my anxiety lest it upset her? When did she start growing so thin and calling me names that were not mine?

I began to sing without realizing it. It was a song Ma often sang to me. Even though its verses carried notes of sadness, the tune proved to be comforting.

A name on the wind.
A voice full of sorrow.
Grey rings stand silent.
Never will I, never will I follow.

Stay in my shelter
within walls of stone.
My memory to hold you,
Hold you in safety alone.

A shadow to hide
A path laid below.
Cold tower offers solace.
Never will I, never will I follow.

Stay in my shelter
within walls of stone.
My memory to hold you,
Hold you in safety alone.

I repeatedly hummed the chorus until her breathing evened and a soft sigh escaped her lips, then I reached for the rushlight nip I kept by my side of the bed and touched the rushlight to the candle flame.

I continued to hum as I straightened and eased across the chamber, and that was when I heard it. The song died in my throat. I froze like a hare hidden among purple heather.

Outside, a voice called. I could not discern the words.

I scrambled for the ladder to the loft and balanced precariously on the squeaking rungs as I climbed one-handed. The rushlight was little more than a sad spark in the thick blackness of the broch. Still, I twisted my body to hide the light as I wove among the hanging herbs to the hollowed upper gallery and the window, which sat behind a wall of thick furs.

When I pushed aside the covering, the first thing I saw was dark blue sky and a fading red horizon. The first thing I heard was the stranger.

"Hello?" he called.

I crouched in the narrow gallery beneath the window and set aside my rushlight.

"Is anyone there?"

I bit at the chapped, peeling skin on my lips. He'd heard me. He'd heard me singing. He knew someone was here.

You heard nothing, I wanted to scream down at him.

It was a ghost.

It was me.

Two things Ma never spoke of: my father and her past. Whatever it was my mother feared — whatever her reason for begging me to stay in the broch and the darkness — must have lain behind one of those two silences. It must have been the reason the stranger could not know we existed, and so I barely breathed for the longest time.

A clatter echoed from below. I imagined horse hooves kicking at loose stones as the stranger descended the path, but I dared not look.

He's leaving. He has to be leaving. I only hoped it was true.

I braced a shoulder against the wall and shivered. My fingers worried the edges of my arisaid. The tartan was so faded, I couldn't tell if it was once purple or blue, only that it was old, and that it was hers before it was mine.

What would happen when Ma's fever finally broke? What would happen when Ma wanted wool for weaving and there was no wool or thread? What would happen when she learned there was a stranger asking about our home? She'd never let me out of her sight. She'd never give me the chance to escape the broch even for a moment.

No! No. I dragged in a deep breath and held on to the exhale as long as I could. I pulled my hair over my shoulder and combed through it with trembling fingers, then separated it into three strands and began to braid it back.

This was what I would do, I thought calmly as I braided. I would take my pillow — thin as it was. I would empty it of its loose wool filling and stuff it with an old skirt instead. There wouldn't be much, but it would keep her busy, and she'd never know anything was amiss. No one would ever know.

And until then, I would stay here — silent, afraid, and not knowing why — until I could be sure the stranger was gone.

I thought once again of the offer of the wool merchant's widow, and of Shaw's words. I did not know what I desired, but in that moment, I could think of three things I knew I didn't want.

I didn't want things to change, and yet...

I didn't want to live the rest of my life behind secrets and darkness...

But I also didn't want to leave my mother.

The moor beyond the window became so still the silence had a voice. I tucked my cold feet beneath me, looked up at the gathering stars, and hummed on a breath so soft I could barely hear myself. The words were in my head though, and I let myself believe they were comfort enough.

Stay in my shelter
Within walls of stone.

~~~~~

I didn't think I slept, but I must have, because when I woke, night had fully unfolded, and a man was falling through the window.

He tripped over me, breath sawing in his throat, and his boots caught on my skirt.

I twisted away with a cry and fell back against the fur divider.

"Who are you? What do you want?"

"I mean you no harm."

I blinked frantically. My fingers skittered to the rushlight and I thrust it between us like a weapon. "You're... You're the stranger from the market."

"Dougal."

"What?" The word squeezed out on a breath. I should have said or done something, but I couldn't think enough to know what.

"My name is Dougal," he said, breath blowing hard. "And you—you are that girl from town."

"How did you get up here? Did... did you climb?"

He shrugged a shoulder. "I couldnae find the door."

"You couldnae find... are you *insane*?"

"No. Just a bit of a chancer." He stretched a hand toward me and I froze, my own breath uncertain, but instead of touching me, he reached for the divider and peered into the darkness of the broch over my shoulder. "You said no one lived here. Only ghosts."

I slapped his hand away and pulled the divider shut once again. "M-maybe I am a ghost. You cannae be certain."

He looked at me a long time. It was the same empty, indecipherable expression he'd given the tower earlier, yet this close, I saw a myriad of thoughts flashing behind his eyes. The already small space seemed suddenly smaller as I became aware that we were pressed knee to knee in a gallery that could barely fit one person.

"You do not feel like a ghost," he finally said.

"Please, you must go." My voice quavered and lacked the force it should have had.

Dougal leaned closer still. His voiced dropped to a grave whisper. "Why are you here? Are you being held against your will? That man from the village—"

"No!" I hissed. "Shaw would never. It's my màthair—"

"Is she a danger to you?"

"No! This is my home, and my màthair is not well, and you cannot simply climb into people's homes. She cannot find you here!" And then — I prided myself for it — I looked him square in the eye and said, "Get out."

His voice dropped lower still. Urgency threaded his words. "I seek only answers — please — and a moment to catch my breath. Then I will be gone."

A brittle, breathy laugh escaped me. "What could you wish to know so desperately?"

"What happened here?" Rushlight flickered across his severe features. "This tower should be in ruins."

I warred with myself longer than I should have. Our secrets were our own, true, but what harm was there in answering this? Maybe the sooner someone bucked up and said it, the sooner he would leave.

"It was rebuilt in a time when a fierce conqueror ruled the mainland." The words flooded from me before I could rethink them. "Immigrants fled to our isle, seeking the asylum of the sacred standing stones. A man, once a king in his own right, came with his family. He rebuilt this tower to ensure their safety, and his wife, grieved by the lack of light, demanded a window be added to the upper floor. That is how the story goes."

"And what happened to them?"

"I dinnae ken."

"You mean to tell me an entire village is oblivious to their own history?"

My lips parted even before I knew what response I would give.

"Zelia?" called a faint voice from below.

I bowed my head and pinched the bridge of my nose. "It's Rhapona," I said under my breath. Not that it mattered. Nothing mattered more than this: My mother was awake, and a stranger was in my home asking questions I could not answer. I lifted the fur divider. "I'm here, Ma. I'll be down in a moment."

I twisted back to face the man. "You must go. Now!"

He scooted back. His hand already rested on the stone windowsill, but he hesitated and made no further move to leave. "Is there anything more you can tell me?"

"Why does this matter so much to you?" I said, choking on a half laugh that did little to mask my panic.

"I'm here to right a wrong."

"What wrong could you have to right? Surely this happened before both of us were even born."

"There are rumors of a daughter — a princess — living still upon this isle. Do you know if this is true?"

"It is just that. Rumor. The family disappeared and never returned. They vanished without a trace, and that — that is the truth."

"Zelia?" Ma called again. She'd risen from her bed already. I heard her moving across the floor.

"Rhapona?" Dougal said, a question in his tone.

"Wheesht!" I pressed a finger lightly to his lips. A shiver of awkward unease rushed through my arms to my shoulders. I wanted to take back the gesture as soon as I'd done it, but I could not bring myself to move, so I stayed there, pressed close to him, and for the first time, he remained silent.

Ma was on the ladder. I heard the creaky third rung.

"Go!" I wheezed. I blew out the rushlight, plunging us into blackness. "Just... Go."

Dougal pulled himself quickly to his feet. His boots scraped stone and his body blocked the starlight as he threw one leg out the window.

He wasn't fast enough.

The fur covering was thrown back, and Ma stood less than a step away, the lantern swinging in her fist.

For a moment, time froze. Ma remained in the doorway, lips parted. Dougal stayed perched in the window, eyes narrowed and assessing.

"Ma, I can explain..." My voice was explosive in the stillness. It shattered whatever fae spell there might have been upon us.

"Rhapona?" Dougal said, slowly, carefully.

This time, I knew what he was thinking as his eyes darted between us. I looked nothing like her. She was not my mother — not my mother by blood.

The woman who stood before us was frail, and if anyone looked like a ghost it was certainly her. Her once-dark hair, now bleached of color, haloed around her slight figure.

"Out!" she screamed. Her foot collided with my shin as she sprang toward him. "Get out! Out!"

I didn't see what happened next. I only remembered Ma rushing forward, her hands clawing at his face. Then — I must have blinked — there was only starlight and an empty window.

A scream tore from my throat. "Dougal!"

No response. I never even heard him hit the ground, and my mind told me that if I didn't hear it, then it never happened. It couldn't have happened.

"What have you done?" My voice, part shriek, scraped in my throat.

Meanwhile, my mother — the woman who had never been able to butcher a chicken or stand the sight of blood — just stood there with a hand braced against the window's curved edge.

"What have you done?" I said again.

"It has happened." Ma was pale as a wraith as she turned on me. "It has finally happened. We must run, Zelia."

"What?"

Ma's hand found my wrist before I could think to pull away. She dragged me from the gallery. Hanging herbs smacked me in the face, making my eyes tear and my nose tingle with an approaching sneeze.

I slipped from the last rungs of the ladder, banging my knees on the floor of our bedchamber, but Ma's iron grip was relentless. She pulled me to my feet and towed me down the stairs to the ground floor.

"Ma. Ma, please!" I pleaded. She acted as if she couldn't hear me.

She paused only once to snatch the chopping knife from the dirty pile by the hearth. Ice spread down my spine to my legs.

Down the tunnel to the entrance we went. Then, with her lantern hooked in two fingers and the knife tucked into her palm with the other three, she fumbled. Her hold on me vanished as she fought with the door. I darted half a step back into the tower before she snagged my wrist again.

My nails scraped against rock and dirt before my fingers latched onto the doorframe. I braced myself.

"Don't fight me, Zelia. Just once. I beg you!" Ma cried. She spun on me. The lantern swung wildly. The knife flashed in the candlelight. It slashed across my arm as she wrenched me from the doorway.

I felt no pain in that moment. There was only the sensation of something wet on my arm.

Ma stared. Her mouth twisted in horror.

"It's Rhapona." I spat the words in her face as if they were poison. "My name is Rhapona!"

Her eyes met mine.

For a moment, I thought maybe she'd finally heard me. I thought maybe she'd let me go, we'd both return to bed, and I'd wake up in the morning to find this was all a terrible dream.

But Ma's gaze remained vacant and empty. She turned toward the night, hauling me along in her wake. The door in the bog myrtle banged behind us, abandoned in the wind.

My gaze snapped back toward the broch. "Dougal!" I screamed.

Again, nothing.

I twisted toward the village, pulling against my mother and straining toward the second cottage down the path. "Shaw!"

Nothing, again. There was only my voice, empty on the wind, my mother's hand shackling my wrist, the kitchen knife clenched tight by her side, and my blood dripping, dripping, dripping across the desolate, wind-burned moor.

~~~~~

The wind cut at my cheeks and fingers and toes. Above, a black, star-studded sky arced against the blacker rise and fall of the moor.

I did not know how long we had been walking. I no longer felt Ma's hand around my wrist as I staggered after her on numb feet.

Was she even wearing shoes when she dragged me from the tower? I didn't remember, but I couldn't imagine treading barefoot across this ground. Neither could I imagine what doggedly drove her on and continued to lend her strength.

Only one thing ran circles in my mind: the memory of Dougal asking if I was in danger.

No, I had said.

No. My mother would never hurt me.

A lie? A truth?

I didn't know. I didn't know anything anymore.

My teeth chattered and my eyes began to sting and blur. When I first caught sight of the hill, I couldn't be sure what I was seeing. I swiped the back of my hand across my eyes.

A ring of standing stones crested the top of the mound before us like fingers reaching for the sky. The cold notes of the song skated across my mind.

A name on the wind.
A voice full of sorrow.
Grey rings stand silent.
Never will I, never will I follow.

Ma did not hesitate. She didn't even look back when I tripped and stubbed my toes on the rocks.

A dark rectangular hole lay in the side of the hill. Ma tugged me into a crouch and we plunged into the narrow tunnel entrance. My head banged on stone as we descended deeper. At my back, the wind howled past the narrow opening like a creature on the prowl.

A moment later, the tunnel widened, and she stopped. Her hand slipped from mine.

Run, screamed a voice in the back of my head, but I was too cold and too lost to move. Deep within, the little girl I once was wished to cry out, but I was not a lost lamb, and I doubted my mother would answer me.

Instead, I watched her ghost around the shape of a chamber. She removed the candle from her lantern, unmindful of the hot wax dripping over her fingertips. Her lips shaped frantic, silent words.

As she moved, rushlights winked awake from nips fastened to the walls. The chambered cairn glowed warm and orange in the light as if I were in cozy cottage and not sheathed underground, surrounded by stone.

Then, I knew — I knew what this place was, and a tremor gripped me. I couldn't pull in a deep enough breath.

This was the place the stories spoke of — a place of refuge and ancient worship, a place free of bloodshed and sorrow. But now... now it was a tomb.

Bones rested in the corner — a femur, a ribcage, a skull. I couldn't look. My skin crawled, and I tried not to peer into the unblinking, adjoining chambers.

Ma's own hands shook as she set down her lantern and stared at the far wall marked with ink. No, not ink. Dried blood smeared across the layered stones.

The second verse of the song tumbled through my head. Ma was singing it under her breath, too. She rocked back and forth on unsteady feet as she reached for the wall and the blood.

A shadow to hide
A path laid below.
Cold towers offer solace.
Never will I, never will I follow.

The words were different. I had always thought the verse referred to the broch, but it was really speaking of the standing stones. It was speaking of this place.

I shook harder and hugged myself. I understood, even though I desperately didn't want to. The family from the tower disappeared — father, mother, and daughter. They came here. They were murdered.

I jumped as Ma dropped to her knees with a keening cry. The knife rose. I leapt forward a step, unsure of what to do, heart pounding beneath my ribs, but I wasn't fast enough. She gathered her hair in a fist and hacked at it with the knife, sobbing as pale clumps fell among the rubble and the bones.

"Ma..." I clapped a hand to my mouth.

She looked up as the last strands fell. Her hair hung ragged and frayed around her tear-stained face.

"Wh — what happened here?" I knew it was the wrong thing to say as soon as I said it.

She shook her head and cried harder. She reached for me.

For the length of a breath I hesitated, torn between running away and running to her. I might not have been her blood, but she was still my mother. She would never hurt me on purpose, would she?

One slow step forward. Two. She teetered. I latched onto her elbow to steady her as she caught my braid and wrenched my head to the side. I cried out, more from shock than pain.

"Ma—!" Tears pricked my eyes. More than anything, I wanted to tell her to stop, but the knife caught the lantern light and wild sorrow gleamed in my mother's eyes.

Her gaze darted past me as a sound caught in the doorway of the tunnel. It took me a moment to realize it wasn't the wind. She shoved me behind her and thrust the knife at the man half-crouched in the chamber entrance.

Shaw.

He straightened slowly and raised both hands. "Easy," he said. His voice was gentle and kind, as if we were merely crossing paths on the street instead of in this forgotten place with a knife between us. He glanced only fleetingly at the darkening blood that edged the blade.

"Easy," he said again.

"It's fine, Ma." I skirted carefully around her until she could see Shaw and me in the same glance. A feral glint still lay behind her eyes. I swallowed hard. "It's just Shaw. You know Shaw."

Slowly, I stretched until my fingers found her elbow again. I slide my touch up her arm toward the knife, and she remained statue-still.

Perhaps all would have been well in another moment, but beyond the wind came the scrape of more steps in the tunnel. Dougal climbed stiffly into the chamber behind Shaw. His face was scratched, his eyes red and swollen, and his hairline bloody, but he was alive. How was he alive? A juddering breath escaped me.

It was then that Ma lunged. The knife drove forward.

"No!" I grabbed her wrists and threw my weight against her.

In the next moment, Shaw was beside me. His steady hands enfolded my mother's white-knuckled grip on the knife handle. A drop of blood welled along a nick on the edge of his palm, but he didn't flinch.

"Let go," he said, soft as a greeting. His steady, sea-troubled eyes never left my mother's. "Let go, Zelia."

Zelia?

I staggered backward against the stone wall. My knees threatened to buckle. Dust rained on my shoulders and head, and I choked on the stale air as I watched the woman who had once been my safe tower crumble to the ground.

Shaw tossed aside the knife. It rattled among old bones, and I winced.

"Rhapona." He held out a hand. "Come. Come to me."

I studied him for a long time, so long that his thick eyebrows lowered in confusion, but I stayed where I was, braced against the wall.

"She's not Zelia," I heard myself say.

His eyebrows dipped lower. His hand continued to hover in the space between us, and something in his eyes begged me to take it, but I turned away.

"Ma." I eased a foot forward in the dust. She stared back at me with dead eyes and caved in on herself a little more. "Who is Zelia?"

I traced my index and middle finger along the wall over a small, bloody handprint.

"Ma?"

"It was supposed to be me," she murmured.

I shook my head. "*What* was supposed to be you?"

"It was a trap." The words rasped past her lips, dry and half-formed. "It was a trap and they knew it. So they called me Zelia. They dressed me as Zelia."

I drifted closer still. *Stay in my shelter, within walls of stone...* "The family who lived in the tower — they had a daughter. Her name was Zelia, wasn't it? They told her to stay in the tower and they took you in her stead, hoping she would be safe, but she didn't stay. She followed, and she died here with them."

Pain flashed across Ma's face and her eyes pinched closed. "It was supposed to be me."

I glanced back at Shaw. Confusion furrowed his brow. His lips pressed into a tight, taciturn line.

Callanway's secrets are ours to keep. I'd heard that said all my life by elders who knew more than me, but I never understood our silence... until now.

I turned back to Ma and knelt before her. I rested my fingertips on her knee and laid my other hand gently over the hands clenched in her lap. "When you returned, the village thought you were her, didn't they? So you stayed in the tower, because that was what Zelia should have done."

A sob wrenched from my mother. She pressed her forehead to the floor and wailed into her hands.

I bowed over her shuddering body and wrapped her in my arms. My heart ached as I rocked with her back and forth. Something in her was splintering, and there was nothing I could do. Nothing at all.

This woman both was and was not my mother.

She both was and was not Zelia.

Did she even remember that she had her own name?

The rushlights eventually burned low. Some vanished into ash, but still I held onto my mother. Neither Shaw nor Dougal left or said a word, but when mother finally ran out of tears and I led her back to the village, Shaw stayed at my side and Dougal limped closely behind, leading his horse.

Did they say nothing because they were afraid to speak? Or was it because we were all hurting in our own way?

Instead of going to the tower, Shaw turned us toward his cottage, and I didn't argue. Dougal did not follow us inside.

Ma curled up in the back room on Shaw's cot with little prompting. She shivered when I touched her forehead, but her skin was finally cool. The fever had broken.

"Rhapona," she rasped.

I blinked back tears. "Yes, Ma?"

But her eyes were already closing. I removed my belt and covered her with my arisaid, murmuring empty words until I knew she'd fallen asleep.

In the main room, a crude table with a single chair sat near the newly banked hearth fire. Shaw waited for me there. He gestured me to sit, then knelt and took my injured arm in his calloused fingers. He ran a damp cloth over the wound and scrubbed away the dust and blood from my skin, then smeared salve across the cut. He was so focused and lost to his own thoughts, I was afraid to speak at first. I drew in a breath and exhaled slowly.

"I know now what I desire," I said.

Shaw met my eyes for the first time since the cairn. "What is that, lass?"

"I want to know the truth." I paused and wetted my chapped lips. "Are—are you my father?"

"Aye, lass." His voice broke around the words. "I am."

Inhale. Exhale. Each breath ached.

Shaw's movements became slow and methodical as he finished wrapping my arm. "Your màthair — your first màthair— she died when you were still an infant. The same illness that took her threatened you. I didnae ken what to do, but Zelia did. Or at least, we all thought it was Zelia, so we never said a word. Not one. She'd been through enough." He paused for a long moment, like the realization was still sinking in, then he cleared his throat. "I told myself you were better with her. She could care for you more than I at the time. Crivvens, I've mucked this up, haven't I?"

He pushed away from me and crossed to the window. Silence cocooned us once again. Finally, he continued, "I... I wanted to tell you — truly — but it did you good to have a màthair, and it did her good to have someone to care for. It was the first I ever remembered her smiling."

He ran a hand over his eyes. "Then every time after when I would see you, I'd say the words in my head, but I didn't know what you would do or think. The last thing I ever meant to do was hurt you. So like the selfish coward I am, I said nothing day after month after year, just for the chance to speak with you in passing and see you smile back at me."

I stood and joined him. He refused to look at me.

"Aither..." I touched his arm. "Pa."

There were more words in my throat that I didn't know how to say aloud — at least not yet. One day, though, I would know how to say them, and when I did, they wouldn't stop coming.

Tears gathered in his eyes. "I was so afraid, Rhapona. When that boy came, pounding upon every door until he arrived at mine and telling me that you were in trouble and that your màthair... I don't know what I would have done if—"

I threw myself at him before he could finish and buried my face in his chest. He wrapped his arms around me in return.

~~~~

Later, as day woke to an overcast dawn, I found Dougal outside, sitting under the cottage eaves.

He started when I approached, as if I'd caught him dozing.

"Are you well?" he said quickly.

"Are you?"

He'd cleaned up. The blood was gone, but there were bruises at his temple and his eyes were red and teary.

I held out a poultice and motioned to his head. "It's made with willow bark. It will help with the pain and the swelling."

He hesitated and blinked sharply. One arm remained tucked protectively to his stomach, but after a moment, he reached with the other hand and took the poultice. "My thanks."

I tore my gaze away as he pressed the poultice to the side of his head. I wanted to apologize for my mother. I wanted to tell him I was very glad he was not dead, even though he was the worst kind of idiot for ever climbing that tower.

"Why are you here? Really?" I said instead.

He didn't answer for the longest time, but his jaw shifted as if he were chewing over his words. "There is a story in my family. My grandfather's brother vanished into the north. We were told his leaving was over family disputes and brotherly differences. When my grandfather found his whereabouts years later, he went there himself with my father, who was still just a boy at the time, to make amends. Or so our history states.

"But there was also a rumor of the rebellious north amassing under my great-uncle's name. My grandfather was a zealous man. I have little doubt forgiveness was never his intention."

I forced my hands to unclench. "And was your grandfather also a great conqueror?"

"There are many words I've heard describe my grandfather. *Great* was never one of them." He lowered the poultice and released a heavy sigh. "After his death, my father never spoke of him, but there was something else he never spoke of that grieves him still. I always suspected whatever it was happened here." His eyes strayed to the tower.

There was more he wanted to say. I saw him working through the details. Each thought seemed to pain him. I pressed my lips into a thin line and waited.

"My father was quite ill when I left home," he eventually said. "Whether this is to be his end or not, I do not know. But the last thing I want is for him to go to his death with unanswered questions and a head full of guilt because I did nothing. Neither do I wish that to be my legacy. That is why I came here — to seek a truth he will never utter, and to right a wrong that should never have been made. Perhaps I was a fool to think it could be righted at all."

"Not a fool," I said. "Just a chancer."

His lips crooked upward, and despite his severe features, he was handsome in that moment.

"Did you think I was the princess?" I joked, and offered a small smile in return.

"No. But for a time, I thought you were her daughter."

My smile faded. I pictured him perched in the tower window, looking between my mother and me. He knew I was no princess even then, yet he still helped me. He found Shaw and he followed.

"What would you have done... if I really was family?"

"I suppose I would have taken you and your mother back to the mainland. I would have shown you the forest where I grew up and the plains where I first saw my father staring to the north. I would have introduced you to my sister, and given you a wing in the castle all your own, and I'd have done all in my power to ensure you were given a good life beyond the tower."

I swallowed hard. "It is a fanciful future indeed."

"Which part? Living in a castle or traveling to the mainland?" he said. His swollen eyes fixed on me, then he caught himself and looked away.

I wasn't sure how to answer. I didn't know what a castle looked like, and the only forests I had seen were the straggly trees that grew along the coast. I'd never considered leaving the island. I'd never thought of anything beyond survival and caring for Ma. Now, I was as untethered as a boat that had lost sight of shore, and I did not yet know if I was headed for disaster or adventure.

"Also," he continued, "I would like to provide for your mother until the end of her days, if you would allow it. You both needn't live in the darkness of the tower any longer. It's the least that can be done."

"My thanks." I stared at my hands.

He fingered the edges of the poultice. "What will you do?"

I wondered if the widow's offer still stood, and I felt both guilt and relief for considering it. "I will see my mother settled and happy — wherever that may be. I will take the time to get to know my father. And maybe one day, I will go across the water to the mainland, and see this castle and forest that you speak of."

He offered a sheepish, sideways grin. "I could... I could show it to you one day. All of it. If that is something you desire."

My gaze drifted to the sea and I smiled. "Aye. I would like that."

END

The Dragon-Keep's Servant
Michaela Bush

Galena was only sure of two things: one, the sacred egg was still wrapped in its warm nest, safe. Two, she had never heard such a ruckus in her entire life.

At the sound of clattering and shouting outside her window, she seized a knife and her wooden broomstick, uncertain which would be most effective against intruders. She risked leaning out the window, a thing that the Dragon-Keep told her never to do when passersby were near.

The thing she saw took her by surprise for the second time in less than ten minutes. A young man was crumpled in a heap, meters below at the base of her tower. The thundering of four hooves beyond the thicket of trees told her the man had been abandoned.

He appeared quite unconscious too. She bit her lip, then quietly called out. "Sir!"

No response.

She raised her voice, then shouted twice, to no avail. She could see the glimmer of red blood trickling across his forehead now.

"Hang it all," she muttered. Thinking quickly, she rushed to the center of her tower, where a small cistern kept water. She dipped a bucket from the frigid depths and then rushed back to the window. Aiming for the man's head, she dumped the bucket out the window.

Still nothing. She sent up a quiet prayer the man wasn't, in fact, dead. Who knew how long it would be before the Dragon-Keep reappeared with supplies? She had recently restocked the tower, so it would be quite some time. Yet, Galena couldn't bear the thought of a mangled body decaying just beneath her window.

With a grimace, she abandoned the window and raced for the second level of the tower, where the treasure was kept. It was still safe, indeed. And its time to arrive in the world was soon; the egg's scaly, iridescent black surface glimmered as it jostled. It would be another day or two before the creature was outside its protection and into the world that wanted it dead. According to the Dragon-Keep, that is.

Galena couldn't imagine a world otherwise.

She gnawed her bottom lip, weighing her options. Then she dashed for the window again, retrieved the bucket she'd left on the sill, and filled it with water once more. She chucked it out the window unceremoniously and waited.

"Ack!"

"Oh, hallelujah," she whispered, crossing herself as her shoulders slumped with relief. The man was awake.

And in her moment of jubilance, she'd wasted too much time. The man's eyes tilted up, his gaze following the tower wall, and met hers squarely.

She covered her mouth and fell backward away from the window, muffling a squeak. She couldn't be seen; couldn't let anyone believe someone was living inside the tower. The Dragon-Keep told her of rumors, of rumblings that the kingdom wished the Dragon-Keep dead. Surely they would know who kept a servant girl hidden in a tower deep in the woods, which no one else lived in.

"Who are you?" called the man outside.

She stayed silent, willing him to leave. To forget. To believe that maybe he'd hit his head a little harder than he'd thought and had simply imagined everything. That had happened to Galena once; she'd fallen whilst dusting and hadn't woke until the sun had retired.

It was easy to ignore the man's calls; it was harder to ignore the moan she heard after, followed by another *thud*.

"Tell me you didn't..." she trailed off. *He couldn't have fainted again. Could he?*

She leaned out the window, searching for the man's form. He had only made it a few paces away from the tower, but was now slumped on the ground, clutching his head.

The breath fled from her lungs. *What do I do now?* She wavered between calling out and slipping away from the window once more -- announcing her existence and disappearing as a specter -- but fate would decide for her, it seemed.

Again, the man's face turned upward to meet her gaze. She didn't back away this time, eyes widening in fear as she took in his apparent injury. Blood painted one side of his face, darkening his auburn hair. She opened her mouth to ask of the man's health, but then he stood, still gazing up at her. Her mouth snapped shut so hard her teeth clacked together.

"Lady, did you see which direction my mount took off?" he called.

"No," she said. At least it was truthful, and a simple answer yet. At his crestfallen expression, she wet her lips and added, "Are you all right?"

"I...believe my brains were addled quite well," he said, rubbing his temples and then wiping the blood off his fingers with his tunic.

"You dashed your brains on the tower, so I'd say so," she blurted.

The man looked up and, to her surprise, laughed. "I believe you." He winced again and a fresh trickle of blood slid down his cheekbone.

Galena took a deep breath, then took a step away from the window as she realized she was too taken in by the young man. She couldn't help him any further, anyway, so why prolong the discussion?

"Wait!" The muffled, deep voice came again. "Don't go yet. What is your name?"

"A good Samaritan," she said.

A grin quirked the side of his mouth. "Witty, I see. I mean you no harm, I would simply like to express my appreciation. Surely there is something I can do for you."

Leaving quietly and falling off your horse somewhere else next time would be a start, Galena almost said. Instead, it occurred to her that she ought to ask why he was in the woods alone. So deep in the wilderness, falling off a horse or getting injured was dangerous.

Or so the Dragon-Keep said.

So why was he there, alone?

"What are you doing so deep in the forest? It's not safe. Obviously. You could have been left for dead."

"Yet, you were here." The man took a step closer to the tower, and she felt herself bristle.

"Well, I couldn't let you rot there. I'm not a complete monster."

"And yet, one lives on this piece of property."

"What?"

The man glanced up at the sky suddenly, shaking his head. "I'm sorry, that was untoward of me. But surely...are you a squatter? Passing through? Are you a servant?"

"I believe I asked *you* the question, not...not the other way around," Galena stammered.

The young man refocused on her. "I am Ansel, if that helps ease your nerves. I'm no threat to you. But surely, you know who owns this property. Don't you?"

She shook her head for safety's sake. "I believe—"

"The Dragon-Keep of the Westside owns this property. It will do you well to leave as soon as possible."

Galena's brows furrowed. *He knows the Dragon-Keep?* "I will stay with my own business, and you would do well to stay with your own, sir. Please, be on your way."

It was Ansel's turn to look confused as he took a step closer to the tower. "That is a rather harsh manner to deal with someone who is offering you life-saving advice."

She glanced back inside the tower. "I am well. If you are well, I'd recommend that you leave as quickly as possible. If you say it's as dangerous as you believe..."

And with that, she disappeared into the depths of the tower, wishing the window locked and that the Dragon-Keep would return swiftly for the precious egg.

Even though she knew what would happen next, when the Dragon-Keep no longer needed her services.

~~~~~

Ansel reappeared the next day, and instead of knocking against the tower with his *head* as the day before, he called out instead.

"Mystery damsel deep in the woods!"

The wooden bowl in Galena's hands crashed against the stone floor with a crack. Grimacing, she didn't bend to pick it up until she listened closely. Was he on foot again? Had he truly left the forest last night, or had he – the thought made her shudder – waited by the tower all night?

"Are you still there?"

She cleared her throat to rid herself of the initial shock of hearing his voice again. "Are you in need of assistance?"

"I'm not, but are *you*?"

A shudder ran up her spine as she, again, weighed her options. Silence seemed like the best choice.

"I know only one person owns this land. I know the Dragon-Keep is an elusive, eccentric old woman, one I won't chance to find here. But I know what the Dragon-Keep does to her servants. I know she is keeping a servant in this tower. Are you here by choice?"

No, I'm not. She tried to swallow, but her throat constricted. "I... if you are not in need of help or waking-from-unconsciousness, please be on your way, sir."

"Miss, please." He called from the ground below, and she backed away from the window until she couldn't see him anymore. He called again, and she realized that no matter where she went, she would still hear his voice.

Unless the second floor was an option.

She sucked in a deep breath and fled for the staircase, leaving his shouts behind. Protecting the egg, that was all that mattered. All that *should* matter to her, anyway. She was selfish for even thinking anything otherwise.

She rounded the corner into the room in which the egg nestled and neared it. A few more cracks cobwebbed around the shell. It would still be several hours until the little creature clawed its way out into the open air, and then...

Then, she didn't know how many minutes or hours or weeks she would have before the Dragon-Keep arrived and relieved her of the burden she'd carried since childhood.

Her sigh turned into a shudder, and she whispered to the egg.

"You're not at fault, are you? It was me. My fault that I'm here. My fault that I caught the attention of a stranger, too."

A muffled thump, the squeak of a rusty hinge, caught her ear, and she spun around. Surely it wasn't the Dragon-Keep already, was it? A frigid blast of fear shot through her as she realized it very well could be Ansel, breaking in on whatever distress mission he believed himself to be on. And if that were the case, it would be the end for her charge. The treasure she'd guarded all her life.

She grabbed a broom from the corner of the room and raced for the staircase, then down the stone steps until she hit the main floor of the tower. Sure enough, the trap door had been opened – the one the Dragon-Keep entered and exited through, locking it from the outside always. But the Dragon-Keep wouldn't be snooping in the kitchen.

Not like Ansel was.

"Just because I'm alone doesn't mean you're safe!" she cried, snatching his attention away from the fruit on the table. His eyes swung toward hers, and she found she couldn't hold his gaze. Another shot of fear doused her system, and she brandished the broom.

"I've been beaten by brooms before," he said conversationally, tossing a grin her way. "But I'm most concerned —"

"*I'm* concerned you hit your head too hard yesterday. Go have the healer tend to it; mayhap you must be kept in the prison for your actions!"

He snorted a bit. "Dear lady, there are many people who should be kept in prison for their actions and yet roam freely. Your mistress is one."

"You don't know that I —"

"My mother was kept here. In this very tower. I do know," he said, with a voice both certain and quiet with loss.

His eyes, a staggering deep green, locked onto hers and she stumbled back a step.

"There has never been another person here save for the Dragon-Keep, and I've been here eighteen years."

"Yes. Are you here of your own accord? Working? Being paid?"

"She gives me a roof, food, and protection," Galena countered.

"Yes, until her use for you is over."

"Obviously your mother survived," she pointed out. "And you live freely."

Oops. The moment she said as much, his gaze sharpened. "So you don't work here of your own accord, and you know what happens to the Dragon-Keep's servants. What happened?"

She shook her head so hard her hair fell into her eyes like a curtain. She shoved it aside. "I can't say. Get out. Please."

He dampened his lips, letting his gaze flick around the room. "I'm here because I am the King's son. Prince Ansel. He has a special order for a certain dragon, which should be hatching soon. He has grown impatient."

Galena's brows furrowed. "You should have said that first. The Dragon-Keep never said that you would be arriving to pick it up. And still, it's not..." She trailed off. How much should she tell him? "How am I to believe you are supposed to be here?"

His mouth twitched. "Isn't my title enough?" He chuckled, then pulled a small ring from his pocket. He held it out in his palm to her, but she simply stared at him blankly. What did a ring have to do with anything? He cleared his throat. "It's my signet ring, for sealing letters and whatnot. Have you sincerely been kept here since childhood?"

She dipped her head. "Yes, but my time for freedom is...quickly approaching. The Dragon-Keep says so."

"Have you struck a deal with anyone?" he asked.

"A...deal?" She shook her head, feeling her stomach knot as she realized what Ansel meant. The Dragon-Keep would be willing to give up her servants...for a price. "No one's interested in small maidservants these days. The Dragon-Keep said so."

He swallowed audibly. "So, the other kind of freedom then. What's your name?"

She glanced at the broom in her hands, then slowly set it down. If he was the King's own son, he posed no risk to the treasure anyway. "My name doesn't matter."

"Of course it does. Besides, I've told you mine." He glanced around and, finding the options of seating lacking, sat down on the stone floor cross-legged.

She cleared her throat, wrapping her hands in her skirts. "It is Galena."

"Of...?" He trailed off, rolling his hand in the air as if waiting for more information.

She shook her head. "Just Galena."

He nodded slowly. "Why don't I tell you about my mother?"

She glanced around the tower. Were all men as conversational as this? Did they all simply invite themselves in and make themselves cozy?

He chuckled. "I suppose you think I'm mad, yes?"

"I believe I've stated that before," she said with a grin despite herself.

"Well, it's my hope that you'll see I'm not mad. Perhaps a little odd, but not out of my own mind."

She cleared her throat. "What happened of your mother, then?"

He nodded, seeming pleased with himself. "She was sold by her parents as a teen and kept here to protect a rare breed of small dragon, which the Dragon-Keep was afraid would be stolen under unprotected circumstances. She has several abandoned watchtowers she uses for such purposes. One night, my father – a young prince himself at the time – found this tower, which he believed to be abandoned, and sought refuge in it during a terrible storm. When he realized that it was, in fact, inhabited by a young woman, he found her quite lovely. Now, everyone in the land knows that the Dragon-Keep is a mystical woman, one who evades capture and clutches some rulers in her hand—"

"I didn't," Galena blurted.

His brows furrowed. "Didn't what?"

"Know that she was feared. She has always told me that if anyone knew I was being kept here, they would come for *her*."

Ansel's lips pressed together. "I see." He paused a few moments, then continued as if Galena had said nothing. "My father was quite pleased with the young woman that he found, and though she wasn't royalty as his parents wished for him to marry, he realized that a new deal could be sprung: he would aid the Dragon-Keep in all of her expeditions and conquests as a young ruler, if the Dragon-Keep released her servant to him for marriage."

"And she did, and so you were born?" Galena asked.

"And so I was born," Ansel said with a nod and a deep sigh.

"That is a lovely story." Galena glanced around the tower, then wiped her palms on her skirt. "But please tell your father, his highness, that the dragon's egg will not be ready until—"

Ansel stood. "Won't you tell me your story? How did the Dragon-Keep find you?"

An ache seared through her chest. "I've been here since a babe, and that's the only thing that matters."

"Of course not! Surely you have family."

"If they are still alive, I would be quite blessed and amazed." Galena bit her lip and turned toward the window. "You must leave."

"Please, tell me. Maybe..." He trailed off. "Tell me you will be safe once the egg hatches."

She shrugged him off. "That is nothing of royalty's concern, I'm certain."

"Don't be so assumptive of what stands before you," he tossed back. When she turned to look back at him, a strange expression passed over his face, clouding it for a few moments. "What caused you to become the Dragon-Keep's servant? Even telling me this will help me...understand."

"I'm fine. Perhaps your imaginings have gotten you addled more than the head injury." She laughed lightly, though it was forced.

Ansel huffed, then chuckled. "Hardheaded as a goat and a spirit as wild as the untamed islands, I see."

"What?"

"You. You're very stubborn. Hardheaded. And you're quite witty.

Spirited."

"I don't know what I am." She shook her head. "Except the Dragon-Keep's servant, and that's all that matters."

"What of your parents? Don't they care?"

Galena chewed her lip, sizing Ansel up. *Maybe he would know exactly what I'm facing if he knows what the Dragon-Keep does to servants she no longer needs, if he knew the circumstances. Or he may know of someone who wants a servant. A wild-goat-servant, if that's what he wants to call me.* She snorted a bit at her own thoughts, then sat down at the table. "I'm here because... well, it's my fault."

"How so?"

"My parents were starving, poor, and my mother had a craving. My mother stole from the Dragon-Keep's gardens when she was bearing me. As punishment, they were forced under threat of death to give up their firstborn... me. Ever since, I've been here." She twisted her hands together and swallowed hard. It was the story she'd been told by the Dragon-Keep every time she'd misbehaved as a child. The woman held a remarkable grudge against her parents. Galena knew they had only been foraging because they couldn't afford to eat, and her mother wanted to keep her baby healthy. It was all her fault they had stolen from the Dragon-Keep. She didn't even know if they were dead or alive, but she imagined... she imagined they weren't alive.

Ansel's face drained of all color. "What did you say?"

"My mother stole from the Dragon-Keep's gardens."

"You're certain?"

She laughed drily. "Yes, I believe I would know so. The Dragon-Keep herself has told me as much. Every time I..." She trailed off, her gaze flitting over to the window.

"Every time you ask to leave the tower?" Ansel finished for her.

"Among other things." She nodded, swallowed hard, and turned her gaze to her lap, where her fingers twisted nervously.

"Did they survive?" he asked gently.

"That is one thing she never told me; and I don't expect she ever will."

The expression on Ansel's face told her everything she needed to know. A lump swelled in her throat. She always thought as much – that they were dead – but *knowing* it... She took a deep, shuddering breath.

"It's not your fault, you know."

"What?"

"Your parents. I can see it written on your face, the guilt. Shame. It's not your fault. You deserve... much more." He shook his head and stood by the table near her. "You know you could escape, yes? Before the Dragon-Keep kills you and feeds you to her breeding pairs? You could go right now. I would help you."

Galena's eyes bulged at his bluntness, and she grabbed a lock of her long hair, twisting it around her finger until it cut in. "You don't know she'll kill me—that...that way."

Ansel shook his head. "I don't know that is exactly how she plans to kill you, but no one serves the Dragon-Keep and lives past their sole mission. It's how she instills fear into those who wish to rebel against her."

She felt her heart fall. The finality of it all. *As my parents died, so shall I.* She shook her head to clear it. "So, now that you know everything about my entire life, including what is yet to come...what right do you have, coming in here? Into my home? You could have at least told me you were the king's son before you came barreling in here. I would have understood your mission."

Ansel cleared his throat, and it was only then she realized he'd been gazing intently at her. His gaze dropped to the floor. "Checking in on the egg is my formal mission; the one my impatient father sent me on. It's not the real reason I'm here. You need to know what you're guarding. It's for your own safety."

"What?" Galena laughed. "It's just a tiny dragon pup, not yet hatched."

"Where do you keep it?"

"Upstairs. It's quite safe, I assure you."

Ansel cocked his head. "Upstairs?"

"Yes. Here, I will show you." Galena gestured and invited him up the stairs. He politely followed behind, and she swung the door open, allowing him entrance to see the dragon egg. He approached its nest slowly, taking in the warmth, the heaps of blankets and materials protecting it. "See, it is quite safe with me."

"That's not what I mean. *You* won't be safe, nor anyone else, as soon as the Dragon-Keep lays hands upon it. My father asked for a rare beast that could be trained and used in battle, an intelligent monster to safeguard our kingdom and conquer others. When it came down to it, the Dragon-Keep asked for a hefty price and he gave it all to her. He sold me as well as my birthright to her for this egg. His firstborn." Ansel's gaze roamed over the cracked egg. "I know her plans; she delivers them to me, as well as my own missions, through a young messenger. Untold lives will be lost if you keep this safe."

"Is it born a destroyer?" Galena asked, twisting her hands in her rough skirts.

"Nay, but easily trained for such." Ansel's fingers twitched at his side, and she knew he yearned to snatch the egg, to destroy it.

Galena bit her bottom lip. When Ansel seized her shoulder, she stiffened.

"You must understand, Galena. What she is doing, it's nothing good. There's nothing heroic about the slaughter of innocents. What my father does is wrong too. I aim to make a right—"

"Two wrongs won't justify this third wrongness," Galena murmured. "You know that, right? Killing an innocent thing—"

"It's not even alive yet—"

"The egg is cracked, it has begun to hatch. It breathes. Listen!" Galena cautiously moved aside, pressing her ear to the scaly egg's side. "Its heartbeat."

Ansel gulped. "That doesn't change—"

"It's not evil yet; and it will only become evil when someone misuses it. And...Ansel, we could run away," Galena whispered, meeting his eyes over the egg. When Ansel fell silent, eyes wide, she continued. It felt like her head was floating off elsewhere with what she was suggesting, but she steeled herself. "How many servants does the Dragon-Keep hold captive?"

"I only know of...three other locations."

"We could rescue them. Flee to the islands you mentioned earlier, tame the land all on our own. The dragon would grow there, safe. It wouldn't be trained for evil. And we would be safe from the Dragon-Keep. And you from your father...Prince Ansel." She let the words roll off her tongue, barely believing them. She, a servant, talking to the disowned prince. A sympathetic sort of hurt flared in her chest; at least her parents had been forced to give her away; she hadn't been sold like Ansel. She had never been unwanted like that. She bit her lip.

"It might work for you, but..." Ansel shoved his hands through his hair. "It's harder when you're royalty. Or *were*."

"Would it be easier if someone stood alongside you?" Galena asked. "Simply because I disagree with killing the dragon in no way means that I have disdain for *you*. I want to help you just as much as this little beast. And I know the other servants would feel the same."

A shadow passed over Ansel's face. "You wouldn't if you knew..."

"Knew what?"

"The anger I've harbored in my heart. The things I've wished upon the Dragon-Keep, my father, my entire legacy."

"Maybe you were exposed to evil from the start. But that doesn't mean you can't un-learn it," Galena said.

Another crack appeared across the egg, and a chunk of shell slid to the floor with a thin snap. They stared at the debris for several long moments, Ansel's jaw twitching. Finally, he drew a breath.

"You believe this?" he asked.

"Wholeheartedly," she said with a nod. To prove it, she gently gathered up the cracking egg in the bundle it was nestled in. She held it

with one hand to her chest.
He held out his hand. "So be it."

END

Ocean Shackles
Cassandra Hamm

A deep gasp cuts through the silence of the underwater cave.

From my place on the cave's shore, I stiffen as a head emerges from the water blocking the entrance. The figure starts cutting through the water with swift, measured strokes, much unlike Casimir's choppy aggressiveness.

Someone has found our sanctuary.

I dart into the shadows and hide behind a stalagmite. The damp rock is gritty beneath my trembling fingers.

I just have to last long enough for Casimir to return from the village. Then he will evict this stranger and make us safe again.

The person swims closer and closer to the shore, taking great lungsful of air every few moments. The inhales sound feminine, but I can't be sure. Perhaps she's simply exploring the island's many caverns and fissures... or perhaps she's here for *me*.

I measure my breathing and sink into the darkness, which isn't a difficult feat. Cas teases me that I'm so small I still look like a child, even though I'm seventeen now.

The swimmer drags herself onto the shore. Her back is arched, her limbs tense, but something about her athletic figure pricks my memory.

I fight the urge to slip forward and investigate. Casimir would be furious if I put myself in danger for such a small thing. Without magic to protect myself, I need to stay hidden.

She pushes herself to her feet. In the dim light, I see rounded cheeks and large, wide-set eyes. I rub my own eyes, as though to banish the apparition, but when I open them again, she's still there.

It can't be.

"Estelle?" she calls. "Are you here?"

I ignore Casimir's voice in my head and stumble away from the stalagmite, my legs barely holding me up. Her words tear at my seams, unraveling my thoughts and inhibitions. *Lucia.*

"Estelle!" Lucia claps a hand to her mouth. "Oh, gods, I can't believe..."

My steps falter. I haven't seen my best friend since I moved into Casimir's home. Still the same red-brown hair, almost black when wet; still the same expressive eyebrows and dark eyes ready to spill tears. A few escape, creating a trail down her freckled cheeks.

Lucia closes the distance and throws her arms around me, her amulet pressing against my neck.

I've missed her, I realize—the nights we braided each other's hair and talked about boys, her compassion for anything wounded and broken, the way her laugh filled my bones. I let myself sink into her embrace.

Lucia rests her chin on top of my head. "I've been trying to get here for ages."

Whenever someone tries to enter our home, Casimir uses mighty waves to push them away until they relent. Lucia must've been one of those people who'd tried and failed to enter our sanctuary—until now.

Lucia isn't a danger. He didn't need to keep her away.

A lump forms in my throat. *Then why did he?*

"Gods, Estelle, I can practically feel your ribs!" Lucia says.

Cas likes it when I'm thin. I pull away, shoulders hunched. Water drips from the ceiling, a cold shock against my bare arms. "Lucia, what are you doing here?"

"I wanted to see you." She wipes tears from her lashes. "It's been a whole year."

A year? Has it really been that long? Time is skewed in our cavern. Minutes seem like lifetimes, and each embrace passes by in a breath.

Lucia squeezes the ocean from her hair, but it doesn't reach the ground. Instead, droplets dance around her hands, her magic calling to the water even here.

I miss the days when magical energy collected in my amulet, the orange-and-gold firestone I pried from the volcano itself. I miss how the ocean answered to me, how saltwater seemed to run in my blood, how releasing the magic was as easy as breathing.

I shake away the thoughts. *I don't need an amulet—I have Cas.*

Lucia fingers her own amulet—an opal, dull in the cavern's dim light, but I remember how it seemed to carry the sun's rays. She, of course, couldn't help but burn every time she went outside. Her skin never grew any darker, just redder. I remember teasing her that she wasn't a real island girl.

Now I just want to feel the warmth of sunlight on my dark skin.

"Is he here?" Lucia asks, not quite able to hide the edge in her voice.

The joy inside me sours as I glance back at the water. It laps against the stone floor in soft ripples—not strong enough to tell me Casimir is coming back. Every second I'm alone with someone besides him, my skin itches.

"Estelle."

"You know he's not." The words come out clipped. "If he were, you wouldn't have made it into the cave."

"Because he would've tried to drown me?"

"He doesn't *drown* people!" I snap. "He just doesn't like it when people come into his home."

She shakes her head. I can't stand that familiar look on her freckled face—saying she knows better than me. "That's what worries me," she says. "You think it's *all right.*"

"He just wants to protect me!"

"From *what*? From *me*?"

I massage my temples, trying to stave off the headache—a frequent occurrence since I gave up my amulet. *I knew that was the only reason she came — to lecture me about Cas.*

When I first told Lucia about Casimir, she'd wrinkled her nose at our six-year age gap. Perhaps it was strange then—me just fifteen, Cas fully a man—but love doesn't recognize age. Now, she won't stop worrying about his protectiveness. How am I supposed to explain that it hurts Cas to think of me in danger?

It's always been Cas and me against a world that tries to destroy us, but that's all right. We don't need anyone else. Not even Lucia.

Lucia's eyebrows tug together as she looks me over. She's already lectured me about my weight—*now* what?

"Estelle, where's your amulet?"

I look away. I *know* what she's going to say. I *know* how she's going to react.

"He took it from you, didn't he?" Her lips flatten into a thin line. "Estelle—"

"He didn't take it. I *gave* it to him." Everything I have is his—my heart, my body. Why not my magic?

"You *gave* it to him?" She covers her face with her hands, muffling her voice. "I thought you had more sense than that. Your magic—"

"You should go, Lucia."

She steps back, her shoulders hunched, her expression wounded. I bite the inside of my cheek until I taste blood.

It's for her own good. If Cas comes back and finds her here...

"Ask him for the amulet back," Lucia says. "See what he does."

I recoil. I gave him the amulet the night I gave him my heart. If I took it back, he'd think I was withdrawing my love.

"Why would I need to do that?" I say in as nonchalant a tone as I can.

"If you're not willing to understand, there's no point in me explaining it to you."

My jaw clenches, exacerbating my headache. Why was this girl ever my best friend?

I'm about to tell her to get out when she says, "When was the last time you left?"

The question catches me off guard. "I have everything I need here," I say vaguely.

"When was the last time you left, Estelle?" she repeats, louder this time.

I *know* it seems weird that I haven't left since I moved in. But it's only because he loves me so much. If he didn't care, he wouldn't try to stop me from leaving.

"He's protective," I finally say.

"He's controlling you!"

"He loves me!" I'm shouting now, my words bouncing off the cave walls. Sweat gathers on my temples. If Cas is anywhere near, he will have heard it. And if he finds out I allowed Lucia to stay for so long...

But what could I have done? I have no magic, no way to turn her out. I suppose I should've stayed hidden, but what's done is done.

Lucia blows out a breath. "I don't know *what* it is, Estelle, but it's not love."

What does *she* know about it? She's never had a lover. She doesn't understand how when he's around, nothing exists but us — we are infinite, blinding, whole.

Maybe she has a lover now. I haven't seen her in a year. Her life has gone on without me. I swallow hard.

"It just... hurts to see you like this," Lucia says.

Oh, gods, is she *crying*? The sight almost breaks me. Lucia is many things — an athlete, a perfectionist, a secret romantic — but *not* a crier.

"You've changed, Estelle. I barely even recognize you."

Maybe I have. But all that matters is that Casimir loves me. I don't need Lucia's approval or anyone else's.

Still... sometimes I feel small, and not just in stature. Small and insignificant and worthless, ready to crumble if I go too long without Casimir by my side. An addict, unable to live without him, like my mama can't live without daily pinches of gem dust.

Is that really a bad thing, though? Casimir is my oxygen, my reason for living, and I am his. What could be more beautiful than that?

"I wanted to rescue you." Lucia wipes her nose. "But I can't rescue someone who wants to stay."

"I don't need to be rescued!"

But the word — *rescue* — pokes and prods at me, finding root in traitorous thoughts — *I don't like it when Cas tells me I can't eat meat or wear baggy clothing. Or when he compares me to a child. Or when he uses his magic to drag me back to shore if I ever swim too close to the entrance. Maybe... maybe I am trapped.*

"Cas adores me," I say as firmly as I can. "What more could I want?"

Waves lap against the shore, harder this time. They slosh over the rock lip and gush onto the ground, soaking my boots. I look to the cave's entrance and find the ocean rushing toward us, carrying a man on its crest.

My blood turns to ice. *Casimir is back.* "Hide!" I hiss to Lucia.

She darts behind a stalagmite farther into the cave's depths and is swallowed by the shadows.

Casimir rides toward us, his arms outstretched as he manipulates the water to his will. His face is triumphant, his body language sure. He alights on the shore, letting the water settle down behind him.

"Cas!" I run toward him and throw myself into his arms, hoping he can't feel my heart hammering. "I've missed you."

"Estelle," he murmurs against my hair.

His skin is damp—he must've submerged at some point. I press my face to his neck and breathe in the scent of sweat. Two pendants hang from his neck, one a sapphire, the other my old firestone. His amulets.

Seeing them reminds me of what Lucia said, and I can't bear to think about her, what Cas will do if he finds out she's here. Impulsively, I press a kiss to his bare collarbone. His arms tighten around me. I lean into him, reveling in his solid warmth.

A gem digs into my cheek. I pull back just enough to register that it's the firestone—*my* firestone, if I can still think of it as such.

Without thinking, I touch the amulet. My breath hitches as its power tingles against my fingertips. I remember when I found it, how *I* discovered it on the volcano's flank, how *I* was the one to dig it up. I remember the first time I touched it, how it felt so truly, perfectly *mine*. It wasn't something my mama could take away. It was power—it was freedom.

Lucia told me to ask him for the amulet. Maybe I *could*. Maybe he wouldn't get mad.

"Do you think...?" My voice falters, but I push on. "Could I wear my firestone? For old time's sake."

He pulls back, frowning. "Why would you want to do that?"

"I... I don't know." I clear my throat. "To protect myself, I suppose."

He laughs. "Why would you need magic when you have my protection?"

"Well, yes, but when you're gone, I don't always feel... safe." Not that I ever feel unsafe around *him*. Just when he's gone. That's all. I'm tired of feeling powerless while he's away.

His eyes soften. "It's not like you had enough power to protect yourself, anyway. You really were terrible with that amulet."

I shrink back, but his grip tightens.

"Just do as I told you and hide if anyone comes by. You'll be fine until I return. If anyone makes it into the cave..." His grin turns feral. "Don't worry. They won't make it out."

My throat tightens. I can't respond, can't think of anything except that Lucia is here, and if he finds her—

"I'm famished." Casimir releases me and takes off his pack, which I'm sure is full of grains and produce and meat. The meat isn't for me, but that's all right. I only miss it sometimes. "How about I start a fire, and you can get cooking."

He won't go far into the cave. He won't find her. I have to believe it, or I'll fall apart. "Anything special for tonight's meal?"

"Nah." He smirks. "Let's just hope you won't burn anything this time."

I flinch. I know my cooking skills aren't up to his standards. Even after a whole year of making his meals, I'm still just passable. I think of how, when she wasn't high on gem dust, Mama would roast freshly caught boar—tough, savory meat cooked in redcurrant, sweet fennel, woody cloves, and honey. My stomach growls.

"Sounds like you're hungry too," he says.

My cheeks warm as I nod. *I can't eat what I want, though.*

These dissatisfied thoughts driving a wedge between Cas and me are all Lucia's fault. I never would've doubted Casimir like this if not for her. I wish she'd never come.

"You look lovely, by the way," Casimir says in a low, husky voice.

His gaze runs over my body, warm and appreciative, and I revel in it. His hands encircle my waist as he tugs me against his chest. I peer up at him, taking in the smooth planes of his face, the rich tan of his unblemished skin, the firm lines of his jaw and cheekbones. His golden hair falls in thick waves over his forehead, curling behind his ears, and I want to run my fingers through it.

He is beautiful, and he is mine.

He presses a kiss to my lips, over far too quickly, and lets me go. "Now, about dinner."

I stifle a sigh. It's better if we don't get intimate right now, anyway, since Lucia is here. *Besides,* I remind myself, *I don't deserve anything from him or anyone.*

Lucia said he was no good for me, but she's wrong. He's *too* good for me.

Casimir wanders farther into the cave—*too far.* My heart rate triples as I rush toward him. "Wait!" I blurt.

He turns back to face me, his full lips twisting into a scowl. "What is it, my love?"

"I just—I thought we could—I don't know. Could we wait a little before eating?"

"I heard your stomach growl, Estelle." He laughs. "Not that you need any more food."

I swallow hard, looking down at my body. I thought I was getting better, but my thighs are still too big, my hips too wide, my stomach not flat enough. I wrap my arms around my torso in an attempt to hide the imperfections.

"That's *enough*." The words are sharp and clear, the voice all too familiar and feminine.

I freeze. But it's too late—Lucia is stepping out from behind the stalagmite, her head held high, her stride purposeful. Her amulet sparks white-hot.

Casimir goes rigid, his hands straying to his own amulets.

They're going to fight each other.

"You remember Lucia, don't you?" I force a light tone. "I would have mentioned her earlier, but I didn't want to startle you right when you got home. She just dropped by while you were away."

"Of course I do." His voice is nearly glacial.

"Hello, Casimir."

I want to tell her to drop her fighting stance, that it will make him react more calmly, but somehow, I doubt that anything Lucia does will make him relax.

"She was about to go when you returned," I say. "Weren't you, Lucia?"

"Leaving so soon?" Casimir says, right when Lucia snaps, "I'm not going anywhere without you, Estelle."

My stomach clenches into a cold, hard knot. *This can't be happening.*

Casimir holds up his hands. The water swirls ominously behind us. "I don't think I heard you correctly. You seem to have said something about taking my beloved from me."

"She doesn't belong to you, old man." Lucia extends her own hands. Her opal glows, a pinprick of light against her pale skin.

"Please, Lucia," I beg. "You need to go."

"Oh, it's too late for that." The soft blue of Casimir's eyes turns to frost. "This girl trespassed in *my* home. Now she will pay the price."

"You can't! Please, Cas, I'll do anything!"

He flicks his hand toward me, sending an icy wave crashing over me. I nearly collapse under its weight. The chill spreads to my core.

"I knew you were planning to leave me." His voice is low, almost a whisper, but it cuts straight to my bones. "Even after all I've done for you."

"I wasn't—I didn't—"

"Don't you *dare* manipulate her like that!" Lucia launches herself at Casimir, whipping up a water funnel of her own. He twists, sweeping his long, lithe fingers in a curving motion. The funnel pauses before turning back on its creator.

"Watch out!" I cry.

But it's too late. Lucia gasps as it slams against her body, nearly knocking her off her feet.

Casimir turns burning eyes on me. I flinch. His fingers twitch, sending water toward my face. It pushes its way through my lips and into my throat, choking, burning. I wheeze, trying to expel the water and drag air into my lungs, but the ocean is winning.

"Don't touch her!" Lucia snarls, launching herself at Casimir.

"I *didn't* touch her." He withdraws the water from my mouth.

I heave in ragged breaths, tears stinging my eyes. *He tried to drown me.*

Lucia lets out an animalistic growl. "You bastard."

He forms the fallen water into a long rope. My eyes widen, but before I can say anything, the whip cracks against Lucia. She flies backward, hitting the cave wall with a sickening *thud*.

"Lucia!" My shriek is raspy, my vision blurred. Bile surges to my throat, nearly making me gag.

We were supposed to grow old together, raising our babies alongside each other, being honorary aunties. We were supposed to sit by the sea and listen to the volcano complain, much like we would complain about the aches in our bones and the ways our husbands annoyed us.

Cas took that away from me. The realization swells inside me, pressing against my skull until all I can do is scream and scream, my lungs weak but my grief fierce. Each keening wail rubs me raw.

She's gone.

Casimir claps a hand over my mouth, silencing me. I struggle against his grip.

"It's what she deserves," Casimir says. "She trespassed in *our* sanctuary."

She just wanted to see me! If you'd let her come here, this never would've happened! Tears pour down my cheeks and soak his fingers.

"You know I hate doing things like that, Estelle. But I wouldn't have had to if you hadn't let her stay."

Maybe it is my fault. If not for me revealing myself to her, Cas wouldn't have gotten upset. *He was just scared because he thought I was going to leave him, that's all.*

I collapse against him, my body aching, my heart in pieces. His hand slides down my jaw, my neck. He presses a kiss to the hollow of my throat.

My eyes find Lucia, crumpled against the stone floor. Pain lances through my sternum, as though I've been physically stabbed.

But then—she shifts. Her body moves, just a fraction. Is that a groan?

Casimir doesn't seem to notice, his face still buried in my neck. Did I imagine it? Am I just seeing what my desperate eyes want me to see?

Then her foot twitches. I hold back a sob. *She's alive. He didn't kill her.*

"I know it's hard." He twists me around to face him. His eyes have calmed to the gentle blue of the ocean at dawn. "But she wanted to separate us. Everyone does. You remember how your family disowned you simply because you wanted to be with me? Their judgment and scorn, just because I'm a few years older."

"You tried to drown me." The reckless words slip out. I wish I could bite them back, but his eyes have already shifted to something hard and unfamiliar.

"It was just a bit of water. You're overreacting, Estelle."

He just did it because I tried to warn Lucia. That's all. I chose her over him. He had a right to be mad. My eyes find Lucia again. She isn't currently moving, but I *didn't* imagine it. She's alive. She has to be.

"Hey. Look at me." He forms a wall of water, surrounding us on all four sides, so I can't see Lucia anymore. I stare at the slick floor.

He grips my chin with frigid fingers, forcing my face toward his. "I love you. You know that, right?"

"I know." The tears won't stop falling. Lucia's words echo in my head: *"It's not love."* What if she's right? What if this all-consuming, desperate thing between us is something else entirely?

"They don't love you. Not like I do." His hand tightens on my chin. I yelp as pain shoots through my jaw. "You're lucky I stay with you."

"I know." I'm shaking so badly I can barely stand. "I'm very grateful. But... I was thinking... well, I get lonely sometimes."

"You have me. How could you ever be lonely?"

"I know, but you're not always here, so... maybe you could let me go out to the village again sometime."

He laughs, a cruel, hard sound. "No one wants to see you there."

Lucia does. Maybe even my mama misses me. Or maybe she's lost herself completely in a haze of gem dust now that I'm not there to stop her.

"Then... can I at least have visitors?" My voice squeaks. "I love you, but... I miss people sometimes."

"You don't need anyone but me." He's smiling, but his tone is harsh.

"We have a lovely cave. You can show it off, you know." I'm babbling now. "You don't have to drown the people who try to come here—"

"This is our *sanctuary*, Estelle!" His voice bounces off the walls.

I close my eyes. *I shouldn't have asked. I should've just stayed quiet. Then he would be happy.*

"I'm sorry. I didn't mean to shout." His fingers trail along my jaw. "I know it's hard for you to understand, Estelle, but this is what's best for you."

What's best? How is trying to kill Lucia what's *best*? How could killing a girl whose only crime was wanting to see her best friend be *best*?

My body begins to shake. *This isn't right,* my mind screams. *This isn't right.*

All the things I've ignored come rushing back—the way he won't let me eat enough or see anyone but him or use magic anymore. I stare at the firestone swinging from his neck and remember the burst of power I felt when I touched it—how alive I felt, more alive than I have since we moved in together.

I'm not strong enough to save Lucia. But maybe if he had only one amulet, I could save my best friend, damn the consequences.

Lucia's life is more important than my happiness.

"What's best," I whisper.

"Yes." He smiles. "Someday you'll understand."

One of my hands snakes up to wrap around the back of his neck, the other touching his chest. I wrap my fingers around the firestone. It tingles, filling me with the strength I've lacked for so long. I work at the knot keeping the necklace together, unraveling it just slightly.

He blinks at me, the strange motion registering in his eyes, but he's too late. I rip the amulet from his neck. I stagger backward, clutching the firestone in my palm. My back presses against the wall of water before it disintegrates, splashing onto my head and coursing down my body.

I rub the wetness from my eyes and blink. My heartbeat stutters as I see the cold fury on his too-perfect face. I scramble to my feet and hurry toward Lucia, who is standing and rubbing her head.

Her eyes are dazed, her expression shocked. "Estelle! You... how...?"

I thrust the firestone toward her. "Take it."

She reaches for it, but a wave slams into me from the side. The amulet slips from my grasp as I land hard on my hip. Groaning, I look up to see Casimir is running for the fallen firestone. I crawl toward it and tuck it into my fingers, then curl into a ball, readying myself for the inevitable kick.

But it never comes. Instead, I hear a grunt. I look up. Casimir strains against a watery rope.

"Run!" Lucia shouts.

I drag myself to my feet, hesitating at the edge of the lake. Casimir is distracted. I might actually be able to leave.

Do I want to? Casimir is my entire life. This cave is my *home.* And Lucia needs this amulet—

"Damn it, Estelle, just *go!*" Lucia cries. Then water slams against my back, sending me toppling into the lake.

Water closes around me, fierce and cool and familiar. I force my limbs to move despite the shock and the terror, my feet kicking, my arms pushing me toward the surface. The amulet digs into my palm with the force of my grip.

But the water rebels against me, churning and foaming, pressing against my skin so painfully I gasp, letting water in. *He really will drown me.* Panic is a vise around my throat. Air streams through my nose and forms a cloud of bubbles.

Then a watery force heaves me back onto shore. I land hard, ribs complaining, and hack up what feels like half the ocean.

This is Casimir's home, his dominion. It's always been *his*, not *ours*. There's nothing I can do but bend and beg and hope he forgives me for my treachery.

The firestone floods my hand with sudden heat, and I drop it, palm stinging. It pulses orange, showing more life than it has since the day I gave it to Cas, as though it knows it's back with its master.

You found me, it seems to say. *I belong to none but you.*

I reach for it hesitantly. Its heat doesn't bother me anymore. Weak as I am, I can feel magic flowing from my skin into its molten exterior. Soon, it will be usable.

Lungs rattling, I look up at Casimir and Lucia, locked in combat. Without the extra amulet, he is almost evenly matched with Lucia, but she still seems weak from her head injury. He pushes her back, farther and farther, until she is nearly against the wall of the cave.

I look down at the firestone again. *You can't use that amulet,* Casimir once said. *You don't have enough power.*

Maybe the person he wanted me to be doesn't have that kind of power. But I am a girl of the islands, raised by the volcano, baptized in fire and water, and I cannot help but rise.

I close my eyes and breathe in, clutching the amulet tight. Its facets press against my hand so hard they almost draw blood. *For Lucia,* I think.

Casimir turns his face toward me, pale eyes widening as he pauses the fight. "You gave that amulet to me," he hisses. "That power is *mine*."

"No," I say. "It's always been mine."

Energy surges into my body, burning away the terror and filling me with love instead—not the blinding love I had for Cas, but love for Lucia, the girl who didn't give up on me even when I pushed her away.

I thrust my hand—my small, thin, trembling hand—toward the wall of water separating Lucia from Casimir. His hold on it breaks, and it roars toward him. He staggers beneath the weight of the wave, then collapses. His head slams against the stone floor. He doesn't rise.

Lucia and I release the power. The water falls to the stone and bleeds back into the lake.

I stare at my lovely Casimir, limp on the ground. A strangled cry bursts from my mouth. *I killed him. I killed him!*

Lucia grabs my arm before I can move. "Wait."

She approaches him hesitantly, then flips him over. His face—his beautiful face—is pale and ghostlike. My stomach lurches, but I haven't eaten since a biscuit this morning.

"He's alive."

Though Lucia sounds annoyed, my shoulders slump at her words. *I didn't kill him.* I'm not sure I could've handled it if I had.

"Perhaps we should…" She trails away.

My heart skips painfully in my chest. "You want to kill him?"

"Estelle—"

"We can't. Please."

She looks at me, her eyebrows knitting together. "He'll come for you, Estelle."

"I know." My voice is small, raw after the almost-drowning. "Please forgive me. I couldn't… I wasn't…"

Lucia crushes my hand in hers. Her fingers are wet but warm, unlike Casimir's icy grip.

When I enter the lake, I half-expect Casimir's power to pull me back to the shore. The water surrounding me feels like a prison instead of a second home, like it used to be. Part of me wants to drown, to let the ocean take me after what I did to my beloved. How I betrayed him.

In my head, I hear Casimir say, *You can't leave me. We are nothing without each other.*

But then I see Lucia swimming ahead of me, her magic pushing and pulling the water, her movements strong and sure as we surge toward the underwater entrance. Toward sunlight and sand and new beginnings.

I might be a dying fire, but I won't let these embers fade. I will prove him wrong. I will *live*.

I take a deep breath and dive to freedom.

END

The Tower
Deborah Cullins Smith

"The Tower of London was originally built in 1066 by William the Conqueror. It took twenty years to build and was first conceived as a military fortress. It was a massive keep with twenty towers and an enormous moat. Double walls kept the English safe from all invaders..."The guide droned on, but Dorothy Wexfield tuned him out. She had read the literature before booking this tour, and her mind already churned with the stories she wanted to write about the people who had been imprisoned within these cold stone walls.

Few noticed the young American woman. She had learned long ago to fade into the background wherever she went. Some authors developed flamboyant styles, and they announced their presence wherever they might appear, but Dorothy preferred to keep a low profile. The fewer questions she raised, the better she liked it. She wanted to absorb atmosphere, not stir it up. She sought to study the places and the people in the settings she planned to use in her next books and novellas; she didn't want to be the center of attention for a clamoring public. Her figure was trim, but not remarkable. Her hair was clean, but not lavishly styled. She kept her wardrobe so conservative that her friends had accused her of prudishness, and one went so far as to call her "mousey." She kept her skirts knee-length, her necklines ridiculously high or buttoned to the chin. She could "dress up" if the occasion demanded—or rather, if her father demanded—but for research trips, she maintained an anonymous frumpiness.

Dorothy stepped through the portcullis, looking up to see the sharp spikes above her head. She shivered as she imagined that heavy gate slamming down and locking her inside the Tower. Or worse, coming down on top of her and skewering her to the path at her feet. Her heart thumped a little harder and she scurried through the portal, pausing to stare back at the gears that held the gate high above their heads. *Such heavy chains!* The little group passed between the sections of double walls as the guide continued with his lecture.

"If invaders did manage to breach the portcullis, the double walls of the fortress served to stop them before they could get past this inner door. Defenders would rain arrows down from above and anyone caught between the walls, where we are right now, would be sitting ducks."

Nervous chuckles fluttered through the visitors as they scanned the walls for signs of archers poised above them. When none appeared, their guide ushered them through the heavy inner door into the courtyard beyond the Tower walls.

Nearby, a chubby woman in a brightly flowered dress shrieked and scrambled away from a sleek cat, bumping into others, treading toes and banging elbows. Titters ran through the crowd.

"Here now," protested a large man with a bulbous nose. "It's only a cat."

"But it's a black cat," the woman squealed.

"You'll see cats everywhere in the Tower," the guide said with a reassuring smile. "Black cats have always been considered especially good omens here. In fact, so much so, there are some black cats buried in the very foundations. To this day, there are always cats in the Tower, and many are black."

"Well, keep 'em away from me," the woman muttered, to the amusement of those standing closest to her.

"Superstitious blather," the large man snorted. "Black cats are just black cats."

Dorothy smiled indulgently at the banter, but something shivered over her skin, like a breeze that lifted the hair on her arms. Was it the cats? Surely not. She was fond of animals, even black cats. Why would a cat cause her discomfort? She looked about her. Her companions were a jovial lot. No threat from that quarter. But something caused her senses to tingle. What was it?

As they moved toward the buildings, the guide talked about the many guests of the Tower. One of the first was Bishop Ranoud Flambard in the year 1100.

"Flambard was clever and ambitious, quite the livewire," the guide said with a grin. "Today we would call him a hotshot." That comment drew a few laughs. "He had been a tax collector for the previous king, and was suspected of, shall we say, creative bookkeeping. He frequently entertained his guards and was quite the party animal. One night, he got his guards roaringly drunk, then he took a rope and rappelled down the wall. He managed to escape across the sea.

"But a little over a hundred years later, in 1241, a prisoner of Henry III tried the same stunt and fell to his death. So not all stories ended well." The laughter remaining from the tale of Flambard died away.

"Who remembers the movie *Braveheart*?" the guide asked. Murmurs drifted through the little group. "Of course! Everyone knows the fabulous Mel Gibson movie." He paused on the Green in the middle of the tall towers. "King Edward I, also known as Edward the Longshanks, was determined to bring the Scottish people to their knees. He began by capturing the heads of the Balliol clans, John Balliol and his son Edward. They were imprisoned together with several other nobles here in the Tower, after Edward put their border town to the sword and defeated them at Dunbar in 1296. He seized Edinburgh, then forced King Balliol to abdicate his throne. With the Balliols locked in the Tower, Edward thought he had Scotland under control. The Balliols actually lived in comfort, at least for the first six months. They had rooms off the great hall in the White Tower. Their personal household consisted of a chaplain, assistant chaplain, tailor, pantry attendant, butler, barber, two chamberlains, two grooms, and horses for exercise riding. They were even given an allowance to maintain this staff. As Balliol's value as a political prisoner decreased, he was moved to the cramped confines of the Salt Tower and his allowance was cut. Two years later, his pleas to the Pope finally bore fruit. Until his death in 1314, Balliol was a dependent of the Pontiff in France, who paid the bills for his upkeep.

"But in 1297, William Wallace beat Edward at Stirling Bridge. Edward was furious that an upstart Scotsman of no particular breeding could rise up against the greatest army in the known world. He bribed the other chieftains and, with their betrayal, managed to defeat Wallace at Falkirk in 1298. After that, Wallace resorted to guerilla tactics. And those tactics were hugely successful. The Scotsmen cringed as Wallace took revenge on those who had betrayed him. Englishmen shook in their armor for fear that Wallace would rise from the mists and slaughter them where they stood. In 1305, Wallace was betrayed by Sir John Menteith in return for a hefty English bribe. Wallace broke the back of one captor and literally brained a second man. He was brought to London in chains and treated as a common rebel and traitor. He was held at the Tower until his trial at Westminster Hall."

Dorothy felt that chill again. The wind picked up and lifted her hair from her shoulders.

"Here on this Green, William Wallace was hanged, then racked. When they released the ropes, he had to be dragged to a wooden table, and that's when the real torture began." Silence lay heavy over the group. "His genitals were removed, then he was disemboweled while the crowds called for his blood. At last, he was beheaded, then drawn and quartered. His head was placed on a pike along that wall." He pointed to the walls towering above them. "His arms and legs were sent to the four corners of Scotland as a warning to other rebels."

"Didn't work out very well for old Edward though, did it?" muttered a voice in the crowd.

The guide smiled ruefully. "No, it didn't. The Scots rose up under Robert the Bruce and gained their freedom. But at a terrible, terrible cost. After Edward's reign, the Tower became known as a place of murder."

Dorothy looked around the beautifully kept Green. Suddenly the scenery shifted, as if centuries fell away. Peasants watched a giant with long red hair hanging by his neck. He was no Mel Gibson, but he was an amazing specimen of a man. Long limbs flailed against the air as he strangled, to the sound of Englishmen calling for his death. Then suddenly the rope released and he crumpled to the wooden platform. Dorothy strained to see past the shoulders of the people in their dirty homespun clothing. Then she shrank back, afraid of being seen herself. But these people seemed unaware of her presence. She turned her attention back to the man on the platform. Ropes circled his arms and legs, and a horse pulled his legs straight out from the poles that held his arms. She heard the snap of cartilage and bones, yet the giant man made no outcry.

How can he stand the pain? Her heart beat wildly against her ribs. They stretched him forever, until Dorothy wanted to scream. By the time they released the ropes, Wallace dropped to the platform with a thud that shook the ground beneath her feet. Unable to rise to his feet, he was dragged to the wooden table and thrown rudely onto its stained surface. His clothing was cut away and a brazier was pulled nearer. The crowds cheered as the butcher held up the big Scot's manhood. Dorothy looked away, tears in her eyes. Barbarians! How could people do this to one another? She heard the sizzle and smelled flesh hit the fire. Then she saw the butcher pulling organs from the body of the wretched man. Still, he uttered no cries. With every organ the butcher held aloft, there was a cheer, then the sound and smell of sizzling meat hitting the fire. Dorothy choked. His entrails seemed to go on forever, and the smell almost doubled her over. Then she saw the enormous axe rise in the air and descend...

Dorothy shook her head. The group was moving on along, the guide chatting about other famous or infamous inmates of the Tower through the years. She hurried to catch up with them. Thankfully no one had noticed her lagging behind. She took one more look over her shoulder at the Green.

And shivered.

Dorothy caught up with her group inside the White Tower. The guide paused long enough to scan his charges. Satisfied that he had everyone in his tour, he proceeded down a dank stairwell.

"Many of you may remember the tales of Richard III, one of our most notorious kings, who was known for murdering his way to the throne."

A shiver crawled up Dorothy's spine, and the stones in the stairwell felt like they were closing in on her. She reached out to steady herself and jerked her hand away from the wall with a sharp gasp.

I'm losing my grip! Dorothy swallowed hard. *I could swear I felt a sob coming from that wall. But walls don't breathe. Or cry.*

"Edward IV and his queen, Elizabeth, arranged for their sons, young Prince Edward V and Richard, the Duke of York, to be brought here to the Tower—to the upper rooms, of course—to be kept under guard while the King fought his enemies in what we know as the War of the Roses. Their care was entrusted to the one person King Edward still believed in—his younger brother Richard.

"But Richard had plans of his own. He had already turned the King against their brother, Clarence, arranged for his arrest, then paid to have him murdered before Edward could change his mind and pardon Clarence in a moment of mercy. Now the only people standing between Richard and the throne were his brother the King—on the front lines of battle daily—and his two young nephews."

Fear rushed at Dorothy so strongly, she stumbled and fell against the stone wall. She felt the room grow dark around her. Her surroundings had changed. She stood in the corner of a bed chamber fitted with two narrow beds, and two blond boys who lay sleeping. A bent figure slipped through the darkness, little more than a shadow, until he stood over the older boy. His face twisted, and he hesitated only a moment before grabbing a pillow and stuffing it over the child's face. The boy thrashed and beat at his attacker, but his fists did nothing against the man's brute strength.

In the other bed, the smaller boy sat up and scrubbed his sleepy eyes with his fists.

"Edward, are you dreaming?" he asked, blinking across the room by the dim moonlight shifting through the narrow window. "Edward?"

Then Edward's body lay still and the shadow over him moved toward the little boy.

Dorothy felt his terror grow, saw his face drain of color as his eyes filled with tears. "My f-f-father is the King! You mustn't hurt us! Edward! Wake up! Edward!"

"Don' you cry, little Prince," the shadow said. "You'll see your bruvver in just a moment. Won't hurt much. It's sorry I am, but I does as I'm told."

The pillow came down and Dorothy felt the air leave her own lungs. She fell against the wall in horror as the child's cries ended.

The man picked up both boys and slung them over each shoulder like sacks of potatoes, before shuffling down the stone staircase.

"...no longer seen by the window playing together. The Queen was always certain Richard had killed her sons, but no one could find their bodies."

Dorothy slowly became aware of the guide's voice. She shook her head.

What is happening to me?

"Are you all right, Miss?" An elderly man peered at her with concern etched on his face. His voice carried a thick Australian accent. His wife hovered at his shoulder, equally concerned.

Dorothy managed a weak smile. "Yes, thank you," she whispered. "Just felt a bit faint there for a moment."

"That tale always gives me the willies." The plump wife shuddered. "Poor little tikes." Her accent was much more British than her husband's. Two pairs of brilliant blue eyes watched Dorothy's reactions carefully.

"In 1604, a box was discovered under these stairs." The guide pointed to a place commemorated by a plaque under the stairwell. "It contained the bones of two children and was believed to be the remains of the young princes. Their bones were removed and interred at Westminster Abbey."

"Can we find some nicer place to visit?" an American teenager whined. "This is creeping me out."

The guide smiled as a few other tourists snickered. "Well, before we leave the lower levels, we do have one more stop to make."

"Must be the dungeons." A red-haired American man laughed. He was one of three young men. Dorothy had overheard enough of their banter to know they were Americans stationed at one of the nearby air bases, and this was their first opportunity to "see the sights."

"Don't need to see no dungeon," grumbled a young African American. "That's a place of misery."

"You afraid it's haunted, Teddy?" A skinny guy with black-framed glasses and an unmistakable Brooklyn accent laughed.

"Nope." Teddy shook his head. "Don't believe in ghosts. But sometimes the misery sticks around."

His buddies elbowed him good-naturedly. The guide picked up on their comments and affirmed that, yes, they were headed for the dungeon.

"And you might be right about misery lingering in a place, young man," the guide said. "For this place has certainly seen its share."

The dismal area they entered was filled with medieval torture devices, from racks to whips and the wickedly curved axes, long favored by Tower guards in days long ago.

Dorothy held her breath as the sobs and screams echoed around her, crying out from the stone walls of the chambers that surrounded her. Men screamed in rage and pain. Women's shrieks carried terror, humiliation, horror. All screamed, "Why did this happen to me?"

Dimly, Dorothy heard the guide's voice.

"Queen Mary, daughter of Henry VIII, filled these dungeons with Protestants during her reign. She was violently bitter over the death of her mother and the changes in policy wrought during her father's marriage to Anne Boleyn. Her goal was to stamp out what she called 'heresy' and return the country to its Catholic roots. She tortured Protestant Christians in wholesale lots, then burned them at the stake. She's known today as

'Bloody Mary.'"
"Why, God?"
"I am forsaken!"
"I am lost!"
"I can't take the pain!"
"No, don't touch me!"
"I'll say whatever you want! Just stop! Please! Pleeeeease stop...."
"I'll confess..."

Dorothy stumbled, overwhelmed. She squeezed her eyes shut, but still saw visions of men and women chained to the walls, stretched on the racks, their screams echoing in the dim recesses of the dungeon. Others hung by their arms from chains attached to hooks in the ceiling while men beat them with barbed whips or burned them with heated iron rods. Their sobs and curses soaked into the stones.

"Miss? Miss? Are you all right? Does anyone have a bottle of water?"

The guide's voice above her pulled Dorothy back to the twenty-first century. A bottle of water pressed against her lips, and some liquid dribbled into her mouth. She gulped, struggling to open her eyes, and found herself staring up into the eyes of the guide and several of her fellow tourists. The elderly British lady held her upper body cradled in her arms. The rest of her had landed on the cold stone floor.

"There we are," the guide said a bit too cheerfully. "Bit of fresh air and you'll be right as rain. Sorry to say, but the dungeon often proves to be a bit much for some of our visitors."

"I-I-I'm so sorry," Dorothy murmured, as she tried to stagger to her feet. The guide and the Australian man steadied her.

"Quite all right, miss," the guide said with a smile. "This can be a pretty intense place to visit."

"No kidding," muttered the G.I. named Teddy, still looking around the dungeon uncomfortably while his buddies teased him about ghosts.

The other tourists moved away after casting a few curious glances her way. The elderly couple remained close.

"You know, mate, my wife and I have been on this tour before. You'll head up to Thomas More's chamber next. Right?" The old man's bright blue eyes held a twinkle.

The guide's smile crinkled the corners of his eyes. "Guess you have visited us before. Yes, sir. That's the next stop."

"There's a nice window at the top of the stairs. How about we take the lady up to that window for a little air? I promise we won't go no further than that."

"Well, the group is supposed to stay together..."

"You haven't got but about five more minutes to your spiel. And me and Abby ain't apt to be running no foot races through the Tower, are we?"

The guide laughed.

"We just want to help the lady here."

"All right, best behavior then. I'll trust you both to be at the top of the steps in five minutes or I'll call out the guards on you. Might have to chain you three down in the dungeon for more than a tour if you're pulling one over on me." He tried to frown as he said the last bit and utterly failed when the elderly couple crowed with delight.

"You have our word, young man," the lady said in her crisp English accent. She nodded brightly and linked her arm through Dorothy's. "Come, my dear."

"You're too kind," Dorothy murmured, as they made their way up the stone steps. "I'm sorry you're missing out on the tour."

"Oh, pish posh," she said. "We've seen it before. Anytime Horace's relatives visit, they all want a tour of the Tower. We could probably give it as well as our young guide back there by now."

They reached the landing and Dorothy leaned out the window, breathing deeply.

"Besides, Miss Wexfield, it's an honor to be of assistance to one of my favorite authors." The old man smiled at the shock on Dorothy's face. "Horace Dellacourt at your service. And this is my wife, Abigail."

"How did... But..." She stammered a moment, then fell silent.

Abigail patted the white knuckles that clutched the window ledge. "Don't worry, my dear. We won't say a word. It's obvious you don't want to be recognized. We know how to keep a confidence."

Dorothy dared to look at her and saw compassion in the wrinkled face, gentleness in the smile.

"Thank you," she whispered.

"You're welcome," Horace said, bowing his head. She stared up into merry blue eyes with a trace of mischief. A courtly man though. A man who could be trusted.

How do I know that? She wondered at this instant relief she felt. She relaxed, her shoulders slumping as she breathed deeply.

"New book?" Horace asked.

She grimaced. "One I'm beginning to regret."

"Thought as much." He chuckled. "The Tower tends to have that effect on people. And don't worry. I won't ask questions."

"Dorothy laughed. "Now that's refreshing!"

"Well, I will ask one," said Abigail. "Might I ask the era?"

"Actually, I'm researching several at one time," Dorothy confessed. "The Tower may figure into more than one project. And I'm certainly finding more than I bargained for." She looked out over the Green and frowned. "Tell me something. You've been on this tour before. Have you ever ... sensed or seen ... or felt strange things here?"

Horace and Abigail exchanged an odd look. Then Abigail's eyes met Dorothy's. "Every time, dear."

Dorothy felt her eyebrows rise. Just then, Horace glanced toward the stairwell as footsteps and voices came their way.

"We'll have to continue this discussion later, ladies. We're about to rejoin the tour."

"You need to brace yourself, my dear," whispered Abigail, squeezing Dorothy's arm briefly. She covered her surprise just before the guide came around the corner and up the stairs with his charges.

Their group surrounded them. Dorothy overheard the guide as he clapped Horace on the shoulder and murmured, "Glad I didn't have to call out the Beefeaters, mate."

Horace chuckled and shook his head, muttering about being too old for such antics, which made the guide laugh.

Neither looked her way. But Horace and Abigail managed to remain close to Dorothy as they moved along through the Tower.

The next stop was relatively close. The chamber was small, containing only a cot with some straw, a table, and a chair. The ceiling was low, and the table was positioned by the window to catch the few hours of daylight. Iron grid doors barred the entry, giving the prisoner no privacy whatsoever. Dorothy felt agitation rise the minute she stepped into the room. Frustration and anger clawed at her.

"Failure!"

"Weakling!"

"Fool!"

"What are you doing?"

Dorothy clenched her jaw. Abigail sidled up next to her and slipped a comforting arm around her waist. The voices eased a little.

"This was the cell of Thomas More," the guide began. "Once one of Henry VIII's greatest friends and supporters, he withdrew when Henry demanded that his political allies embrace Anne Boleyn as the next Queen of England, replacing Queen Catherine of Aragon, who had been his wife for fifteen years. Besides replacing his queen, Henry was determined to replace the Catholic Church with a new Church of England, in which he would be named the head of the church instead of the Pope. Both were radical moves that would change the course of English history, and he rocked the foundations of all his people believed at that time.

"Thomas More tried to remain quietly in the country with his family, but those on both sides of the issue refused to let him remain neutral. In the end, when pressed, he could not deny his conscience and advocate for a divorce he felt was unwarranted and misguided. In this room, his wife came to plead with him to sign the King's Oath of Supremacy, which would have meant swearing loyalty to the Church of England and renouncing the Roman Catholic Church. It would have also meant that any children of Anne's would inherit the throne, while Catherine's daughter, Mary would be cast from the line of succession. This Thomas would not do, though it meant his life."

Dorothy frowned. What she felt in this room was different. But why? Why? There was frenzy here, but beneath it was a calm resolve. Was it Abigail's arm around her waist that made the difference?

"In the end, Henry had Thomas More beheaded for defying him. But it was believed to be one of his greatest regrets."

They moved to the next chamber.

"And this room belonged to Bishop Fisher. Like Thomas More, he refused to recognize the divorce of Henry from Queen Catherine. The Pope tried to save Fisher's life by declaring him a Cardinal. He dispatched a courier with the Cardinal's mitre — the tall hat signifying the office. In a fit of fury, Henry had Fisher charged with treason and beheaded before the vestments of office could arrive from Rome."

Dorothy felt insane laughter bubble from the walls followed by rage, fury, a loathing beyond any she'd ever known. She shivered.

"Hold on," Abigail whispered.

They moved on to the kitchens and the guide droned on about the various poisons used, particularly during the medieval era. White arsenic in place of salt was popular. Also effective was grinding up diamonds to a fine powder, which had the effect of lacerating the digestive tract, much like ingesting glass.

"Waste of jewelry, if you ask me," said a lovely European tourist with a sniff. She had a handful of rings and hung on the arm of a smirking playboy.

"When you are a king and you want your enemies to disappear," the guide shrugged, "what are a few diamonds?"

"Note to self — don't upset da Queen," muttered the Brooklyn G.I., which drew laughter from his buddies.

They continued through various chambers, hearing of King Henry VI, who was imprisoned for five years in the Tower during the War of the Roses. He was murdered while at prayer in the Tower Chapel.

"That's cold," rumbled Teddy. "Killing a guy while he prays? That's real cold."

"You sure these dudes ain't from da Bronx?" quipped Brooklyn.

"Ain't funny, man," Teddy said, shaking his head.

Dorothy wondered if Teddy was responding to the Tower's influence too. But she didn't want to draw more attention to herself today than she already had by asking him.

And then to the rooms of Robert, Lord Essex, who was executed by

Queen Elizabeth I for treason.

Was he the lover who spurned the older queen? Dorothy wondered. She'd seen movies and read books that suggested that Essex had been highly ambitious and over-reached his station. Likely. Was it love? Or lust? Or lust for power? She shook her head.

They entered the next chamber and Dorothy felt the air leave her lungs.

"And here we have a most interesting room in the Tower's history. Anne Boleyn's chambers. She began her reign as Henry VIII's second wife by spending the night right here in this room before her coronation. She was pregnant with Elizabeth I at the time. Three years later, she would return to these rooms for her final months of life before facing the executioner's sword herself for treason."

The guide's voice receded and once again, screams issued from the stones in the floors and around the windows. The walls were paneled with wood, now aged and lacking the luster of days long ago, but Dorothy watched as the rooms around her began to glow with the care of dozens of servants.

The door opened and Dorothy watched a white-faced young woman enter the room, her lips pressed together so tightly they were colorless. And elderly man held the door open for her and she swept into the room, her manner as imperious as her royal gown. Beneath the haughty exterior, she reeked of fear, and those who accompanied her seemed to know it. The man was followed by four dour women in simple black dresses.

She looked around with a raised eyebrow. "So I am to be kept in the same chambers I occupied before my coronation? Is this Henry's final slap in my face, Sir Kingston?" she asked sharply.

"No, my lady," he said, bowing his head respectfully. "I believe the King wishes only for you to be given some measure of dignity."

"I am not your 'lady'," she snapped. "I am your Queen."

"I apologize, my lady," he said, his face growing pale. "But the King has forbidden us to call you by royal titles. We cannot disobey his Majesty."

She started to argue, then waved her hand impatiently. "Go—just go. And take your flock of crows with you."

"I'm sorry, my lady, but the King has ordered that they remain with you night and day," Sir Kingston said gently.

"The King! The King! The King! What about what I want?" she shrieked. She saw them glance at one another. "Oh, I see those shifty-eyed looks. They're here to report my every utterance back to Henry. Is that it? He's trapped me here with four spies to watch my every move. Is that it? Well, is it?" Her voice rose, angry and harsh, and a vein bulged in her forehead.

Sir Kingston looked her squarely in the eye. "Yes, it is."

She staggered back as if she'd been struck.

"You've been charged with treason, my lady. The others charged with you have far less glamorous quarters below and they are accorded a great deal less respect." Sir Kingston's words took Anne's breath away. "You will not be mistreated. No one will harm you in any way. Please, my lady, I beg you to see the King's generosity to you."

He nodded to the servants and they silently set about tidying the room, making the bed, setting out candles, and generally making it a suitable area for a woman of station.

Anne stared, white-faced, at her captors for a moment. She frowned.

"You said 'others.'" Her voice came out in a raspy whisper.

Sir Kingston sighed. "The... er... the men who are said to have been treasonously allied with your Maj—with you."

"Treasonously allied?"

"The ones accused of ... bedding with you."

"But I didn't! I never did! Not with anyone else. Unlike Henry, who took every opportunity to find a new lover. I never did!" Bitterness dripped from her voice and rotted in the room, leaving behind a rancid feeling in the air. The servants gasped at her bold accusation.

"Please, my lady, I beg you to watch your words." Sir Kingston lowered his voice, but it still held an edge of warning.

"Why?" Anne began to laugh hysterically. "Henry can only kill me once. He's going to do that anyway." Her laughter broke into a sob.

"Quite possibly. But how is the question."

"Does that really matter to a dead woman?" Anne shook, caught between laughter and tears.

"There is a vast difference between a beheading by an expert and burning at the stake."

His words were like cold water dumped over her. Her knees gave out and Anne crumbled to the floor.

"He wouldn't do that to me," she whispered. "He couldn't..."

"Are you so sure of that?" Sir Kingston gave her a long, steady look.

"He loves me," she whispers. "He'll remember he loves me. He'll come..."

"I wonder if that's what Catherine said from her exile. I heard she called for him, asked for him all those years, never doubting he'd come back to her." Dorothy saw her eyes narrow at Sir Kingston's words, as she thought of Catherine pining for her husband while Anne and Henry partied and lived their romance out without giving her a second thought. And she knew that pretty little Jane Seymour had already captured Henry's attention, even as she sat here in her royal prison awaiting her fate.

"Your ladies will set up an altar for your prayer time. If you desire a priest, you need only ask." Sir Kingston sighed. Anne Boleyn was a hard woman, accustomed to getting her own way. This one would not go quietly.

"I want to see my daughter," Anne said suddenly. "I want Elizabeth."

"I was told that was not permitted, but I will issue the request in your name."

"Thank you, Sir Kingston." Anne's voice was little more than a whisper.

"Try to rest," he said gently before leaving the women alone.

Days passed, and Dorothy watched it all in fast forward as tempers flared and bitterness, anger, hatred, and murderous thoughts clung to the rafters and oozed like tar from every surface.

Anne picked up her Bible and the anger and bitterness screamed in fury. Dorothy leaned close to hear her prayers and caught phrases.

"If only I had not berated him."

"If only I had been more understanding, or just looked the other way as other wives do."

"If only I had been more kind."

But it came down to Elizabeth's claim to the throne.

Notes came from Henry. Just sign away Elizabeth's right of succession and I'll let you live.

"How can I live in a little cottage in a dirty village somewhere when I have been the Queen? No. I am Queen or I am nothing. But my Elizabeth will not be a little nothing."

One of the servants sat quietly in the corner reading her Bible. She tilted her head and muttered something unintelligible under her breath.

"An interesting verse, Mistress Helena?" Anne asked, expecting a jab of some sort, as was the woman's tendency. "Pray read it aloud that we may all be edified."

"Oh, just a little verse from the Apostle Peter. Humble yourselves therefore under the mighty hand of God, that He may exalt you in due time. That was 1 Peter 5:6, your ladyship, should you wish to read it yourself." Mistress Helena's self-righteousness dripped from her voice.

"So you think if I just humble myself, Henry will suddenly see the error of his ways and take me back? That's a fairy tale, you silly girl, not a Bible story."

Anne stared out the window, not truly seeing the activity on the Green below. "Besides, Henry doesn't want to see me humbled. He wants to see me die." Her chest heaved once... twice. Then Anne rose abruptly from her place by the window. "I'm weary. I wish to rest for a while."

She laid herself on the four-poster bed and curled her body away from the women, who sat quietly sewing or reading on this sunny day.

Dorothy drew nearer and saw tiny shudders, barely perceptible, as Anne cried soundlessly into her pillow. Sorrow and self-pity soaked the bedding and dripped into the carpets on the floor.

Days continued to roll by, and Anne roiled in the tempest of her stormy disposition. All she had set in motion when she had decided to fight her way to the throne came back to haunt her. One moment, she would be remembering her coronation in great detail, all the fabulous dishes they had served, who wore what, and who had been the most outrageous flirt. The next minute, she would remember something Henry said or did to hurt her and the tears would come, only to be choked back by pride.

"I wonder if Catherine ever railed at the loss of Henry's favor," Anne mused softly. "Did you curse him too, Catherine?" She gave a bitter laugh.

"No, she did not." The low voice came from the elderly Mistress Hawkins, a plump little hen of a woman whose piety was often offended by Anne's lack of decorum.

"I beg your pardon?" Anne turned sharp eyes upon Mistress Hawkins. "Did I hear you talk back to me?"

"No, my lady, I did not talk back to you," Mistress Hawkins said, yanking on her needle so hard the thread snapped. "I simply answered your question."

"And just how would you know about Catherine's household?" Anne's eyes held a dangerous glint.

Mistress Hawkins glanced up at her, then back to her tangled thread. As her fingers set to work undoing knots, she spoke softly. "My best friend served in Queen Catherine's household, and she wrote me every week. She said her thoughts were always for the King's welfare and happiness. She even said that Queen Catherine grieved when you lost your son because she knew how deeply the King would be grieving. That's how she bore her exile. She prayed for her King and wished him well."

Anne's voice was low, strangled by emotion. "When I want such charming little tidbits, I'll ask for them. I may be forced to endure your presence, but I do not have to endure your tongue. So if you wish to keep it, I suggest you keep your comments to yourself."

"But you did ask, Madam," said Lady Margaret, the leader of the quartet. "You wondered what Queen Catherine's reactions to the King were during her exile. Mistress Hawkins simply happened to be in a position to have the information you sought."

"From now on," Anne seethed, her rage building, "you will consider such musings to be rhetorical."

Voices came out of the walls and surrounded Dorothy and Anne.

"They called her Queen Catherine."

"They respect her but not you..."

"She was a better queen than you..."

"A better wife than you..."

"If she hadn't died, Henry would have her back on your throne."

"He's blaming you for her death, you know."

"And it *is* your fault, Anne. It's all your fault..."

"Catherine is looking down on you and she's laughing."

Anne leaned her head against the window and tried not to weep.

The crowds roared outside Anne's windows. She had refused breakfast, knowing it would not stay down. She clutched the window frame as a wagon rolled into sight. Four men sat on the benches in the wagon and one lay sprawled on the floorboards between them.

One by one they were dragged to the platform and laid out prone, arms outstretched. Down the axe fell amid the cheers of the villagers, then men would set to work, soaking up the blood with handfuls of straw while the body, still twitching, was hauled away. Frances Weston, William Brereton, Henry Norris, men who had danced with her, laughed with her, protected her, cared for her — because they were the King's friends. And now he was discarding them to get rid of her. George Boleyn, Lord Rochefort — the title given by the King himself — and her own brother... How could Henry imagine she would bed her own brother?

"How could you, Henry?" she whispered to the window. "How could you even think it?" She winced and closed her eyes at the last minute, unable to bear the sight of George's body twitching and pumping out blood on the wooden platform. Anne heard the ka-thunk-ka-thunk of a body being dragged up the steps. He was so badly mangled she almost didn't recognize the gentle musician who had been her favorite at court. Poor Mark Smeaton had been racked until he could no longer stand or walk. Death would be a mercy for him. But Anne sighed. The world would be a sadder place without Mark's music.

She closed her eyes. "Oh, Henry! Henry! What have we done?"

She heard the axe fall as the crowds cheered wildly. The raucous caws of the Tower's ravens caught her attention as they took flight and soared over the Green. Despair and sorrow clutched at Anne's skirts, and she would never be free of them again.

Dorothy found herself clinging to Abigail's hand as they stood at the window overlooking the Green. The guide still droned on about the era of Henry VIII and his many wives. Horace stood between the rest of the tour group and his wife and Dorothy, shielding them from curious eyes.

"How long...?" Dorothy whispered, her glance darting about furtively.

"Only moments," murmured Abigail. "But you covered months, didn't you?"

"How did you know that?" Dorothy whispered.

"Perhaps we should have a nice spot of tea after the tour, Miss Wexfield," Horace said, turning to face the ladies as the rest of the group began to file out of the room. "We're nearly done here."

Dorothy took another look around the room. The light flickered. A very young girl threw herself across the bed, her long golden hair falling in tangles around her swollen face.

"It's just not fair! I'm too young to die! I don't want to die!" She kicked her feet and beat the silken bedclothes with her tiny fists. "I never wanted to marry a bloated old man in the first place. This isn't fair."

"Hush now, girl," said a stern-faced matron. "You brought this on yourself."

"You know you might give a thought for your lover. Thomas Culpepper was the King's best friend before you turned his head, you little trollop," grumbled a wrinkled old woman who picked at her sewing in the corner.

"I'm not a trollop," the girl screamed. "I'm the Queen! And I'll have you whipped for that!"

"Humph..." The old woman sniffed. "Not much of a queen now, are you?"

The stones laughed at the girl's pain. Bitterness mocked her, and vanity scorned her.

"Poor King Henry." Dorothy recognized Mistress Hawkins, sitting with her Bible. "He saw another Catherine and thought he was getting a dove like the first Queen Catherine. What a cruel irony." She sighed in sympathy with her sovereign.

"Failure!"

"Whore!"

"It's all over now, little Catherine Howard." That voice sneered at her. She was never good enough. Never measured up. Never made the family proud.

And now she would die.

Dorothy stumbled for the door.

"I've had enough. I can't take anymore. I need to leave this place." Her words tumbled over and over, as she made her escape from the Tower with Horace and Abigail fast upon her heels.

~~~~~

Abigail poured Dorothy another cup of tea and pushed the raspberry tart closer.

"You really should eat something, my dear," she urged. "It will do you good. You've had some pretty hard shocks today."

Dorothy picked at the tart with her fork. "Do you think that boy Teddy's friends were right? Is the Tower haunted by ghosts?"

Horace and Abigail glanced at each other, then Horace took up the gauntlet and tried to find a way to answer. "We believe that the Tower is inhabited by demons, spirits that tormented those incarcerated all those many years. They were powerful spirits, and they have kept up a forceful presence. We've sensed them before. Every time we come here, we experience much the same thing you did today. At least near as we could tell. You saw the past, right?"

Dorothy nodded.

Abigail nodded. "I've seen it too. The little boys?" Dorothy's eyes filled with tears. "The dungeon? Yes, of course. That was obvious. Thomas More?" Dorothy frowned and shook her head. Abigail sighed. "Then you were lucky, my dear. His imprisonment and Bishop Fisher's are quite painful to watch."

"I-I-I saw William Wallace first," Dorothy stammered. She set her fork down. "It was horrible."

"Oh, my goodness!" Abigail paled. "No wonder you were shaken. That was a particularly grisly portion of the Tower's history. I'm so sorry. And we weren't there for you either."

"Why were you there?" Dorothy asked. "I mean, if this is such a miserable experience for you, and obviously no one is visiting you right now. Why were you there today?"

The couple smiled at one another. "We prayed this morning, as we do every morning," Horace explained. "The Lord told us we would be needed at the Tower today and that we should come take the tour. We weren't too happy about that, but when the General gives you marching orders, you do as you're told."

"Why would the Lord tell you to go on a tour that you've been on so many times?" Dorothy asked.

"Why, for your benefit, Miss Wexfield," Abigail said, her blue eyes smiling clearly. "You need answers, and we have them."

"Call me Dorothy," she said slowly. "I think we're going to be spending a lot of time together. Too much to stand on formalities."

~~~~~

Dorothy checked out of her hotel at Horace and Abigail's insistence and they settled her into their cozy guest room. For the next five days, they toured London with her, and spent their evenings in discourse before the fireplace with Abigail's endless pots of tea.

"You see, there has been no one to cast these spirits out of the Tower and keep them out," Horace explained. "It's not an easy process, and it requires diligence. Even if we managed to do the exorcism, we're getting on. We won't be here forever. What happens when we're gone? Those nasty demons can slip back in and wreak havoc on the place all over again."

"So after much prayer, we decided to just go and help anyone who seemed to be getting in over their heads," Abigail added. "Like you, Dorothy. We could see right away that you were being hounded by those wicked spirits. The least we could do was to try to protect you through the tour, then help you afterwards to learn to protect yourself."

"Well, I assure you, I will never go back to that place again." Dorothy laughed.

Horace and Abigail exchanged a troubled look but did not share her humor. "No, but you may carry some of that influence with you. You see, you wouldn't have been able to see what you did—feel what you did— unless those spirits somehow already had a hold on you somewhere. You reacted to the very worst points in the entire tour. You saw and felt the rage of William Wallace, the fury of the crowds, the fear of the children, the despair of the dungeons, the wild array that was Anne Boleyn. And you felt the anger against Thomas More and Bishop Fisher, but you didn't see their brave stories, their selfless journeys from this life to the next one." Horace clasped his hands, his blue eyes holding her attention closely. "I am concerned about your welfare when you leave us to return to America. What are you returning to, Dorothy Wexfield? Are you returning to a Tower of your own?"

"Why… no, I don't think so. How do you mean?"

"How close is your walk with God, Dorothy?"

"As close as anyone, I suppose," she stammered. "I make it to church as often as I can. When I'm not traveling, that is." She thought about their comment in the tea shop. They prayed, as they always did, and God told them to go to the Tower. Somehow, she knew they had something she knew nothing about.

"Let's get you closer to your Maker, shall we?" Abigail smiled as she said it, and Dorothy found herself nodding.

Dorothy got the crash course in walking with God. She learned about prayer, she learned the importance of Bible reading, and she learned about the power of calling on God and her friends in times of crisis.

"That was the difference between More and Fisher and the others," Horace said, expounding on the subject one day. "More and Fisher never gave in. They knew where to place their faith, and they didn't let anyone sway them. The voices you heard in their chambers didn't come from those men. They came from the demons sent to torment those men in their final hours. But they still did not surrender to evil. They stood strong, and they prevailed. That's why those spirits are so very angry. They're still spiteful to this day because they lost huge battles with those two old warriors. The dungeon? You heard what they did to those poor people, the nightmares they put those folks through."

Horace paused to sip his tea and bite into a cucumber sandwich.

Abigail took up the tale.

"Then there was Anne Boleyn. We remember her for helping to bring about the Reformation, giving us our Protestant faith, but so much of her life was embroiled in self-promotion. She set herself up to fail by tearing down a good woman, Catherine of Aragon. You can't base your own success on someone else's misery. She predicated her future success on what Catherine had not been able to do—have a son. But then she could not bring a son to term either. Quite the irony. Then there were rumors of promiscuous behavior long before the charges of treason. She was so different from the pious Catherine of Aragon, and I think Henry was besotted at first. Sin usually is beguiling in the beginning. Then the fruit is seen to be rotten, and it becomes harder to ignore. Henry longed for purity in his Queen again. That was what drew him to Jane Seymour."

"So the voices in their rooms stay there out of anger..."

"At their own failure," Horace finished for her, nodding. "Yes, and perhaps remaining in those rooms is their punishment for that failure. Who knows? I've seen other spirits latch onto visitors from time to time and leave the Tower with them."

"That's why it's so important for you to walk daily with God, Dorothy." Abigail refilled Dorothy's teacup. "You must not give the enemy even the smallest crevice to creep into. He can turn your fortress into a tower of misery and it will become a prison in a blink of an eye. Your writing can mean freedom as Thomas More's did, or it can become a chain around your neck, tying you down."

For the rest of the week, they talked and prayed and talked some more. By the time she flew away from London, she thought she was prepared for anything.

Horace and Abigail prayed all that night for their new friend.

~~~~~

Dorothy's taxi pulled up to her apartment building. She hesitated a moment before paying the driver and exiting the cab. Why did she feel that moment's hesitation? She was home. It usually felt good to return to her penthouse apartment. She waited while the driver unloaded her suitcase from the trunk, and Tony, the doorman, hurried to collect her bags. She smiled at his enthusiastic greeting and entered the foyer ahead of him. He asked about her trip, and the weather in London as the elevator climbed higher and higher. Dorothy unlocked the door to her apartment and allowed Tony to set the luggage inside the door, then tipped him generously and ushered him back out again. He was a nice man, but rather like an over-enthusiastic puppy.

With a sigh of relief, Dorothy sank into a soft chair overlooking her view of Central Park and picked up the phone. Dialing her publisher was first on her list of priorities. She'd been eager to make this call for days.

"Sid Farnsby, please. This is Dorothy Wexfield... Yes, I'll hold." She leaned back and sighed. Historical fiction had been her passion for the past seven years. And she'd been making a good name for herself too. Her research was meticulous. Did she really dare to make this move?

"Hey, Sid." She straightened up a bit in her chair. "Yeah, I just got in a few minutes ago... No, the trip was fine. I got a lot of information. Look, Sid, I actually got more than I bargained for over there. How would you feel about branching out into something a little — well, a little different?"

She listened for a minute. "Well, a little more along spiritual themes, or supernatural angles. Like good and evil, God and the devil, the war between right and wrong. ... Yeah, I know I've never done that sort of thing before... Yeah, I get it, Sid. ... Yeah, I'd be sticking my neck out too. But I really want to do this."

She listened intently. "Who? Allan Custer? No, I don't think I've met him before. Is he new? ... He's not? ... We have a supernatural division? ... No, I didn't know that. Sure, I'd be willing to meet with him. When can you arrange it? ... Yeah, call me back. Thanks, Sid."

Dorothy hung up the phone and bowed her head in thankful prayer. Her hands shook. That was answered prayer and fast! She had been so afraid that Sid would cut her loose and cancel her contract. He had loved her last eight books, but a new one on demons in the Tower of London? She hadn't been at all sure he would even listen to her. This could bring a new dimension to history if she could tell the story by including the influence of evil spirits throughout the ages. Then again, she might become the laughingstock of the publishing world.

Her doorbell rang. Dorothy opened the door, and her heart sank to her toes.

"Tony said you just got home." Her father pushed past her and entered the apartment.

She knew it would do no good to chastise the doorman for not respecting her privacy when it came to her father, since he still paid for the penthouse, and he considered it his right to know her comings and goings. She sighed and closed the door.

"Good Lord, please tell me you haven't been running around London dressed like that!" Her father eyed her from head to toe. "Dorothy, your mother would be aghast. Simply aghast. I know you have more stylish clothes in your closet than — what is that ensemble you're wearing?"

Dorothy smoothed the tan a-line skirt and dark brown silk blouse. The matching tan jacket was cut in simple lines, and was attractive, but not overly flattering. "Father, you know that I prefer to keep a low profile when I go on these research trips. I don't like to draw attention to myself. I keep my wardrobe simple and modest. Very little jewelry, no show of wealth or status. Nothing to attract attention."

"I told you I could assign a bodyguard," he fumed.

"I didn't want a bodyguard," she stated. "I wanted to be able to wander around without anybody knowing who I was."

"Well, I certainly hope you succeeded. Your mother would die of embarrassment if your picture showed up in any of the papers looking like that."

"Thanks, Father," she said. "You know just how to make a daughter feel loved."

"Don't be cheeky with me, young lady. I think we've been more than tolerant of your eccentric behavior. It's time for you to live up to your familial obligations. Now, your mother has arranged for a homecoming party for you this evening. Cocktails at seven. I trust you have an evening dress that will be appropriate? If you don't, get one. And it had better not look like that!" He motioned toward her ensemble.

"Father, I just got home. I'm tired." Dorothy moaned, thinking of the hours of small talk, the drinks, dinner, more drinks, questions, but little of it would be real interest in what she was doing. It would all be about the gossip of the day, or the men in the room.

"The term is jet-lagged," he said tersely. "Too bad. Your mother has her heart set on this, and you will not let her down. She has arranged for a couple of very eligible young men to be there this evening. It's an opportunity, Dorothy. A very good opportunity. One of them is the son of Nelson Eddington. I've been trying to coax him into a business merger for years. A match between you and his son might just get the job done."

"How many times do I have to tell you both, Father? I am not ready to settle down and marry some socialite just for the sake of the *New York Times* gossip column?" Dorothy felt her temper rising.

"Are you forgetting that I pay for your continuing lifestyle, Dorothy?" Her father loomed over her. "Just how long do you think this writing career of yours will keep you going if you have to pay your own bills? Certainly not in this apartment, my dear. Accept a little reality check. You've had your fun. Now it's time to pay the piper. Get with the program, Dorothy."

Her father fixed steely eyes on her before heading for the door. "See you at seven o'clock sharp. Do not be late, Dorothy."

He slammed out the door. Dorothy sank into her chair and covered her face with her hands.

"You can't make it without Daddy's money."

"Failure!"

"Coward!"

"Just do what you're expected to do. Who do you think you are?"

"You can't take off on your own. You'll never make it."

Dorothy's head came up and she looked around the apartment. She walked to the window and looked out over Central Park. How much it suddenly reminded her of the Green outside the Tower of London! Was she trapped in her own Tower?

No, she wasn't a prisoner.

Slowly she walked to her bedroom and opened the closet door. Rifling through hangers, she found the forest green evening dress. Off the shoulder, sweetheart neckline, dropped waistline—it was flattering and the color was fabulous. She had the perfect jewelry too—an exquisite set of emeralds her father had given her for her sixteenth birthday. She held it up and looked at herself in the mirror. She could go to her mother's party. It would make them both happy.

But it wouldn't stop there.

It would never stop.

And a husband would just replace dear old Dad when it came to demands. Book deadlines would mean nothing when stacked up against corporate dinners or social obligations. A husband would expect her to lay aside her personal needs to fulfill his calendar first.

"What do I do, Lord? Show me, please." She laid the dress carefully across the end of the bed and walked over to the bedside chair. She picked up the extension phone and dialed her best friend, Katie. Her parents detested Katie, who was another writer with Sid's firm. Though not as successful as Dorothy had been, Katie had a kind heart.

"Hey, Katie ... Yeah, just got back about an hour ago." Dorothy gulped back her tears. "No, I'm okay. ... Well, yeah... you're right, I'm not really okay. Hey, do you know if that vacancy is still available in your building? ... Yeah, I'm serious. I might need it. ... Well, right away... Well, honey, if I don't go to my mother's party tonight, I might need it by morning."

Tears rolled down Dorothy's cheeks. "Stay with you? But Katie, you don't have enough room... Are you sure? Really? ... Yeah, I won't be bringing much. Just clothes and a box or two of personal stuff. The furniture goes with the apartment. I'm pretty sure my father will be cutting me off completely... Yeah, he's trying to map out my future tonight—right down to a husband, son of his future business partner. ... Nope, not kidding one little bit... Yeah, give me about an hour to pack and I'll be over there. But only until an apartment opens up, kiddo. Listen, could you call Sid and explain I'll be camping with you? He's supposed to be calling me back about a meeting. I'll have to take my calls at your place until I can get a cell phone that's not in my father's name. ... Yeah, thanks, Katie."

Dorothy hung up and sat quietly for a moment. Then she pulled a couple of suitcases from the closet and began to fill them. She packed her books and mementoes, moving carefully from room to room, then stacking everything by the front door next to the luggage she had just come home with. She left the green evening dress on the bed with the emerald jewelry. For Father.

As she stood and looked around, the voices were curiously silent. She smiled.

"Yes," she said to the room. "You can be quiet. I won't be stifled. I won't be cowed. I won't be forced to submit to someone else's plan for my life. God controls my life. No one else. I'll succeed or fail, but I won't give up the fight."

She picked up the phone. "Tony? I'm going to need a cab and a luggage cart, please. Right away."

She hung up, hesitated, then picked up the phone and dialed her parent's home on Long Island.

"Yes, good afternoon, Graves." She was instantly grateful that the butler had picked up instead of her mother. "Please tell my mother I will be unable to attend this evening. Thank you." She hung up quickly, leaving the butler to stammer his objections to a dial tone.

She answered Tony's brisk knock on her door, loaded her belongings on the cart, and left the penthouse without a backward glance.

END

MEET THE AUTHORS

Kathleen Bird is the author of the *Adven Trilogy*, a Christian fantasy series which includes her debut novel (*To Love in Peace*), and the *Isles of Miadhra*, a series of steampunk fairytale retellings. She has been a lifetime lover of stories: reading, writing, or watching them. Basically, anything that takes her away to a fantasy world whether it's Narnia, the TARDIS, outer space or beyond! She grew up with a passion for reading fairytales, especially those by Hans Christian Anderson and continues to enjoy exploring retellings of those same stories as an adult. Be sure to check out her website (*www.adventrilogy.wordpress.com*) for more information about her books and where to find them.

Michaela Bush is a Christian author, editor, and crazy cat lady. When she isn't spinning her next story, she's spending time with her family, horseback riding, or playing violin. She is the author of a Rapunzel retelling titled *The Lady of Lanaria*, and has published a wide variety of Christian fiction from contemporary to historical fantasy! Readers can find her online at *www.tangledupinwriting.com* or *@tangledupinwriting* for publishing updates.

Rachel Dib is a stay-at-home mom of three small children. After marrying a soldier, she left her home state of South Carolina to live in random places across the United States. Her other published work consists of micro fiction found in *On the Premises* Magazine, flash fiction published by Havok Publishing, and short stories in *Toasted Cheese Literary Journal* (the latter under the name R.J Snowberger). In her limited spare time, she enjoys reading, writing, and playing board games.

Kaitlyn Emery was obsessed with dragons and fantasy at a young age, but as she grew up learned the harsh truth that reality was darker than anything she read in a book. Through writing, Kaitlyn learned to cope with the world around her and find her voice again in fiction. Giving a voice to the voiceless is a common theme in Kaitlyn's writing. Her love for short stories has led her to be featured in various magazines, flash fiction for Havok Publishing, and published in several anthologies including *Rebirth, Sensational, Prismatic, Casting Call, When Your Beauty Is the Beast, Moonlight and Claws, The Depths We'll Go To, Aphotic Love, Fool's Honor*, and *The Heights We'll Fly To* (coming soon). You can learn more about her writing and other creative endeavors at her website *Kaitlyn-Emery.com*.

Believing firmly in magic and merriment, valor and peace, **Abigail Falanga** is an author of fantasy and science fiction. She lives in New Mexico with family, books, too many hobbies, and many wild ambitions. Along with her sister Sarah, she's the editor of the *Whitstead Anthologies* of speculative stories set in a small Victorian English town. Besides short stories published in various anthologies, she has released her first book, *A Time of Mourning and Dancing*, and is working on follow-up books in the same dark fantasy universe. (Editor's note: Ms. Falanga also had a lovely story in *When Your Beauty Is the Beast* last year!)

Beka Gremikova writes folkloric fantasy from her little nook in the Ottawa Valley, Ontario, Canada. Her flash fiction can be found on Havok Publishing's website and in several of their anthologies (*Bingeworthy, Sensational, Prismatic,* and *Casting Call*). Her other short stories can be found in various anthologies, the latest of which include *Aphotic Love, Fool's Honor, The Heights We'll Fly To, The Depths We'll Go To, Whitstead Harvestide, What Darkness Fears,* and *Moonlight and Claws*. When she's not travelling, playing video games, or sketching, she's often curled up in a corner with a mystery novel. Currently, she's plotting a plethora of retellings and planning to release her dark fantasy thriller short, *Perchance to Dream*, in late 2022.

Pam Halter is a children's book author and editor. Her picture book series, *Willoughby and Friends,* have won Purple Dragonfly awards, and a Realm Award. Parents have told her they hide the books because they're tired of reading them. Pam considers this a WIN.

She also published a YA fantasy, *Fairyeater* (Love2ReadLove2Write Publishing), which is also a recipient of a Purple Dragonfly. She attended her local community college for cosmetology in 1977-78. While she doesn't work as a hair stylist, she has cut, colored, and permed friends and family's hair over the years. Pam lives in South Jersey where she enjoys writing, gardening, cooking, quilting and playing the piano. She enjoys walking on long country roads where she finds fairy homes, emerging dragons, and trees eating wood gnomes. Learn more about her at *www.pamhalter.com*. (Editor's note: Pam also has a lovely tale in *Moonlight and Claws* called *Growls and Meows*!)

Cassandra Hamm is a psychology nerd, art collector, jigsaw puzzler, and hopeless romantic who spends most of her time lost in another realm. She is a mental health advocate with a passion for social justice, and many of her stories focus on shattered girls finding their way in the world. Her work appears in various anthologies, including several of Havok Publishing's collections, *Warriors Against the Storm, When Your Beauty Is the Beast, The Depths We'll Go To, Aphotic Love, Exquisite Poison,* and *The Lady in the Tower.*

Michelle Houston loves creating new worlds and civilizations and occasionally getting them on paper. She is a Christian, wife, mother, teacher, and scientist, who strives to connect young adults with the wonders found around us. She spends her free time reading everything in sight, going outside as much as possible (to the relief of the dust bunnies inside), trying new recipes and of course, writing. She has a wonderful loving and supportive husband and three crazy kids who will together take over the world (or at least North America) someday. Her story *Recovery* can be found in *Moonlight and Claws* anthology.

On the road to publication, **Michelle Levigne** fell into fandom in college and has 40+ stories in various SF and fantasy universes. She has a bunch of useless degrees in theater, English, film/communication, and writing. Even worse, she has over 100 books and novellas with multiple small presses, in science fiction and fantasy, YA, suspense, women's fiction, and sub-genres of romance. Her training includes the Institute for Children's

Literature; proofreading at an advertising agency; and working at a community newspaper. She is a tea snob and freelance edits for a living. (MichelleLevigne@gmail.com for info/rates), but only enough to give her time to write. Her newest crime against the literary world is to be co-managing editor at Mt. Zion Ridge Press and launching the publishing co-op, Ye Olde Dragon Books. This book launches her second year under this new banner. Be afraid... be very afraid.

Cortney Manning resides in Florida but has always loved traveling the world. She holds a master's degree in Victorian Literature from the University of Glasgow and has a not-so-secret love of fantasy and fairy tales as well. In her free time, Cortney enjoys walking, drawing, and afternoon tea. Cortney's fantasy, mystery, and fairy tale retellings can be found on Amazon and Havok. Her novellas and short stories have been featured in several anthologies: *Five Poisoned Apples*, *The Depths We'll Go To*, and Havok's *Season Six: Casting Call*. In addition, Cortney's novel retelling of the fairy tale *Snow White and Rose Red* was released in conjunction with the *Six Frosted Roses* book release and can be found on Amazon as well. More information about Cortney and her writing can be found on her website, *https://cortneymanning.wixsite.com/author*, or on Instagram *@cortneymanningauthor*.

Lindsi McIntyre is a linguaphile from Texas who hopes to use her words, both written and spoken, to bring glory to the Lord Most High. When not writing she can be found within the pages of a good book, or watching the latest episode of her favorite TV shows, and drinking way too much tea while doing both. You can check out more of her work on Havok, grab a copy of *Moonlight and Claws* from Ye Olde Dragon books, and look for her award-winning novella, *Broken Pieces*.

Stoney M. Setzer lives south of Atlanta, GA. He has a beautiful wife, three wonderful children, and one crazy dog. He has written a trilogy of novels about small-town amateur sleuth Wesley Winter (*Dead of Winter*, *Valley of the Shadow*, and *Day of Reckoning*). He has also written a number of Twilight Zone-like short stories with Christian themes that have been published in several anthologies and online magazines. Mr. Setzer is currently writing the Tremble Town stories, centering on the fictional community of Sardis County, Tennessee. His previous contributions to the Ye Olde Dragons anthologies are part of this series. He has also written historical fiction stories about Zacchaeus, Samson, and Barabbas for Faith Journeys app, available on your app store. Learn more at *www.tinniepress.blogspot.com* or on Facebook *@stoneymsetzerofficial*.

Deborah Cullins Smith participated in several anthologies before publishing back-to-back releases of her Hippies trilogy — *Shroud of Darkness*, *The Birth of the Storm*, and *Victoria's War*, all with CWG Press. Deborah is the grandmother of twelve and loves nothing more than a rousing tea party with a table full of children. Her newest series is a remake of the Mina Harker legend, beginning with *Mina: Warrior in the Shadows*, just released December 2021. Mina's follow-on story appeared in *Moonlight and Claws* in a novella called *Habitations of Violence*. She also has stories in the anthologies *When Your Beauty is the Beast* and *Two Olde Dragons Writing Wyrd Stories*. Deborah is co-editor and partner in Ye Olde Dragons Books.

Meaghan Elizabeth Ward is an author, youtuber, and freelance illustrator with a passion for storytelling. She mainly writes high fantasy with low magic and loves drawing inspiration from world-wide cultures and myths. She has written three stories for Havok publishing, one which made Editor's Choice in their *Stories That Sing* Anthology. Her newest story *Iron Hood* can be found in their *Casting Call* Anthology. When not writing or reading, Meaghan can be found drawing her story-worlds, creating fanart, or making funny bookish comics. You can find her on Instagram *@meaghaneward* or on Youtube *@meaghanunabridged*.

Raised in a family obsessed with science fiction, fantasy, and role-play, it was only a matter of time before **Etta-Tamara Wilson** began trying her hand at her own stories. A childhood spent haunting the forests, villages, castles and abbeys of Central Europe resulted in a deep-seated fascination with fairy tales, especially the rarely told ones. Etta-Tamara pursued a degree in Mass Communications and Creative Writing, which she hopes to finish someday. After wandering lost in the woods for a time, she now focuses on spending her time negotiating with a myriad of fairy tale characters, working out plotlines and determining who to write about first. She looks forward to seeing who ends up winning the argument: Rumplestiltskin, Puss-in-Boots, the Big Bad Wolf, or the twins of the Juniper Tree. *Blood Gold* is her first fiction publication.

CPSIA information can be obtained
at www.ICGtesting.com
Printed in the USA
LVHW090846250422
717138LV00018B/1372

9 781952 345678